The Knight's Gambit

The Alternate History Novel of the Battlesh

Book 2 of the Malta Fulcrum Alternate History Series

Preface

Entry from the personal diary of Count Gian Galeazzo Ciano, Foreign Minister of Italy:

"July 1, 1942.

Returned from Leghorn (Livorno) on the anniversary of my father's death. Was met at the Railway station by Kesselring among others. He wanted to discuss the supply situation in Africa and the actions taken by the Regia Marina to deliver supplies closer to the front now that Malta is in our hands. As always, the picture painted is of German triumph betrayed by Italian cowardice. I pointed out to the Field Marshall that fuel allocations from Germany for our naval escorts have not met the promised levels and that our navy has just fought a pitched battle with the British and suffered serious damage as a result. 'K' mutters about 'excuses'. I briefly lost my temper and asked 'K' if the German navy is expected to perform any better in the coming operation against the Allies' next Arctic convoy. I should try not to provoke 'K' as he is among the least beastly of all the Germans."

PART 1: THE CHESS BOARD IS SET.

CHAPTER 1

The Admiralty, Whitehall, London

June 29, 1942

Sir Dudley Pound looked pensively out his office window onto the Horse Guards parade below. Fluffy white clouds were giving way to darker more ominous skies. The Royal Navy Meteorological office predicted rain for the morrow, the last day of June 1942 after an unusually dry month. Afternoon shadows lengthened, but summertime daylight still had long hours before time to draw the blackout curtains. Pound sighed and turned back to the set of maps covering one paneled wall of his office.

The First Sea Lord of the Royal Navy reviewed for the hundredth time that day the worldwide dispositions of his ships and fleets, looking for an answer to the problem that bedeviled him. But the answer was always the same. That is to say, there was no answer. Everywhere, in the Pacific, Atlantic and Indian Oceans, from the far north to the tips of Africa and South America and Australia, there was too much water and too few ships to properly patrol and defend it all.

His eyes lit for the thousandth time on the islands of Malta in the Mediterranean Sea. The story of the Axis invasion of Malta is told in Book One of the Malta Fulcrum Series, "OPERATION HERKULES" and details are to be found in that book.

Pound knew communications with the Malta garrison were lost some eighteen hours earlier and news broadcasts from Berlin and Rome radio now claimed the islands were in Axis hands despite all Pound and his navy had done to thwart the German and Italian invasion of Malta. He had dispatched a powerful fleet from the Royal Navy base at Gibraltar to rescue the situation and to throw back the tide of Axis advance, but now it seemed certain the effort had been futile. Futile and costly too, in resources and lives and ships. He ran through the butcher's bill in silence. Two aircraft carriers, *HMS Eagle* and *Furious* and the battlecruiser *Renown* lost along with nearly a dozen other warships, gone to enemy air and submarine attack and in the surface action fought in the waters west of Malta with the Italian Navy, the Regia Marina. Gone along with nearly two thousand Royal Navy seamen and officers, dead, wounded or missing. All for nothing as Malta, with the finest natural harbors in all the Med and three crucial airfields now lay in enemy hands, along presumably with the island's entire garrison of over 25,000 men. He knew that, within days the

Italian navy would escort convoys of troops, supplies and weapons across the Mediterranean to the Axis Army in North Africa to threaten Cairo and the Suez Canal and his other great Mediterranean naval base, at Alexandria, Egypt.

Worse still, two of his three remaining Aircraft Carriers sat trapped in the Eastern Basin of the Mediterranean. *HMS Illustrious* and *Indomitable* were in the Indian Ocean supporting the Allied occupation of Madagascar when Malta was attacked. They'd left Operation Ironclad as the Madagascar invasion was dubbed and raced north up the coast of East Africa, through the Red Sea and Suez Canal in a desperate attempt to reach the Med and Malta in time to tip the scales back to the British forces on the island, but were too late to take part in the battle. Now, with Malta occupied by the German and Italian Air Forces it would be suicidal for them to try to run the Mediterranean gauntlet to Gibraltar. Axis airbases pushed deep into Egypt also gave the enemy the chance to shut the Suez Canal against their return to the Indian Ocean.

Pound's eyes shifted to the chalkboard next to his maps. It listed the position and status of all his surviving capital ships, the battleships and aircraft carriers. Too many were out of position or incapacitated. The old battleship *Ramillies* in dry dock, Durban S. Africa, torpedoed by a

Japanese midget sub at Diego Suarez in Madagascar. *HMS Queen Elizabeth* and her sister battleship *HMS Valiant* on their way to dry docks in America for repairs to damage done by Italian frogmen in Alexandria Harbor. Preliminary reports indicated they would be out of action for a year or more as repairs were effected. The modern, powerful battleship *HMS King George V* was scheduled to leave port next day after extensive repairs to her bows, damaged when she'd run down the Tribal Class Destroyer *HMS Punjabi* in a heavy fog off Iceland. *Royal Oak, Hood, Prince of Wales, Repulse, Barham, Courageous, Glorious, Ark Royal* all lost in the preceding three years to enemy action. He sighed, wondering how to juggle the demands for his remaining vessels.

He surveyed his map of the Atlantic Ocean next. Two convoys on the North Atlantic and a third in the south already put heavy demand on the Royal Navy's escort vessels. His eye landed on Iceland and the track of his latest burden, convoy PQ17 bound for the North Russian ports of Murmansk and Archangel. Thirty-five merchant ships carrying Lend-Lease weapons and war material had left Iceland two days prior with a large, close escort of destroyers, anti-aircraft and anti-submarine ships and, ominously to the merchant crews who sailed the cargo ships, three rescue vessels, sent with the convoy to pluck survivors from the icy waters of the Arctic Sea.

He checked the progress of the second track on his Arctic map, the cruiser force assigned to PQ17 as close cover against enemy surface attack. The cruisers traced a course parallel to the convoy to its north and west. His eyes dropped to Scapa Flow, the Royal Navy's Home Fleet anchorage in Scotland's Orkney Islands. There he knew the last naval elements of PQ17's escort prepared to sail. The battleship *HMS Duke of York* and carrier *Victorious* were joined by the American battleship *USS Washington* and four heavy cruisers to provide the distant heavy cover for the convoy.

That they were needed he held no doubt. His eyes flicked across the map to the north coast of Norway and the ports of Narvik and Trondheim. The German Navy's heavy fleet units were assembled there and British Intelligence estimates predicted they would sail to attack the convoy in an effort to wipe it out, down to the last ship. Pound knew that if roles were reversed the Royal navy could almost guarantee this outcome. He was opposed to sending the convoy, at least in June and July when the endless daylight hours of the Arctic summer made it impossible to evade German aircraft and submarines stationed in Norway's North Cape. In mid-May

1942 Admiral Pound had confided his fears to the American Chief of Naval Operations, Admiral Ernest King.

"These Russian convoys are becoming a regular millstone round our necks," he told King. "The whole thing is a most unsound operation, with the dice loaded against us in every direction."

And yet, political pressure from 10 Downing Street and even from the White House in Washington, D.C., ensured the convoys must proceed at almost any cost in the effort to provide aid to the Russians, that they might remain in the war against Germany. The Americans set the value of the convoy's cargo at the staggering sum of $750 Million. It included weapons and supplies to equip an army of fifty thousand men in the field.

Now Pound faced his worst nightmare. With his Navy stretched to the breaking point and beyond, fulfilling commitments the world over he now was responsible for sending the ships and escorts of PQ17 to face the German surface fleet, including the ship called the most powerful in the word, the Battleship *Tirpitz*.

Sister ship to the infamous German battleship *Bismarck*, the *Tirpitz* struck fear in the hearts of Allied seaman and strategist alike. More than a match for any Allied battleship afloat, she was heavily armored and displaced 51,000 tons. Despite her bulk, she was fast, capable of prolonged speed in excess of 30 knots and able to sail nearly 9,000 nautical miles without refueling. She carried a massive ship's compliment of over 2,500 officers and men. Her armament included over 60 anti-aircraft and dual-purpose guns and she was even capable of launching torpedoes against her enemies. But the dread she inspired came from her main battery of eight naval rifles, firing armor penetrating shells of 15-inch diameter to distances over 30,000 yards. These same model guns aboard *Bismarck* had put the mighty *HMS Hood* down in just minutes in May 1941 in the Battle of the Denmark Strait. The thought of *Tirpitz* breaking out onto the North Atlantic or Arctic convoy routes was Pound's biggest worry. The possibility kept his precious, heavy ships tied down on constant watch, compounded by the fact that it would take at least two of his battleships to stand an even chance against *Tirpitz* in open battle. The one thing that made sending PQ17 into the path of this monster worthwhile was the chance of luring *Tirpitz* far enough from her Norwegian lair that she could be brought to battle and sunk or at least damaged sufficiently to break the hold she had on British naval strategy. It weighed on Pound's conscience that the men and ships of PQ17 were used as bait for the German battleship.

A soft knock and his door swung silently open. A discreet cough and Pound turned to his aide, an RN Commander.

"Excuse me, Sir," his aide said. "Admiral Tovey on the telephone."

"Thank you," Pound said and returned to his desk. He waited until his aide had left the room before lifting the phone from its cradle. "First Sea Lord," he said.

"Yes, Sir," the voice of Sir John Tovey, Home Fleet Commander came to him down the secure line from Scapa Flow in Scotland. "We're to sail shortly and I wish to review last minute changes to plans or intelligence. In particular, I should like to cover once more the plan for the cruiser covering force. On consideration, I think it unwise to commit the cruisers east of Bear Island. Their exposure to air and submarine attack will be extreme there, as we've seen with *Trinidad* and *Edinburgh*." Tovey referred to two Royal Navy cruisers lost that spring already in Arctic waters.

"I understand, Admiral," answered Pound, "but the convoy must have protection against German surface ships. Without those cruisers the Kriegsmarine's destroyers on the North Cape could wipe the whole show out unhindered. It would be a slaughter. In any case, I may order the convoy to scatter if threatened by the German heavies east of Bear Island."

There was a brief pause before Tovey asked, "And what of *Tirpitz*? What shall it be if she gets loose?" A long moment of silence followed the question.

"Good luck, good hunting Admiral," said Pound. "Do keep the Americans in line won't you?" He set the phone back gently in its cradle and returned to the silent study of his maps.

Chapter 2

June 29, 1942

Scapa Flow

Sea water shot at high pressure from fire hoses, washing the mud and silt from *USS Washington's* anchor chains and the deck vibrated as her mighty Babcock & Wilcox boilers powered her GE turbine engines to full power. A snow squall swept across her decks and visibility dropped to less than fifty feet as she swung round and headed down the deep-water channel from Scapa Flow through Hoxa Sound. The squall passed within minutes and visibility rose to several miles beneath a heavy, grey sky over a pewter sea. Ahead of *Washington* the Flagship of the Royal Navy's Home Fleet, *HMS Duke of York* led the Allied fleet from Scapa. Four miles past the southernmost tip of South Ronaldsay Island the fleet executed a turn to port into the Pentland Firth and on towards the North Sea.

Gunner's Mate 1st Class Reggie Elkins pulled his heavy pea coat closed at the neck and hunched his shoulders against the cold. *Washington* set to sea buttoned up at battle stations; all guns and magazines manned, watertight bulkheads snugged shut and ready lockers filled with ammunition. The ship's three mighty 16 inch turrets were manned too, the guns 'trained-in', pointing fore and aft. The ship would remain at some level of battle station alert during daylight hours for the duration of the cruise. Reggie stood to at his battle station, the forward 5-inch starboard turret. He shivered and knew he was lucky to be buttoned up in the turret. Crews manning the many light anti-aircraft guns aboard were exposed to the elements.

"Summer my Aunt Elma," he muttered bitterly, stamping his feet to warm his toes. Reggie hailed from Ft. Lauderdale, Florida and before the war had never been fifty miles from home. He'd never seen real snow before joining the navy and certainly was not prepared to deal with freezing conditions at the end of June, when temps at home would have been nearer 90 degrees Fahrenheit.

"Watsa mattuh, Elkins?" his buddy, Taylor Wynn chided him. "Hot water bottle let you down again?" Wynn was from Detroit and was no stranger to cold.

"Screw you Tay," Reggie answered good-naturedly, but he was too cold to spare the energy to keep the banter up.

The gun crew busied themselves assuring their weapon was in perfect working order. The turret housed two of the 5-inch, dual-purpose guns and the men to serve them and was quite crowded and claustrophobic. Sometimes, especially when at battle stations for prolonged periods, the crew was allowed to leave the rear hatch entrance open for fresh air, but today the turret was buttoned up tight against the bitter cold wind.

High above his head *Washington's* radar aerials turned, the invisible beam of their eyes searching the heavens for any threat, but this didn't satisfy Captain Benson, Master of the American battleship. Every watch and lookout position aboard was filled with men scanning the skies with binoculars. German air raids still threatened Scapa Flow, the Royal Navy's primary northern anchorage in home waters and there was even the possibility of submarine attack. During her stay at Scapa, *Washington* anchored two miles from the rusting, overturned hulk of the battleship *HMS Royal Oak*, torpedoed by a German sub right in the heart of the anchorage shortly after war broke out in 1939. She'd capsized taking over 800 of her crew with her. *Washington's* sailors knew all too well the fate awaiting the unlucky.

Reggie watched a US Navy destroyer charge down the starboard side of the great battleship. He knew little of the science of war, and unknown to him the 'tin-can' was using its active sonar, pinging pulses of sound beneath the sea and listening for the return echo as the sound pulse bounced back from a submarine's hull. Reggie felt better for the 'little boys' presence despite his ignorance of the destroyer's role.

Reggie and the rest of *Washington's* crew knew they were headed to the far north in the Arctic Sea and that it would get far colder before it got any warmer. Their officers told them they were serving under the temporary command of the British Royal Navy to assist in protecting an important Lend-Lease convoy to Russia, but far more ominously they'd also been told of the possibility the German battleship *Tirpitz* might sail to attack the convoy. The men felt a strange combination of fear mixed with eager anticipation for their first time in battle.

Ahead of *Washington,* a Royal Navy battleship led them to sea. *HMS Duke of York* had been at war now for only a little longer than *Washington*. She had commissioned the prior November 1941. Even so, most of her crew were experienced men drafted from other ships of the Royal Navy, and ashore at Scapa they'd affected a bored nonchalance for the benefit of the Americans when asked about their combat experiences. Now "The Duke", as the American seamen inevitably dubbed her, began the process of exercising her machinery. The great four-barreled aft turret of 14 inch guns swung out from the 'trained in' position pointing straight aft, first to port then all the way round to starboard before settling back to trained in. Soon *Washington* began the same process with her three triple 16-inch gun turrets humming round on their armored barbettes.

Aft of *Washington* the aircraft carrier *HMS Victorious* followed in their wake. The high, buff sides of the carrier tipped the ship up on the waves like some playground teeter-totter, the planes on deck alternately appearing and disappearing behind the rearing bows.

The wind gusted and another snow squall moved over *Washington*, obscuring the ships of the fleet from each other's view. Reggie sighed and rubbed his arms against the cold. It was going to be a long watch with many more like it to follow.

Eight hundred yards ahead of *Washington*, *Duke of York* finished her machinery tests and settled in for the run to the Arctic Sea. Her 43,000 ton displacement helped her shoulder aside the rising seas without difficulty. Not so the escorting destroyers. Already they were being tossed about like flotsam on a beach with white seas breaking over their bows.

Throughout *Duke of York*, men went about their duties with the stoicism for which Royal Navy seamen have been renowned for centuries. Among these was a young man named Norbert Lamb, known to his few friends as "Nobby" and about as completely unremarkable a nineteen year old as could then be found serving in the Royal Navy. Gangly, all arms and legs, with straw colored hair and still prone to acne, Lamb seemed never to have escaped that awkward stage between adolescence and manhood. He was painfully shy, especially around girls and would often forego his liberty to avoid social interactions ashore. Lacking formal education, he was nonetheless an intelligent lad and his Royal Navy Petty Officer saw him as obedient and reliable in carrying out his duties. Those who called him Nobby also referred to him as "A Good Egg."

Lamb's duties aboard *HMS Duke of York* were simple. He was a member of a division responsible for maintaining various emergency equipment. He and his mates inspected and repaired watertight hatches, emergency lighting and power supplies as well as firefighting apparatus, extinguishers, and water pumps, valves and hoses throughout the ship. His action station was below decks forward, adjacent to the armored barbette, the great steel cylinder upon which 'A' Turret turned and which protected the hoists and elevators that lifted ammunition from the magazine below.

He was from a small village called Tynesbury in the Midlands near the Welsh border, the only child of Charles and Edna Lamb, second cousins. Charles was a blacksmith twenty years senior to Edna and the couple's relationship was such that strangers often wondered if they weren't in fact father and daughter. No home life could better prescribe the introversion of the boy.

Before the war, Nobby had never even been down to the sea, much less sailed upon it. As *Duke of York* left Scapa Flow that day he went about his business, testing a circuit of emergency lights, replacing a bulb he found burnt out. He was virtually unknown outside the small circle of men he worked with, a nearly anonymous cog in a machine of war. Within one month, all England would know Nobby Lamb.

High up in the armored superstructure on the Flag Bridge, Commander of the Royal Navy's Home Fleet, Sir John Tovey conferred with *Duke of York's* Captain, Cecil Halliday.

"The escorts cannot sustain these speeds if the sea freshens any further," commented Halliday watching the bows of a destroyer plunge into a wave, green water cascading from her decks as she popped back to the surface.

"True enough, Captain," answered Tovey. "But while we can I want to make seaway from land and prying eyes." He gestured at the sky.

Halliday nodded. He understood the Admiral wished to evade Luftwaffe reconnaissance aircraft by getting as far clear of Scapa Flow as quickly as possible. He waited a moment, then asked the question every man aboard the fleet was burning to ask.

"Do we have an estimate of when and where we might meet *Tirpitz*?"

"Were I in command of the German surface force I should attempt to attack the convoy to the north and west of Bear Island in four days' time," Tovey answered. "He can use the island to screen his approach then after putting paid to the convoy he can withdraw again behind the island where his air force and submarines will try to prevent our following."

Captain Halliday tugged at his ear for a moment, about to question the logic of the Germans in attacking to the west of Bear Island, but stopped himself when he saw his Malay steward at the back of the bridge.

"Ah, Tembam," he addressed the man. "Tea or Kai Admiral?" he asked Tovey.

"Tea please," answered Tovey.

"A pot of tea please Tembam, that's a good fellow," Halliday ordered. The Captain would have preferred Kai, the hot, viscous chocolate drink favored by the Royal Navy of the time. Tembam bowed silently and left the bridge.

"Why wouldn't Jerry simply await the convoy to the east of Bear Island?" Halliday returned to his line of thought. "He must suspect our reluctance to commit our heavies in his sub and air infested waters."

"Just so," said Tovey. "That's why we and the Russians have thrown three patrol lines of submarines above the North Cape on east-west bearings. To attack east of Bear he must pass through those subs on the way out and on return to base. They'll have not forgotten *Bismarck* so quickly."

Halliday nodded thoughtfully. The other great German battleship had been brought to heel only after a lucky torpedo hit had disabled her rudder in mid-Atlantic and left her unable to steer. But in that case the torpedo was dropped from a Swordfish bi-plane launched from an aircraft carrier. He wondered if the Germans wouldn't be more concerned to avoid the Royal Navy's air power at sea than a handful of subs strung along a patrol line.

Tembam appeared with a tray and a small teapot with two mugs. He deftly poured tea for the two officers then soundlessly retreated again from the bridge. Halliday and Tovey sipped their tea in silence for a few moments before Halliday spoke again.

"If you will excuse me, Sir, it is time for the watch change."

Tovey nodded absently and watched the sea and sky, alone with his hopes, ambitions and fears.

Chapter 3

Trondheim, Norway

July 2, 1942

"Gentlemen, the great opportunity for the surface navy to strike a blow in this war has come." Admiral Otto Schniewind looked from face to face around the conference table in his flag quarters aboard *DKM Tirpitz*. The commanders of his fleet all attended to go over the plan for "Operation Rosselsprung", or "The Knight's Gambit" in English.

"We sail this evening for the North Cape," he went on. "We sail through the inner channel to shield us from enemy submarines, then join *Scheer* and *Lutzow* at Altenfiord. From there we set out to attack the Allied convoy which has sailed from Iceland for destinations in the north Russian ports." He paused again to build a moment of drama. "It is to be our duty and honor to see that not one Allied vessel delivers its cargo to the communists!"

An excited murmur ran round the table as the eight officers digested this news. Schniewind turned and pulled away a drape from the bulkhead, revealing a map of Arctic waters, bounding the sea from the Russian island Novya Zemlya in the east, the Denmark Strait between Iceland and

Greenland in the west and north to the summer limits of the Arctic ice pack. A black ribbon was pinned to the map originating at Iceland and extending northeast past Jan Mayen Island and on towards Bear Island.

"This is the convoy's course, Gentlemen," Schniewind said pointing along the ribbon. His finger stopped briefly, where the ribbon ended, 600 kilometers to the southwest of Bear Island. "And here is its most recent position confirmed by U-boat sighting several hours ago. It is traveling at about eight knots and we estimate it will pass to the north of Bear Island around midnight July 3, tomorrow night." He surveyed the officers. He held their rapt attention.

"Of course, in these latitudes at this time of year there is barely an hour of twilight that passes for darkness and the Luftwaffe and our own submarines are already shadowing the convoy round the clock."

Schniewind stabbed his finger down on the map northeast of Bear Island. "We attack here!" he exclaimed. "*Scheer, Tirpitz, Hipper* and *Lutzow* all together along with our destroyer escorts in the morning hours of July 6. The four heavy ships will converge on the convoy, like four fingers of a hand, *Scheer* and *Lutzow* on the west and east flanks, *Tirpitz* and *Hipper* in the middle, all spread out over a forty-mile front to assure we cannot miss the convoy. We will set upon the merchantmen with the big guns of the heavy ships while our destroyers hold any British escort vessels at bay."

"What constitutes the convoy escort?" Captain Karl Topp of *Tirpitz* interjected the first question. "Surely the Allies have not entrusted such a valuable convoy to the usual mix of light anti-submarine and flak ships. Where are the enemy's heavy fleet units, especially the battleships and airplane carriers?"

"Quite right, Captain!" exclaimed Schniewind. "We are tracking two or three battleships and a single aircraft carrier to the southwest of the convoy, but are confident these will not venture within range of our shore based Luftwaffe airfields around the North Cape." He waved his hand at the far northern tip of Norway. "There is also a force of enemy cruisers operating as a shadow to the convoy. We also expect these to withdraw to the west at Bear Island, but should they continue with the convoy we have more than enough firepower to dispense with them and still shatter the cargo vessels." He leaned down on the table and looked at each Captain in turn.

"Our orders are straight from Berlin, gentlemen, from the Fuhrer himself. For the sake of our Army's renewed offensive on the eastern front, we must annihilate this convoy and prevent one single ton of the supplies it carries from reaching the Russians. A comprehensive defeat of this kind will force the Allies to suspend these Arctic supply missions entirely, at least until winter darkness gives them some hope of hiding from our forces. By then the Army will have broken the Eastern Front open and crushed the Bolsheviks!"

"What if the enemy heavy units do not behave as predicted?" asked Wilhelm Meisel, Commander of the *Admiral Hipper*. "What are your orders if the battleships appear east of Bear Island, or," and here he lowered his voice as if the British might be listening, "what if the carrier comes within range to fly off an attack against us?"

Schniewind nodded his head. "The Fuhrer's orders in this case are clear. Under no circumstances are we to risk battle with superior or even with equal enemy forces. Our powerful, but small fleet is all that stands against an Allied landing in Norway. *Tirpitz* especially is not to be risked against enemy battleships and carriers. In this case we are to leave the convoy to the Luftwaffe and the U-boat boys."

Chapter 4

Berlin

July 2, 1942

Field Marshall Wilhelm Keitel settled in for another interminable Fuhrer briefing in the bunker under the garden of the Reich Chancellery in Berlin. In fact, there were of course major developments on several fronts and important decisions to be taken. As head of the OberKommando der Wehrmacht, or OKW, Keitel served as Adolph Hitler's de facto War Minister and the daily strain of gently steering the Fuhrer towards sound decisions based on military logic was wearing on him. There were days when Keitel wondered whose side God truly favored, that he should have to labor so in guiding a military novice in matters of strategy. Keitel waited until the Fuhrer was comfortably settled in his chair before beginning the briefing.

"My Fuhrer," he began with a nod to Hitler at the head of the table. He pointed at a map of the southern Soviet Union. "Our advance of Army Group South in Russia continues to make headway against fierce resistance. In the Crimea, the port of Sebastopol is almost entirely cleared of enemy troops and our engineers have begun the task of clearing the harbor and restoring the port to operation." He paused to assess the Fuhrer's mood. So far, so good. Hitler was listening attentively, showing no sign of the explosive temper displayed so often of late.

"Meanwhile," he continued, "further north at Voronezh the 2nd and 4th Panzer Armies in cooperation with 6th Army to the south have completed the encirclement of the Soviet 40th Army. We expect tens of thousands of prisoners to fall into our bag."

"Yes, Keitel," Hitler growled, speaking for the first time. "Another great encirclement with staggering Soviet losses, yet somehow they always make them good! We must break the Russian resistance once and for all! Drive to the Volga and split their armies with the Caspian Sea as our fulcrum!"

Keitel drew a quick, deep breath and bit his tongue. The entire German offensive for 1942 was geared to exactly this strategy.

"Yes, my Fuhrer," he bowed. He then spent the better part of a half hour delivering specifics about the German position on the Eastern Front. Hitler often demanded details down to the company level and Keitel struggled to satisfy the Fuhrer's insatiable need for minutiae. Keitel was also forced to explain for the hundredth time the many logistics problems facing German forces in the east, with shortages of nearly everything, but especially of fuel, plaguing and delaying the German advance.

"I will accept no excuses, Keitel," the Fuhrer growled in a voice low and filled with menace. Hitler's face was turning red and Keitel, sensing the leader's mood souring, changed the subject before the Fuhrer exploded.

"Turning now to the Mediterranean Theater," he said, switching to another smaller map. "Our forces on Malta are still tallying the enemy's losses there, but to date it seems in excess of 25,000 military prisoners have been taken. Add these to the British losses at Tobruk ten days ago and the British have suffered over 50,000 recent casualties." He held a sheet of paper in the air. "I have here a report from Dr. Goebbels' office that in the English Parliament today a vote of no confidence was tendered against Churchill's war leadership."

Hitler perked up. "Is that drunken Jewish sot deposed then?" he demanded with evident glee.

"Er," Keitel stammered, regretting now that he'd brought the matter up. "No, it seems that Churchill passed this vote, but his leadership is being openly challenged now. It can only be a matter of time before he follows Chamberlain into history." Hitler sat back in his chair and said nothing, but the scowl on his face foretold a building anger. Keitel once again sought to change the subject.

"Naval operations in the north are now underway which may bear the most profound influence in the east," he began. "The western Allies have sailed a major convoy bound for the north Russian ports carrying a cargo of war materiel, weapons and supplies. If safely delivered these supplies will soon be used against our forces in the east." He arched his eyebrows to emphasize the profound influence this would have on the struggle in the east. "Grand Admiral Raeder will now describe the Navy's plan to prevent this convoy reaching its destination."

Erich Raeder rose from his chair and with a slight bow first to Hitler, then to Keitel he strode to the map board and addressed himself to a map nearly identical to the one used earlier that day in Norway by Admiral Schniewind in the briefing to his senior officers.

"Our operation in the north is known as 'The Knight's Gambit'," began Raeder, "and its purpose is to bring the heavy guns of our surface fleet to bear against the ships of the Allied convoy." He pointed at Trondheim, halfway up the Norwegian coast. "In a few short hours the battleship *Tirpitz* and the cruiser *Admiral Hipper* will sortie from Trondheim. They will sail north to a rendezvous at the North Cape with the heavy cruisers *Scheer* and *Lutzow.* The four heavy ships, along with their escorting destroyers will sail at high speed to the north to intercept the allied convoy in the area east of Bear Island where they will sweep aside the light warships of the convoy's close escort and sink the vulnerable merchantmen."

Raeder turned to assess the Fuhrer's reaction to the briefing. Hitler's eyes were narrowed to slits and he glared at Raeder unblinking. The Admiral hurried on, anticipating the outburst he'd been expecting all day.

"Admiral Schniewind in command of our northern fleet has orders to avoid combat with superior enemy forces including battleships and especially airplane carriers at all costs and to preserve his heavy vessels, particularly *Tirpitz* from battle damage."

Hitler was about to speak, but Keitel beat him to the punch.

"I received an interesting communication on this topic this morning from Field Marshall Kesselring in Italy," he said, a feigned innocence in his voice. Hitler closed his mouth. Field Marshall Kesselring was theater commander in the Mediterranean. Hitler was surprised that Keitel would find anything Kesselring might say on this Arctic naval situation to be of interest.

"It seems Kesselring had a conversation with Count Ciano," Keitel went on, referring to the Italian Foreign Minister. "It seems the Italians are quite well informed of events in the far north and are eagerly anticipating our navy's performance against the British." He shrugged. "Apparently they are offended over the criticism they've taken over their own fleet's performance at Malta, especially the decision to turn and flee from the British Royal Navy."

Raeder stared at Keitel with barely concealed malevolence at this deliberate provocation in the middle of his presentation.

"The German War Navy does not run from battle!" he spat. "Our U-boat men and the crew of *Bismarck* can attest to this!"

"No doubt, no doubt!" Keitel answered breezily. "Still, Ciano is prepared to offer his sympathy and understanding in the event our fleet is over matched and makes a strategic withdrawal."

Hitler jumped to his feet, confronting Keitel

"Those strutting, dago peacocks!" he stormed, spittle forming at the corners of his mouth. "How dare they question the courage of our German commanders? The Italians have never once stood their ground against the British, on land or at sea! Not without strong German forces at their sides to stiffen their spines!" He turned to Raeder.

"Admiral," he growled. "Our heavy naval units are not to withdraw unless faced with overwhelming enemy sea power, including airplane carriers and threat of air attack! This convoy must be smashed before reaching Russia and the Royal Navy must be humbled! You are authorized to greater risks in pursuit of these strategic goals!" His fists clenched and breathing barely controlled, madness flared in the Fuhrer's eyes.

Admiral Raeder clicked his heels and gave a short bow to Hitler. Keitel fought to keep the smile from his face. For at least one Fuhrer Conference someone else bore the brunt of Hitler's anger.

Chapter 5

HMS Victorious on the Norwegian Sea

July 3, 1942

Duncan Butterweck huddled in the relative shelter of the forward pom-pom battery. A bitter wind whipped across the flight deck of *HMS Victorious* as aircraft for the dawn patrol readied for flight. Smoke from the pot burning up in the bows hugged tight to the centerline of the deck, indicating the wind was fresh and from directly ahead. He'd already inspected his own aircraft, a Fairey Albacore of 817 Squadron. It sat now on deck. He had only to wait for enough sunlight to permit flying off the carrier safely.

"Off you go now, Duncan," Flight Commander MacAdams patted him on the shoulder. "Keep yerr feet dr-ry laddie." The flight commander was a proud Scotsmen.

Duncan nodded, tightened the strap of his flight cap under his chin and stepped out on deck followed by his navigator, Charlie Oswald and radio operator Tim Butten. Immediately the wind nearly knocked him from his feet and the bitter cold stung his cheeks and eyes. He pulled his goggles down and raised his gloved hand to shield his face as he raced across deck to his aircraft. Climbing aboard, it took just moments to start the motor and begin his warm-up and pre-flight checklist.

When his engine and oil temperature gauges showed in the green, he gave a hand signal to a miserable looking crewman on the flight deck who waved him forward for take-off. For this flight his Albacore was not carrying a torpedo or depth bomb, but was laden with an extra 40 gallons of aviation fuel to extend his range. His mission today was to scout the seas around the fleet of US Navy and Royal Navy ships, looking for signs of German surface ships or submarines. His assigned sector was a vast, pie shaped wedge of sea to the southeast of the fleet, out to a range of 200 miles at a right angle to the fleet's course. Turning on a northeasterly heading to parallel the fleet's course he was to maintain the most economical speed for fuel consumption, covering another 400 nautical miles before turning back to the west to land on the carrier. All told, a six and a half hour flight lay ahead.

Duncan released his brakes and shoved the throttles forward, then gripped the flight stick and hung on through the stomach churning dip from the end of the flight deck before the Albacore had enough speed to sustain flight. He thanked his lucky stars for the closed cockpit of the Albacore. He'd taken his initial flight training and served aboard his first carrier assignment in the navy while flying the older Fairey Swordfish. Like the Albacore, the Swordfish was a bi-plane torpedo bomber, but with open cockpit was brutal for aircrew to fly in the harsh conditions of the arctic, even in what passed for summer in those latitudes. Temperatures in the Albacore's cockpit would still be below freezing, but without the punishing wind to which a Swordfish subjected its crew.

He checked his compass and worked his flaps and rudder. Satisfied his control surfaces were working properly he began his climb to altitude and settled down for the long patrol that lay ahead. A serious challenge for him and the other two members of his crew would be to stay alert for over six hours while flying across the mind-numbing emptiness of the frigid sea. One mistake, one momentary lapse of focus could plunge the three of them into waters so cold as to sap their lives away in minutes.

Behind Duncan on the flight deck of *Victorious,* two more Albacores waited their turn to take flight and assume their own patrol routes. The second bi-plane thundered from the deck and winged away to the front of the fleet. Its job would be to patrol the path directly ahead of the ships with a special eye for U-boat threats. Unlike Duncan's Albacore this bi-plane carried a 1,000-pound depth bomb for use in the event a sub was spotted.

The third Albacore's pilot was a young man from a good family in the Midlands. He was on his first war voyage. He went through his pre-flight checklist with a curiously excited feeling in the pit of his stomach. He knew he'd been given the route to the west of the fleet because he lacked experience and because that was the least likely direction from which a threat might materialize, but he was determined that if the enemy lurked in his sector he would find it.

He finished his checklist and pulled his goggles down over his eyes. Signaling the deck hand, he released his brakes and throttled up. The Albacore surged down the deck nearly two hundred feet when the carburetor coughed and backfired. Power to the engine fell off, then surged back. With a start, the young pilot realized he had forgotten to verify his engine temperature. The carburetor coughed again and the bi-plane bucked up onto its two front landing wheels. He hauled back on the stick, but it was no use. The plane nosed over and dug its propeller onto the armored steel flight deck. Sparks cascaded back over his windshield as the Albacore skidded down the deck, towards the bow and the leaden sea beyond. Screams from his two crewmen in the back cockpit indicated the terror they both felt, but the pilot could not utter a sound. He pushed himself back in his seat and braced for the impact of hitting the water.

As the Albacore reached the bows in its skid, the fixed undercarriage collapsed and at the last moment as the plane teetered on the brink of plunging overboard a strut snagged in the smoke-pot recessed in the steel flight deck. It stuck and the plane whipped round until its tail plane and rudder hung out over the bows, holding a precarious balance that still threatened to dump the plane overboard, taking the crew to their deaths. The bows reared up on the crest of a wave and plunged back down, slamming the crew and the one thin strut by which their fate hung with four times the force of gravity.

Even before the Albacore came to rest over a dozen men were racing toward her. The first to arrive grabbed the engine cowling and propeller and threw their weight in to the balance of holding the plane on the deck, but they too were bounced mercilessly by the plunging, rearing bows and their efforts were of small avail against the physics of holding the 11,000-pound aircraft on the deck. Finally, a rope arrived, and then another and these were looped over the engine cowling and snugged to the tie-downs on the deck used to keep parked aircraft from blowing overboard in high winds.

The pilot unhooked his harness and began to struggle with releasing the canopy above his head, but a deck crewman slapped his palm against the thin aluminum skin of the plane to grab his attention. The deck hand shook his hand and pointed to the two men in the rear cockpit, then made a tipping motion. The pilot nodded his understanding. He would have to wait until his two crew were off the plane before his own weight could leave, lest the shift would tip the bi-plane overboard. He craned his head to look over the back cockpit and saw the two men releasing themselves from their harnesses, then reach to unpin the canopy. It stuck! They banged against it, even threw their shoulders against it with what little leverage they could achieve from inside the cockpit, but it did not come free.

Victorious' bows plunged down again from the height of an especially tall wave and the two men slammed painfully into their seats. The motion of the deck beneath continued to hinder their efforts to escape until, to their amazement a deck hand clambered up over the engine cowling, the pilot's cockpit and the upper wing. He carried a heavy hammer and bracing himself with legs straddling the dome of the aft cockpit dealt three swift blows to the snaps holding the canopy locked. The snaps sheared away and the canopy popped open. The deck crewman scuttle crawled backwards the way he'd come as the radio operator and navigator gingerly climbed free of the canopy.

The bows plunged again and the two men were nearly flung from the airplane. Somehow, they hung on long enough to regain their balance. First one, then the other timed his escape over the wing and back onto the flight deck. Now the pilot got the thumbs up signal that it was his turn. He unsnapped his canopy. It released without a problem and he clambered up until he was standing on his seat. The bows plunged and his knees buckled against the force, but he held on and as the bows reared up again he crawled out over the engine cowling. He'd reached the propeller hub when the bows crashed down, yanking him free and tossing him from his hold. He crashed down on the flight deck where willing hands grabbed and held him from pitching out over the bows.

With the crew safe the deck hands of *Victorious* turned their attention to what to do with the Albacore, still delicately perched at the very edge of the carrier's bow ramp. First impulse was to pitch the wreck over the bows into the sea, until it was pointed out there was no guarantee the wreckage would not foul the propellers or rudder as it slid beneath the ship. Finally, more ropes and cables were taken forward and 200 men of the ship's company were brought on deck where, by main strength they heaved the Albacore back aboard. They dragged it back to the forward elevator and lowered it to the hangar deck below. Just another nearly deadly mishap aboard a ship at war.

From the moment of the accident until the flight deck was cleared and a fresh Albacore was launched in place of the crashed machine nearly an hour elapsed. The young pilot from the Midlands watched it wing away to the west and wondered if his career in naval aviation was over. As it turned out, this was the least of his worries.

Chapter 6

SS Carlton in the Barents Sea

July 2, 1942

Nineteen-year-old Willard Cipresso, known to his friends as Willie checked his watch as he scuttled along the port side weather deck of the *SS Carlton.* It was the shortest path to his bunk. Willie grew up in hardscrabble Weehawken, New Jersey and was no stranger to winter weather. The eldest child, his father was a dockyard Longshoreman who moonlighted as Mafia muscle, delivering beatings to debtors late with their payments. His mother was the daughter of Irish immigrants and twenty years younger than the old man. When Willie was sixteen she died giving birth to Willie's little sister, Colleen, the last of seven children. A year later, tired of minding his younger siblings Willie took a job on the docks and never went back to school. It was a short jump from the docks to a freighter with forged papers for the Merchant Marine, acquired through his father's outlaw contacts. If Willie had learned a thing in life, it was that the world did not believe it owed him a damn thing, and he pretty much returned that outlook. He was very good at watching out for number one.

It was 6.30 PM in what passed for local time, but the sun still rode high in the sky. In fact, it would barely set that night before rising again. Willie was coming off watch aboard the rusty old tramp steamer and was dreaming of being warm again. Even so, he paused a moment to look at the sight of the ships of the convoy, drawn up tight in short columns and wide rows as they steamed slowly to the northeast. His ship was second of three ships in the starboard column of PQ17. That is to say, she was furthest south and closest to land of any of the merchantmen in the convoy and the entire crew believed they'd been assigned this exposed station because they, their ship and its cargo of explosives, tanks and tank ammunition were deemed most expendable among the convoy.

Willie drew his pea coat tighter about him, put his head down against the biting wind and hurried on his way, but he'd not gone far when the sounds of a ship's horn came to him on the wind. He stopped and looked out at the convoy stretched away to the north, but saw nothing out of place. The horn sounded again. This time he clambered around the number one hatch cover and passed over to the *Carlton's* starboard side.

The British escort ships protecting the convoy's flank were dashing about at high speed, horns blaring and signal lamps flashing. Willie looked up at the bridge of the *Carlton*. Her master, a Norwegian named Hansen stood there watching the action among the escorts through his binoculars. A moment later, the men of *Carlton's* US Navy Armed Guard detachment appeared on the bridge wings and uncovered the two .50 caliber machine guns the ship carried as her only protection.

The crack of guns wafted across the water and he turned back to the escort ships. Black streaks and puffs of smoke were appearing in the sky to the convoy's south and Willie assumed enemy aircraft were sighted, but he could not make them out. Looking back at the bridge, he saw Captain Hansen holding his binoculars to his eyes with one hand while pointing with the other. He followed the captain's line of sight and finally picked up the black dots of approaching airplanes mixed amongst the exploding anti-aircraft shells. Within seconds, the planes were close enough to begin to recognize the details of twin floats on fixed undercarriage and the menacing long, thin tube of a torpedo slung below each plane.

The planes began to descend towards the sea and the height above water from which they could drop their torpedoes. The flak fire from the escorts followed them and intensified, with red and green tracer shells distinguishable among red and black explosions. One of the float planes tipped over on its port wing, straightened momentarily, then tipped right into the sea with a mighty splash of white water. A ragged cheer erupted from *Carlton's* bridge and Willie laughed aloud.

The destruction of their companion seemed to take the courage from the remaining enemy bombers. One by one, they each dropped their single torpedoes and even Willie knew they were far too distant to hope for anything but the luckiest of hits. The convoy sailed serenely on as the six surviving floatplanes turned tail and ran for home.

"Round one to us!" Willie exclaimed aloud before hurrying on to his bunk.

Chapter 7

DKM Tirpitz on the North Cape of Norway

July 4, 1942

Tirpitz rocked in the gentle swell inside the protection of Altenfiord near Norway's North Cape. *Admiral Hipper* stood in her lee and across the fiord *Lutzow* and *Scheer* swung gently at anchor. They'd arrived several hours earlier from their previous anchorage at Narvik. Along with a pair of torpedo boats, several of the combined fleets' escort destroyers guarded Altenfiord's entrance while the others waited their turns to take on fuel from the oiler sent ahead there for that purpose.

Elsewhere in the world that day, the German hero of "Operation Herkules", German Army Major Kuno Schacht first awakened in a Benghazi, Libya hospital from the delirium he suffered due to the Amoebic Dysentery he contracted during the invasion of Malta. American farm boy and RAF volunteer pilot Kenneth Wiltshire's odyssey continued. Rescued at sea from the Malta harbor launch on which he'd escaped the island, he was on his way to join a new RAF Spitfire squadron flying from an airbase in Egypt's Nile River Delta. *HMS Sirius* and her Gunnery Officer Roland Webster sailed through the Suez Canal on their surprising return to the Mediterranean Sea. Maggie Reed suffered the cruel effects of oxygen deprivation during a ten-day journey aboard a Royal Navy submarine. The sub had to remain submerged through the long daylight hours and its crew and the forty Malta evacuees it carried consumed the oxygen in the sub each day until carbon dioxide in their atmosphere reached dangerous levels. The Baron von der Heydte, Colonel Friedrich August fought for his life at a Sicilian evacuation hospital jam packed with Luftwaffe wounded from the Maltese invasion.

However, in Altenfiord the crews of the German heavy ships were enjoying a brief respite from continuous watch keeping. Hot meals were served and the men given a chance for a few hours of sleep. The fleet would sail again within hours after successfully navigating the run from the anchorages further south on the Norwegian coastline. *Tirpitz* and *Hipper* left their anchorage near Trondheim at 8pm the evening of July 2 along with their escorting destroyers, their crews watching the rocky, jagged shoreline of the Norwegian coast flit by to either side in the mist. *Tirpitz* slid with a soft, quiet swish through The Leads, the narrow channel separating the Norwegian mainland from the rugged islands that closely hug the coast. *Admiral Hipper* sailed close behind, staying in the wake of the larger ship, relying on the outstanding seamanship of Captain Topp to see them safely through the dangerous passage.

In the early hours of July 3 they left behind The Leads and sailed into open waters of the Norwegian Sea. But while danger from submerged rocks was gone, the need for vigilance was re-doubled, for now the ships were exposed to lurking Royal Navy submarines, sent to spy on them and always willing to throw a spread of torpedoes on the chance of a lucky hit. The destroyers took up screening positions two kilometers to port and the watch on every ship was on heightened alert.

Once in open water the ships' engines went to full power and the fleet came to 29 knots, close to the top speed of its slowest member, the *Tirpitz* herself. The great battleship could sustain bursts of speed close to 32 knots and *Hipper* and the destroyers could all exceed 32, but the time to push machinery and the men who operated it to their limits was not yet upon the Germans. Now, in Altenfiord the time for maximum effort was near to hand. Once the destroyers were all refueled the fleet would sail on a due north heading to intercept the Allied convoy steaming east near Bear Island.

The German plan had already escaped a brush with disaster. The "Pocket Battleship" *Lutzow* scraped an uncharted rock in the channel outside Narvik the day before and several compartments below the water line were flooded. Quick reaction from the ship's damage control parties isolated the damage and on the run to Altenfiord, her captain found her top speed of 28 knots slowed only to 27 knots. As her engines and armament were uninjured and given the vital need to stop the Allied convoy, it was decided she could proceed as planned with the operation.

As final preparations were made on all the ships of the fleet to leave Altenfiord for the attack on the convoy Admiral Schniewind hosted another conference aboard *Tirpitz*. This time Vice-Admiral Kummetz in command of the *Scheer/Lutzow* battle group along with the commanders of the two pocket battleships, Captains Meendsen-Bohlken and Stange respectively attended along with the previous participants. Schniewind had changes to the planned operation to cover.

"Gentlemen," he began in his courtly manner. "I have received fresh instructions from Berlin in the past hour, sent by land-line teletype." He held up a message slip to emphasize the point. He referred to the slip and read aloud from the message sent by Admiral Raeder following the Fuhrer conference earlier that day.

"Along with the utter destruction of convoy PQ17 it is also imperative that the German Navy establish superiority over the British Royal Navy in northern waters. For that purpose, you are authorized to accept battle with enemy surface forces up to parity to your own strength. While it remains vital that the heavy fleet units be preserved for further action, it is also vital that if the Royal Navy dares to send its heavy units into the zone of U-boat and Luftwaffe operations that the German Navy should not concede these areas."

The other officers were briefly dumbfounded, but Admiral Kummetz recovered quickly.

"Well!" he exclaimed. "Do you have any indication what is behind this change of spirit?" he asked of Schniewind. "Does Berlin know something they are not sharing with us? Up till now we've operated with hands tied behind our backs with regard to risking our heavy ships."

"Quite so, Kummetz," answered Schniewind. "I can think of only one condition which would result in such an extraordinary change in outlook in Berlin. The High Command must have information concerning the British airplane carrier sighted this past week. I can only assume it is out of action somehow, perhaps sunk or damaged by one of our U-boats, an accident as nearly befell *Lutzow* on her transit north or an engineering casualty. Only with threat of air attack at sea removed can I imagine being given this kind of operational freedom." He waved the message slip again. "There is only one way for me to interpret these new orders. I am to press the attack on the convoy, until confronted by superior surface forces of the enemy. That can only happen if we are confronted by an allied fleet that includes at least two battleships, plus supporting heavy cruisers." He stabbed his finger on the same map he'd used at Trondheim.

"Here, to the east of Bear Island we shall attack and annihilate the enemy convoy and any surface fleet that tries to stop us!" He placed his hands flat on the table and met each of his senior officer's eyes. "Return to your ships, gentlemen. See that they and your crews are ready in all respects. We sail this afternoon to make history!"

Chapter 8

Whitehall, London

July 4, 1942

Prime Minister Winston Churchill puffed one of his famous cigars in his right hand and held a nearly empty brandy snifter in the other. While most other members of the British War Cabinet eschewed these vices, Churchill reveled in them and made little effort to hide either, even from the public. Late the evening of July 4, 1942 Churchill and the War Cabinet met in the underground chambers beneath the New Public Offices building in Whitehall, London. Finished just days before the outbreak of hostilities in September 1939 the basement's War Cabinet Rooms as they came to be known had returned their investment many times. They allowed the senior civilian leaders of Britain's government to remain in London, setting policy and direction of the war effort in the relative safety of the underground bunker, even at the height of the Luftwaffe blitz in the summer and autumn of 1940.

On this night, the War Cabinet had many challenges to consider. The situation in the Mediterranean and North Africa held center stage. Tobruk and Malta had both fallen to the combined air, sea and land strength of the Axis powers, Germany and Italy and now the newly minted German Field Marshall Erwin Rommel seemed intent to make Cairo and the Suez Canal the next dominos to fall in Hitler's grand game of world domination.

Only two days earlier, Churchill survived a No Confidence vote in the House of Commons, the second such vote he'd passed already that year of 1942. Triggered by the fall of the Libyan port of Tobruk and reinforced by the loss of Malta, the vote was passed with a wide margin, 425 -75, but that 75 Members of Parliament should vote against the government and its war direction was itself a clear statement of the unease felt by the public at large.

That evening the war cabinet voted to reinforce Egypt by pulling yet more men and resources from the Far East where Commonwealth forces were hard-pressed by advances of the Japanese. Defense of India was a high priority, but not nearly as vital as stopping a German advance to the oil fields of Iraq and Iran.

Minister of Production, Mr. Lyttelton expounded on the choices to be made among the various aircraft types being demanded by the Royal Air Force and the Royal Navy's Fleet Air Arm. Fundamentally, not all demands could be met. The choices between them boiled down to whether or not to favor heavy bomber production in support of Bomber Command and its mission to attack German industry from the air, or to meet the requirements of the Navy and of Fighter Command and Coastal Command in defense of the home islands and the transatlantic convoy routes. This decision was tabled, with the majority of the Ministers seeming to favor defense of the Home Islands, while Churchill vigorously fought for the fleet of heavy bombers.

The final topic of the evening, at the end of a very long day, involved the convoy to Russia, designated PQ17, then underway, and of the heavy commitment of escort ships for it. Someone suggested, history is not clear by whom, to cancel the convoy in the face of British Intelligence estimates that the Germans might send the dreaded *Tirpitz* out against the convoy. Here too Churchill disagreed and used his imposing rhetorical skills in support of his preference.

"If we are to ever see an end to the drain on our naval resources that *Tirpitz* imposes upon us, she must be brought to battle and destroyed, or at least crippled for many months," he argued, "even should this mean losses of our own in the short term. For if we should even disable *Tirpitz* such that she should spend the better part of a year in dock for repairs, the freedom this would give us in disposing the heavy units of our Home

Fleet would be worth the cost of a battleship of our own, and even dare I say it, of an aircraft carrier as well. And should we succeed in sinking *Tirpitz*, even at such a high price, why then the entire direction and focus of our naval war effort would open and broaden before us, no longer confronted with the task of keeping our thumb on her and being ready always to defend the shipping lanes from her." He took a drink of his brandy. "No gentlemen, we should NOT recall the convoy at all, but rather should direct our forces to the greatest effort to lure *Tirpitz* from her lair and to come to grips with her. In the scheme of things the convoy, as important to our Russian allies as it is, is of small measure compared to the opportunity to destroy or disable *Tirpitz*."

And so it was that in both Berlin and London, the fall of Malta was the event that tipped the antagonists' highest leadership to decisions involving PQ17 that bordered on desperation. Orders were given that effectively gambled dozens of ships, including the most powerful naval forces then available, hundreds of aircraft and the lives of thousands of men, either to press the convoy through and to sink *Tirpitz*, or to smash the convoy and to drive the Royal Navy from northern waters once and for all.

For the Germans, the vital strategic goal of denying a huge delivery of war materiel to the hated Soviets was paramount. In addition, they sought to defend their claims of superiority over their own allies, the Italians. To Hitler, and indeed to his entire High Command, the idea that the Italians could claim to show more courage in confronting the Royal Navy than the Germans could not be contemplated.

In Britain, there was an air that the war had taken several giant slips away from the Allied grasp in recent weeks with the losses suffered in the Mediterranean and that without a genuine success in battle somewhere and soon, that the political direction of the war could yet be lost.

Together these two viewpoints reinforced one another and led to the greatest surface battle of the war in European waters.

PART 2: OPENING MOVES

Chapter 9

Over the Norwegian Sea

July 4, 1942

The Focke-Wulfe 200 Condor thundered toward the North Pole, its four BMW radial engines performing flawlessly. Six hours into the planned twelve hour flight on the great half-circle from Vaernes Air base outside Trondheim in central Norway to Bardufoss Air Field near North Cape, the crew was tense and alert, scanning the sea for any sign of their prey, the allied convoy. At the same time they watched the sky for dangerous predators, British naval fighters flown from the airplane carrier believed to be operating somewhere in the vicinity of Bear Island.

Weather conditions that day were a rarity for the Arctic, even near high summer. A calm, flat sea and clear blue skies combined for startling clarity and visibility. From its cruising height of 3,000 meters, the crew of the Condor had an unobstructed view of the sea and sky in all directions to the horizon. Flying at the center of a circle nearly 400 kilometers in diameter, they surveyed a sea surface area of over 100,000 square kilometers.

So far, on this reconnaissance flight the sea and sky were both incredibly empty. Apart from a handful of fishing trawlers hugging the Norwegian coastline they'd seen nothing. The flight engineer plotted a course that took them to the west of Bear Island, near the limits of visibility, but near enough to make an accurate landmark to confirm his navigation. At 6pm that afternoon, the island came into view, away to the northeast.

The FW 200 continued on, past Bear Island, deeper into the Arctic until the shimmering white line of the ice barrier emerged on the horizon dead ahead. The pilot banked the plane to the right and, keeping the line of the ice barrier in sight off his left wingtip began the long eastbound leg of the flight. With Bear Island still visible now on his right wingtip the crew of the Condor had a clear and unobstructed view of the sea between the island and the ice. It seemed inevitable that they would soon sight the convoy.

"No sleeping now," the pilot announced jovially to his crew over the ship's intercom. "We could sight the enemy convoy anytime now, and if there is an airplane carrier lurking about its fighter patrol could find us just as easily. Stay alert." Ersatz coffee in insulated flasks, fortified with artificial caffeine served to jolt the crew to heightened watchfulness.

An hour after passing Bear Island they found the convoy, flying up from behind the fleet of merchantmen at 8pm. The sun was still high in the sky on that summer day and it took only minutes to confirm the thin, white streaks that appeared on the sea far ahead were in fact the wakes of the convoy, drawn up in nine columns of three to five ships each. A coded sighting report flew through the ether within minutes, followed by a much lengthier and more detailed message on the composition of the convoy. Thirty-four merchant vessels on a due east heading with a dozen light escort vessels in close attendance. Unknown to the Germans, one of the original thirty-five merchantmen had turned back to Iceland with a mechanical failure. The pilot settled his airplane into a great circle around the convoy, keeping a respectful five kilometers outside the range of the escort ships' anti-aircraft guns. Coded signals every twenty minutes provided a constant confirmation of the convoy position, course and speed. PQ17 had been pinned to the map like a fly in an insect collection. Four hundred miles away these sighting reports were monitored with great interest aboard every ship in the German fleet. Operation Rosselsprung was about to begin.

Chapter 10

The Admiralty, Whitehall, London

July 4, 1942

The Germans were not the only interested parties listening to the sighting reports from the FW 200. Covert listening stations of the British 'Y' Service, the wireless intercept organization picked up the signals as well. Though coded, the wireless stations nonetheless recorded the signals, then forwarded them on to Station 'X', the super-secret code-breaking unit outside London in Bletchley Park. Working round the clock, a team of dedicated and talented scientists and mathematicians succeeded in gaining a working understanding of the German Military's most secret wireless communications. On this day the Condor's sighting reports were decoded and distributed to senior officers of the Royal Navy in the Admiralty almost before Admiral Schniewind and his staff aboard *Tirpitz* saw them.

From these intercepts, the Admiralty knew that the Germans had PQ17's position pinned to the mile and that concerted air and U-boat attacks might commence at any time, but their gravest concern was the whereabouts of the German surface fleet and its intentions. A gap in the

British signals intelligence existed. While the British had an excellent and extensive 'Y' Service, dedicated to intercepting enemy wireless transmissions and forwarding them to Bletchley Park for rapid decoding, they had no such coverage over the enemy's landline network of telephone and teletype messages. At this moment, the most dangerous communication amongst the German commands was the one the British were completely unaware of, from Berlin to Admiral Schniewind authorizing him to take greater risks in pursuit of PQ17.

Norwegian spies alerted the British through their embassy in Stockholm, Sweden that *Tirpitz*, Hipper had left their lair at Trondheim, and the British assumed that so too had *Lutzow* and *Scheer* put to sea. But with no sighting reports of their own on the German ships they could not be certain of their up-to-date locations. They could only estimate where the Germans might be, based on the top speeds of each of the enemy vessels and the last time they were known to be at anchor. On this basis the German heavies could be as little as four hours sailing time from PQ17, about as close as the Anglo-American cruiser force sailing 120 miles to the northwest of the convoy. Worse, even if the four heavy cruisers of this covering force went to top speed to close up with the convoy they were no match to take on *Tirpitz* and her consorts. They'd likely be swept aside and simply fall onto the casualty list along with the merchantmen and close escorts.

Only the distant covering force with the battleships *HMS Duke of York*, *USS Washington* and aircraft carrier *HMS Victorious* could possibly tackle the Germans with any hope of success and these ships were nearly four hundred miles to the west of the convoy. They were much too far away to arrive in time. Worse still, the heavy ships and escorts of Admiral Tovey's distant covering force were all low on fuel. A high speed run to the east, and battle with the German surface force while exposed to air and U-boat attack would drain their thin reserves of fuel and might require them to replenish at sea. Underway refueling was a dicey proposition when the Arctic weather could turn on a whim and blow up gale force winds and mountainous seas for days at a time. As the war progressed, the US Navy in the Pacific Theater would master the techniques of refueling and replenishing while underway. Before War's end, the Americans could keep whole fleets at sea for months at a time. A massive and complex network of forward supply depots and ships was required. In the Arctic, none such existed.

First Sea Lord, Admiral Sir Dudley Pound and his Admiralty staff faced a dilemma. To allow the convoy to sail on would be to hand them to the depredations of the German battle fleet. Another possibility discussed between Pound and Admiral Tovey now aboard *Duke of York,* before the latter left Scapa Flow, was to scatter the convoy and leave every ship to make its own way to the Russian ports. Doing so would reduce the size of the target available to the German surface ships and force them to hunt down individual merchantmen in a time consuming venture that might expose the Germans to British submarine attack. But it would also deprive the merchantmen of the advantage of their close escort ships and leave them nearly defenseless against German aircraft and U-boats. Either way, a slaughter seemed imminent.

Now the Admiralty staff revisited a proposal made by Admiral Tovey before his departure, that in the event the convoy should find itself east of Bear Island and in danger of *Tirpitz* or other German surface ships and without the Anglo-American distant covering force to hand for protection, that the convoy itself should reverse course. Backtracking to the west could add several hours to the time it would take the Germans to reach the convoy. At the same time, it would reduce the time needed for the allied battleships to close the distance and would bring the convoy in range of *Victorious*' fighter and torpedo aircraft sooner as well. Finally, reversing course would put the convoy more distant to the German air bases in northern Norway.

Drawbacks to the idea were that the convoy would remain exposed to U-boat attack regardless of the direction it sailed and any hours spent backtracking would simply have to be made up when the convoy eventually resumed its course for Russia.

Debate went back and forth in the Admiralty conference rooms, but left unsaid was Admiral Pound's orders from the War Cabinet expressing the desire that *Tirpitz* be brought to action if at all possible, even using PQ17 as bait to achieve this end. Ultimately, this seems to have been the deciding factor in his decision.

At 10PM the Admiralty Signals Section sent the message ordering Convoy PQ17 and its close escorts to reverse course and backtrack to the west, back towards Bear Island.

Chapter 11

U-355 on the Norwegian Sea

July 2-5, 1942

It had been a frustrating war patrol for Lt. Commander Gunther La Baume, Captain of the German submarine U-355. In the morning on July 2, he and his boat reached their assigned station in a patrol line of six subs southwest of Bear Island, along the line of the convoy's expected course. His orders were to find the convoy and report its position, then to follow it and keep it under observation until other boats came in for a mass attack. Only then would he be free to launch his own attack. Bad luck seemed to dog his efforts though. A heavy fog descended over his boat and kept visibility to under 200 meters all day on July 2nd. Not until the morning of the 3rd did it clear and by then the convoy was presumed to have passed him to the northeast.

La Baume turned east by northeast and ran his twin diesel engines up to full speed, intending to cut inside the arc of the convoy's course to Bear Island. The sea was in a strange, flat calm, U-355 knifed across the surface at an optimal speed of 14 knots and La Baume hoped to leap ahead of the convoy, find and report it. The cold, dreary fog of the day before gave way to bright sunshine and unlimited visibility and he conned the boat from the exposed bridge. Constant reminders and frequent changes of the watch kept the crew alert to detect the convoy or the approach of enemy aircraft, but neither appeared through all the long hours of the day.

At midnight, during the brief interval of twilight that passed for darkness in the Arctic summer he dived the boat. With his executive officer standing watch in the control room La Baume retired to his tiny sea cabin and snatched a few hours of sleep; waking at 0300 he resumed command and made a thorough inspection of the surrounding sea through his periscope before surfacing. Another long, frustrating day followed with U-355 patrolling a box 25 nautical miles on a side centered some 50 nautical miles northwest of Bear Island. By the end of the day it was clear that the convoy had eluded him and must be many miles to the east by now. Even at top speed, it was highly unlikely he could catch it, but his orders precluded him from even trying. The sea zone to the east of Bear Island was to be kept free of U-boats to allow the German surface ships free reign there.

La Baume wrote a message for transmission to flotilla HQ in Norway with his position and situation He resigned himself to settle down awaiting a reply with new orders. He leaned pensively on the binnacle, staring out over the sea, wondering where and how the British had slipped past him. His reverie was interrupted.

"Kapitan!" a shout came up through the conning tower hatch. La Baume knelt and looked down the hatch.

"Yes, what is it, Kubein?" he asked the boat's wireless operator.

"Captain, I am unable to send the signal you ordered," replied Kubein standing at the bottom of the conning tower ladder. "There is a fault in the wireless and I have not yet been able to solve it."

"When did this fault occur?" demanded La Baume.

"I am uncertain, Sir," answered Kubein. "This is the first message we've attempted to send in two days. The problem may have come at any time since. We are able to receive messages, Sir," Kubein went on hopefully. "You've seen several this past day. The fault is in the transmitter."

La Baume considered then shrugged.

"Begin your diagnosis, Kubein," he ordered. "Report to me when it is complete. I may amend the message depending on how much time has elapsed."

In any event, La Baume was not greatly concerned. With the convoy already past him and the area east of Bear Island excluded to him the only orders he conceived he might receive in response to his own message were to return to port or to remain on station for the time being. He resolved to sit tight, watchful and alert until his wireless was again functional.

Chapter 12

HMS Duke of York on the Norwegian Sea

July 4, 1942

Tembam, the Malay steward brought two steaming mugs of Kai to Captain Halliday and Admiral Tovey on the flag bridge of *HMS Duke of York*. Tembam made the hot, viscous drinks himself, melting two bars of milk chocolate into a pot of hot milk. He bowed and left the two officers alone on the flag bridge.

"It seems we are to roll the dice after all," said Admiral Tovey, carefully sipping from his steaming Kai. He'd just read the latest Admiralty signal, including the decision to turn PQ17 back on its course to bring it closer to the Anglo-American covering force.

"So it does, Sir," answered Captain Halliday, wrapping his hands around the heavy porcelain on tin mug. "How do you rate our chances of luring *Tirpitz* west of Bear Island?" he asked.

"I should have thought better had we turned the convoy back on its course before they'd passed the island rather than after," responded Tovey. "At this point the Germans can't believe we'd sail the convoy all the way back to Iceland. They've got to figure this is some sort of ruse or lure."

The two men stood quietly, with only the sound of the wind and the soft swish as *Duke of York* parted the slight swell. Heavy sea gear muffled both to the ears, but thankfully, they had only to contend with the bitter cold.

"My fuel situation is chancy," said Halliday. "Doubtless the same for *Washington* and *Victorious*. We can't spend days prancing about east of Bear Island, else we shall have to refuel at sea or accept a tow home. Good that we've already topped up the destroyers, or else they'd be falling out of line by tomorrow morning."

"Yes," nodded Tovey. "And to conserve fuel we shall have to avoid high speed sailing until the critical moment."

"All the more critical that our weather should hold," agreed Halliday. "So long as *Victorious* can fly off search planes we oughtn't to have to conduct any kind of grid search."

"We'd best get started," said Tovey. "Signal to the fleet by Aldis Lamp to turn due east at 22 knots. I'll prepare a more comprehensive message for *Washington* and *Victorious* explaining the latest developments."

"At 22 knots we're 20 hours from Bear Island," said Halliday. "By this time tomorrow we'll have the convoy in hand again. What if *Tirpitz* declines the invitation?"

"Their Lordships will know," answered Tovey without the slightest hint of sarcasm. "See to your ship Captain and do keep me informed on your fuel reserves."

"Yes, Sir," said Halliday, leaving Tovey alone on his flag bridge to contemplate the expanse of frigid sea.

Chapter 13

Convoy PQ17. Westbound, east of Bear Island

July 5, 1942

Willie Cipresso and his shipmates aboard the old tramp steamer *Carlton* were initially ecstatic over their change of course. With no explanation offered them, most believed the effort to reach Russia was cancelled and that they were destined now for return to Iceland. A few of the more die-hard cynics of the crew were more skeptical. Their view was that some diabolical danger threatened the convoy and the course reversal to the west was temporary while this new threat played out. Only when the Master, Captain Hansen ordered the crew to break the hatch seals on the tanks on deck and to bring tank ammunition up from the for'ard hold did the somber mood of the crew return. He also ordered that empty oil drums filled with oil soaked rags and bits and pieces of broken wooden packing crates be placed on deck over the number two hold behind the bridge. He did not explain this strange command. In any case, the course reversal still left *Carlton* on the south edge of the convoy, but now the German airbases on land were to port, not starboard.

Through the day, the convoy was never without its aerial shadow. The German Focke-Wulfe 200 Condor stayed frustratingly clear of the anti-aircraft guns of the close escort, but always in sight. Its size made it hard to miss even staying several miles outside the radius of the convoy as it maintained its vigil. At mid-day, another replaced it. The departing pilot had the gall, some said the panache, to overfly the convoy at high altitude and to waggle his wings in a goodbye gesture. That the shadowing enemy planes had reported their change of course, none in the convoy had the slightest doubt.

Four hours after reversing course the convoy suffered its first concerted air attack of the voyage. Twenty-six He 111 torpedo bombers with 12 Ju 88 dive-bombers flying from the German bases at Banak and Bardufoss Norway came at them in three waves. Eight of the torpedo bombers approached from low on the southern horizon while the flight of Ju88's attacked moments later from high altitude. A blizzard of anti-aircraft fire erupted from the convoy, first from the escort ships, and then the merchantmen themselves added their own puny firepower to the defense.

Convoy Commodore Dowding aboard the *River Afton* decided this was the time to use his CAM launched Hurricane fighter aboard the British freighter *Empire Tide.* The CAM was a catapult device loaded amidships that launched a Hurricane fighter to break up enemy air attack. For the pilot it was a one-way ride. There was no provision for recovering the aircraft. If damaged in battle or when out of fuel the pilot's only choices were to ditch the aircraft near one of the covering escort vessels or to abandon his ship by parachute and hope to be recovered quickly. Either way, once he was in the frigid water he had only moments to inflate the small dingy he carried under his parachute and to haul himself out of the water before hypothermia killed him. Calculated life expectancy for CAM pilots was one flight.

With *Empire Tide* flying her 'aeroplane flag' the CAM Hurricane was shot into the air, a process capable of delivering a nasty case of whiplash to any pilot not properly harnessed in and braced. Away it raced, out to the fringes of the convoy and with more than one gun aboard the freighters mistaking it for a German. As the Ju 88's began their diving attack, the Hurricane pilot took his craft in against the He 111 torpedo bombers on the convoy's port flank, and coincidentally right through the hail of anti-aircraft fire directed toward the Germans. When the enemy bomber pilots realized they were facing a British Hurricane fighter plane here in the Arctic where none should be so far from any land base they appeared to lose their nerve. One after another, they dropped the twin torpedoes carried under their fuselages and turned for home. The deadly fish, dropped too far from their targets to be effective raced through the screen of escort ships and on to the convoy. But even the cumbersome freighters had plenty of time to turn out of line to avoid their paths.

At the same moment, the Ju 88's high above tipped over in their dives and hurtled down towards the milling ships of PQ17. Aboard the *Carlton* Willie Cipresso was back on watch on the bridge when the attack began and he found himself barely able to take his eyes from the spectacle of the German torpedo bombers running for home. For the second time in the voyage it appeared that PQ17 had driven off an air attack. Only when flak shells began exploding over his head did he realize his mistake.

"Airplane straight overhead!" he shouted, pointing into the sky. Captain Hansen turned to see the threat.

"Hard a-port!" he shouted. "Left full rudder!"

The deck vibrated under Willie's feet and he leaned to brace himself against the turn just as two bombs fell from beneath the airplane. The German aircraft immediately began pulling out of its dive, even as a line of machine gun bullets from the *Carlton's* Naval Armed Guard crew stitched through its right wing. The two bombs plunged down. To Willie it seemed both were aimed directly for him and he ducked down behind the canvas screen on the bridge railing and flattened himself to the deck. Both bombs carried over the ship and into the water to starboard. Fused to either penetrate below decks or to sink fifty feet before exploding it seemed for a moment to those watching that they must be duds as nothing more than a large splash erupted at first, but a moment later the two bombs went off almost simultaneously.

The underwater concussion seemed to lift the *Carlton* in the air and slam her back into the water. Willie's body was lifted off the deck and he felt as if he hung suspended a foot in the air for a moment before a giant hand swatted him painfully back down.

"WOOF!" the breath was knocked from him and he lay on the deck writhing and gasping for air.

"Right rudder!" shouted Hansen. "Steady amidships!"

Willie picked himself slowly to his knees. Still seeing stars, he hung on the bridge rail until he could fill his lungs with a deep breath. He nearly retched on the icy bite of the frigid air in his windpipe, but he cleared his head and got to his feet. He turned and looked out over the convoy. Black, oily smoke rose from two other ships, one in the next column to starboard that he knew to be the American flagged *Fairfield City*. The other burning ship was in the middle of the convoy and he could not see which it was.

As Willie watched in horror *Fairfield City* began to list to port and her speed fell off. She slewed round until she wallowed between swells. Behind her in line, the *SS Honomu* turned hard to starboard, but her vast bulk carried too much momentum and she continued on. Her foghorn sounded a collision warning and she scraped down the starboard side of *Fairfield City*, shouldering into the stricken freighter with a dull crunch, then the tortured scream of steel plate tearing and bending like cardboard. *Honomu* seemed to bounce away from the impact as if she'd been punched by a heavyweight boxer, rocking back and forth as she steadied on course. As she cleared *Fairfield City's* bows Willie saw a forty foot gash in *Honomu's* port side. The damage was above the waterline and for now, *Honomu* was lucky, but she'd be in serious danger if the sea freshened.

Captain Hansen was on the telephone to the engine room demanding a damage report and the rest of the bridge watch was as shaken as Willie. They'd had a very close brush with disaster and all were rapt, watching as

Fairfield City fell behind, her crew fighting to swing her port side lifeboats out before her list grew too great.

Willie turned his attention back to port and scanned the sky there for any more aircraft. The flak fire had all died out and a haze of black smoke trailed away behind the convoy and her escorts, from the two burning ships and the barrage. Willie could see the German planes escaping to the south, keeping low to the water and running at top speed for home. So far as he could tell none had been shot down or were seriously damaged. He looked aft, down the port side of the ship. *Carlton* appeared to have escaped with no visible damage. His gaze carried on aft to the fantail where the Stars and Stripes snapped and whipped in the wind. Behind the ship, a smoke screen lay upon the water and he could only see the one ship behind them in the port column, the *Daniel Morgan* three hundred yards behind.

Willie exhaled a long held breath and was turning away when an aircraft burst from the shroud of smoke behind the convoy. Two more quickly followed. He gave an incoherent startled cry and pointed aft. The three planes flew right between the two port columns of the convoy at masthead height. Nose mounted machine guns sprayed the decks of *Daniel Morgan*, bright sparks banging at crazy angles along with green tracer ricochets like water thrown on hot oil in a frying pan. One by one, the three planes passed *Carlton* then tipped over on their right wings and turned into the middle of the convoy. They steadied back on level flight before launching their six torpedoes one after the other, then turned back in the direction from which they'd come, from behind the convoy and, machine guns still blazing away, disappeared back into the smoke.

Seconds later the hits began. Launching their torpedoes from within the very confines of the convoy the Germans could hardly fail to score multiple hits. One after another, a loud report followed by a fountain of water towering hundreds of feet into the sky indicated a hit. Willie could not even be certain how many explosions he heard, but was sure there were at least five. In fact, the second wave of eighteen torpedo bombers attacking from astern hit six different ships with eight torpedoes.

The eighth torpedo to score a hit caught the *SS Olapana* in her forward hold. The fish burst into the hold before detonating amongst her cargo of explosives and ammunition. A volcanic explosion rocketed the hold's hatch cover over a hundred feet in the sky atop of a pillar of fire. Debris rained down on nearby ships, injuring eight men and killing one aboard *Bolton Castle*.

The Germans had conducted a brilliant attack with precision coordination, no doubt facilitated by the crew of the Condor circling high overhead. Now, too late the Hurricane returned from chasing the first wave of torpedo bombers and began climbing to altitude. If nothing else, its pilot was determined to take a shot at the Condor with his few remaining rounds of machine gun ammo.

But the crew of the Focke-Wulfe was alert to this danger and turned away to the south long before the Hurricane could rise to an altitude to challenge them. With eight burning pyres in the heart of the convoy, serving as homing beacons for any ship or aircraft within a hundred miles it was not necessary that the Condor stay in close touch with PQ17. With its four powerful BMW radial engines straining, it fled before the Hurricane could get close. Nearly fifteen minutes later the Hurricane returned. It circled the scene of the disaster, the pilot watching rescue operations as all three rescue ships assigned to the convoy plucked survivors from lifeboats, rafts and in a few cases the open sea. Men in shock from their wounds or simply from emersion in the frigid waters were hustled below decks where they were stripped of sodden, burned or torn clothing, swaddled in fresh duffel gear and bundled up near the engineering spaces where warmth from the ships' engines brought the temperature into the 60 degree range on the Fahrenheit scale. Nonetheless, men succumbed to hypothermia who were otherwise uninjured.

Once it was clear all survivors had been plucked from the sea the Hurricane pilot set his fighter down on the water with a gentle splash. He climbed out on the wing as the plane settled in the water. He inflated his dingy and stepped carefully into it before paddling away from his sinking aircraft. Rescued less than ten minutes later by one of the escort ships he was among the luckiest of all CAM pilots. He did not even get his feet wet before being taken aboard *HMS Ledbury*, a Royal Navy destroyer of the convoy escort.

The German Air Force had drawn blood and not a man in the convoy doubted the enemy's thirst for more.

Chapter 14

DKM Tirpitz hunting PQ17.

July 5, 1942

Admiral Schniewind paced the flag bridge of *Tirpitz* as the great battleship led his fleet northward into the Arctic. The fleet started from Altenfiord on a north by northeast heading, on a course to catch the allied convoy 300 nautical miles east of Bear Island. But early that morning the ships' wireless operators listened in on the sighting report of the 4-engine FW 200 flying over the convoy when it reported the convoy's course reversal. Schniewind immediately ordered course altered to north by northwest to converge on PQ17's new track just 100 miles east of Bear.

He knew this would put his fleet on the very fringe of the zone in which he was authorized to operate without clear intelligence that the allied battle fleet, especially that damned airplane carrier, was in no position to threaten him. To reach the convoy in time he ordered his force to increase speed to 26 knots, just below the maximum *Lutzow* could attain with her damage and at which his escorting destroyers would consume their fuel supply at a shocking rate. If sustained for more than a few hours or if followed by a protracted period of maneuver in battle his escorts would not have fuel to reach harbor and he'd be forced to try to refuel them at sea, a procedure in which his crews had little practice. Worse yet, the unpredictable Arctic weather could close in on very short notice. Foul weather would make any refueling effort nearly impossible.

But Schniewind was determined. He felt this could be the German Surface Navy's last opportunity to strike a blow for the Fatherland in this war and to validate the expense committed to its construction. He knew that if *Tirpitz* and the others returned to port empty handed they would likely never sail a combat sortie again. Their crews would be broken up and assigned to the U-boats, the ships themselves turned into little more than floating gun batteries defending some harbor, like the old stone fortifications of a bygone time, and just as obsolete. He'd rather that *Tirpitz* should go down in battle than rust away swinging at anchor. He stepped to the back of his bridge.

"Anything?" he demanded, knowing he'd only just asked minutes earlier.

"No, Admiral," his flag signals officer answered, with more patience than even Schniewind felt was justified. "Our last wireless reception remains the report from the Luftwaffe reconnaissance flight forty minutes ago. The convoy remains on a westerly course and is now 160 miles to the east of Bear Island."

Schniewind turned and looked out over the peaceful sea. He was no stranger to Arctic conditions and knew the fleet was enjoying an extraordinary run of good weather, even for high summer in those latitudes and he wondered how much longer it might last. He leaned down to the voice tube and spoke.

"Plot, this is the Admiral. Time to intercept?"

"Seven hours, forty minutes at present course and speed Admiral, assuming the enemy holds to its present course and speed," came the ready reply. The Chart Room was as used to his frequent inquiries as the Wireless Office.

For the hundredth time he ran the timeline in his head. Intercept the convoy at 0600 hours the morning of July 6, 100 miles to the east of Bear Island. Engage the close escort and sweep aside the enemy destroyers and any cruisers that might be in company as quickly as possible. If necessary, leave *Scheer* and *Lutzow* to finish mopping up the escort while *Tirpitz* and *Hipper* chased down the merchantmen. He assumed they would scatter in every direction the moment they detected his fleet. Every moment of delay the British escorts could force upon him raised the chances that some of the freighters might slip from his grasp.

Once more, he weighed the option of racing ahead with *Tirpitz* and *Hipper* at their top speeds of 31 knots, leaving *Scheer* and *Lutzow* behind with half the destroyers to catch up. He could trim an hour or more from the time needed to catch the convoy, but once again, he shook his head. He had to resist this impulsive temptation. With just the guns of *Tirpitz* and *Hipper* and only four of his eight destroyers, the British close escort might succeed in shielding him, however briefly from reaching the convoy and wrecking it. Further, there was little point in reaching the convoy just at the time when the only brief interval of relative darkness could help the merchantmen make their escape. No, he must arrive with his fleet intact and together and with enough daylight for maximum effect.

He closed his eyes and tried to put himself into the mind of his English counterpart, the Royal Navy Admiral in command of the enemy battleships and carrier. Schniewind had to assume the Royal Navy knew *Tirpitz* and the others were at sea, attempting to close with the convoy. Why else would the British have ordered it to reverse course? But what was the English Admiral doing right now? What decision had he taken?

Was the British battle fleet still far to the northwest, or had it too changed course to meet the convoy. Might the Germans arrive at PQ17 to find it defended by two or more battleships? Worse, might the British know his own position and course, perhaps from a submarine sighting and even now be flying a strike of torpedo bombers from the carrier to hit him? He stepped to the back of his bridge.

"Anything?" he demanded.

"No, Sir," came the same patient reply.

Chapter 15

USS Washington bound for Bear Island.

July 5, 1942

Reggie Elkins shivered inside the 5-inch gun turret. Even with shortened watches of two hours to reduce the men's exposure he found himself barely able to function. There could be no question of suspending battle stations nor even of bringing the crews of the light anti-aircraft guns on the weather decks under cover. Not in a war zone with enemy aircraft and submarines known to be lurking about. Other men worked on the weather decks. Using hammers and picks, they chiseled away the build-up of ice that made the ship 'stiff'. The added weight of ice above decks made *Washington* top-heavy and could even threaten her sea-worthiness if allowed to accumulate. Reggie and his shipmates suffered in silence and dreamt of being warm again.

He tried to distract himself from his discomfort by thinking back on what had already been an eventful cruise. Some of the crew used stronger language, believing that something of a curse followed *Washington* since she'd left her last American port of call, Casco Bay, Maine for the voyage to Scapa Flow in March. Less than twenty-four hours out of port and in a state six sea, the cry of "Man overboard" rang out. The body was never recovered, though no fewer than six men aboard the battleship and others on the cruiser *Tuscaloosa* sailing in company had seen him in the water.

The mystery deepened when a muster of the ship's crew found all hands present and accounted for. Only when Captain Benson tried to alert Admiral Wilcox of the situation did it begin to dawn that the Admiral himself was missing. Eventually it was determined that the Admiral had gone overboard through mishap or accident after inspecting the starboard floatplane and its hangar deck on the fantail, then proceeding back along the weather decks toward his flag quarters. An inquest found no fault or deficiency in the crew or equipment, though rumors circulated among the crew that the Admiral had committed suicide, unable to bear the strain of command. There were even whispered stories of an even more lurid explanation for the Admiral's death. According to some, Wilcox was pushed overboard by a member of the crew with a grievance, or who was an Axis agent, planted aboard *Washington* to make mischief at any opportunity.

Following the loss of Wilcox, Admiral Giffen, commander of the cruiser division sailing with *Washington* took command of the whole American fleet and transferred his flag from *USS Wichita* to the battleship. Giffen stood on the bridge wing above Reggie's head, binoculars pressed to his eyes, scanning the sea to the south.

Rumors swirl aboard any ship at sea, especially one at war and the *USS Washington* was no different. Talk among the crew that day involved the whereabouts of the German fleet and its mighty battleship *Tirpitz*. Some said the Germans were luring the combined allied fleet to the east, into a trap ready to be sprung with waves of aircraft and submarines, all capped off by *Tirpitz*' big guns. A few of the men circulated a more mundane sort of rumor; *Washington* did not have enough fuel left aboard to return safely to Scapa Flow. They would be forced to accept a tow back to harbor, an embarrassment of the first order for the US Navy, still suffering an inferiority complex of its own against the Royal Navy.

Up on the flag bridge Admiral Giffen moved to the port wing to survey the sea on that side of the fleet, but there was nothing more to be seen than the cold, empty sea on the starboard.

"Signal from flagship, Sir!" his Flag Lieutenant said.

Giffen turned his attention to *Duke of York*, sailing a thousand yards ahead of *Washington*. A signal lamp flickered and flashed in Morse code with a lengthy message. A few moments later, his aide handed him the decoded message, then stepped back a respectful pace. Giffen read the message and his eyebrows shot up.

"You've read this?" he asked his aide.

"Yes, Sir," responded the officer, something of a celebrity aboard *Washington* now as he had been aboard *Wichita*. Giffen's aide was Lieutenant Douglas Fairbanks, Jr., USNR, the well-known American actor and cinema star. On a recent movie night in port, the entire crew watched one of Fairbanks' most recent films, 'Gunga Din'. The crew took delight in Fairbanks' famous mustache and more than a few cultivated one they thought its match. Giffen leaned down and spoke into the voice tube that connected his tiny flag bridge to the navigation bridge below.

"Ask Captain Benson to join me on the flag bridge at his convenience please," he said.

"Aye-aye, Captain Benson to the flag bridge at his convenience," the acknowledgement.

"Yes, Admiral?" Captain Benson said as he came up the ladder.

Giffen said nothing, but handed Benson the message. The Captain read it and nodded his head before handing the message back to Giffen.

"Into the Lion's Den?" he asked rhetorically.

"We're ordered east of Bear Island if necessary to bring *Tirpitz* to battle at all costs," Giffen nodded his head. "Into the Lion's Den indeed. Where are we now Captain?" Giffen stepped to the back of his flag bridge and looked down at the small chart table against the bulkhead.

"We're here, Sir," Benson said, pointing at a spot on the map 160 miles northwest of Bear Island. "We're just outside the range of German strike aircraft operating from the north Norwegian airfields, though within range of their long-range reconnaissance planes. Lucky in my view not to have been seen by one of them yet."

"They are probably all focused on the convoy," answered Giffen. "Less interested in us." He put his finger on a spot 100 miles east of Bear Island. "At top speed, how long?" he asked.

Benson shrugged. "A little over seven hours," he answered, "skirting the island to the north and at my best speed of 28 knots and assuming *Duke of York* and *Victorious* can sustain that speed."

"Any question that *Washington* can?" queried Giffen.

"None!" said Giffen. "We can sail for days at 28 knots from a machinery point of view."

"But that's not the issue, is it," said the Admiral rhetorically. "Fuel?"

"Exactly, Sir," nodded Benson. "Seven hours at top speed followed by a surface action or even just dodging torpedo planes out of Norway and our fuel situation looks critical. We'll be on the razor's edge of getting back to Iceland without a tow. Scapa Flow will be out of the question."

"All right, Captain," said Giffen straightening. "We're following the Brits here. Let's hope their Lordships know what they are doing. Set course for Bear Island."

Chapter 16

U-355, 40 miles northwest of Bear Island

July 5-6, 1942

Gunther La Baume grew more anxious through the twilight hours before midnight on July 5. His wireless operator Kubein struggled to diagnose and repair his radio transmitter. He replaced tubes and wiring from the boat's store of spare parts, but the transmitter remained stubbornly silent. La Baume's one consolation was that aside from a position update and meteorological report he had no information to transmit anyway. He conned the boat from the exposed bridge and read all the signals his functioning wireless receiver picked up. These fell into two broad categories.

First were the sighting reports of the German Luftwaffe reconnaissance and strike aircraft and of other U-boats. From these he was certain there was no doubt of the Allied convoy's position. The Luftwaffe had it pinned down to the mile and so long as the clear weather held there was little prospect of the convoy disappearing. Reports from the strike aircraft operating out of the north Norway fields suggested the Luftwaffe was already grabbing its share of the credit for inflicting damage against the enemy.

Reports from other U-boats told a different story. Excluded from operating in the area from Bear Island east for some 500 miles the submarines were finding little but empty sea to report. With the convoy doubled back to Bear Island it seemed the only chance at action for the U-boats would be for those west of the island still in position to attack should the Allies withdraw the convoy all the way to Iceland.

The second kind of messages he intercepted were those sent by the German Naval establishment to its forces at sea. One of these messages was addressed expressly to his boat, the U-355 and demanded the exact report he wished to send, that of his own position and the weather. In this respect, the morning of July 5 presaged a change. High clouds gathered from the north and west until the bright sunshine of the prior days was replaced by a flat, leaden sky. Aerial reconnaissance would become more difficult as this new weather pattern spread over the entire region. Unable to respond to this request La Baume knew his U-Boat flotilla would eventually assume him and his boat to be lost at sea.

Losing patience La Baume increased the frequency of his demands for a status update on the transmitter from Kubein, but this added pressure did little to help the man find and repair the fault. The transmitter remained silent.

He leaned down to speak into the voice tube to ask Kubein for another report, but was beaten to the punch.

"Captain, Conn," La Baume recognized the voice of his XO, Leutnant Kohl.

"Conn, Captain," he answered. "What is it Kohl? Is the wireless functional?"

"No, Sir," Kohl answered. "Still no resolution there. But our sound location equipment has picked something up."

"What have we heard?" La Baume's ears perked up.

"Sounds of a vessel using its active sound location equipment," answered Kohl. "There is a vessel to our west pinging for contacts. The sound comes and goes, but is intensifying."

"Bearing and range?" La Baume demanded. He lifted his Zeiss binoculars and began scanning the western horizon in the strange, grey twilight.

"Bearing perhaps one or two degrees north of due west," answered Kohl. "Range is more difficult to estimate. The ping fades and then returns, but each time the cycle is stronger. It could be quite close, or many miles away," Kohl went on. "The sound could be bouncing off a thermal layer and skipping to us."

La Baume nodded his head in understanding. A layer of cold, dense water beneath the surface might cause the sound of an echo locating device to literally skip many miles further than it otherwise might. But regardless, this discovery was important. Somewhere to his west, a surface vessel was on the defensive against submarines, using active ASDIC as it was known to the British, Sonar to the Americans, to find and defend against a U-boat threat.

"Come right to a due north course, heading zero-zero-zero," La Baume ordered. "Hold speed at four knots. We'll see what we have. And keep the reports on that ping coming!"

"Yes, Sir!" acknowledged Kohl.

U-355 swung softly round to the right until it was on a due north course, or as near to one as could be estimated. In such northern latitudes, so close to both the magnetic and geographic poles a compass heading could not always be trusted completely.

"Ping intensifying, Captain," Kohl told him through the voice tube. "Now straight west of us."

La Baume continued to scan the western horizon for any sign of a vessel, but could find nothing. A shiver ran up his spine. Acting purely on instinct he leaned down to the voice tube.

"Cut the diesels, Kohl. Let her drift," he ordered.

A moment later the steady rumble of the diesel motors died and only the soft swish of the gentle swell washing against the boat's hull relieved the silence. La Baume and his lookouts all kept silent now, listening and watching intently.

"Aircraft sounds!" the port side lookout hissed in a stage whisper.

La Baume lowered his head and pulled the scarf away from his ears to listen better. There it was! He heard it now too, the distant sputter of an aircraft engine somewhere above the clouds over their heads. With an airplane about, he knew he should dive the boat, but he was loathe to do so before he had sighted the vessel to his west.

“Ping intensifies,” said Kohl softly. “Moving again a point to the north of west.”

La Baume listened as the aircraft motor faded away. He thought the sound disappeared to the east, but could not be certain.

“Maintain due north heading, resume four knots,” he said down the voice tube. The diesel motors started again, sounding overloud after the silence. He turned to address the lookouts on the bridge.

“Keep a sharp eye to your sectors!” he commanded. “If that aircraft returns from another direction it could surprise and sink us in a moment!” The men all acknowledged the command and tended to their own sectors, despite the temptation to watch the western horizon.

La Baume lifted his glasses and swept the western horizon to 45 degrees either side of due west.

“Do you still have the ping?” he demanded in frustration.

“Confirmed Captain!” said Kohl. “Now about five degrees north of west and growing stronger!”

“Could we have been detected?” asked La Baume. He turned to ensure his lookouts were all paying close attention to their sectors. All appeared to be alert.

“Doubtful, Sir,” said Kohl, “but a thermal layer at play can be tricky.”

“Shut down the diesels,” commanded La Baume.

The boat settled into the water and drifted on the gentle swell. La Baume listened intently for any sound that might indicate a threat to his boat. Nothing. He listened for a full two minutes and was about to order the diesels started again when he decided to check the western horizon first. There! A smudge of smoke to the west-north-west. There for a moment then gone, but he was certain of what he’d seen.

“Diesels to full power, all ahead flank!” he shouted down the tube. “Come right to zero-two-zero!”

U-355 surged ahead, knifing through the water and throwing off a boiling white wake that would be visible for miles from the upper works of a destroyer or other warship. Nerves taut, he watched the horizon, balancing the need to cover distance against the chance his wake might be seen. He knew the area of disturbed water already in his wake would last for many minutes after he slowed the boat. Another smudge of smoke.

"Slow to four knots!" he ordered. The throb of the engines died down and the bow settled back into the water. He looked back behind the boat. Evidence of his wake stretched behind him like an arrow pointed right at U-355. Certainly, no airborne enemy could miss it and with the sea in such a calm state, he was sure it could be seen by a warship's lookouts as well. A second smudge of smoke appeared to the northwest and quickly grew.

"Shut down the main induction vent and settle the boat two meters into the water," he ordered. The louvers over the induction vent closed. The diesel motors, still powering the boat through the water demanded oxygen and began sucking it from the rest of the boat, creating a strong draft down the conning tower hatch that whistled past the hatch rim. Diesel fumes continued out the trunk exhaust pipe. Even so, the stink of diesel would permeate the boat and take weeks to clear.

U-355 now bulled its way through the sea with water flowing across her deck and around the conning tower and 88mm deck gun. La Baume kept his Zeiss glasses pressed to his eyes scanning the northwestern horizon. Within minutes he had isolated the first of the ships there, a destroyer moving at high speed from west to east at a range of nine miles. A moment later, a breathtaking sight swam into his view. A magnificent battleship with towering superstructure appeared and behind it another a minute later. Two more destroyers and then the crucial piece of the puzzle, a broad, slab-sided airplane carrier came into view.

The ships were much too distant to attack. On their present course and speed they'd pass many miles out of his range, but if he had a functional transmitter none of that would matter, he could send a sighting report that might tip the balance of the action to the German Navy. He pounded his fist in frustration against the binnacle.

"Any progress on that damn transmitter?" he demanded. "I've got two battleships and a carrier up here to report!" La Baume could hear urgent voices below and from their tone he understood his answer without hearing the words.

"No resolution to the problem, Sir," Kohl reported, disappointment in his own voice.

La Baume kept watch on the enemy fleet as U-355 continued on its slow northeasterly course and as the enemy kept moving at high speed to the east. When the leading of the two battleships was straight north of him one of the enemy destroyers turned out of line and charged directly at him and he knew it was time to disappear.

"Clear the bridge!" he ordered. "Dive the boat!"

The diesel motors shut down and the exhaust manifold closed behind him. As his lookouts hurried down the conning tower hatch La Baume took one last look at the enemy fleet through his glasses. Startled, he checked the wind with his hand. Freshening and blowing from the southeast. Finally he was the last man topside and the conning tower was almost awash. He turned and swung his legs into the hatch, then pressed the insoles of his boots against the conning tower ladder and slid to the bottom. His senior chief was waiting for him to clear the hatch rim. He slammed the hatch down and dogged it shut the moment the Captain was clear. Even so, a shower of icy water drenched him at the bottom of the ladder.

"Periscope depth!" he ordered, spluttering in the cold water. Kohl handed him a towel and he dried his face and hands. "Up periscope!"

He pressed his face to the eyepiece as the tube of the periscope rose from its well. "Stop 'scope," he said when it broke the surface of the water above his head. He began a running commentary on what he saw.

"The destroyer is suspicious and is moving down on us to see what he may find. Bearing, Mark!"

"Bearing, three-nine-zero," answered Kohl, reading the bearing from the ring round the periscope tube.

"Range, Mark!" said La Baume.

"Range, 4,000 meters!"

"Is he pinging?" he asked.

"No, Sir," answered his sound location operator, Tennemann. "The pings continue, but from a more distant source, bearing zero-one-zero."

"That's the leading destroyer," said La Baume. "Our suspicious friend was second in line on the starboard side of the fleet. Down 'scope."

The periscope slid back down into its well.

"Stopwatch!" snapped La Baume. Kohl clicked the watch and started it ticking.

"Fast screw sounds now," Tennemann said. His headset was clamped over one ear to listen to the enemy. The other ear was free to listen for orders. "Bearing three-nine-five, closing."

"Thirty seconds," said Kohl.

"Fast screw bearing zero-zero-zero," said Tennemann. "He's turning. Bearing zero-one

-zero, range 2,000 meters."

"One minute," said Kohl.

"He's found nothing so he is going away," said La Baume. He waited another minute before ordering the periscope back up. This time he kept it very low in the water, so that the gentle swell would alternately cover and uncover the glass.

"Bearing, mark," said La Baume.

"Bearing three-nine-zero," answered Kohl.

"Range, mark."

"Range, 9,000 meters."

"Prepare all four forward tubes. Set the fish for maximum distance, depth five meters," La Baume ordered. "There is just a chance we may get a chance at a shot. Down 'scope. Stopwatch." Click, Kohl started the watch.

"Range on the destroyer?"

"Range, 3,000 meters, still bearing zero-one-zero," answered Tennemann.

"One minute," said Kohl.

La Baume closed his eyes and visualized the movement of the ships up on the surface. The bridge crew all kept silent to respect his concentration.

"Two minutes," said Kohl.

"Up 'scope." This time La Baume made a complete 360 degree circuit of the surface and the sky above it looking for any danger before focusing back on the enemy fleet.

"Bearing, mark," he said.

"Bearing, zero-zero-zero," said Kohl.

"Range, mark."

"Range, 8,500 meters."

"Down 'scope! Stopwatch." La Baume stepped away from the tube and rubbed his eyes. "It is as I first suspected," La Baume said, excitement rising in his voice.

Chapter 17

HMS Victorious west of Bear Island.

July 5, 1942

In the surreal twilight of a pre-midnight arctic sunset, Duncan Butterweck sat in the cockpit of his Albacore, once again going through his pre-flight warm-up and checklist. Two more Albacores sat on deck behind his, each of the three loaded with a 21-inch torpedo. His orders were to fly to the southeast, skirting the southern shore of Bear Island and to scout a route that would take him south of Convoy PQ17 in a great half-circle to a point east of the convoy before turning straight west for home aboard the carrier. Each of the three Albacores was to follow roughly the same route, but twenty miles apart, spread over a forty-mile wide span.

The Anglo-American heavy covering force was now just six hours from its rendezvous with the convoy and Admiral Tovey was said to be very keen for information on any German surface ships in the area. It was Duncan's job to find them and report their whereabouts by wireless. Whichever pilot found the enemy was to file his report and stay out of anti-aircraft range until joined by the other two torpedo bombers. If circumstances permitted, they were to launch their torpedoes against the Germans.

Smoke from the pot in the bows blew back over the port quarter of the ship. When Duncan signaled he was ready, Captain Bovell turned *Victorious* to starboard to bring her bows into the wind. Smoke from the pot began to fly down the deck until it was racing along right down the centerline. Duncan got his go-ahead signal from the deck crew. He brought the engine to full power and let off the brakes. The Albacore surged down the deck, but weighted by the torpedo the take-off was not as fast as the last time he'd left *Victorious*. He kept the plane on the deck right onto the bow ramp and only pulled back on the stick as the bomber shot out over water.

Duncan was thrilled to have another chance to strike at *Tirpitz*. Just over three months earlier Duncan had flown his Albacore from the deck of *Victorious* as part of a strike force sent to attack the German battleship in Norwegian waters. Twenty-five Albacores attacked *Tirpitz* as she ran for the shelter of the Lofoten Islands. Ever afterwards, the Germans admitted amongst themselves they'd been lucky to avoid any of the torpedoes dropped against her. The British were deeply disappointed at the failure to sink or injure the one ship whose existence so controlled their own strategy and none felt the disappointment more keenly than the aircrew who survived the fruitless attack.

Duncan circled the ship once and watched as the second Albacore launched, then set out on his pre-determined course to the southeast. Bear Island reared up on his left a scant few minutes after flying off the carrier. The forbidding peaks disappeared into the cloud base at just 2,000 feet altitude. He gave the island a wide birth, not wanting to end his career by flying into a fog-shrouded mountain.

The second Albacore off the deck was assigned to a route twenty miles to the north of Duncan's and the third plane twenty miles further south, each hoping to scout the sea ten miles on either side of their flight paths. In this fashion, the British hoped to cover a strip of sea some sixty miles wide to find the German battle fleet. After the final Albacore launched, one remaining task remained before *Victorious* could resume her course. An Albacore launched hours earlier was returning to land aboard. The ship's radar had detected it at a range of over twenty miles, but with the lowering cloud deck, it was feared the pilot might not be able to find the ship.

One simple means of directing him home was out of the question. No ship of the fleet could break radio silence, so the simple expedient of transmitting a homing beacon could not be used. The Captain could only wait and watch hopefully as the pilot searched for the carrier, remaining on course into the wind so that the plane could land on, once the ship was found. Finally, the wayward Albacore dipped below the cloud deck and spotted the fleet. Its pilot, the same young man who'd made such a mess of his takeoff the day before, waggled his wings and to observers aboard ship the plane itself seemed to increase speed with relief at finding its way home.

As the Albacore lighted on deck its arresting hook found the taut wire stretched across the deck and the plane jolted to a stop, its young pilot nearly weeping with relief at having accomplished his mission and returned his crew safely to the ship. History does not record the reaction of his observer and wireless operator, but it can be assumed they were hardly less affected at finding themselves safely aboard the carrier again.

Victorious turned smoothly and her great bulk began to swing to port, resuming her base course to the east. Captain Bovell on the navigation bridge was quite pleased with his ship and its crew's performance. He ran a taut ship at war and discipline was rigid, but nonetheless *Victorious* was a happy ship and her crew were proud to serve aboard her.

She was already a famous ship as well. Commissioned just over a year previously, *Victorious* sailed on her maiden war voyage to provide cover for an Atlantic convoy in May 1941, but almost immediately was pulled away from the convoy and assigned a historic role in the hunt for *Tirpitz'* elder sister, the *Bismarck*. Just when it seemed *Bismarck* would escape to the safety of Luftwaffe air cover flying out of airfields in western France, a flight of Fairey Swordfish torpedo bombers flown from the carrier caught the German ship and damaged her rudder with one lucky, or well-placed, depending on one's perspective, hit. Left unable to steer *Bismarck* succumbed to the combined firepower of several British battleships, with a coup de grace delivered by torpedoes launched from Royal Navy cruisers.

Today, *Victorious* sailed as part of a powerful fleet tasked with accomplishing the same feat against *Tirpitz*. Bovell watched as smoke from the smudge pot drifted back over the port quarter as his ship resumed her course.

"Signal from American destroyer, Sir!" shouted the young lookout on the starboard side of the bridge. For a brief moment, Bovell was startled from his reverie, but he recovered quickly as he looked to his signals officer.

"Torpedoes in water!" the young officer shouted as he interpreted the flashes from the American's lamp.

Bovell leapt to his feet and raced to the side of the bridge, scanning the sea for tracks of the fish.

"Where?" he demanded. Just then the light anti-aircraft guns aboard the American opened fire. Automatic cannon fire lashed the sea and now Bovell saw the track of the torpedo. From its course, he could see it would pass well ahead of his ship and he breathed a silent word of thanks. But a lone gunner on the aft deck of the American ship opened fire against a second target, over a hundred yards to the right of the first torpedo.

"Hard right rudder," he shouted. "All ahead port, all back starboard emergency!" But even as he shouted the command he felt the hollow, empty feeling of defeat in the pit of his stomach for he knew *Victorious* would be hit. "Sound the collision alarm!" and he braced himself on the armored splinter shield.

As the collision klaxon sounded, the torpedo ran in under the great carrier's starboard side 'island', the superstructure built on the very edge of the flight deck and from which flight operations were controlled and the ship navigated. It exploded twelve feet below the waterline and burst in a space that housed the starboard propeller shaft. The shaft was severed instantly. The ship rocked and bucked from the blast with men in every corner of the carrier thrown off their feet. On the flight deck, the crew of the Albacore just landed were thrown to the deck by the blast, the young pilot suffering a dislocated shoulder. In the officer's wardroom, all the fine china flew from the sideboard and smashed upon the floor. Power throughout the ship flickered off and on for several seconds, then went out briefly until emergency generators were started and electricity started to flow again.

The shaft tunnel flooded within seconds and the ship began to list almost immediately. Damage control parties slammed watertight doors and set to work within minutes to shore up damaged bulkheads. In her engine rooms, all three of her Parsons turbines shut down while her chief engineer assessed the damage.

By the time he reported his findings to the Captain it was clear that *Victorious* had been very lucky indeed. Her port and central turbines were restarted and pumps were already working to keep the flooding from spreading. Bilge compartments on the port side were flooded to counter her list and within a half hour *Victorious* was making 17 knots on an even keel.

So much for the good news. With her starboard propeller out of action, just two of her three great brass propellers drove the ship. This, combined with the thousands of tons of seawater she'd taken aboard meant her top speed of over 30 knots would not be restored without a lengthy time in a dry dock for repairs. She could no longer keep up with *Duke of York* and *Washington*, nor could she even launch aircraft, though it was thought she might be able to recover those already in the air.

When he received the news aboard *Duke of York*, Admiral Tovey faced with two big decisions. The first of these he took very quickly. He concluded almost immediately that *Victorious* was out of the current operation. She could not continue with the battleships and would only be a liability henceforth. He gave orders for her to begin making her slow, cautious way home to the British Isles, to the shipyards of Greenock, Scotland.

His second decision was much more difficult, for now he had to ponder if he should proceed on his current orders and take the two battleships to the east of Bear Island without air cover. More complex yet, he had to decide if this decision were even his to make, or should he break wireless discipline to inform the Admiralty of developments and to receive new orders.

As *Victorious* moved away to the south with a retinue of destroyers and the cruiser *HMS Norfolk* in attendance, Tovey called Captain Halliday to the flag bridge for a council of war.

"East of Bear Island we shall be exposed to German air attack, of course," observed Halliday when apprised of the choices. Tovey nodded his head, but said nothing, preferring to let Halliday lay out the options.

"If you break silence and signal Whitehall for instructions you might as well send up a beacon as to our whereabouts," the Captain went on.

"It seems the Germans know where we are already," Tovey said wryly.

"Interesting that we've not detected any signal that might have originated from the sub that did the deed to *Victorious*," Halliday countered. "It's just possible that our destroyer's counter attack has done for the U-boat. She certainly broke from normal German practice by not signaling before attacking."

"We might have missed the signal," objected Tovey. "They could be using a new frequency for example that we're not monitoring."

"Even if we missed it," said Halliday, "any signal would have been picked up at home and Whitehall alerted us to the presence of a sub in our area." He shook his head. "No. There may yet be a message, but I don't believe one has been sent already."

"In that case the German command and any surface force at sea are still ignorant of our present location," Tovey picked up Halliday's line of thought.

"Yes," agreed Halliday. "Which means that whatever decision you take, you must do so without breaking radio silence. You are on your own until we detect evidence the Germans are aware of our location."

"So, then," said Tovey. "The difficult choice remains. Go on, or scrub the operation?"

"What of the convoy if we scrub?" asked Halliday.

"The losses they've already suffered make this one of our worst efforts," answered Tovey. "They've only been turned round and offered up as sacrifices to make it possible for us to bring *Tirpitz* under our guns. We've either to turn them round again, back on their way to Russia or bring them home to Iceland. I had my way, it'd be Iceland. Never should have sailed this convoy in the first place."

"Er, um," coughed Halliday. "Is that your decision or the First Sea Lord's?"

"Quite," said Tovey, taking Halliday's point. "It is his, and for him to make it I have to break radio silence and if I break radio silence he's really left only the one choice, isn't he? To sail the convoy home for Iceland. I will have forced his hand."

"And *Tirpitz* will retire to her lair to await the next convoy," Halliday finished. The two men sat in a long moment of silence while Tovey came to grips with his options. Finally, Halliday broke the silence.

"What of the Americans?" he asked. "Should they be consulted?"

Tovey smiled. "Ya s'pose they will say?"

"On to Berlin!" laughed Halliday.

"Still," relented Tovey. "Form requires I should."

Moments later a similar meeting took place aboard *Washington*, with the ship's commander, Captain Benson in attendance with Admiral Giffen and his flag officer, Lt. Fairbanks. Much has been made of Fairbanks' presence at this and other meetings, but it is from his journal that so much is known of the inner councils of the Allied fleet during PQ17. Without his personal and contemporary notes there would be much more conjecture over subsequent events.

"Admiral Tovey proposes to proceed east of Bear without naval air cover," Admiral Giffen got straight to the point. A low whistle escaped Fairbanks' lips and Captain Benson's eyebrows arched in surprise.

"The Germans certainly won't lack air cover there," he replied. "What do you suppose is behind this move?"

"Has to be the convoy," answered Giffen. "They've already taken a mauling from the Luftwaffe. Now they may be exposed to the German surface heavies as well. I think he feels we either go east of Bear or take them back to Iceland," he finished in a remarkably accurate assessment of Tovey's frame of mind.

"We'll be within range of the German bomber fleet in Norway," Benson objected, "without so much as a single fighter to break them up."

"The imperative is to catch *Tirpitz*," said Giffen firmly. "Nothing else, not *Washington*, not *Duke of York*, not the convoy, NOTHING else matters."

Benson shrugged. "In that case, in for a penny...," he left the thought unfinished.

Giffen slapped his thighs, stood and turned to Fairbanks.

"Signal to *Duke of York*," he said. "With you all the way."

Chapter 18

DKM Tirpitz southeast of Bear Island

July 6, 1942

Schniewind paced the flag bridge. He knew he should sleep, but knew also there was no chance he could sleep. He was about to lead the most powerful German fleet since Jutland into battle and a thousand things could go wrong. If by some mistake, he led his force to disaster it could turn what up to now seemed likely German victory to defeat. He reviewed his dispositions and orders to his other ships.

His destroyers sailed out front and to either side of his fleet as a screen against submarines or torpedo attack from enemy destroyers. *Tirpitz* led his heavy force, her mighty 15 inch, 52 caliber guns prepared to deal long rang death and destruction to the Allies. *Admiral Hipper* was next. Her 8-inch guns would suppress the convoy's light escort forces, while *Scheer* and *Lutzow* brought up the rear. When the convoy was in range, they were to advance on the two wings while *Tirpitz* and *Hipper* held the center. All would fire on the convoy with their heavy guns, and use their secondary batteries to fight off the escorts.

“But where are the enemy heavies?” he muttered to himself over and over. There’d been no sighting reports on them for three days. For all he knew they lurked just over the horizon beyond the convoy, ready to spring their trap the moment he attacked.

A FW 200 Condor still accompanied the convoy, slipping beneath the cloud layer periodically to confirm the enemy’s course and speed. Now, just two hours sailing from the convoy he knew that only an air attack from enemy carrier borne planes could stop him from reaching PQ17 and beginning the slaughter.

A discrete cough behind him roused him from his reverie. His Flag Lt. stood behind holding a message slip.

“Pardon the interruption, Admiral,” Lt. Krause said. “You will want to see this immediately.”

“News on the enemy surface force?” he asked hopefully, reaching for the message. Krause handed him the paper, but kept silent.

Schniewind read the message through quickly, closed his eyes for a moment then re-read it again carefully.

"Dammit!" he swore under his breath. "Ask Captain Topp to join me please, Krause," he ordered.

When Topp reached the flag bridge, Schniewind handed him the message.

"No air support to be had for at least six hours," he concluded after reading the message. "Airfields fogged in. Nothing else?"

"Very terse, hmm Topp," said Schniewind. Topp nodded his head.

"Do we go on without air cover, or return to port," he asked, giving no hint of his own opinion on the matter.

"We can be in range to attack the convoy in under two hours," responded Schniewind in frustration.

"Or be under attack ourselves by British torpedo bombers," answered Topp, dutifully playing Devil's Advocate.

"The Condor has not given any indication of heavy ships in the convoy's vicinity, nor of any aircraft. The British fleet must be at least twenty nautical miles north or west of the convoy."

"Yes, nodded Topp, "and if the enemy surface force makes an appearance in the next two hours we should hear about it from the

Condor." He checked his watch. "It should remain on station for another three hours before turning for base."

"I wonder," said Schniewind, a new thought occurring to him. "If the bombers cannot take off from the north Norway fields, how would this Condor hope to land?"

Topp's eyes widened. "Meaning they might have to fly all the way back to Trondheim to land. If that is the case, low fuel might force the Condor to leave much sooner." He looked out at the leaden sky and freshening sea. "Our Luftwaffe flyers are likely to balk at launching under these conditions."

"Indeed," said Schniewind. "Send for the flight officer. Have him join us here."

"Right away," agreed Topp.

Within minutes, feet banging on ladders resounded through 'Flag Country' aboard *Tirpitz* until a young officer in Luftwaffe uniform skidded to a stop in front of Schniewind and Topp.

"Leutnant Wahl, reporting as ordered." He threw out a Nazi salute. "Heil Hitler!"

Schniewind returned the salute, but said nothing, appraising the young man. About twenty-five years of age the Admiral estimated, Wahl was a remarkably fit looking young man with broad shoulders, narrow hips and glowing blonde hair. His Luftwaffe uniform was in impeccable order, as if he'd been waiting in his quarters for just this summons. It occurred to Schniewind that perhaps Wahl had been ready.

"Relax Wahl," the Admiral began. "How long have you been in the Luftwaffe?" he asked.

"Since 1939, Admiral," Wahl replied, still somewhat woodenly.

"Sit down, Wahl," Schniewind ordered. "Would you like a cigarette?"

"Thank you, Sir," said Wahl, taking the offered chair. Schniewind held out a Swastika emblazoned lighter and lit the young man's smoke. Schniewind was among the many German Naval officers who regretted the decision that precluded the navy from conducting its own aviation program. In the pre-war years, the navy lobbied extensively for this freedom as had the British Royal Navy in opposition to the RAF, but Luftwaffe Chief Goering successfully countered their arguments, convincing Hitler that anything that flew in Germany should be under the auspices of a single branch of the armed forces. So it was that the German navy had no aircraft or pilots of its own. Coastal and maritime patrol aircraft, even scout planes launched from cruisers or battleships were under Luftwaffe command with Luftwaffe pilots. This ridiculous policy extended even so far as the new airplane carrier, the *Graf Zeppelin* then under construction for the Navy. The airplanes she was intended to carry were in almost all cases nothing more than slightly modified variations of Luftwaffe land fighters and bombers. Her embarked air wing was to be under Luftwaffe control.

"How much do you know about the operations of the Condor reconnaissance aircraft in Norway, Wahl?" asked Schniewind.

Wahl looked surprised by the question, but recovered quickly.

"They fly several different routes, Admiral," he replied. "Their main base is at Vaernes Airfield outside Trondheim. From there they fly an Atlantic route that takes them far to the west of Ireland and then back to the mainland in France. They then make the return flight several days later." He puffed on his smoke and exhaled. "Here in the north they fly from Vaernes in a half-circle sometimes as far as Iceland then north past Jan Mayen and Bear Islands and then on to Bardufoss or Banak near the North Cape."

"Very good, Wahl," Schniewind said.

"Thank you, Sir!" beamed Wahl.

"There is a Condor involved in our current operation, Wahl, did you know that?"

"No, Sir," said Wahl, "but I am not surprised. The Condor has the range and endurance to make long reconnaissance flights over water."

"Very true," nodded Schniewind. "This one left Trondheim over seven hours ago and has been shadowing the enemy convoy now for almost four hours. It has been providing excellent intelligence on the enemy's location, course, speed, and so on."

Wahl smiled again, but said nothing.

"Our wireless, right here aboard ship has just received another message," Schniewind went on. "This one however was sent by your Luftwaffe command in the North Cape," he said. Schniewind now began to pace, worry and concern written on his features.

"You see, Wahl," he went on, shaking his head, "it seems the airfields in the North Cape region are all fogged in."

Wahl's eyebrows shot up. "Oh!" he exclaimed.

"Good Wahl," said Schniewind. "You are a bright young man. You see the dilemma right away, don't you?" he asked rhetorically. "With those airfields in the North Cape fogged in, nothing can get in or out until the fog lifts. And that includes your comrades in the Condor."

"Yes, Sir!" said Wahl.

"What will the pilot of the Condor do under this circumstance Wahl?"

Wahl thought a moment.

"I should think he will be forced to fly back to Trondheim before his fuel is exhausted," answered Wahl.

"That is just what I was thinking, Wahl," agreed the Admiral. "The problem we have is that the next Condor in the rotation has not even left Trondheim yet and it seems likely the one currently shadowing the convoy must leave very soon if it is to have the fuel to return to Trondheim. There will be several hours, several crucial hours when we have no aircraft scouting the enemy. The Englanders are sure to realize this and change course and speed in an effort to evade us. Do you see my problem, Wahl?"

"Yes, Admiral, I think so," said Wahl. "Without a reconnaissance flight over the enemy they might escape your grasp."

"Just so!" exclaimed Schniewind. He turned to Captain Topp. "You were correct about this young man, Captain. He is very quick. Of course, Wahl, just locating the convoy is only part of the problem. It is only fifty miles or so ahead of us now and the enemy commanders of the convoy have been quite lax with their wireless discipline. We intercept two or three messages an hour, which confirm its location. I am confident the convoy can be found. I was relying on that Condor to locate the enemy heavy warships as well."

Wahl beamed. Topp smiled and nodded.

Schniewind continued pacing. "Without accurate information on the enemy, especially his heavy fleet units I shall be forced to turn back," he sighed, "before attacking the convoy. I shall have to explain to the Fuhrer himself I am afraid."

"Em, uh, Admiral," stammered Wahl. "What about the aircraft we carry aboard? One could be launched in time to locate the convoy and to maintain our surveillance of it."

"Ah, yes, of course Wahl, that idea has occurred to me," said Schniewind. "But these weather conditions are less than ideal. In fact, they are outside the normal operational parameters for our scout planes."

"It is true, Admiral that visibility is less than generally required, but as you've said, we already have a very close estimate of the enemy's current location," Wahl said. "I would not actually have to search for the convoy, only fly to it and maintain contact while also guarding against the enemy fleet. Even in these conditions such should be possible."

Schniewind pursed his slips and appeared deep in thought. "You make a point, Wahl," he said. "But such a flight would be very dangerous. It might be quite difficult to recover the launched aircraft later. Survival in this sea for any airmen out of fuel...," he let the thought hang in the air like an airplane out of gas.

"Admiral, Bear Island is well within range. The Luftwaffe has established several emergency landing sites with shelter and supplies including cached fuel for our airmen."

"Such a thing is only possible for the most experienced and confident pilot!" Schniewind exclaimed. "Have you such a man in your group, Leutnant Wahl?"

Wahl sprang to his feet. “Admiral, I am fully confident of my own ability to conduct this flight! I would not assign another of my men to this. I will fly this mission!”

“Wahl!” exclaimed the Admiral. “I do believe you are the right man for this job! Prepare your aircraft for immediate launch as soon as it can be made ready!” Wahl leapt to his feet.

“Heil Hitler!” he saluted the two naval officers then left on the run.

“A shame,” said Topp after a moment.

“Yes,” agreed Schniewind. “A great many fine young men like him are going to die before this war is over.” He shook his head as if to clear an unwanted memory. “Come Topp. Prepare to turn her for the wind.”

The Admiral’s Flag Lt. coughed at the back of the bridge. Schniewind waved him forward and received the message flimsy with the anticipated message that the Condor was leaving station early for the long return flight to Trondheim. The next Condor was not expected on station for at least another three hours.

Twenty minutes later the Admiral stood amidships, just aft of *Tirpitz’* funnel. The Arado AR196 floatplane sat on its launch rail, the BMW radial engine running up to full power in preparation to fly off. Schniewind watched as Wahl climbed into the cockpit after receiving the Admiral's final instructions for this flight. He had impressed upon Wahl two top priorities.

First, with little more than an hour now to intercept the convoy at its last reported position it was imperative that Wahl locate the convoy and report its precise location. The Germans could not afford to spend time in a surface search for the convoy. Wahl should set out for the last enemy position reported by the departing Condor then search widening circles to the west until spotting the convoy.

Once he had pinpointed the convoy and reported its position, Wahl must then scout to the north and west towards Bear Island in an effort to find the enemy heavy warships suspected to be lurking. At this point Schniewind was completely in the dark about the successful torpedo attack launched by U-355 against the British airplane carrier. Had he known the carrier was out of action, or even that it had suffered unknown damage from a torpedo hit it is likely his subsequent actions would have been more aggressive, but in the absence of any news, he was determined to approach the convoy cautiously and not be caught unawares by an air attack.

At last, all was ready with the Arado and the signal was sent to the bridge. *Tirpitz* turned smartly to starboard and brought the wind across her decks at the correct angle. Schniewind watched Wahl checking his instruments in the cockpit, a rather miserable looking observer in the rear cockpit bracing himself for the launch. Wahl gave a hand signal and rammed his throttles to full power. A moment later, the catapult was released and the Arado was flung over the side of the ship. It dipped perilously low to the water, almost touching the wave tops before staggering slowly into the air. It circled the ship once as *Tirpitz* turned back on course, then tipped on a wing and flew away to the northwest at top speed. In less than two minutes, it disappeared from view.

Chapter 19

Albacore 18 looking for Jerry.

July 6, 1942. The Barents Sea

Duncan held his Albacore to its optimal cruising speed of 120 knots to conserve fuel and maximize his range. He hoped to find the enemy, report his whereabouts and deliver a successful torpedo attack. To do all those things, then find *Victorious* and recover to her might well require every mile of endurance he could squeeze from the bi-plane. As Tovey chose to maintain wireless silence Duncan was unaware the carrier was damaged and he might be unable under any circumstances to land back aboard her.

He navigated his way around Bear Island, not wishing to risk running into a cloud shrouded mountain peak by attempting to fly across the island. He skirted it well to the south, then turned due east, staying below the cloud base at 2,000 feet. His assigned course was the middle of the routes given the three Albacores that bitter cold, grey morning. He touched the button in his flight helmet strap that allowed him to talk to his crew.

"Stay alert now chaps," he chided cheerily. "We may find Jerry anywhere now to the east of Bear."

"Bloody cold, Duncan," complained his navigator, Charlie Oswald. "How about a nip then?"

Duncan laughed. Charlie was famous in the squadron for his capacity for alcohol and as a pretend malcontent. Duncan felt there was no more reliable man in the squadron.

"All right, Charlie," he answered. "Just a wee one though. And save one for me when we get home!"

The minutes ticked by with no sight of the enemy, but Duncan knew that flying so low under the clouds vastly limited the area they could see. There were over twenty miles between his own patrol line and the ones to either side that would be out of sight to each plane. If the Germans happened to slip through that gap, they might never be seen. They were an hour into the flight and nearly 100 miles east of Bear Island when Charlie made the first discovery.

"Duncan," he called. "Aircraft off the starboard wing!"

Duncan craned his head but could see nothing so he turned the Albacore to starboard for a better look. Just at the edge of his vision, a black dot moved in the thin, grey stripe of sky above the horizon.

"Hold her steady, Duncan," Charlie scolded. Duncan gripped the control column and did his best to comply. Both his rear seat crewmen used binoculars to identify the aircraft.

"It's a single engine float plane," said Charlie. "Too distant for any markings, but it's certainly not one of ours. He's cutting back behind us. He'll cross our course about four miles behind us. Bearing about three-two-zero I should say."

Duncan's mind went into overdrive. British intelligence briefings to their naval pilots confirmed the Germans operated floatplanes out of their bases in Norway. Several days earlier, a flight of such aircraft had launched an unsuccessful torpedo attack on the convoy. But why would a lone torpedo bomber be out on this course. Far more likely he calculated the floatplane was a scout, launched by a heavy surface ship, a cruiser or a battleship and sent ahead to look for the convoy. He made a snap decision and veered to his right, taking up a course parallel to the float plane, but reciprocal to it on bearing one-three-zero or as near to it as could be based on his wildly gyrating compass. Here in the far north latitudes close proximity to the magnetic north pole made compass reading a dicey proposition.

After fifteen minutes Duncan was worried he'd made a mistake. They'd seen no sign of their quarry and by leaving his assigned route he exposed a much greater area of sea between himself and the Albacore to the north through which the enemy fleet could sail unseen. Perhaps worst of all he was not certain how best to resume his original course. He was about to run the question past Charlie when the third man of his crew, Tim Butten spoke.

"Something to the north of us, Duncan," he said, somewhat tentatively. "Could be a ship's wake."

Duncan turned to his left and swept the leaden grey seas.

"I don't see it, Timmy," said Duncan. "What bearing?"

"Just behind the left wingtips," answered Timmy. "It comes and goes. When it's there it looks just like a string floating on the water."

"I've got it now too, Duncan," said Charlie, a little excitement creeping in to his voice. "Maybe a little oil on the water. A bit of a rainbow sheen to it. Only visible when the sea tips just so to the light."

From his position in the forward cockpit and without binoculars Duncan could see nothing, but he trusted his crew, especially Charlie, so he banked sharply to the left until he was on a bearing just a point or two west of due north. He knew this second course deviation would complicate the task of calling the other two Albacores to his position, if that is he spotted the enemy at all. He flew on, keeping the trail to the left of the plane so Charlie and Tim could keep it in sight.

Another ten minutes and his doubts began to fade. The streak of oil on the water solidified until he could see it plainly with his unaided eye. It stretched off to the north and it was clear it was trailed by some vessel with a leaking oil compartment.

"Duncan!" shouted Charlie. "I can see the upper works of a heavy ship just on the horizon. Range close to thirty miles now, but no doubt of it!" Duncan waited until he could see the ship himself, along with two smaller destroyers at the end of the long wake and trail of oil they'd been following. The Germans themselves were unaware that the underwater damage suffered by *Lutzow* in the Norwegian Leads had produced a small leak from one of her fuel bunkers. No larger than a few liters per minute the telltale sign of the leak escaped the Germans' view as the ship's own propellers churned and mixed the oil in her wake. Only as the wake settled and the oil's natural buoyancy brought it back to the surface did the greasy rainbow sheen appear, several minutes behind the heavy cruiser.

"Charlie, give our position to Tim," Duncan ordered. "Let's get a sighting report out right away! One heavy ship, two destroyer escorts, course zero-zero-zero."

As they came closer to the ship, details of it became clearer. The Nazi Swastika flapped in the breeze at the fantail. Two great armored turrets, one each fore and aft housed triple barreled heavy caliber guns and an impressive array of secondary guns lined her port and starboard sides. A large binocular range finder mounted atop the main mast tracked the Albacore as it circled the big ship to starboard and one of the destroyers came charging towards him to keep him at a distance. Duncan veered away, keeping out of range of the destroyer's guns for now.

"Message transmitted!" said Butten.

"Keep repeating it until it's acknowledged by the other two planes," Duncan ordered. He knew he'd receive no acknowledgement from *Victorious* due to the fleet's wireless discipline, but if sent repeatedly he hoped it would be picked up aboard ship as well as on the other two Albacores.

“Aircraft 22 acknowledges!” said Butten. “They estimate they are twenty minutes flying time from our location.”

Aircraft 22 was the Albacore on the northernmost of the three planned routes. Twenty minutes flying time put it almost sixty miles away, sixty miles closer to the combined British/American fleet.

“Tell 22 to repeat the message continuously,” Duncan ordered. “Maybe the carrier or even the convoy will pick up one of the signals!”

“Right-o, Duncan!” said Butten.

“Duncan!” said Charlie. “We don’t have twenty minutes to wait around for the 22 plane!”

“What’s wrong Charlie?” asked Duncan.

“Jerry is warming up his float plane on the heavy. Through the glasses I can see the propellers turning.”

“Dammit!” swore Duncan.

“No response from the 19 plane,” sang out Butten.

Duncan’s mind raced, balancing chances and possibilities. There were two, nearly evenly weighted choices available to him. He could attack now, before the Arado floatplane was airborne, or delay his attack until joined by either one or both of the other Albacores.

Against a full strike of Albacores and other aircraft from *Victorious* the German float plane would hardly pose a threat. Not much faster than an Albacore the Arado would be hard pressed to even disrupt the attack of one torpedo bomber in a force of a dozen or more. But if left to focus on a lone Albacore the Arado would be a handful, along with dodging defensive flak from the enemy ships and lining up an attack. The Arado could probably prevent him from any chance of scoring a hit. With only the 22 flight acknowledging his signal Duncan could reasonably count on only two aircraft to attack the German heavy ship. If the Arado handled one of them the odds of a hit were cut by at least half.

On the other hand, to attack now and brave the entire combined defensive fire of all three ships hardly seemed a more promising option. Every gun in the German fleet would be lined up against him and if he succeeded in launching his torpedo, the German heavy would have only one fish in the water to avoid. On that basis, he should play cat and mouse with the floatplane, slipping in and out of the clouds to keep the German fleet under observation while avoiding attack by the Arado.

When the aircraft 22 of the Albacore squadron arrived the two could attack together, or perhaps await the arrival of the 19 plane.

But this tactic had its drawbacks as well. Duncan did not know the operational abilities of German radar, but that it was functional on this heavy ship he had little doubt. He could see the characteristic aerial spinning atop the ship's mainmast. If it could be used to direct the pilot of the Arado to an attack against him, hiding in the clouds would be of little use. Indeed, rather than losing the Arado, he might instead be attacked when he could not even see his attacker, or at least be driven far enough away from the German ships as to lose contact with them. He made his choice.

Aboard *Lutzow*, Captain Stange stood on his bridge, watching the Royal Navy Albacore circle his ship. He could clearly see the yellow-nosed torpedo slung under the bomber and understood how deadly it could be to his ship. Like many surface officers, he hated submariners and aviators and the threat they posed to his ship, but the disappointment at being found by the British airplane now hit him in the stomach like a punch. He believed himself to be less than an hour from launching the planned attack on the enemy convoy.

Apart from the alarm he felt at the presence of this lone bomber he was deeply worried that it most certainly meant there was a Royal Navy airplane carrier somewhere within range. He had little doubt other bombers would soon follow. A concerted attack by a dozen or more such airplanes had a high probability of scoring one or more hits.

"Bridge, Radar."

"Radar, Bridge," the Officer of the Watch acknowledged.

"A second target indicated now on our screen, approaching from the northeast."

"How many aircraft?" the OOW asked.

"One aircraft indicated," the radar officer replied. "Bearing one-three-five, range forty nautical miles."

"Get the Arado in the air!" commanded Stange. A glimmer of hope burst to life. Perhaps these were scout aircraft, not part of a concerted strike attack. Single ships approaching from the south and northeast, the most unlikely areas for a carrier to be operating suggested they were on a patrol and were drawn to his ship like moths to flame, brought in by the coded transmission his wireless operators detected from the first

Albacore. In that event there might be a limited number in the area that would arrive in ones or twos. If so, the Arado, already warmed up and ready to go on its launcher could hold the bombers at bay, perhaps even shooting one or more down.

"Come left to three-one-five," he commanded. "Put the launcher into the wind."

"The enemy aircraft has disappeared into the clouds," called out one of his bridge lookouts. Stange stepped directly to the telephone.

"Radar, this is the Captain," he said. Without waiting for an acknowledgement, he went on. "The enemy aircraft has gone into the clouds to line up an attack. I need constant reports on his course and bearing!"

"Yes, Sir!" the telephone crackled. Stange switched the phone circuit to speaker and stepped back to the railing as the radar reports began.

"Aircraft one is moving ahead now, crossing the bows from starboard to port at a range of four miles, altitude estimated 600 meters. Aircraft two still approaching from the southeast on one-three-five, range down to twenty-five nautical miles."

The Arado's engine roared and a moment later it was aloft, climbing for altitude to starboard.

"Come left, steady on three-one-five," ordered Stange.

"Come left, steady on three-one-five," the helmsman repeated the order.

"Gunnery Officer, alert your flak crews to expect an attack at any time."

"Bridge, radar, aircraft one now turning to his left. Four miles ahead on the port quarter. Looks like he's going to come down our port side."

"Helm," barked Stange, "as soon as he drops below the cloud deck I'm going to turn into him, to port to shorten the time he has to line up his attack. We'll present our bows to him and maybe his torpedo won't have time to arm or come back to the surface."

"I understand, Sir," replied the helmsman, a steady old quartermaster from the Kaiser's navy.

"Bridge, radar. Aircraft two, still on one-three-five, range fifteen miles."

"Send the scout plane after aircraft two," ordered Stange. "So long as we are only dealing with one at a time we can evade."

"Bridge, radar, aircraft one now directly to port amidships, range three miles, altitude about 600 meters. No sign yet of a turn."

"Is he going to circle us?" wondered Stange aloud.

"Bridge, radar!" with an edge of excitement. "Aircraft one now turning in towards us on the aft port quarter."

"Bridge, wireless, both enemy aircraft now transmitting continuously."

"Aircraft in sight!" the cry rang out from a dozen different lookouts almost simultaneously. "Port twenty!"

"Helm, hard to port!" shouted Stange. "Gunnery officer, fire as soon as you have the range!"

Guns on the destroyer to port were already firing, a distant staccato crackle as the 20mm cannon carried on the smaller ship burst into action over a mile distant from *Lutzow*. Their POP-POP-POP carried over the waves.

"Aircraft descending!" from the lookouts. "Changing course! He's screening behind our destroyer!"

Stange pounded his fist on the bridge rail. Holding the glasses to his eyes with one hand, he confirmed the lookouts' reports. *Lutzow* could not fire in her own defense for fear of hitting the destroyer. Only after the plane flew over the escort ship and was clear of her could his own guns fire. By then the plane would be just seconds from dropping its torpedo. The plane hopped up over the deck of the destroyer.

Duncan pushed the stick down and over to his left and began his diving turn back towards the German ship. He was pretty certain he had found one of the so-called 'Pocket Battleships', sisters to the infamous *Graf Spee*, sunk in the war's first months by a trio of Royal Navy cruisers off the coast of South America.

He broke through the cloud base and into clear air. As he turned, a destroyer swam into view over a mile in front of him and its guns burst to life almost immediately. Tracers and solid shot hurtled through the air at him and he pushed the throttle forward and the nose down for more speed. He settled on a course aimed directly for the destroyers bridge and held the stick tight.

WHAM. His Albacore bucked and jumped from a hit, but the motor kept turning and his control surfaces responded. Duncan cut to his right, then dove back left in an effort to throw off the aim of the destroyer's gunners. He pulled back on the stick and lifted over the bows of the

German. On the bridge, a startled officer in black uniform shook his fist at Duncan as he roared across the deck. He had to fight the impulse to giggle. Clear of the destroyer he dove back down until it felt as if he were fairly skipping across the wave tops flying by in a blur beneath him.

Flashes twinkled up and down the port side of the German battleship looming up before him like a medieval castle on a hilltop. Her guns were firing and she had begun a turn toward him. He jogged his course to the left to line her up amidships again, though he knew this would allow both enemy ships to target him.

BANG. A shell burst to his right, seemingly just outside the cockpit and shrapnel peppered the starboard side of the plane like hail on a metal roof. The stick was nearly yanked from his hands and he had to fight to bring the nose up to avoid crashing in the sea. He was now too low to drop his torpedo and would have to gain altitude. He pulled back on the stick more, knowing this would present his undercarriage to the gunners aboard the ship.

"Hold on lads!" he called out to his friends. He reached down beside his seat and gripped the release lever with his left hand. The German continued his turn into him and the range was shortening faster than he'd ever seen in any practice drop.

BAM-BAM. The Albacore staggered in mid-air like a prizefighter rocked by a one-two combination punch. He yanked the lever and felt the plane surge upward from release of the 2,000-pound torpedo. He pushed the stick over to his left and dived right down on the wave tops. The gunners from both ships followed him with a pelting rain of fire. A hole punched in the metal skin on his upper wing, just above his head, but the Albacore's engine didn't miss a beat.

"Did we hit her, did we hit her?" he shouted, not bothering to use the intercom. He craned his head to look back over his right shoulder in time to see a fountain of water settling back onto the sea.

Stange watched in helpless rage as the Royal Navy bomber skipped over the deck of his escort destroyer and changed course to attack him amidships. Green and red tracer arced out over the sea from *Lutzow's* many guns, like the arms of an octopus seeking to ensnare its prey. Its pilot had an intuitive feel for flying that let him dance away from the flak fire just as it seemed the octopus must have him. The nose of the plane came up and Stange watched with elation as a series of shells hammered into the belly of the bomber, but it shook the hits off and leveled in flight before suddenly its torpedo was plunging into the water and the plane no longer held the slightest interest to him.

"Keep your helm hard to port!" he shouted.

"Helm hard to port" the quartermaster at the helm repeated. He was straining to push the wheel hard over and to hold the rudder left against its stops. As the torpedo plunged into the frigid sea, Stange visualized its submarine course. First, it dove deep with energy from gravity and the forward momentum it carried from the plane as it dropped. Some reports indicated British aerial torpedoes sank as deep as sixty meters before starting to rise back towards the surface. He scanned forward along the torpedo's track looking for the telltale signs of bubbles rising to the surface, but none appeared. He began to hope the fish had plunged straight to the bottom, perhaps damaged in some way from those last shell hits in the belly of the plane.

Stange realized he was literally holding his breath. He exhaled a dry, strangled gasp and breathed again. Just then the torpedo broke the surface of the sea just fifty meters from his ship abeam of the aft main battery turret. It porpoised once, then sank back below the water as it approached at a nearly forty-five degree angle. With *Lutzow* still turning to port, it seemed possible the torpedo would strike at such an angle that its impact fuse might not even be armed.

Stange leaned out over the railing, heedless of danger to himself from a possible explosion, and watched the side of his ship. A dull thud reverberated through the deck plates, clearly audible even over the banging of the guns still firing at the fleeing bomber. His heart leapt for an instant, but then the torpedo exploded. A huge fountain of water erupted from the sea and deluged the port side weather deck adjacent to the aft turret. The crews manning the exposed flak guns in the area were drenched with icy water. All would have to abandon their positions and be replaced at their guns lest they freeze to death in minutes.

"I want a damage report from the engineering spaces!" Stange shouted over the sound of cascading water.

"Bridge, radar," the intercom interrupted him. "Aircraft two on the starboard beam, range three miles, altitude 300 meters. The scout plane is behind him and attacking."

Stange raced to the starboard side of his bridge and lifted his glasses. Two planes were approaching his ship in a long, gliding dive. The leading plane bobbed and weaved from side to side in an effort to shake its pursuer, but with the weight of its torpedo slung beneath the Albacore was not nimble enough to escape the Arado. The German pilot hung on tenaciously, firing short bursts from his two wing-mounted 20mm guns.

"Hold your helm to port!" commanded the Captain. At a distance of more than two miles, he watched as the torpedo fell away from the bomber and plunged to the sea. It hit with a mighty splash and Stange knew it had been dropped from too high an altitude. Still, it posed a danger to his ship that could not be ignored. As the second Albacore turned away, the Captain visualized the course the torpedo should take.

"Ease your helm," he ordered. "Wheel amidships." He stayed on the starboard bridge wing and watched as the trail of the torpedo's bubbles raced past his ship fifty meters to starboard. He breathed a sigh of relief and looked up in time to see the second bomber crash into the sea five miles away.

"Where's that damage report?" he demanded.

Chapter 20

HMS Duke of York on the Barents Sea.

"Transmissions from our two aircraft have ceased, Admiral."

Sir John Tovey took the news with storied English equanimity.

"What was the last signal received?" he asked his flag signals officer.

"Both report finding one of the German heavies twenty-two miles southeast of the convoy," the man answered. "Both indicate they were initiating their torpedo attacks, then the signals abruptly ended."

"And no indication of results, I suppose?" asked Tovey.

The officer shook his head. "None, Sir."

"Were either of them able to identify the ship they sighted?" this question from Captain Halliday.

Another shake of the head. "Not directly, Sir, but the signals from the first aircraft describe a single heavy ship with two destroyers in attendance. The heavy is described as having two triple gun turrets, one fore, one aft."

"*Scheer* or *Lutzow* then," said Tovey. "No word on *Tirpitz*?"

"No, Sir."

"So," said Tovey. "Three of the four still unaccounted for, the fourth attacked just twenty-five miles from the convoy, but with no word as to whether she was hit or not?"

This time the flag officer said nothing, but stood waiting. There was a discreet knock on the door. The signals officer answered. A messenger handed him a clipboard. The officer signed for it and handed the board to Tovey who quickly scanned it.

"Wireless intercept of a German signal on the same bearing as our two torpedo bombers. In code of course," he said.

"The Jerry will know that our planes reported his position," said Halliday. "No sense in maintaining wireless silence once he's been sighted and reported."

Tovey nodded his agreement. "Yes and alert his friends of the presence of our torpedo planes. I say!" he exclaimed, an idea dawning. "Maybe they really are not aware *Victorious* is out of action! Remember, we never picked up a signal from the U-boat that hit her."

Captain Halliday broke the long silence that followed.

"Perhaps, but we have to assume the convoy is going to be attacked within minutes," he said softly. "We can hope, but not count on this pocket battleship having been damaged or scared off."

"No word from the third Albacore?" Tovey asked.

"None, Sir," said the flag officer. "Not a peep since she left *Victorious* with the others. Not even an acknowledgement of the sighting reports of the other two aircraft."

"Could easily be a wireless fault," said Halliday.

"Or they may be down," countered Tovey, scowling. "Either way is the same to us, no intelligence and we cannot assume they've done the Germans any harm."

"One thing is clear though," said Halliday, sensitive now to the Admiral's foul mood. "The enemy is split in at least two powerful surface forces, maybe three or four. The one to the southeast we're sure of is centered on this pocket battleship, *Scheer* or *Lutzow*. But *Tirpitz, Hipper* and the other pocket are still out there, together or separate."

Tovey nodded his head, deep in thought.

"There is, perhaps a certain symmetry to it," he said finally. He leaned down and pointed at his map. "The Germans are approaching the convoy from the south and even with a scout aircraft to guide me I'd be worried to not bypass it by some slim margin either in front of or behind it." Halliday noted the shift in pronoun. Tovey was beginning to personalize the chess game, to get inside the psyche of his German opponent. Tovey splayed the four fingers of his right hand and laid them on the map.

"Better to spread out a little," he said, "across perhaps a forty mile front the better to assure I don't miss my quarry." He pulled on his earlobe in thought.

"In that case," Halliday said, "the pocket battleship we've sighted is on his right wing and the others are spread to its left."

"Yes," agreed Tovey, "With *Tirpitz* on the left wing I should guess. I'd want my most powerful weapon facing where I thought my enemy most likely to appear in force." Keeping his hand on the table, he wiggled his pinky and ring fingers on his right hand. "Pocket battleships on the right. They're slower than *Tirpitz* or *Hipper*, but could still crush the convoy if left to it with a free hand. *Tirpitz* on the far left," he wiggled his index finger, "with *Hipper* in between," indicating his middle finger.

Admiral Tovey's appreciation of his German counterpart's intentions was remarkably accurate. The German surface force was spread out over a forty-mile line. The German disposition differed only in that Admiral Schniewind had *Scheer* and *Lutzow* on his two flanks, with *Hipper* and *Tirpitz* in the center.

"If *Tirpitz* is our only priority we should rush to pass in front of the west bound convoy and sweep round it to the south to intercept her," said Halliday.

"Yes' said Tovey. "Their Lordships beside their fires in London would probably agree, but here on the spot *Tirpitz* is not my only priority."

"The convoy," said Halliday.

"Right," said Tovey. "If I leave those merchant ships to a pair of pocket battleships I'm signing the death warrants of nearly two thousand men."

"What then?" asked Halliday, glad the decision was not his own.

"We send the Americans to deal with the pocket battleships," said Tovey finally. "We swing down and to the south to find *Tirpitz*."

Halliday's eyebrows shot up. "I've a fine ship and crew, Admiral, but I can't guarantee the result in a one-on-one slugging match with *Tirpitz*!

Her armor is thicker and her guns more powerful than mine. Fortune might smile on us, or *Tirpitz* could treat us as *Bismarck* did *Hood*!"

"I don't believe she will stand to fight, Captain," replied Tovey. "More likely she will turn and run at the first sight of us. All the more reason to have *Washington* to our east. She and her cruiser escorts can drive off the pockets then put *Tirpitz* in a pincer, force her to divide her fire to port and starboard. At that point your heavy guns will outnumber his ten to four, and *Washington* nine to four."

"Of course, this might all be academic at this point," relented Halliday.

"Yes, the time lost standing by the carrier after she was hit may have cost us our chance at intercepting the Germans before they reach the convoy," nodded Tovey. He turned to his flag signals officer. "Prepare the message for *Washington* and her cruiser escorts," he ordered. "Free them of wireless silence as soon as contact with enemy air or surface forces is made."

The signals officer snapped off a quick salute and left the Admiral. After he was gone, Tembam appeared as if by magic at the open door.

"Coffee, Sirs?" he asked, a pot in one hand and two heavy porcelain mugs balanced in the other.

Halliday laughed. “Tembam, you are a wonder. Yes, today is a day for coffee.”

Chapter 21

USS Washington east of Bear Island.

July 6, 1942

Reggie Elkins pulled his collar up around his ears and rubbed his arms. Temperatures were bitter cold for the Florida native, around twenty degrees Fahrenheit as the sun climbed back into the sky that morning. For those unfortunates on the weather decks the wind chill brought the effective temperature down below zero. A dull, diffuse glow that barely penetrated the low clouds and did nothing to warm the sea or the ships that sailed through it was all there was to tell the morning from the twilight that had preceded it. Ice began to build-up on the superstructure of the ships in the fleet and work details were assigned to chip the ice free, lest important machinery or weapons be rendered inoperative and so that the ships would not become 'tender', or top heavy from the weight of accumulated ice.

Ice chopping details and crew at battle stations on the exposed weather decks were rotating every half hour to avoid hypothermia. Reggie thought it was a waste of time, as it didn't seem any warmer to him inside the ship than out, though in truth the crew accommodations were actually above freezing. At least his battle station inside the 5-inch turret was enclosed and sheltered from the biting wind and the ventilation ducts, usually needed to bring cool, fresh air to enclosed spaces was pumping warm air from the engine room into the turret. As men came off ice watch they had to warm up in the engineering spaces where temperatures approached 60 degrees Fahrenheit.

Reggie wondered at the decisions of the Captain and Admiral to bring them to such a God forsaken corner of the world. "They're probably snuggled up in wool pajamas with a hot toddie," snorted Reggie under his breath.

"Watsat Elkins?" asked Taylor Wynn, but even Tay seemed content to stay wrapped up to fend off the cold. Reggie didn't bother to answer. For once, he was glad of the regulation anti-flash gear he wore when on duty in the turret. He tucked in the asbestos mask that covered his face and hung down around his shoulders and swatted himself with the asbestos gloves.

In the Admiral's quarters, a council of war was underway. Admiral Giffen hosted Captain Benson and the Admiral's Flag Officer, Lt. Douglas Fairbanks Jr., the American actor. There were no hot toddies. Alcohol was banned aboard United States Navy warships, but the three men each held a steaming mug of coffee nearly hot enough to boil in the cups. *Washington* and her two cruiser escorts, *USS Wichita* and *USS Tuscaloosa* had parted ways with *HMS Duke of York* twenty minutes earlier, following Admiral Tovey's orders to skirt round behind the convoy to search for the German pocket battleships.

"I certainly don't like splitting the force," said Admiral Giffen, "but if the Germans do plan to attack the convoy spread out like a fan, this gives us some chance of intercepting at least some of them."

"If the Germans are where the British say, relative to the convoy we haven't a hope in hell of intercepting them," said Benson. "We'll have word any minute now that the convoy is under attack and we're still a half hour away, even at top speed."

"Yes, and gulping fuel we cannot afford as well," said Giffen.

"Just two or three hours of this fuel consumption and reaching even Iceland without refueling at sea will be out of the question," nodded Benson.

"We may or may not find the pocket battleships," said Giffen, "But whether we do or not I want to stay as far to the west as possible,

Captain. Crowd the western edge of our assigned search grid. If *Duke of York* finds *Tirpitz* she'll need help as fast as we can get there."

"Not to mention every mile east and south we sail puts us closer to the German airbases in Norway," Benson pointed out.

"Can't understand why the Germans have eased up on the air attacks," pondered the Admiral. "With *Victorious* out of the picture they should have a nearly free hand against the convoy. They'd already sunk six freighters from the air. Why have they stopped?"

"Weather?" asked Lt. Fairbanks. "Maybe this overcast is even worse over their air bases."

"Or maybe they don't want to risk attacking their own ships," said Benson. "Remember how the British almost sank one of their own heavy cruisers while hunting *Bismarck* last year."

"Whatever the cause," concluded Giffen, "we have to do our business smartly and be on our way. If the Germans change their minds and send the Luftwaffe in force we are vulnerable."

The conference broke up on that somber note, *Washington* straining with engines all ahead to reach the convoy in time.

Chapter 22

DKM Tirpitz south of Bear Island.

July 6, 1942

"Dammit!" swore Admiral Schniewind. He and Captain Topp were on *Tirpitz's* bridge. With action imminent Topp deemed it critical that he remain in command minute-to-minute and that he not leave the bridge. They'd just received the message flimsy of the wireless signal from *Lutzow* with the news she'd been torpedoed.

Tirpitz was moving towards the enemy convoy. *Hipper* led the two heavy ships in line ahead formation with their four escorting destroyers fanned out in front. All six ships were sailing at *Tirpitz'* top speed of 31 knots.

"How serious is the damage?" asked Topp.

"Uncertain," Schniewind shook his head. "Stange indicates she is seaworthy, but at reduced speed. He is turning her about to make for port."

"Very bad luck, so close to the convoy," observed Topp, a bit wryly thought Schniewind.

"Indeed," he agreed noncommittally. "So far from home can I dare let her proceed unescorted? What if she is attacked from the air again? She'd be a sitting duck in a pond!"

"*Scheer* is alone also, save for her two destroyer escorts," observed Topp.

Schniewind stroked his chin. Finally he made up his mind. "Signal to *Scheer*. Have her rejoin us. Once she is in company, we'll detach the two destroyers lowest on fuel to join *Lutzow*. With four escorts she'll have a fighting chance to get home, even in the face of another air attack.

"But *Scheer* is over the horizon," objected Topp. "Would you break radio discipline to communicate with her?"

"No, you're right about that aspect, Topp," answered the Admiral. "Sending a wireless message now could prove fatal if that carrier has more aircraft in the air. No, we'll use signal lamps. Send a message to the destroyer in our port screen to pass along to *Scheer* and her escorts. Provide the location they can expect to intercept us."

"Yes, Sir," answered Topp. He moved off behind the armored wheelhouse to the chart house behind the bridge. After ordering his navigator to calculate the intercept position for *Scheer* he returned to stand beside Schniewind. The two stood in silence for several minutes before the clacking of the signal lamp told them the message was on the first leg of its journey to *Scheer*.

"When we sight the convoy, Captain," Schniewind broke the silence, "we must make quick work of the merchantmen. Remember, it is sufficient to disable each ship. Not necessary to sink them. Let the U-boats and Luftwaffe clean up the cripples."

"Yes, Sir," acknowledged Topp. This was a clear feature of the plan from the beginning. The two resumed their silence.

Tension on the bridge was palpable. Men moved and conducted their duties like mimes with as few words as possible, murmured in undertones or near whispers. Throughout the great battleship, every action station was closed up and manned. Watertight doors were dogged shut. In the sick bay, the Chief Medical Officer and his orderlies worked quietly to clean the operating table and to sterilize the surgical instruments. In the officer's mess, all loose fittings were stripped away and the compartment converted to a dressing station where the ship's second Doctor made his action station. Deep below the waterline in the engineering spaces the black gang, as the engine room crew were universally known watched every dial, valve and fitting to ensure optimum performance of the ship's propulsion.

In the radar offices men sat with headphones and telephones hung round their necks, their eyes glued to the electronic line representing the radar beam sweeping a full 360-degree circuit round the ship every twenty seconds. Each time the arm swept across *Hipper* and the destroyer escorts, a brief, bright flash erupted on the screen. Likewise, the two great optical rangefinders mounted behind the forward and after turrets worked back and forth, seeking any indication of prey and at every lookout station aboard ship, men with powerful binoculars swept the horizon.

Inside the armored belt that protected them the magazines stood ready. Ammunition handlers, swathed head-to-foot in their protective anti-flash gear had already sent the first shells and cotton swathed bundles of gunpowder up to the guns above them via the shell hoists. In the turrets, gunners stood ready to unleash the fury of the mightiest battleship afloat.

The four double-barrel turrets of the 380mm, main battery swept around from port to starboard and back again, testing the motors and the ball bearings in the ring on which they rode. In the German navy such turrets aboard a capital ship were named from front to rear in alphabetical order. The two forward turrets were named Anton and Bruno, while the aft turrets were Caesar and Dora. The eight guns of the main battery were capable of hurling 15-inch shells weighing 1,800 pounds an incredible thirty-six kilometers, or nearly twenty-two miles.

Along the port and starboard sides of *Tirpitz* on the main deck level below the bridge were the secondary arms. Three double-barrel turrets carrying 150mm, 5.9-inch guns lined each side. In all ten main and secondary turrets, the guns were loaded and crews waited only the order to fire.

Fewer than half the crew had ever seen combat and of these, the ten-minute action in fighting off the British torpedo bomber attack the prior March was hardly the thing to qualify them as hardened veterans. Of them all there were a handful of veterans of the Great War, the First World War and fewer still had fought at Jutland, the last great fleet action of World War I. Only these few really knew what to expect.

On the bridge, Topp stepped into the wheelhouse and murmured a few words to his helmsman, as much to steady his own nerves as the quartermaster's. Schniewind stood staring out at the gloomy sea. Throughout the ship men stood to their posts and as the minutes ticked by an eerie, expectant hush descended on *Tirpitz*. Not a silence by any means for the noise of engines and machinery and the swish of the swells as she slipped through the water were ever present sounds, but no human voice was raised. Necessary commands were communicated as quietly as possible, often with just hand gestures.

Topp returned to the bridge and with silent nods indicated the armored blast shutters should be lowered and locked in place. Only narrows slits remained for the bridge watch to see outside and the bridge darkened momentarily until the red electric battle lamps came on.

Topp turned to Schniewind to speak, but the intercom crackled to life.

"Bridge, radar!"

Chapter 23

HMS Duke of York east of Bear Island.

July 6, 1942

The crew of *Duke of York* watched their companion now of several months, the *USS Washington* sail away to the southeast, even as their own ship picked up speed, her decks vibrating as her engines geared up for maximum revolutions, and moved southwest on her own rendezvous with convoy PQ17. The Royal Navy crew had viewed the American's with a combination of good natured rivalry and a sense of superiority bred by the knowledge that theirs had been the world's preeminent navy for centuries. Along with this superiority came doubts as to how effective *Washington* and her crew would be if the crisis ever came. Now as they watched the Americans move off many suffered a deep, but vague feeling of unease. Only the more introspective of them realized this was because they no longer sailed as a powerful combined force, and they doubted their own chances against *Tirpitz* alone.

But the Royal Navy had not been the preeminent navy for generations for no good reason. Their officers remained the most highly skilled, self-confident naval leaders and the crews of His Majesty's Ships held a deep belief in their strength, along with an astonishing stoicism in the face of adversity and death. They would not back down or flinch in the face of any enemy. They were the keepers of a long tradition of doing the impossible in war at sea.

Duke of York, the heavy cruiser *London* and the two fleet destroyers that escorted them increased to the battleship's top speed of 28 knots and hurried to the southwest. As aboard *Washington* and her consorts the increased fuel consumption was a matter of great concern to the British officers in command, but there was no alternative. Expectations were that the German surface force could be in place to attack the convoy at any moment.

They monitored German wireless transmissions that from their bearing could only come from an aircraft circling the convoy some 35 nautical miles to the south. They were more than an hour from reaching the convoy and could only hope they'd be in time. It was 0640 hours, Greenwich Mean Time. On the streets of London that morning citizens hurried to their jobs in the shops, factories and offices on a cool and cloudy day for July, but in Berlin the day would turn out fine and hot, and indeed would be the warmest day of 1942 with an unaccustomed afternoon high temperature of nearly 95 degrees Fahrenheit. In a city without air conditioning the populace sweated through the day, a condition made more difficult for all by the shortages of soap.

As on *Tirpitz*, and so too aboard the American ships, the final touches were made to prepare the Royal Navy ships for battle. 'Action stations, Surface' was sounded and all off duty crewmen reported to their assigned stations for a surface battle. Hoists and elevators lifted ammunition from the magazines to the turrets and ready lockers. Guns were loaded, though with safety keys locked, and watertight doors and bulkheads were sealed off throughout the fleet. On the bridge, atop the great armored tower from which the ship was commanded, the steel splinter shields were lowered and locked in place.

Radar aerials spun atop the masts in their ceaseless search for the enemy. The men settled in to their Action Stations and a soft, peaceful quiet descended on the ship. On the bridge, the Officer of the Watch sent a steward on an errand to his cabin. When the mess boy returned the Lt. Commander thumbed through the contents of a small box. With a grunt, he found what he was looking for. Moments later, with *Duke of York's* ship wide address system on, musical notes wafted from the Tannoy speakers on every deck and in every battle station. Men and officers alike went about their duties with an extra measure of quiet in the turrets and gun tubs, in the engineering spaces and every compartment, muffling all sounds to hear the beloved voice of Britain's Sweetheart, Vera Lynn sing "We'll Meet Again".

We'll meet again,

Don't know where, don't know when,

But I know we'll meet again, some sunny day.

Keep smiling through,

Just like you always do,

Till the blue skies drive the dark clouds, far away.

So will you please say hello,

To the folks that I know,

Tell them I won't be long. I won't be long.

They'll be happy to know,

That as you saw me go,

I was singing this song.

We'll meet again,

Don't know where, don't know when,

But I know we'll meet again, some sunny day.

We'll meet again,

Don't know where, don't know when,

But I know we'll meet again, some sunny day.

Keep smiling through,

Just like you always do,

Till the blue skies drive the dark clouds, far away.

So will you please say hello

To the folks that I know,

Tell them I won't be long. I won't be long.

They'll be happy to know,

That as you saw me go

I was singing this song.

We'll meet again,

Don't know where, don't know when.

But I know well meet again, some sunny day.

We'll meet again,

Don't know where, don't know when.

But I know well meet again some sunny day.

keep smiling through,

Just like You always do,

Till the blue skies drive the dark Clouds far away.

So will You please say hello to the folks that I know,

Tell them I won't be long. I won't be long.

They'll be happy to know

That as you saw me go,

I was singing this song.

We'll meet again,

Don't know where, don't know when.

But I know we'll meet again some sunny day.

Keep smiling through just like you always do.

Nobby Lamb paused in his work. He was replacing worn insulation on an electrical harness when the song came over the Tannoy speakers. In a moment, his mind drifted back to his home and his parents and he smiled when he thought of seeing them again.

"Back to work now Lamb," growled his superior, Petty Officer Grisham. But there was no anger in Grisham's voice. Nobby reminded the grizzled Chief of his own son in Cornwall.

"Yes, Chief!" Nobby responded cheerfully. He resumed his repairs, humming the song quietly to himself as he worked.

Tovey and Halliday received another pot of hot coffee from Tembam, the Malay steward who tended to "his gentlemen's" needs with a quiet dignity. He bowed, left the pot and retired to the Admiral's quarters where he set about changing the linens on Tovey's bed and in his small private loo.

Tovey sipped at the scalding African blend with satisfaction. He glanced at the clock above the chart house door.

"One hour to go," he said, sotto voce to Halliday. The Captain nodded and sipped his own coffee.

"Bridge, radar." The intercom crackled to life. "Aerial contact bearing one-eight-zero, range twenty-eight miles appearing on the edge of our field. Looks like the Jerry snoop may be flying a wider search radius."

"Radar, this is the Captain," said Halliday, speaking into the telephone circuit. "Keep an eye on him and report changes."

Below and forward of the bridge, 'A' and 'B' turrets were working through their practice regimen, sweeping first all the way to port, then to starboard and the guns from maximum to minimum elevation. *Duke of York*, like her sisters in the *King George V* class of Royal Navy battleships mounted her main armament in a somewhat unusual arrangement. She carried ten 14-inch guns with six forward in two turrets of two and four guns each and four guns aft in a single turret. Her secondary battery consisted of sixteen dual-purpose 5.25-inch guns mounted two apiece in eight turrets, four to port and four to starboard. These dual-purpose guns were highly prized in the Royal Navy on the belief they were equally effective against surface and air targets. As *Duke of York* was completing in the summer of 1941 manufacturing trouble limited the availability of the 5.25-inch gun tubes. The Admiralty reassigned to *Duke of York* the guns intended for several *Dido* class anti-aircraft cruisers, which were forced to make due with lighter automatic flak cannon.

Tovey glanced back at the clock. Fifty-five minutes still to go, yet with each passing moment he felt more confident they would reach the convoy in time to shield it from the enemy surface force. That no word of an attack against the convoy by the pocket battleship spotted and reported earlier by the Albacores gave him hope they'd somehow managed to damage her. If so, she could prove easy game for the Americans aboard

Washington and for a moment, he almost regretted not keeping his force together to be in on the kill if the pocket battleship were found.

"Radar, bridge," the intercom crackled. "The snoop is back, bearing one-seven-five, range down to eighteen miles. He's flying back and forth on a half arc course roughly east to west, executing a search. Each arc moves five nautical miles further north."

"Altitude?" Halliday leaned down to ask.

"Quite low, Sir," answered the radar officer. "Between 1,000 to 1,500 feet. He's under the cloud deck and should see us when he is in range on his next arc."

Halliday looked at Tovey and arched his eyebrows. Tovey shrugged.

"Nothing to be done about it," he said. "He'll report us as soon as we're spotted, but by then we'll be less than three quarters of an hour from our rendezvous."

Halliday nodded and said nothing.

The chart house door opened and closed behind him as one of the navigation crew came or went on some errand. A moment later the ship's cat, an orange tabby named Whiskey sauntered onto the bridge, a place he'd rarely if ever visited before. Whiskey crossed the bridge and curled up under the binnacle where he began to contentedly clean himself.

"Ya, 'spose he knows?" asked Tovey with a smile.

Halliday flushed with embarrassment, though in truth Tovey had known of Whiskey for weeks and in fact had fed the animal scraps from his own supper. Halliday gestured to the Officer of the Watch and looked pointedly at Whiskey. The man nodded, silently scooped the cat up and put it off the bridge. Tovey moved quietly to Halliday.

"We had a cat aboard *Rodney*," the Admiral reminisced softly, remembering his time in the mid 1930's in command of the battleship *HMS Rodney*. "Used to feed him saucers of milk right on the bridge till one day Admiral Cunningham was to be aboard at Valetta. Of course, I ordered everything shipshape ahead of his visit and I never saw the cat again. Always wished I'd made clear the cat was to stay."

"One of my favorite places, Malta," answered Halliday, grateful to the Admiral for excusing Whiskey. "Ship's band playing and dances beneath the awning on the fantail with all the local beauties aboard." They both fell silent.

“Likely to be sometime before the Maltese see those times again,” said Tovey finally, thinking of the reports he’d read and shared with Halliday on the disaster the Royal Navy suffered at Malta in the last two weeks.

“Bridge, wireless,” the intercom crackled. “*Keppel* signaling, urgent preface.” *HMS Keppel* was the destroyer of the Convoy’s Senior Officer Escort (SOE), Commander J. Broome. Halliday and Tovey both stepped closer to the speaker. “Message reads, ‘Enemy surface vessels detected twenty-two miles south-southeast, course three-five-zero, speed thirty knots. Am engaging.’ Message ends.”

Tovey looked at the clock over the wheelhouse. 0703 hours. Still three quarters of an hour from rendezvous with the convoy and the slaughter already set to begin.

“God help them!” said Halliday under his breath.

“Broome must buy us the time we need to get there!” Tovey responded.

“Bridge, radar,” the intercom crackled again. “Enemy aircraft range eleven miles on a westerly course. If he has not already seen us he will soon.”

"All we need," said Halliday.

"Yes it is!" exclaimed Tovey.

Chapter 24

HMS Keppel. An audience with the Queen.

July 6, 1942

Commander Broome raised his binoculars and scanned the enemy force bearing down on convoy PQ 17. For the moment, he forgot the bitter chill wind blowing across the open bridge of his own ship, *HMS Keppel*, sailing at flank speed and throwing a large bow wave before her as she sped to come between the Germans and the helpless merchantmen he was tasked to protect. The other five destroyers of his escort force were arrayed to his port and starboard with all six ships laying as thick a smoke screen as they could from smoke generators on the fantail and by pumping un-atomized oil into the flames of their boilers. But the smoke was being blown to the southeast, and did little to mask their approach.

He counted four German destroyers facing him, backed by two heavy ships, one a cruiser and the other most certainly *Tirpitz*. Even at a range that still exceeded twelve miles, she filled his vision through his ten power binoculars. On their own, the four enemy destroyers would be a handful for his six Royal Navy destroyers. The German destroyers could have been more accurately classed as light cruisers, with displacements in excess of 3,400 tons compared to *Keppel's* 1,400 tons. The Germans' armament was much heavier as well. Each of the Z Class destroyers mounted a main battery of five guns, each of 5.9- inch diameter and eight pre-loaded torpedo tubes as well as a formidable anti-aircraft array. The Royal Navy destroyers were designed primarily as anti-submarine craft and the largest gun in the group was 4.7-inches. Only *Keppel*, built with the stretch design of a Destroyer Flotilla Leader carried as many as five guns. The other destroyers in his escort force were of the Hunt Class and carried only four, 4-inch guns apiece.

Still, he had confidence his force could fend off the four German destroyers alone. So often in the Arctic convoy battles the Germans shied away from a fight with anything like equal odds and he was sure they would again now, if they were not backed up by the cruiser and battleship. As the range closed to twelve miles, the first salvo of enemy shells began landing in the sea around *Keppel* and it was immediately apparent the enemy was concentrating their firepower on his ship, the leader of the tiny escort force. A dozen shells splashed down within a quarter mile in quick succession as the Germans took the range.

"Port rudder, ten degrees," he shouted down the voice tube to the wheelhouse beneath his feet. The two forces were racing together at combined speeds in excess of seventy knots, but even so the Germans were still just out of his range. Another half-minute and he could open fire.

Another hail of shells fell in the sea, to starboard and all right on his previous course. Cascades of water fell back upon the sea, but even as they did, a new sound reached his ears. Often described as being like hearing a freight train crashing towards one in a railroad tunnel, the deafening roar of heavy caliber shells screamed through the pewter sky. WWHHHIIIRRR. Faster than the speed of sound such that their roar was only heard after they had already passed, the shells erupted in four enormous fountains of water across the line of advance of the Royal Navy ship to his immediate left. SPLAT – CRASH – SPLAT – CRASH – SPLAT – CRASH – SPLAT – CRASH. High explosive shells went off on impact erupting in geysers of icy, white water tinged yellow by chemicals added to the warhead to help in spotting the fall of shot.

"Starboard rudder, ten degrees," Broome shouted and *Keppel* heeled to her right. He took just a moment to look back to port as fountains of water from the shell hits settled back on the sea. *HMS Ledbury,* the destroyer that had rescued the CAM Hurricane pilot the day before wallowed in the disturbed sea, listing to starboard and clearly in desperate condition. Already her fantail was awash and men of her crew were scrambling to release her rafts. Broome quickly calculated she'd either taken a direct hit or a very near miss from a heavy caliber shell. Among *Ledbury's* casualties that morning was the CAM pilot. The law of averages had held up. The airman survived a single flight as a CAM pilot.

Another flurry of shells landed around *Keppel*, momentarily obscuring Broome's view in all directions.

"Starboard rudder, twenty degrees," he shouted.

"Bridge, guns," the speaker crackled to life behind him. "Coming in to range now!"

Broome snatched up the telephone. "Concentrate on the destroyer to our front. Fire when ready!"

The words were not out of his mouth before the two forward 4.7-inch gun mounts spit fire. Ice on the forward decks and superstructure cracked and split, crashing to the decks and over the side from the concussion of the guns. The usually reassuring CRACK of *Keppel's* guns seemed pathetic and weak to Broome as another salvo of shot hurtled down around him.

This time two shells fell close enough to drench the forepeak and a loud THUNK told him a large splinter of shrapnel had struck his ship.

"Port twenty!" he shouted as *Keppel* plowed on through the veil of mist, water cascading from her scuppers back into the sea. The forward 4.7-inch guns were firing at a fever pace now, their crews slamming a fresh round into each breech every six seconds. CRACK – CRACK – CRACK - CRACK. The two guns kept a constant bark of defiance going back at the Germans, but Broome knew that to do any real damage he had to close the range for a torpedo attack. The 21-inch fish were the only weapons at his disposal capable of harming either of the German heavies. Of his five remaining destroyers only *Keppel* carried torpedoes. The torpedoes and launchers on his other destroyers had all been removed and replaced with depth charges and throwers to face the submarine threat.

WHHHHHIIIIIIRRR – SPLAT – CRASH. A heavy shell passed directly over his head, exploding in the sea five hundred yards behind *Keppel*. The German destroyers kept up a deadly rain of 5.9-inch shells with each of their combined twenty guns firing three times a minute while the battleship hurled four of her monstrous 15-inch projectiles from her two forward turrets in the same time. He knew the cruiser would soon add her 8-inch guns to the medley of destruction.

"*Leamington* is hit, Sir," shouted his starboard bridge lookout. Broome turned to starboard and saw *HMS Leamington*, Hunt Class sister of *Ledbury* a funeral pyre from bow to stern. Somehow, her engines still ran pushing her forward in the water, but her upper decks were a mass of twisted, buckled steel with flames pouring from her and gusting on the winds. Her bridge was shattered. As he watched, she turned to her port and slewed round on her beam-ends. Fresh explosions wracked her as her ready ammunition supplies cooked off in the fires.

Broome turned his attention back to the enemy. The German destroyers were now just over five miles away, with *Tirpitz* and her cruiser consort another five miles further. To have any chance of hitting either of them with a torpedo he had to close to no further than 8,000 yards of the heavies. He would have to be inside the screen of German destroyers to be that close. At their combined closing speed it would take only minutes, but he doubted he had that long.

He focused on the battleship and as he watched, she turned to port, now bringing her four aft 15-inch guns to bear as well as her three twin turrets of 5.9- inch guns on her starboard side. Flashes lit her gun muzzles as these new threats were added to the guns already arrayed against him.

BANG! *Keppel* rocked from a direct hit from a 5.9-inch shell low in her hull. The shell punched through the cardboard thin steel plate on her starboard side, burst one of her four boilers in the engineering space and passed out again to port without exploding, splashing in the sea a cable length away. The flat trajectory of the shot showed just how much the range had closed in the brief minutes since the Germans first opened fire.

"One of the Germans is hit!" shouted a lookout. Smoke poured from the after deck of the German destroyer. Broome clenched his fists in satisfaction. This was the moment the Germans always turned to run, unwilling to risk damage to their precious ships in the face of a determined, even if inferior enemy force.

WHHHHIIIIRRRRRR – SPLAT – CRASH – BANG, SPLAT – CRASH – BANG! A pair of gigantic waterspouts erupted to either side of *Keppel*, drenching her with cascades of water and adding to a growing collection of the ship's shrapnel wounds. Broome ducked his head against the icy deluge, but the cold of the water took his breath away. He gasped and coughed, and fought to ignore the cold so intense it was physical pain. The enemy had straddled him with remarkable shooting on their fourth salvo after opening fire, but of far greater concern to Broome was that *Keppel* was becoming stiff and her speed had fallen off.

"Bridge, engine room!" the speaker crackled. "Number four boiler is out! We'll not exceed about 28 knots this side of a shipyard!" Broome leaned down to the telephone.

"Casualties?" he demanded, unable to splutter more than the single word.

"Yes," answered his engineering officer. "Three dead and several wounded. Scalded by live steam when the boiler burst!"

"Give me all you have, Chief," shouted Broome, recovering his breath. "We're going in with torpedoes!"

CRACK – CRACK – CRACK – CRACK! Keppel's two forward 4.7- inch guns hurled their puny shells at the enemy in a steady rhythm of defiance. Broome lifted his glasses to better see the nearest German destroyer barring his way against a torpedo attack on *Tirpitz*. The muzzles of the 5.9-inch guns in the Z Class Destroyer's twin forward turret were pointed right at him as they fired and recoiled, a gust of flame and smoke spouting from their mouths.

CRACK – CRACK – CRACK – CRACK – FLASH! Broome found himself fighting for consciousness in a narrowing field of vision, darkness squeezing down on his sight like the walls of a tunnel collapsing around him. As his world spiraled toward darkness it also went eerily silent, as though he were swimming underwater, trying to listen to a conversation on the shore. He rolled slowly to his left side until a lightning stab of pain in his chest stopped him. Strangely, the sudden pain also served to jolt him back from passing out. He rolled the other way, to his right where the pain was slightly more bearable until he could steady on his hands and knees. He hung his head and closed his eyes, but snapped them open again as a feeling of helpless vertigo threatened to take him back down. He stared at the linoleum on the deck of his bridge just inches from his face and forced himself to concentrate. There was something important, he was sure and he had to remember it, but the harder he tried to remember the more distracted he was by the distant sound of sticks breaking. Crack – Crack. He took a deep breath and retched on the taste of cordite and blood in his mouth. For the first time he noticed the little pool of blood mixed with seawater already turning to ice on the deck in front of him and the steady drip, drip, drip into it. He reached up and wiped his chin with his gloved right hand. Crack- Crack. His glove came away red with his blood.

Crack – Crack. What was that infernal noise? He looked up and reached his hand out to the bridge rail, but it eluded him on the first try and he fell face first into the slush on the deck, pain stabbing through his broken ribs. He pushed himself back up and tried again; this time judging the distance, he gripped the rail and pulled himself up to a kneeling position. He looked around him and saw his entire bridge watch down on the deck with him, save the young lad from Plymouth who stood the starboard lookout. What his name again? Broome thought absently. Powell or Cowell or some such. The lad was draped across the starboard bridge railing, blood trickling down the inside of his trouser leg, filling his boot and overflowing onto the deck. CRACK – CRACK. Finally, he recognized the sound of a 4.7-inch gun firing. His head snapped up and he hauled himself to his feet. He remembered now what was so important.

WHHHIIIRRR – SPLAT – CRASH. Another heavy shell passed over his head, but he had more immediate concerns. Smoke poured over the top of the bridge and a strange warmth emanated from the deck below and toward the bows. The gun shield housing the forward 4.7-inch gun was split like a partially open tin of kippers, with its side torn and blasted outwards. A fire burned on the gun mount and the crew were scattered in bits and pieces about the deck. Already the armored sides were glowing red from the heat. Ahead of it and another deck down 'A' turret continued to fire, but the cadence was different. CRACK – CRACK. With only the one gun for'ard in operation his firepower was cut in half. Broome staggered to the voice tube and prayed the helm would answer.

"Hard right rudder," he croaked into the tube, but could barely hear himself. He coughed and tried again. "Hard right rudder!" he shouted with something like his accustomed vigor. "Prepare the port tubes to launch."

CRACK – CRACK – CLANG! Hit again, this time somewhere in the hull, *Keppel* staggered from the blow. But her helm was answering and she heeled over to her right, obeying his command as he'd prayed she would. CRACK – CRACK – CRACK – CRACK. Now that *Keppel's* aft guns would bear her gunnery officer brought them into the fight. A shell splashed down right under her port bows and exploded. Shrapnel ripped up through the bow and the forepeak deck. Water cascaded down from bow to bridge, drenching Broome again and for the moment damping the fire burning in 'B' turret. He gripped the voice tube stanchion to steady himself and bowed under the waterfall. Once again, he was jolted by the shock of frigid water, yet bore it better on the second deluge. He noted with a curious emotional detachment that the water swept away not only his own pool of blood, but the body of the lad from Plymouth.

"Steady amidships," he croaked down the tube. *Keppel* was now broadside to the enemy and if the junior lieutenant who was his torpedo officer were still alive he'd be sighting the fish. "Fire torpedoes when ready!" He raced to the port bridge rail. Ignoring the other young lookout there still struggling to his feet, Broome leaned over the rail and looked back between *Keppel's* two funnels in time to see a torpedo hurled over the side to dive cleanly into the sea. An instant later a second followed and then a third.

CRACK – CRACK – CRUNCH. A 15-inch shell entered the water just yards from the port side and exploded beneath the ship. The young lookout beside him was cut down by a jagged slice of steel torn from the ship's hull and *HMS Keppel* arched her back, splitting bow from stern just aft of her forward funnel. Her bow, including her bridge, spun 180 degrees till it was pointed back the way she'd come while the stern plunged beneath a wave and just kept on going, never surfacing again. Broome was lifted from his feet and hurled backward across his bridge to slam painfully down on the broken ribs in his left side. His tortured lungs gasped for air and he wondered if a rib had punctured them.

The grinding scream of tortured steel came up through the deck and he felt as much as heard watertight bulkheads collapsing below him as the bow listed to port. The canvas windscreen on the bridge rail was shredded and hung in dripping tatters and on the port side was gone entirely. As Broome lay there trying to breathe and listening to what was left of his ship slowly sink beneath him he looked out through the wide open port side of his bridge across the frigid sea.

There one of the German destroyers passed the remains of *Keppel*. The German was charging at full speed to the north, a bow wave thrown off as she sped across the sea. Her forward twin 5.9 inch gun turret was trained in, that is the guns were pointing straight in the direction she was headed, straight for the helpless ships of the convoy, *Keppel* no longer worthy of attention. Soon after the enemy destroyer passed, *Keppel* was struck by her wake. Broome felt what was left of his ship bob like a cork in a bathtub and a loud crash below decks told him one more bulkhead or watertight hatch had collapsed.

The sound of feet pounding up a ladder helped him clear his head. He was not the only survivor and if any of his crew were to live through the ordeal of being sunk in Arctic waters, they would need his leadership and perhaps seamanship as well. He struggled to his knees just as the helmsman and officer of the watch from the pilothouse beneath his feet reached the bridge.

"Captain, Sir!" exclaimed the coxswain. "Are you hurt, Sir?"

Gentle hands helped him to his feet, but the stab of pain in his ribs was excruciating and he felt as if he was suffocating. He could not speak, and was beginning to shiver uncontrollably, from both cold and shock, but gestured aft towards the stern. The coxswain just shook his head.

"Come, Sir," he said. "We've to get you to a life raft. We'll not float much longer." A groan of metal twisting below them emphasized the point. With the help of the officer and coxswain, Broome made his way to the starboard ladder down to the weather decks. The officer went first and Broome turned to go down backwards.

"C'or, Blimey!" exclaimed the coxswain. Broome looked up and there was *Tirpitz*, barely a quarter mile distant, following in the wake of the German destroyer, her battle ensign snapping from her fantail. She passed by like some ancient monster of the deep sea, producing a bow wave to dwarf the destroyer that went before her. She seemed to shoulder aside the sea, to plow through it rather than to float upon it. Her mighty 15-inch guns were trained in, pointing to the north as if sniffing for a scent of her next victim, but Broome knew the German radar must have a firm fix on the merchantmen, desperately fleeing at their pathetic slow speed of eight knots.

The giant battleship passed like two city blocks sliding along the sidewalk and as the German's bridge came abreast of *Keppel*, Broome saw two officers standing on the bridge wing, holding a stiff salute in his direction. Though it took every ounce of his determination to lift his arm Broome returned the salute and held it, just as the first waves of *Tirpitz'* wake struck *Keppel*.

Broome, the coxswain, the young Lt., and fourteen others of *Keppel's* company made it to the life rafts and the ordeal of survival some of them endured must be fully told another time.

Chapter 25

SS Carlton. Sacrificial pawn.

Flashes of lightning as of an approaching storm lit the southern horizon, followed long moments later by the rumble of distant thunder. Willie Cipresso stood his watch on the port bridge wing of the *Carlton*. His biggest worry had been to stay warm and alert until fifteen minutes ago he'd reported to Captain Hansen that the convoy's destroyer escorts were all sailing away to the south at high speed. None knew for sure what this meant, but all were certain it was not a good omen. Confirmation came moments later when a signal flashed from *River Afton*, the convoy Commodore's ship, ordered an emergency turn to starboard and flank speed for the entire convoy.

Now *Carlton* strained every rivet and weld, squeezing power from her laboring engines. Even so, she barely exceeded eight knots. A strange hush descended on the ship as the crew stood their watches. Willie felt the deck vibrate beneath his feet from his position on *Carlton's* port bridge wing, as if the ship herself was desperate to flee. All eyes on the bridge watched the signs of battle to the south, wondering if the pitiful few Royal Navy destroyers were able to stop or even to slow the German onslaught. Most were skeptical and when the flash of gunfire stopped and the rumble of distant explosions died out they exchanged quiet looks with one another and willed *Carlton* to one more knot of speed, but the tired old tub was not up to any more. Eight knots was all she could do.

Minutes passed in unbearable tension for Willie, expecting at any moment to spot the superstructure of German ships appearing on the grey horizon. The convoy's carefully plotted structure dissolved as every ship strained for maximum speed. Tiny differences in performance began to separate slightly faster ships from the slower, with the speedier vessels breaking formation to pass and leave behind the slower prey. *Carlton*, already on the southern fringe of the convoy found herself also one of the slower ships and soon she brought up the rear of the entire stampeding fleet, with only the few pitiful remnants of the convoy escort lagging to the south. The armed trawlers, anti-aircraft ships and anti-submarine corvettes now placed themselves between the convoy and its pursuers, but none believed they'd achieve so much as a moment's delay in the inevitable.

Willie swept the southern horizon in a long, slow arc using his ten power binoculars. Smudges of smoke lingered from the battle just ended, but no ships had yet appeared.

"Maybe the Krauts have called it off after all," he said hopefully.

Before anyone else on the bridge could answer, his hopes were dashed. The terrifying sound of heavy artillery roared over his head. WWWHHHIIIIIIRRRR-SPLAT-CRASH, repeated as four 15-inch shells screamed over *Carlton*, erupting in fountains that shot a hundred feet in the air a half mile to the north of the freighter.

Captain Hansen jumped to the engine room telegraph ph. Already set to ALL AHEAD he rang it down and back up to ALL AHEAD again, the pre-arranged signal with the Chief Engineer that an attack had begun. Willie thought the gesture needless as even deep below the waterline the engine room crew could not have failed to hear or feel the impact of those four great shells.

WWWHHHIIIIRRRR-SPLAT-CRASH, the cycle repeated with four more geysers shot into the sky, this time on the port, or western edge of the convoy where they straddled the American flagged *William Hooper*, the closest shell hitting just a hundred yards ahead and abeam of her. Willie strained through his binoculars to see the source of the firing, but the hazy southern horizon remained stubbornly free of any clear ship silhouettes. With no knowledge of radar it was a complete mystery to him how the enemy could possibly fire from such a range and still achieve such accuracy.

"Cipresso!" Barked the Master. "Get down to the after deck and light fire to all the oil drums above the number two hold!" Captain Hanson commanded. "Take the bridge fire extinguisher with you and make sure the fire doesn't get out of hand." Willie stared at him blankly for a moment. "MOVE!" shouted Hanson, breaking Willie from his torpor. Willie dashed down the bridge wing ladder to obey.

Nineteen miles to the south Admiral Schniewind and Captain Topp were elated to at long last bring the Allied convoy under *Tirpitz's* guns, even at such extreme range. Each minute the four forward guns fired, hurling 800-kilogram high-explosive shells towards the convoy. *Tirpitz's* radar suite was tracking the convoy, but the south-most ships of the convoy were in visual range from the highest point in the battleship's superstructure where the great twenty-five power optical range finder was able to bring the enemy into sharp focus. The German optics industry was justly renowned as the world's finest. In peacetime, German cameras, astronomical telescopes and even eyeglasses were the best available. At war, this technological advantage was exploited, with gun sights for artillery and tanks and naval guns. Under daylight conditions, even with the heavy cloud cover at 600 meters altitude, their optical devices were superior even to radar in directing accurate fire against targets above the horizon.

For the moment however, only the forward main battery on *Tirpitz* could fire. *Hipper* and the destroyers were still well out of range and to turn the battleship to bring her aft guns in turrets Caesar and Dora to bear would delay them in their quest to catch the entire convoy and to slaughter it. The German fleet was then moving nearly 22 knots faster than their quarry. At this differential, they closed by more than a mile each three minutes. Within ten minutes, the furthest Allied merchantman would be at extreme range of *Tirpitz* while *Hipper* would also be able to open fire on the closer ships.

Schniewind gestured to his signals officer. "Send the prearranged signal that the attack on the enemy convoy has begun," he ordered. "Add our position, time and so forth and get it off immediately." The young officer saluted smartly then hurried from the bridge. "No need for wireless silence now, hmm Topp?" asked the Admiral rhetorically with a smile.

"Large ship on the western horizon!" sang out the port bridge wing lookout.

"That will be *Scheer*," commented Schniewind happily. He'd already been alerted by the radar office that the pocket battleship was closing to rejoin the fleet. Soon he would have three powerful warships tearing into the enemy. He sensed a great victory within his grasp.

Turrets Anton and Bruno each fired their 15-inch guns again. CRASH-CRASH-CRASH-CRASH. The shells travelled in great arcs through the sky before plunging down at their targets. Captain and Admiral listened to the tactical telephone circuit as *Tirpitz's* gunnery officer guided her fire onto target. Nearly a minute elapsed from the time the guns fired until the shells reached their destinations. While the last shells fired were still in flight the gun crews in the turrets worked to prepare and load the next salvo to be fired. As soon as the splash of falling shells was spotted through the range finder mounted high above, the gunnery officer issued orders to correct the aim.

"Left one hundred, down three hundred," the speaker on the bridge crackled. Minute adjustments were fed into the mechanical computer deep below the ship's waterline where all the many factors affecting the accuracy of her gunnery were calculated. Range and bearing are the obvious variables, but the Computing Station also factored more esoteric readings into the equation. The enemy's speed and the battleship's own speed along with temperature, barometric pressure, humidity and even the sea state all went into the computation to arrive at the precise aiming instructions fed automatically to each gun. Tiny adjustments only just discernible to the naked eye were made, the gun barrels twitched minutely and then fired again. CRASH-CRASH-CRASH-CRASH. The officers and bridge crew waited expectantly for results.

"HIT!" The single word crackled over the speaker. The Bridge crew exchanged smiles with one another and observed the looks of satisfaction on Topp's and Schniewind's faces. Topp picked up the telephone.

"Gunnery, this is the Captain," he said. "Shift your target! One hit per merchantman. Leave the cripples for our destroyers!"

"Yes, Herr Kapitan!"

The four guns of 'A' and 'B' turrets swung back to starboard, elevated and thundered out again and again. CRASH-CRASH-CRASH-CRASH. One by one they struck the ships of PQ17, first hitting those on the southern fringes of the convoy, but quickly reaching further north to smash the freighters in the middle of the formation. Five miles away to the west guns flashed and seconds later the sound of *Scheer's* forward main guns joined the attack.

"Bridge, Radar," the intercom speaker crackled. "Range now fourteen miles."

As if on cue, *Hipper* fired her four forward 8-inch guns. Now a hail of heavy shells assaulted the ships of the Allied convoy. Those freighters yet undamaged continued their efforts to flee, ignoring all pleas from their wounded consorts to render aid or rescue. Four pyres of black, oily smoke rose already from the convoy, the plumes disappearing into the cloud base that still covered the one-sided battle.

CRASH-CRASH-CRASH-CRASH, now interspersed with distant BOOM-BOOM-BOOM from *Scheer* and CRACK-CRACK-CRACK-CRACK from the nearer *Hipper*. A bright flash lit the northern horizon, as another ship was hit. Seconds later an even brighter flash lit the same location as the freighter's cargo of ammunition exploded.

"Time to bring your after battery into the attack, Captain," Schniewind said to Topp. The Captain nodded an acknowledgement and leaned to the window of the armored wheelhouse.

"Come left thirty degrees," he ordered. "Then make your helm amidships."

Tirpitz heeled to port altering course to allow her aft turrets, Caesar and Dora to bring her remaining four 15-inch guns on target. Within seconds, the first rounds from the aft guns were on their way, hurtling off to the north. Now fifteen heavy guns joined the attack and with the range shortening the pace of hits accelerated. Only ten minutes since the first shot was fired at the convoy and already ten merchant ships had been hit and damaged to varying degrees. Once *Hipper* and *Scheer* were also able to bring their after batteries to bear, the slaughter would be swift and merciless.

"Bridge, Radar," the intercom crackled. "Range now ten miles."

Ammunition rose on hydraulic elevators from the magazines deep in the three German ships, up to the turrets above. A short while earlier the shell handlers and gun crews in the main turrets had complained of the cold, but now they worked themselves into a sweat feeding shells and powder bales to the insatiable main batteries. Officers and gun captains, connected to the tactical telephone circuits via their headsets, kept up a continuous report as they ran up the score with hit after hit on the ships of the enemy convoy. The men worked with a bloodthirsty attitude that helped keep them going beyond normal limits of exhaustion; nonetheless, after fifteen minutes steady fire from *Tirpitz'* forward guns the pace of their fire began to slacken ever so slightly, with a few extra seconds passing between each salvo. This went largely unnoticed by Schniewind and Topp, as *Tirpitz*' aft guns and the forward batteries of *Hipper* and *Scheer* more than compensated for the reduction in fire with the sounds of the three ships' firing melding into one endless cacophony of destruction. CRACK-CRASH-BOOM in a relentless deluge of noise.

"BRIDGE, WIRELESS!" The barrage drowned out all other sounds and no one on the bridge heard the intercom crackle. Only when the wireless office sent a runner down to the bridge did the Captain and Admiral become aware there was a message. Topp picked up the telephone and with one palm flat against the other ear strained to hear.

"WIRELESS! BRIDGE! This is the Captain!" he shouted. He closed his eyes to concentrate on listening. "What!?" he shouted, his eyes popping wide in alarm. "REPEAT!"

PART THREE: CHECK AND COUNTER-CHECK

CHAPTER 26

The Battle of Bear Island

Admiral Tovey and Captain Halliday listened in silent frustration to the radio pleas for help coming from the ships of Convoy PQ17. The convoy's wireless discipline was completely broken. It seemed that every ship was screaming out voice transmissions calling for help. Only the Commodore aboard *River Afton* seemed able to keep his wits, providing detailed descriptions of the ships attacking his convoy and of the hits registered against the freighters one by one. The Royal Navy ships were all buttoned up at Action Stations, turrets and magazines manned, watertight doors and bulkheads shut and lookouts posted at every vantage point aboard each ship.

"Bridge, Radar," the intercom crackled to life.

"Radar, Bridge," the Officer of the Watch responded, flipping the speaker switch.

"Bridge, Radar, enemy aircraft on his east bound leg now," the radar officer reported. "All he has to do is drop out of the clouds and he can't miss us. Range, eight miles, about midway between us and the northernmost ships of the convoy."

"This Jerry observer's been a bit dull to this point," said Tovey. "Let's be certain he doesn't overlook us. Signal the leading destroyers by Aldis to fire on him, even if out of range, the moment they spot him."

The signals staff set about preparing the message to be sent via the Aldis signal lamps. Halliday stepped close to Tovey.

"You want the Germans to know we're here?" he asked, lowering his voice so only the Admiral could hear.

"Yes," Tovey murmured back. "Perhaps they'll break off their attack on the convoy, spare a ship or two."

"Why not just send a wireless signal to the Commodore that we're coming, or to the Admiralty? Jerry'd be sure to pick it up."

"True," replied Tovey, keeping his voice down. "But they'd also suspect the real reason for the message, might give them the idea they have the stronger force right now."

"Bridge, Wireless," the intercom crackled again. The radio operator went on without awaiting the acknowledgement. "Picking up an enemy signal now on bearing one-seven-zero, very strong. Difficult to say the range, but quite close. I should say no more than thirty miles. Coded. Almost certainly the enemy surface force signaling home."

"Ten more minutes and we'll be in range," Tovey said as the OOW acknowledged the message.

The crackle of automatic cannon fire drifted across the sea. Tovey and Halliday both lifted their binoculars and watched as the two destroyers leading the Royal Navy fleet fired on a distant target, too small to see, but presumably the German scout aircraft. A mood of tense expectation pervaded the bridge, with every man from Admiral to lowliest seaman anticipating the coming battle. The bridge became a beehive of activity. Barely noticed, so circumspect was he, Tembam, the Captain's steward lurked at the back of the bridge, watching and listening intently as he had always done when *Duke of York* went to Action Stations.

"Bridge, Wireless."

"Wireless, Bridge."

"Picking up another signal on bearing one-eight-zero. Plain voice in German. The scout plane is reporting our position."

Halliday stepped to the intercom box and flipped the switch. "Wireless, Bridge. Translation!" he demanded simply.

"Two heavy ships, two destroyers, fifteen nautical miles due north of convoy," said the radio man.

"That's it, Sir. Repeated over and over. The signal is weak and intermittent."

"Report immediately when he is acknowledged," snapped Halliday.

"Bridge, Radar!"

"Radar, Bridge," Halliday responded himself.

"Three heavy ships appearing at the southern edge of our range, bearing from one-seven-zero to one-seven-five, range twenty-six miles. Targets not yet distinct. There is a lot of intervening clutter with the ships of the convoy between us."

"The convoy is directly between us and the Germans," scowled Tovey. "We shall have to skirt to the west to avoid having to dodge through the merchantmen." Halliday nodded his understanding.

“Signal to fleet,” the Captain ordered. “Come right to course one-nine-zero, flank speed, action imminent.” The signals staff dashed to send the message and soon the clatter of the Aldis lamps resounded on the bridge.

“Smoke on the horizon, directly over the bows,” sang out one of the bridge wing lookouts.

“The convoy, poor devils,” said Tovey.

Halliday leaned down to the speaker. “Radar, Bridge, keep the range and bearing on the enemy heavies coming!”

“Range, twenty-five miles, bearings from one-six-nine to one-seven-four.”

“Guns, Captain!” Halliday barked into the intercom.

“Guns here, Captain!” The call was anticipated, the response instant. *HMS Duke of York’s* gunnery officer was ready.

“Just minutes from being in range, Guns,” said the Captain. “Almost certainly we’ll be inside his range first. We want the largest of the enemy targets, ignore the others for now.”

“Yes, Captain,” ‘Guns’ responded. “As soon as the radar image clarifies we’ll isolate the largest ship and be prepared to concentrate on her.”

"Thank you, Guns," said Halliday. "Good shooting." He turned to the officer of the watch. "Break out the battle ensign please Leftenant." Halliday glanced up at the clock on the bulkhead above the binnacle. 07.48 hours London time.

"Aye, Sir!" The young officer scurried away and within moments, the eight yard long silk banner rose atop the foremast and was unfurled, the White Ensign snapping and whipping behind. Miles away aboard the ships of Convoy PQ17 sailors felt a surge of hope and pride at the sight.

"Bridge, Radar. Range twenty-four miles. Heavy targets shifting bearing, now show an easterly course from one-six-nine to one-six-five, west to east. Largest target appears to be furthest east."

"She's turning away!" said Tovey with satisfaction. "Directly towards *Washington*!"

"Yes, but also so as to keep the convoy between us and her," answered Halliday. "We should have to fire over the convoy to hit her."

"All right," said Tovey. "They know we're here, but don't know about *Washington* just yet. Make a wireless signal to the Admiralty with the situation. Use the shared code for the Americans to pick it up too. Repeat the Germans position and heading several times. If Admiral Giffen knows his business he'll cut them off and we'll trap *Tirpitz* in a crossfire!"

Several tall plumes of oily, black smoke were now clearly visible to the south, rising from the sea up to the cloud base at 1,800 feet altitude.

"Bridge, Wireless, fresh transmission from the enemy surface units," crackled through the Tannoy loudspeaker intercom on the bridge. "Coded Morse signal."

"Bridge, Radar." The reports were coming atop each other now. "Two of the enemy surface units have turned to a southerly bearing, but the biggest is holding station. Range to it now twenty-three miles, bearing one-six-seven."

"*Tirpitz* is going to play rear-guard while her consorts scuttle away," observed Tovey.

"Bridge, Wireless. *River Afton* reports the shelling has ceased. Convoy holding course to the northwest."

"We're within range now," observed Halliday. "Shall I fire?" he asked Tovey.

"No," the Admiral shook his head. "Not yet. It would only tip our hand that we've only one battleship in range. With the low cloud deck and the smoke from the convoy between Tirpitz and us we'd have to rely on radar targeting anyway; not very accurate. Let's close the range further. We're at least as fast as the pocket battleships. If she's going to try to shield them *Tirpitz* has to hang back at less than full speed."

Halliday nodded. He understood Tovey was thinking out loud, reasoning through his own logic, looking for holes. He decided to play Devil's Advocate.

"The enemy is on a straight course due south now," he observed. "Doesn't lend itself to *Washington* closing as quickly on her from the northeast."

Tovey tugged at his earlobe and nodded thoughtfully.

"Quite right," he agreed. He looked at Halliday. "Thoughts?"

Halliday gave a slight shrug. "You could send *London* south and to the west of *Tirpitz*. With her superior speed she could begin to push the Germans from the west. Maybe they react by altering to the east. Give *Washington* the chance to close on them. Split the German's fire too, when the time comes."

As if to emphasize his point three widely separated spouts of water erupted to port of *Duke of York*. The furthest more than a mile distant and radar directed they were the opening salvo as the German's sought to establish the range. This first salvo adhered to standard German procedure to fire a partial salvo of ranging shots with practice shells. In this fashion, the German Navy's doctrine was to use lighter practice shells to quickly range in on the target, and then switch to live warheads.

Tovey turned to Halliday, nodding his head.

"Wireless to *London*," he said. "Have them stay to the west and no closer than twenty-four miles. She's to stay at arm's length of *Tirpitz*!" he emphasized.

The two great forward turrets of *Duke of York* now turned slightly to port, taking aim on the enemy's bearing. Six 14-inch guns, four in the foremost turret, two more in the turret directly below the bridge gave the battleship a mighty punch forward with four more 14-inch guns in a single turret aft. The smooth whir of the turret motors seemed overloud in the hush of the bridge until the guns came to a gentle stop, elevated to 45 degrees for maximum range, loaded with shells and powder bales and awaiting only the order for the gun captains to launch the 14-inch diameter projectiles on their way.

Three more great spouts of water leapt into the air, again to port, but this time the nearest was little more than three hundred yards distant.

"Come right twenty degrees!" ordered Halliday and the great ship heeled over, the momentum of her massive bulk carrying her forward on her original course for many seconds before her rudder bit into the water and she began to turn. "Damn fine radar directed fire!" Halliday commented.

"Not radar!" Tovey retorted. "Her scout plane is calling the fall of shot for her!"

"Let's give him something to think of on his own then," suggested Halliday.

"Agreed," nodded the Admiral. "You may open fire, Captain!"

Halliday jumped to the intercom and flipped the switch to open the gunnery circuit.

"Fire when ready!" he shouted.

"Shoot!" shouted the Gunnery Officer. The six forward guns rang out in a deafening salvo. Ice cracked and crashed around the forward turrets and superstructure. The concussion of the guns accomplished in minutes what hundreds of men had labored hours to achieve. Great chunks and sheets of ice slipped and slithered across the decks, sliding over the side under the cables of the side rails.

The guns fired one-by-one, in turn rather than simultaneously. Long experience in the Royal Navy showed that firing the heavy guns of a battleship at the same time shocked the structural support of the ship, requiring costly repairs. As soon as each gun fired, it drooped back towards its horizontal elevation for the reloading procedure.

Shell hoists hummed, rising up from the magazines, passing through the heavy anti-flash curtains and delivering first the enormous 1,600 pounds shells. These were then tipped gently from vertical to horizontal onto the loading tray. Hydraulic rams pushed the shells through the gun breech and into the fire chamber, even as the hoists delivered the powder bags to the turrets. Made of the finest silk and impregnated with a special flash explosive, the bags were designed to explode and burn completely in an instant, leaving not the slightest ash or ember behind in the barrel. A single glowing spark left in the barrel could spell disaster if it came into contact with the next powder bag before the breech was closed. It could trigger an explosion that could send a sheet of flame back down the shell hoist shaft, reaching directly into the magazine and destroying the entire ship.

Three powder bags followed each shell into the breech, in order that the shells be propelled the maximum distance, 37,000 yards, or nearly twenty-two miles. *Duke of York's* first salvo was fired from near the maximum range of her guns. Once loaded the guns began to elevate and train as tiny adjustments were made to the targeting calculations. Even as the first of the guns started to elevate for their second shot, the third German salvo began to fall.

Fired from a distance of twenty-two miles the German shells, *Tirpitz's* third salvo, fired now from her aft turrets "Caesar" and "Dora" also benefitted from the finer adjustments in aim made possible by the observations of Leutnant Wahl and his wireless operator aboard the Arado float plane shadowing the Royal Navy ships. The first shell fell four hundred yards off the port beam of *Duke of York* and the next three fell in a straight line across her path. The third shell of the salvo fell just fifty yards to starboard. All were fused to not explode unless a direct hit was scored, so none did damage, but that *Duke of York* had made a narrow escape was not lost on Tovey and Halliday.

"Come left!" shouted Halliday. "Put your wheel hard over to port!"

The British battleship heeled over now the other way in her ponderous turn, changing course and bearing to complicate the German gunnery. Halliday turned back to Tovey.

"Her range advantage over my guns is at least a mile, perhaps as much as two," he said. "I'm barely within range to hit her, but she's just bracketed me!"

"We must either find a way to close the range quickly, get close enough to hit *Tirpitz* or maneuver her onto *Washington's* guns in that cross-fire," agreed Tovey.

"*London* taking fire!" sang out one of the lookouts.

Tovey and Halliday lifted their binoculars and watched as *London*, now more than three miles away, changed course, veering away to the west to avoid the next salvo. A minute later three more, large caliber shells plopped into the sea. They fell a good mile short of target, to port of the cruiser.

“That would be the pocket battleship firing,” commented Tovey, lowering his glasses.

Halliday nodded. “Three shell pattern,” he agreed. “When *London* does not return fire they will know she hasn’t the gun range to reach back.”

WHHIIIRRR- SPLAT-CRACK. The first of a four shot salvo roared overhead. Even in the enclosed, armored bridge the scream of the shell passing over sent a shiver up Halliday’s spine.

“Come right to bearing one-eight zero!” he ordered.

Tovey nodded his silent approval. The Captain was presenting his ship’s narrowest aspect to the German gunners, cutting down the width of target while also cutting the straightest path to shorten the range.

“Bridge, Radar. Main target now bearing one-seven-nine, range 33,000 yards.” Once within gun range of the target the ranges would henceforth be expressed in the more granular yards.

Duke of York’s forward main battery fired in salvo again, the six guns thundering out one-by-one before dropping back to the reload position.

“Barely within range,” commented Halliday. “I shouldn’t want to exhaust the gun crews now.”

"Quite!" agreed Tovey emphatically. "Slow your fire till we can close the range and be more effective." Halliday nodded and moved off to give the necessary orders.

Forty miles away Admiral Giffen and Captain Benson stood on the armored bridge of *USS Washington*, their backs to the massive foot thick steel walls of the armored wheel house behind them. The US Navy battleship was at full speed, straining every rivet and weld, and just exceeding 28 knots. They'd just been handed the text of the coded signal intercepted some minutes before, sent by Admiral Tovey aboard *Duke of York*. *Washington's* radio officer had decrypted the unfamiliar British code as quickly as possible and hurried the printed text directly to the bridge.

They read the message flimsy silently together, then without saying a word turned and walked round to the back of the wheel house to the navigator's station. Benson quickly plotted the relative positions of the German and Royal Navy fleets. *Washington's* own position formed the third point of a triangle, forty miles east-southeast of the British, thirty-five miles east-northeast of the Germans.

"Almost eleven miles out of range," concluded Benson, looking at the chart.

“Yes, and with relative speeds only closing the gap by about one mile per hour,” said Giffen pensively. “At that rate it’ll take us eleven hours just to reach maximum range.”

“May as well plan to drop anchor on the North Cape!” snorted Benson.

“But if Tovey could turn *Tirpitz* back, even for ten minutes, or force her to hold her ground for fifteen, we could make that eleven miles up and bring her under a cross-fire.” Giffen scratched his chin. “I don’t dare make a signal, and anyway, Tovey knows his game as well as I do. He’ll be looking for any chance to slow *Tirpitz* down.”

“Even if he only pushes the Germans to the east we can make up the gap,” said Benson.

“Meantime, keep pouring on the coal, Captain,” said Giffen, straightening from the chart table. “All we can do at our end is maximize our speed to the southwest.”

“We’ll never reach Iceland now without refueling at sea,” said Benson, voicing what was on both men’s mind.

Giffen lowered his voice. "You understand my orders?" he asked quietly. "*Washington*, the cruisers, the whole task force and the Brits too, we're all expendable if it means putting *Tirpitz* down."

Benson nodded. "Understood," he said as Giffen walked back to the bridge.

Several decks below the bridge Reggie Elkins sat buttoned up in the forward 5-inch gun turret on *Washington's* starboard side. The entire ship was buttoned up in a state of expectant readiness and had been for hours. In some places, the crew found the chance to sleep or at least doze off, but many of the crew had now been going for twenty hours without sleep and Reggie was one of these. Even in his bunk, he found sleep difficult in this bitter cold, which penetrated below decks with a strange, dank humidity. Reggie wondered that the men on the smaller ships slept at all.

Men at every station noted the increased vibration as *Washington* pushed her engines to flank speed. Though comprised mainly of men new to the Navy, including many draftees who'd never been to sea before joining her company, the crew of *Washington* had enough 'old salts' among them to know the Captain would not push the ship's engines to their maximum power except in a combat emergency. They looked at one another silently and checked for the thousandth time the tiny details of properly securing their battle stations. Reggie checked the auto loader for the 5-inch shells, ensuring the rounds were all lined up straight and unobstructed. The 5-inch guns were capable of firing ten shots a minute each at their maximum rate and the autoloader apparatus with its ten shell ready rack of ammunition was integral to this performance. Throughout the ship, men took deep breaths, said silent prayers and looked forward to the prospect of action with the enemy, with either dread or eager anticipation, depending on each man's temperament.

Back aboard *Tirpitz*, Admiral Schniewind and Captain Topp quickly recovered their aplomb after the initial shock they received when their Arado scout aircraft reported a British fleet approaching from the northwest. With the warning provided him by the Arado, Schniewind ordered his fleet to turn about onto a southerly heading immediately at 28 knots, the maximum speed of his slowest ship, the heavy cruiser *Scheer*. *Tirpitz*, though capable of over 30 knots herself, held back and brought up the rear of the withdrawal in order to shield both *Scheer* and *Hipper* from the guns of the oncoming Allied battleship. Once his fleet was on a southerly course, Schniewind's first action was to alert Berlin of the latest development via wireless, signaling his intention to withdraw. His second action was to send an urgent appeal to Luftwaffe Northern Command, asking for air support from the North Cape bomber bases although he was already well aware the airfields were fogged in. His flag officer, Leutnant Herbst shuttled back and forth from the port bridge wing to the wireless office, carrying out these signals and bringing fresh reports.

"The Arado reports the enemy battleship is equipped with three main turrets," Herbst reported. "One forward turret carries four barrels as does the after turret while the other forward turret is twin-barreled. Ten main guns in all. The other large ship appears to be a heavy cruiser with eight guns in four twin-barrel turrets."

"The battleship is of the *King George V* class," commented Schniewind. "14-inch guns and heavily armored, but slower than *Tirpitz*. Not much faster than *Scheer*, in fact, if at all."

"A powerful opponent," said Topp, noncommittally, glancing up at the clock on the bulkhead. 08.58 hours, Berlin time, one hour later than in London.

“Yes and new,” agreed Schniewind. “The first ship did not complete until after war had already started.”

Tirpitz’ aft gun battery interrupted him with a salvo of four shells. BOOM-BOOM-BOOM-BOOM. The great guns thundered out in sequence. Seconds later a salvo of six British shells fell short of *Tirpitz’* fantail, lifting a veil of water spouts. Topp took advantage of this momentary advantage to change course.

“Helm to port, new course one-five-zero,” he ordered. Unwittingly he shifted *Tirpitz’* path ever so slightly towards *USS Washington*, still undetected by the Germans to the northeast.

“Message from *Scheer* via signal lamp,” announced a lookout from the front of the bridge.

“See to it, Herbst!” ordered Schniewind. He was busy trying to spot the fall of shells from *Tirpitz*’ most recent salvo. Four shells of the third salvo from the aft turrets Caesar and Dora fell well to starboard of the enemy.

“Admiral!” shouted Herbst moments later as he rushed back to the bridge wing. “*Scheer* reports developing an engineering fault!” he reported breathlessly. “Her speed is down to 25 knots and they are trying to determine the cause of the fault!”

"Damnation!" exclaimed Schniewind. He rushed to the front of the bridge and lifted his binoculars to look at the heavy cruiser, now barely three miles ahead of *Tirpitz*. "That settles it!" he sputtered. "We have no choice now, Captain! We must turn and fight the British battleship, delay her to give *Scheer* time to solve this problem and escape." Topp nodded his understanding.

"Right rudder!" he ordered. "Come about to course two-seven-zero, speed 30 knots. All main guns to fire in salvo!"

Schniewind turned to Herbst.

"Signal *Hipper* to stay with us, speed 30 knots," he commanded. "She is to handle the British cruiser should it venture within range." Herbst clicked his heels together and hurried off to carry out the order. The bridge watch all leaned into the turn as *Tirpitz* heeled over to starboard, veering onto a westerly course and bringing all eight of her mighty 15-inch guns to bear. The aft turret fired again, BOOM-BOOM-BOOM-BOOM. Seconds later the forward turret added her roar as soon as the guns could train past the ship's own superstructure to target the enemy. BOOM-BOOM-BOOM-BOOM.

WHIIIRRR-SPLAT, WHIIIRRR-SPLAT. A pair of British shells roared overhead to explode in the sea, along the path *Tirpitz* would have been on had she held her course. Four others fell just short.

"The British have the range, Captain!" said Schniewind ominously.

"Come right to three-one-zero!" Topp shouted.

"Hit!" shouted a bridge lookout. "Enemy battleship hit amidships!"

Duke of York rocked from stem to stern and men throughout the ship knew immediately she'd been hit. Captain Halliday and Admiral Tovey were knocked from their feet, along with the rest of the bridge watch. The 800 kilogram 15-inch armor piercing shell fell at the base of the armored conning tower, right behind the barbette of the forward 14-inch twin barrel gun turret. It hit in one of the most heavily armored areas of the ship. The barbette or armored cylinder atop which the turret turned was protected by nearly thirteen inches of cast steel to protect the hoists and elevators that delivered shells and powder bags from the magazine to the guns above. The main magazine sat five decks deep beneath the gun deck and was further protected by an eight-inch thick slab of steel built horizontally into the ship's structure. It capped the magazine, folded over down its sides and enveloped it from below to defend against a torpedo exploding the magazine.

The shell exploded three decks deep and had it plunged directly to the armored cap over the magazine no one can say if it would have penetrated the steel slab. Had it done so the results would have been catastrophic for *Duke of York*. The prior year the battlecruiser *HMS Hood* was destroyed when a 15-inch shell from *Tirpitz'* sister ship, the *Bismarck*, detonated her main magazine. From a crew of over 1,600 men, *Hood's* disaster produced three survivors. Of World War I design, as a battlecruiser, *Hood's* armor was substantially lighter than the *KGV* class battleships of later construction.

In any event, the shell did not penetrate the magazine, but its results were serious enough for all that. The twin-barreled forward turret was immediately jammed in its ring from the force of the concussion. The guns were no longer able to train, and though they could elevate and fire they could not be aimed and were effectively knocked out of action. The Royal Navy were aware from their own gun trials that the MK II and MK III turrets installed aboard the *KGV* class battleships were sensitive and prone to jam in combat. Proposed solutions were costly in labor and material, but more importantly in time. Several months in a shipyard were needed for each of the four surviving members of the class to effect these changes and so far the Royal Navy had not been able to spare the ships from service long enough to do the work.

The blast from the explosion was kept from the magazine, turret and shell hoists by the thick armor, but this also served to channel the force of the blast. With the magazine cap below it, the armored conning tower behind and the barbette forward, the blast was forced sideways and up. The explosion shredded numerous compartments in the hull above the magazine. A volcanic eruption of flame rocketed up from the impact site and struck the underside of the bridge overhang above, peppering it with shrapnel and steel fragments. Half a dozen holes were opened in the bridge deck, but miraculously none of the bridge watch were struck. Electrical conduits and water pipes were severed by the blast, plunging other compartments forward into darkness until alternate circuits were opened. A raging fire broke out between decks fed by furnishings, electrical wiring and anything else that would burn. The first damage parties on the scene were driven back by the intense heat and toxic smoke, and from lack of water due to the severed pipes. Not until men arrived with asbestos suits and re-breather air tanks and masks were they able to attack the fire near its heart.

Nobby Lamb was among those who responded immediately to the blast. He took his place in a gang tasked with connecting fires hoses to the nearest operational valves and with fighting back the flames. Thrown from their feet by the explosion he and his mates had to sort themselves out in darkness until a battery-powered lamp was lit. Soon, the tween decks area filled with thick, choking smoke and his damage party was forced to retreat until more help arrived. We shall see more of Nobby later.

On the bridge, Captain Halliday struggled to his knees with the help of Tembam. No sooner had the shell struck than the Malay Steward appeared as from nowhere, gently lifting Halliday to his feet, checking him quickly for injuries, even smoothing his uniform.

“I’m fine!” snapped Halliday over loud, brushing away Tembam’s fluttering hands. Then more gently, “See to the Admiral, that’s a good fellow,” he said, nodding to his steward. “Hard port rudder. Come left thirty degrees.” The helmsman regained control of the wheel and the ship heeled over to its left, to the south, into the teeth of the German fire.

Tembam released the Captain and turned to Tovey who was still face down on the deck. He rolled the Admiral over and gently lifted the tin helmet off his head. Tovey's left eye was covered with blood from a gash on his temple where his own tin hat had cut him when jammed down on his head. He struggled to a sitting position and mopped at his eye with his handkerchief, then stood. He wobbled for just a moment then steadied himself on the binnacle. Blood dripped onto the face of the magnetic compass. A fresh, white towel appeared as if by magic from Tembam's tunic. The steward deftly placed it under the Admiral's helmet and tucked it up to put pressure on the cut, then took the handkerchief from Tovey's hands and wiped at the blood filling his eye. In moments, Tovey was blinking to clear his eye.

"How badly hurt are we?" he demanded.

The four-barreled forward turret cut off any response as it fired its next salvo. BOOM-BOOM-BOOM-BOOM. Halliday hung up the telephone and spoke with Tovey, looking the Admiral over carefully to assess his condition.

"'B' Turret is out of commission," he said. "Jammed in its ring. Dockyard job. Fire between decks doesn't pose a major threat just yet. The magazine armor held up."

"Propulsion?" demanded Tovey. "Steering?"

"Unaffected," answered Halliday.

WHHIIIRRR, WHHIIIRRR-SPLAT, WHHIIIRRR-SPLAT, SPLAT, SPLAT. Four shells passed overhead, close enough together that their sounds were indistinguishable. They exploded on impact with the sea two hundred yards away. Tembam pressed a fresh handkerchief into the Admiral's hands, taking away the now sodden one.

Halliday picked up the telephone. "Radar, Bridge," he barked, then flicked the switch to put the reply on the bridge intercom speaker.

"Bridge, Radar. Enemy battleship turning to course one-seven-zero, speed 28 knots, range 30,000 yards. The smaller cruiser is with her 2,500 yards to starboard, range 31,500 yards. The larger cruiser has held course one-seven-zero throughout, speed down to 24 knots, range 40,000 yards."

"That's it then!" exclaimed Tovey. "The one cruiser has developed a fault of some sort that affects her engines. She's slowed, and *Tirpitz* and the other cruiser are holding back to cover her withdrawal."

"A fine job of it she's doing too," said Halliday. "She's straddled me twice and hit me once."

A trickle of blood ran down Tovey's chin and dripped onto his uniform, but he ignored it. "It's our only chance to bring her to heel, Captain! We must pursue her at top speed!"

"Resume course one-seven-zero," Halliday ordered. "Flank speed, all ahead full!" BOOM-BOOM-BOOM-BOOM. The bridge shook from the blast of 'A' turret's four guns firing.

"Bridge, Radar. Targets turning to port. The battleship and the near cruiser both coming to an easterly heading, ranges down to 30,000 yards. The other cruiser is holding her course due south."

"Follow *Tirpitz*, Captain!" ordered Tovey. "She's all that matters!"

"This turn," said Halliday, holding his binoculars to his eyes. "She's already in range. She's coming broadside to give us all eight guns, then may turn right into us." Even as he watched the foredeck of *Tirpitz* came clear and puffs of smoke billowed from her guns.

"Port rudder," he ordered. "Steady on one-four-zero."

"Port rudder," acknowledged the helm. "Steady on one-four-zero."

"Enemy cruiser firing!" sang out the starboard bridge lookout even as Halliday saw the four aft guns on the battleship also fire. At that moment, the Germans had sixteen shells in the air directed against his ship, flung at him from two different bearings.

WHHIIIRRR-SPLAT-THUNK. A piece of shell casing smashed into *Duke of York*, somewhere in the aft superstructure. WHHIIIRRR-SPLAT, WHHIIIRRR-SPLAT, WHHIIIRRR-SPLAT. Three near misses, all long. WHIIZZ-SPLASH, WHIIZZ-SPLASH, WHIIZZ-BANG-BANG. Two direct hits, this time from the enemy cruiser's 8-inch guns, also aft. WHHIIIRRR-SPLAT, WHHIIIRRR-SPLAT, WHHIIIRRR-SPLAT, CRASH! Three 15-inch shots fell long, with the fourth crashing down on *Duke of York's* bows. It exploded in the port side anchor chain locker, severing the chain and sending the anchor plunging to the depths of the Arctic Sea. The explosion lifted the weather deck and unseated the port anchor's capstan, pitching it across the deck like a cricket ball bowled at the wickets. It crashed through the port side rail and also plunged into the sea. Oils and lubricants used for the Capstan motor burst into flame and black, oily smoke boiled out of the shell hole to mingle with the smoke still rising from the first hit near the conning tower.

"HIT!" shouted two lookouts simultaneously. "Enemy battleship hit amidships!"

BOOM-BOOM-BOOM-BOOM. 'B' turret thundered out another salvo, its eleventh of the battle.

"Good shooting, Captain!" said Tovey, his binoculars pressed to his eyes. "You've hit aft of her funnel!"

Halliday grabbed up the telephone. "Damage report!" he demanded. "Yes, I can see the hit forward," he shouted. "What about aft? It felt like we're hit twice aft?" He waited a moment, listening with a finger in his other ear to block out unwanted noise. "Keep me informed!" he said, slamming the phone down in its cradle. More 8-inch shells splashed down around *Duke of York*. *Hipper's* 8-inch guns had a maximum rate of fire of five rounds per minute per gun. Now she unleashed a torrent of some forty rounds a minute. Incapable of inflicting mortal wounds against *Duke of York*, they were nonetheless a deadly threat to anyone in an exposed or thinly armored area of the ship and were especially dangerous to the damage parties fighting the fires fore and aft.

"Two 8-inch hits aft," Halliday said to Tovey. "The Walruses are both destroyed and their petrol is afire. The aft most starboard five and a quarter inch gun mount took the other hit. Crew there dead, gears smashed."

"Main combat power not affected then," said Tovey grimly dismissing the casualties just reported. The Walrus seaplanes would not be needed and the loss of two out of sixteen 5.25-inch guns would only be a problem in event of air attack or close range gunnery duel.

"Yes, but the damage parties have asked that I put the ship over for the wind to blow the fires over the side," replied Halliday. Tovey started to demur, but then thought better of it.

"Do so briefly and while broadside you can bring both the fore and aft turret into the fight," he agreed. "Our eight against his eight."

"Come left to course zero-nine-zero!" Halliday ordered.

"Come left to zero-nine-zero," the quartermaster at the helm repeated.

BOOM-BOOM-BOOM-BOOM. The turret aft took its turn hurling 14-inch shells at *Tirpitz*.

"Bridge, Radar," the intercom crackled. "Range narrowing, now 24,000 yards."

"Be in range for the five and a quarter inch guns soon," said Tovey, mopping blood from his face. Tembam was there, changing the now sodden towel under the Admiral's helmet.

Halliday said nothing, but knew *Duke of York* would also be in range of *Tirpitz'* own secondary armament, the rapid-fire 5.9-inch guns. *Tirpitz* carried twelve of these, six to both port and starboard in three double turrets. He snatched up the telephone.

"Guns, Bridge," he shouted over the rising din. "Starboard side secondary guns to fire on the cruiser. Keep her at arms-length!"

"Bridge, Guns, Aye."

Within seconds, the six surviving guns of the starboard battery were firing, each hurling an eighty-pound shell at *Hipper* every six seconds, but at the same time *Tirpitz* added her own 5.9-inch guns to the battle, hurling a one hundred pound shell from each gun three times a minute. Now the BOOM from the main batteries was accompanied by a constant crackle from the lighter guns.

"Come right twenty degrees!" ordered Halliday.

"Come right twenty degrees," confirmed the quartermaster.

A plume of fire burst over the bows as an 8-inch shell exploded forward of 'A' turret. Fountains of water erupted on every side as Halliday conned his ship through a hail of armor piercing shot. Smoke and flame still licked from the three fires burning aboard *Duke of York*. From a distance as seen from *HMS London* the British battleship presented a scene like something straight from hell, with boiling brimstone spitting and sputtering all about. WHHIIIRRR-SPLAT, WHHIIIRRR-SPLAT, WHHIIIRRR-SPLAT-BANG. Shrapnel from a 15-inch shell casing rang against the hull.

"Bridge, Radar! Cruiser turning away, resuming her due south heading. Range widening to 26,000 yards. *Tirpitz* holding course due east."

"Hold her Captain!" exhorted Tovey. "Ten more minutes on an easterly heading and we may get help from *Washington*!"

"Bridge, Radar. *Tirpitz* turning away to due south now. Range widening."

BOOM-BOOM-BOOM-BOOM. The forward turret fired its salvo through the veil of water that surrounded the ship.

"Turn with her, Captain!" Tovey urged. "Don't let her widen the range!" Halliday grabbed up the telephone.

"Damage report!" he barked. He listened for a moment, then, "I shall be turning to starboard on a southerly course," he said. "Don't let your crews be caught by the shift in wind!" He slammed the phone back down.

The fire from the 5.25-inch guns went silent as the range to the target now exceeded their reach.

Halliday turned to Tovey. Tembam was once more tending to the Admiral's wound, applying a piece of tape to a dressing over the gash in his forehead.

"The fire between decks is under control and should be out soon," the Captain reported. "The fire aft is more serious. Fed by the aviation petrol and has gotten ahold of the ship's boats as well. We'll lose them all if we turn south. Forward, the fire in the anchor locker is out of control, but will burn itself out soon enough."

"Pursue *Tirpitz*!" said Tovey sternly. "Nothing else matters."

"Come right to one-seven-zero," Halliday ordered.

"Come right to one-seven-zero," the helmsman acknowledged.

"Perhaps we can recall *London*?" asked Halliday. "When the Germans combine the cruiser with *Tirpitz* I've more than I can cope with single handed."

"Agreed," nodded Tovey. "But keep her on a separate bearing. No sense simplifying Jerry's fire control."

"Bridge, Radar," the intercom rattled. Halliday looked up and noticed the Tannoy speaker had a bright slash across its box where a piece of shrapnel had scored it after ripping through the bridge deck. "Cruiser now at 32 knots, course one-seven-zero, range 30,000 yards. *Tirpitz* on one-seven-zero, speed 28 knots, range now 28,000 yards."

The veil of mist that had surrounded the ship for some minutes parted and *Duke of York* sailed into clear water. Tovey and Halliday both lifted their binoculars. *Tirpitz* was showing her fantail, her four aft 15-inch guns trained in and pointing almost directly over her stern. Smoke billowed from the muzzles as they watched. Halliday shifted his gaze further south and for a moment watched *Hipper* as she too fled. The German cruiser appeared to have ceased fire and smoke billowed from her amidships. Halliday wondered if she'd been hit or was deliberately making smoke to screen her withdrawal. WHHIIIRRR-SPLAT. BOOM-BOOM-BOOM-BOOM. The heavy guns raged on. Tovey walked to the wireless office to compose a detailed report to the Admiralty.

Aboard *Tirpitz,* Admiral Schniewind and Captain Topp also conferred. They stood on the port bridge wing, looking aft at the pursuing British battleship through their binoculars. Topp had just received a damage update. *Tirpitz* was hit three times, twice by heavy caliber 14-inch shells and once by a much lighter 5.25-inch round. Damage from this last was minor, but the two heavy hits were of more serious concern. One shell had landed amidships, unseating the launching rail for the Arado scout planes and dumping the three remaining aircraft over on the deck below, where they burned brightly. Shrapnel from this hit peppered the funnel, perforating it in over a dozen places and reducing the air draft from the boilers in the engine rooms below decks. At least temporarily the ship's top speed was reduced to 28 knots.

The other heavy shell struck forward in the port scuppers, adjacent to turret Anton. The shell exploded against the armored barbette three decks deep. The integrity of the turret, barbette and magazines held, but Anton's shell hoists were stopped. A repair crew set to work to find and repair the fault, but it would be some time before Anton could fire again.

"Fortunate it's not Caesar or Dora knocked out," observed Topp. "For now at least we can sustain our fire aft and the British can be kept ignorant that one of our forward turrets is not functioning." Lt. Herbst hustled onto the bridge.

"Two signals, Sir," he said to Schniewind, handing him the message slips. The Admiral scanned each quickly then read the first one aloud.

"Addressed to me from Luftwaffe Northern Command," he began. "Banak and Bardufoss Airfields under heavy fog. Regret cannot meet request for air cover at this time. Suggest request again one hour if air cover still needed."

"No air cover!" exclaimed Topp.

Schniewind held up the second signal. "Our Arado reports fuel running low and must leave for the North Cape in five minutes or for Bear Island in twenty."

"We're going to lose our spotter," sighed Topp. "Still, he has served his function well. Lt. Wahl warned us of the British battleship in time to turn about and our gunnery has benefitted from his observations."

"Wireless to the Arado," said Schniewind to Herbst. "Bear Island is to be his refuge." Herbst hurried away to send the signal.

"A cold harbor for Wahl," said Topp.

"Yes, but if the North Cape is fogged in he would have trouble finding home there anyway," answered the Admiral. Four splashes erupted 500 meters to port. "You notice the enemy is only firing four guns forward?" he asked Topp.

"She must have sustained damage," said the Captain. "There is still at least one fire burning aboard her."

"She is hurt," nodded Schniewind. "Perhaps worse than us, but it's not worth the risk to engage her again at closer range." He stepped to the back of the bridge. "Herbst!" he called. "Signal *Scheer* by lamp. Determine the status of her engine fault!" Topp picked up the bridge telephone.

"Radar, Bridge," he said. "Course and speed for *Scheer*?" He listened a moment. "Danke," he said. Turning back to the Admiral, he shrugged. "Her speed is still only 24 knots," he reported. "She is seven miles south of us, out of range of the British battleship, but only for now. With a 4 knot difference in relative speed the British will be in range of her again in thirty minutes or less."

"Let's hope we've bought her time to find the fault," the Admiral said.

Chapter 27

Outside Influences

What has become known as The Battle of Bear Island settled in for what looked like a lengthy stern chase, in the tradition of the Napoleonic era. *Duke of York* pursued, seeking every advantage of wind, sea and navigation to close the range and keep *Tirpitz* under fire with some chance of hitting and damaging her, of slowing her down enough that *USS Washington* could join the battle. Admiral Tovey was confident the two Allied battleships could overwhelm the German monster if they could bring their main batteries to bear together. During this phase of the battle, the exchange of salvos slowed as each commander tried to outwit the other by guessing the opponent's next course change and hitting her with a long-range shot.

Meanwhile, *Tirpitz* and her accompanying ships fled. Admiral Schniewind knew *Tirpitz* and *Hipper* could outrun a King George V class battleship, and under normal conditions *Scheer* could too if given a head start, but until the engine fault was found and repaired, *Scheer* was vulnerable. Too slow to run away, too thinly armored to withstand 14-

inch hits and too weakly armed herself to counterpunch, she would be an easy victim for the British battleship if left to fend for herself.

Schniewind was also confident that in a majority of cases, *Tirpitz* could battle it out with a KGV and come away the winner, even achieving a great victory, but the specter of *Bismarck's* fate haunted every officer in the German surface navy. *Bismarck* had smashed *HMS Hood*, the most famous warship in the world and until her demise deemed by novice and expert alike to be the world's most powerful as well. But a chance hit from an airborne torpedo had sealed the fate of *Tirpitz'* sister ship, rendering her helpless in the face of overwhelming numbers of Royal Navy battleships.

Who could say what rabbit the Royal Navy could produce here in the Arctic against *Tirpitz*, Schniewind wondered. The temptation to slug it out with the British battleship was powerful, but the risk too great. *Tirpitz* had achieved her mission. She had turned back the Allied convoy to Russia. Almost certainly, none of its cargo would ever reach the Bolsheviks and much of it already rested on the floor of the sea. The Royal Navy had suffered its second great defeat in less than two weeks, following their disastrous effort to relieve Malta in response to the Axis powers' airborne invasion of the Mediterranean island. Further, even if *Tirpitz* won the battle and sank her opponent she might suffer such damage as to be out of the war for months or longer, while the British possessed numerous battleships to replace one lost in battle. Schniewind decided the time had come to collect his winnings and retire from the game. He had only to shield *Scheer* until she was capable of full speed and his entire command would return to port without suffering a loss. He was relieved when turret Anton came back into operation. An electrical fuse had blown on the circuit powering its shell hoists. Replacing the fuse restored power and the turret to full function.

While he nervously awaited a response from *Scheer* on the status of her repairs, Schniewind directed Captain Topp to turn back at their pursuers at odd and unpredictable intervals. Each time *Tirpitz* turned she altered course just enough that her forward battery could fire two quick salvos, adding their weight of firepower to the aft guns to slow and delay the British pursuit. This was somewhat, though not entirely effective. Slowly but surely the British continued to gain on *Scheer* whose base course never deviated from one-seven-zero, the shortest path to the safety of Altenfiord.

"Signal lamp from *Scheer*!" shouted a lookout. Moments later Lt. Herbst appeared with the message.

"Blocked fuel line being replaced," Schniewind said for the benefit of Topp. "Estimate forty more minutes to finish the repair and regain speed."

What neither man knew, what no one could know is that more than three weeks earlier a Polish sailor impressed into the German merchant navy was able to slip a bundle of old rags and cotton waste wrapped around a small aluminum bottle into the hold of a tanker ship which delivered fuel oil to Narvik. The bottle gave the rags just enough buoyancy to float right below the surface of the tanker's hold and went unnoticed as oil was pumped, first into the harbor's fuel storage tanks, then into *Scheer* as she topped off her fuel tanks ahead of sailing on The Knight's Gambit. These rags became stuck in a bend of the fuel line leading to one of the heavy cruiser's engines, reducing the flow of fuel and restricting her speed at the crucial time. *Scheer's* chief engineer raced first to find the problem, then to route a new pipe to bypass the blockage. An after action investigation into the matter would suggest sabotage, but the culprit was never identified.

"Forty more minutes," said Topp. "We'll have to bite at our pursuer again for *Scheer* to complete her repairs."

"Yes, but once she has we'll all be able to outrun the British and return with a great victory in hand," answered Schniewind. "Come, let's plot our next move."

But events in distant capitals were already underway which would alter the course of the battle. In both London and Berlin, senior leadership of the Royal Navy and German Kriegsmarine convened in their respective headquarters' to monitor wireless reports flowing back from the combatants. Neither Schniewind nor Tovey had any reason to maintain wireless silence once the battle joined, since neither could hide his presence from the enemy any longer. Both maintained a steady stream of radio signals to inform their Admiralties of the battle. In Tovey's case, his messages also served to alert Admiral Giffen aboard *Washington* and to vector the American battleship to the scene.

In London, First Sea Lord Admiral Sir Dudley Pound kept watch that morning in his Admiralty HQ in Whitehall and Prime Minister Winston Churchill made the short trip from 10 Downing Street to monitor the battle with him. Churchill had served as First Lord in World War I and again at the start of World War II, before ascending to political leadership in place of Neville Chamberlain. His interest in and love for the Royal Navy were well known and profound, though his wisdom on all things naval was not so universally respected.

As the morning wore on a continuous trickle of brief wireless messages from Admiral Tovey kept both men's attention rapt and Churchill's mood swung from ebullient to melancholy with each successive report. In one respect, Churchill never wavered. He remained iron-willed that everything possible be done to damage or better yet, to sink *Tirpitz*, even if it meant the loss of *Duke of York* and her compliment. He became more and more animated and constantly pressured the First Sea Lord to goad Tovey to greater risk and exertion in pursuit of the prize.

"To trade *Duke of York* for *Tirpitz*, and even at worst ends to trade both *Duke of York* and *Washington* for *Tirpitz* would be an advantageous exchange," he exhorted Pound. He paused a moment to puff on his cigar. "It would be akin to trading a Knight and a Bishop for our opponents Queen," he continued, unwittingly mirroring the chess theme of the German operation named 'The Knight's Gambit'. "It would vastly simplify our task of balancing our available resources against the threats posed by the German navy." History has no record of any American reaction to Churchill's cavalier calculus involving the potential fate of *USS Washington*.

Pound quietly accepted Churchill's guidance for several reasons. Firstly, he knew that Churchill was in fact correct. The Royal Navy's capital ships were tied down by the endless watch against *Tirpitz'* sallying out to threaten the Atlantic and Arctic shipping lanes. With her eliminated, his battleships could be profitably employed elsewhere in the war effort.

The First Sea Lord also understood the tremendous pressure Churchill bore. The Prime Minister had only just survived a Confidence Vote in the House of Commons, precipitated by the losses of Tobruk and Malta in the Mediterranean theater. Churchill badly needed a victory to rally morale and restore faith in his conduct of the war. Another major defeat might lead to a constitutional crisis at a time when Britain needed a steady hand on the tiller.

But it is also known today that Pound was already gravely ill. A cancerous tumor was growing in his brain, diagnosed by the fleet surgeon, but hidden from the Admiralty Board. A number of his decisions have been called into question in the post-war epoch. Critics wonder if the tumor was already adversely affecting him at the time of Malta and Convoy PQ17. In particular, his decisions to press the relief effort of Malta, even after the loss of his fleet's aircraft carriers there and then to reverse convoy PQ17 back toward Bear Island have been torn apart, his detractors and supporters equally adamant in their opposing opinions on the merits.

That night Churchill and Pound were not only privy to the messages sent by Tovey. The British 'Y' Service as their wireless interception bureau was known, kept a keen ear listening for all German signals and passed the coded messages on to Station X, the code-breaking establishment at Bletchley Park Estate outside London. In many cases Station X was able to decode and distribute German messages to senior British Military commands faster than the Germans could do so themselves.

In the last weeks of June 1942, during the battle for Malta, told in *"Operation Herkules"*, the prequel to this work, the Germans captured documents from the British whose analysis began the long process by which the Germans eventually concluded the British were reading their encrypted messages. Major Kuno Schacht, one of the many heroes of the Axis airborne invasion of the island, turned these documents over to an officer of the Reich Signals Intelligence Bureau and Schacht carried knowledge of these documents and their implications for German wireless security on with him to his next posting in North Africa. There, Erwin Rommel made the first use of the information to good effect in the Battle for the Nile Delta. This story is told in the sequel to this work, *"The*

Gates of Victory". But at the time of the events surrounding convoy PQ17 and *"The Knight's Gambit"* Berlin was as yet unaware of the 'Malta File' as the issue came to be known, and anyway it would take several months before official skepticism was overcome and formal changes made to the code system.

As the sun rode to mid-morning over the British capital, Pound and Churchill received the decoded message from Luftwaffe command in Norway politely declining Schniewind's request for air cover. They turned this around in a coded message to Tovey alerting him that "Norwegian intelligence sources" reported the North Cape airfields were unserviceable due to weather and that no Luftwaffe air support could be provided. They urged Tovey to pursue *Tirpitz* "at all costs" in an effort to damage or sink her. To Tovey this message meant only one thing; *Duke of York* and all the Allied warships involved in the operation were considered expendable in pursuit of the strategic imperative to remove the threat *Tirpitz* posed to Allied shipping. Any hesitation he might have had in venturing further south in this effort vanished on receipt of this message. This same message was also received and understood in the same manner by Admiral Giffen aboard *USS Washington*.

In Berlin Grand Admiral Raeder and his Kriegsmarine, staff also monitored the wireless traffic from the Arctic that morning. However, Raeder was obliged to report directly to Adolph Hitler at the Reich Chancellery bunker. The entire German General Staff composed mainly of Army and Luftwaffe officers held an extended session of the nightly Fuhrer briefing. After adjourning for a few brief hours of sleep, they reconvened in the Fuhrer bunker. Among those assembled were Grand Admiral Raeder and Luftwaffe head, Herrmann Goering. The Germans did not have benefit at that time of decrypted British messages, though at different intervals in the war the German code breakers had nearly as much success as their British counterparts in stealing the enemy's message traffic.

They did, however have access to all their own forces' signals, and the key message was the same as the one the Admiralty in London focused upon. First, the request from Schniewind asking for air support was received and read aloud in the bunker by Raeder. Sometime later, the Luftwaffe Northern Command response was received. As this message originated from a Luftwaffe unit, it was given first to Goering. When the fat Reich Marshall read the message, his stomach turned and his face went pale. He stammered uncertainly, looking about the bunker for a friendly face to rescue him. But Goering had few friends in the hierarchy of the Third Reich and none were present that morning. As usual, Hitler lost patience very quickly.

"Come, Goering!" he demanded. "What is the latest message? Are your aircraft on their way to aid Schniewind?"

"Er, um," Goering stammered. "No, my Fuhrer," he said. "There is a problem I must look into. If you will excuse me I will see to it immediately!"

Hitler glared at Goering with a look the Reich Marshall knew all too well, having seen it many times before an officer or government official who had displeased Hitler was sacked, or worse.

"What problem can be keeping our bombers from protecting our only strategic weapon in the north?" demanded Hitler. A low growl emitted from his throat.

"I will see to it immediately, Fuhrer!" Goering assured, snapping to attention. Hitler dismissed him with a disgusted wave of his hand.

Hundreds of kilometers to the north of that Fuhrer briefing, Stefan Vogt set down the most recent letter from his wife and fed another stick into the small stove that heated the hut he shared with three other men. He'd read the letter a dozen times in the three days since it was delivered to him at Banak Airfield on Norway's North Cape, and he expected to read it dozens more times in the days to come. The paper still carried the faint scent of Lorelei's soap and with it under his nose he could close his eyes and almost feel her silky, blond hair sliding through his fingers. He poked the fire in the stove and tucked his scarf in at the collar. He shivered. Early July, yet the dank, dreary weather at Banak left him cold and melancholy, longing for his home near Essen. The only good thing about the fog that smothered the airfield was that flying in such conditions was out of the question. At least he would not die today.

"How much firewood have we left?" asked his hut mate, Gunther Hause, quietly to not waken the hut's other occupants.

Like Vogt, Hause was the pilot of a Heinkel HE 111 torpedo bomber stationed at Banak. Both men had already flown in the mission the prior day against convoy PQ17 recounted earlier and Vogt's aircraft scored one of the eight torpedo hits against Allied merchantmen. Hause was an Austrian from Vienna and fancied himself a sophisticate, with a refined taste for the arts and gentile living, but Vogt knew Hause was just a bricklayer before the war.

"Three more sticks," answered Stefan. "One of us will have to go get more before we retire for the evening." It was a little game they played, Stefan and Gunther, as to which could sound most upper class.

Gunther smiled. "Retire for the evening," he nodded approvingly. "Anyway, it's your turn."

Stefan was prepared to launch the debate as to whose turn it really was, but a knock at the door stopped him.

"Enter!" he answered. A young man attached to the airfield staff leaned in the door, holding it open just enough to be seen, but not let the warmth escape the hut.

"Your pardon, Sir," he said to Stefan. "You are requested in the Operations Shack immediately."

"Very well," sighed Vogt. The young man ducked out and was gone.

"As I said," laughed Hause. "Your turn!" The wood supply was kept under guard outside the Ops Shack.

Vogt ran his fingers through his jet-black hair and wished he had time to shave. He'd done so already that morning, but his beard was very dark and was now more than a "shadow". His squadron mates called him

'Boot Black' or 'Nigger' and alternately accused him of using shoe polish to darken the beard and questioned his parentage. He pulled on his gloves and his flight jacket and stepped out into the gloom of a foggy, high summer morn in the Arctic. He shivered again and set out at a brisk trot from his quarters towards the runway and adjacent Operations Shack. He reached the shack and poked his head round the side of the cinder block walled building. As always, the small woodpile there was under armed guard. Pilferage was a constant problem. He walked on and entered the shack.

A small stage with lectern at the back wall of the building fronted a map of the Arctic region from the Soviet island Novya Zemlya in the east to Iceland in the west and from Trondheim in the south to the arctic summer ice line in the north. A loose jumble of chairs filled the center of the room. This was where pilots and aircrew received their mission briefings. The chairs and room were almost empty, but for two junior staff officers pinning colored yarn to the map in the Arctic Sea region. Vogt knew there was a naval operation underway at sea in pursuit of the allied convoy and he assumed the officers were charting the movements of German and enemy ships. He paused a moment to look at the tracks and his eyes narrowed when he spotted the red and blue threads coming together south of Bear Island. His stomach churned uneasily as he walked to the row of small offices that lined the far sidewall. The door of Major Wegele, Station Commander was open and the Major sat at his desk.

"Reporting as ordered, Herr Major," said Vogt, snapping briefly to attention before flopping down in the extra chair. "What's it about, Mads?" he asked, using his old friend's flight school nickname, earned when he'd cuckolded a Dane of that name.

"I'm leading the 'A' Flight on a sortie in support of the navy in thirty minutes," Wegele told him bluntly. "We're flying northwest to assist the fucking Swabbies in a running battle with a Royal Navy fleet." Vogt sat bolt upright in his chair.

"These conditions are impossible!" he protested. "If you are able to get these boys in 'A' flight off the ground you'll never hold them together for the flight and even if you do find the British none of you will find your way home!"

"Our ships will maintain a steady stream of wireless signals for us to follow in finding the battle," Wegele smiled. "We'll get above the cloud deck, follow the radio beacon and attack the British so *Tirpitz* can escape their clutches!"

"Mads," Vogt pleaded. "There aren't three men in the entire squadron with the experience to carry this off! These boys won't find their own asses with both hands in this shit!" he said, waving vaguely at the weather outside. His heart sank as he watched the smile spread on Wegele's face.

"That's why you will lead the 'B' Flight!" Mads announced triumphantly. "You being the only other pilot capable of this feat."

"Whose brilliant idea is this?" demanded Vogt, but he already knew his protests were in vain.

"That's the good news!" Mads said. "Our orders come directly from Reich Marshall Goering himself! They arrived via landline teletype in the last ten minutes. The Reich Marshall will accept no excuses, not even for shitty weather, as to why the Luftwaffe cannot assist our Kriegsmarine brothers-in-arms."

"What about getting home?" asked Vogt, nearly sick at his stomach. "Has anyone thought of how we are to land?"

"The station wireless will maintain a steady beacon for us to follow home," said Wegele. "I've ordered them to choose music the younger men in the squadron will enjoy. The ground staff are preparing barrels filled with wood soaked in waste oil to line the runway. As we near the airfield on return the drums will be lit for us to find the runway."

"You've thought of everything," said Vogt softly, thinking of Lorelei, doubting now he would ever see her again.

"There'll be decorations in it for you and I Stefan," said Wegele, with just a hint of sarcasm.

"Gute zeiten, schlechte zeiten," answered Vogt. "Good times, bad times."

Chapter 28

Hot Pursuit

"*Tirpitz* turning!" Tovey and Halliday lifted their glasses to see for themselves.

"To starboard this time," said Tovey, disappointed. A turn to port brought *Tirpitz* a little closer to *Washington*, but to starboard took her further away from the Americans. For more than an hour *Duke of York* had chased the German battleship, occasionally firing at extreme range, but most of the time falling slowly behind her quarry. The only thing keeping the chase viable was that *Tirpitz* was forced to hang back to shield the pocket battleship that had evidently developed some kind of fault that slowed her speed. Without the need to protect her weaker consort, *Tirpitz* would already be out of range and safely on her way home. From time to time *Tirpitz* turned, just far enough to uncover her forward guns for one or two salvos and to force *Duke of York* to vary her own course

But whatever the cause, the pocket battleship's speed remained reduced and periodically *Tirpitz* turned back on *Duke of York* to engage her in a short, sharp exchange of heavy guns and to slow the pursuit. What Tovey and Halliday understood, but the German commander apparently failed to appreciate was that had the pocket battleship set off on its own separate course Tovey's orders would have obliged him to ignore her anyway. Only *Tirpitz* mattered to him. Puffs of smoke erupted from the foredeck of *Tirpitz*.

"Her forward guns are uncovered," said Halliday, soto voce to Tovey, then more loudly, "Left rudder twenty degrees."

"Left rudder twenty degrees," the helmsman repeated and the deck tilted ever so slightly as the great ship began her turn. BOOM-BOOM-BOOM-BOOM. The decks rattled as yet another salvo flew from the barrels of the remaining forward turret.

Tovey leaned against the armored bulkhead as the shots were fired and to Halliday he seemed unsteady on his feet. The Captain quietly lifted the telephone from its cradle. Holding his hand over his mouth, he spoke for a moment, listened, flipped a switch and spoke again. He set the telephone back in its cradle as the last shot of the salvo flew on its way. The guns all drooped back to their reload position and Halliday pictured the gun crews working through their well-practiced routine of reloading the giant breeches. He stepped back to Tovey.

“Forward fire nearly out,” he reported. “But the fire aft has gotten hold of the ships boats and is still burning and no hope to repair ‘B’ turret,” he said. “It’s hopelessly jammed in its ring and will have to be lifted out with a dockyard hoist.”

SPLASH-SPLASH-SPLASH-SPLASH. A four-shell salvo from *Tirpitz* fell three hundred yards ahead, across their path. BOOM-BOOM-BOOM-BOOM. The guns of the aft turret cleared and fired.

“We must hit her!” muttered Tovey.

The door to the chart house and wireless office swung open at the back of the bridge.

“Ah, there you are Doctor!” said Halliday cheerfully. “Not much trade for you here I’m glad to report, though now that we have you, perhaps you’ll slap a bandage on the Admiral’s forehead, keep the blood from his eyes, hmm?”

“Yes, Sir! Of course!” said the Ship’s chief Doctor, an experienced surgeon from a major London Hospital. He carried a stereotypical black bag. “Won’t take but a moment I’m sure.”

With no hesitation, the Doctor removed Tovey's tin helmet and the blood-soaked towel Tembam had used to cover the gash. He hung the helmet by its strap from the arm of the Captain's chair and unceremoniously dumped the towel on the deck. Tovey winced as the Doctor probed with his fingers at the wound.

"Let's have you take a seat a moment in the Captain's chair please, Sir," said the Doctor. "This won't take but a moment," he repeated.

"I'm quite alright!" insisted Tovey, but he allowed himself to be gently pushed into the chair.

"That's right, Sir," said the Doctor, ignoring Tovey's protests. He fished in his black bag. "Now if you'll just lean on the arm of the chair Admiral, I'll clean this up and be on my way."

"Casualties, Dr.?" asked Halliday.

"Yes, several dozen so far," the Doctor responded as he swabbed the wound with a cotton ball soaked in medical alcohol. Tovey winced again. "Mostly cuts and abrasions of the sort the Admiral has, a few more serious I'm afraid. Nine fatalities I am aware of." He stepped back and looked at the cut.

"This won't hurt much, Admiral," he said. "Lean forward a moment and close your eyes please."

Tovey did as he was told and the Doctor produced a suture and threaded catgut. Deftly, he ran the fishhook shaped needle through the flap of flesh on Tovey's forehead, down under the cut and back out.

"Do hold still, Sir," he chided Tovey as the Admiral flinched. "I must say these lower deck chaps hold up quite well under this sort of treatment. Not a wince or bit of bother from one of them yet, I can tell you." He ran the needle through four more times, looping and knotting the thread expertly and tying it off with a twist of his wrist.

"That will do Admiral," he said. "Not quite a buccaneer's cutlass scar, but you'll wear this one home to England!" The Doctor sprinkled some sulfa powder on the wound, pressed a dressing on it and wound a bandage round the Admiral's head, then snapped his case shut and left the bridge as quickly as he'd come.

"I've you to thank for that I s'pose?" asked Tovey rhetorically, still in the Captain's chair. Halliday smiled.

SPLASH-SPLASH-SPLASH-SPLASH. BOOM-BOOM-BOOM-BOOM. The gunnery duel continued.

"HIT!" shouted the port bridge lookout. "Smoke from *Tirpitz*, amidships!" he shouted in excitement.

Halliday and Tovey each lifted their binoculars in hopes they'd finally struck the crucial blow, but even as he looked Halliday felt something was amiss. His last salvo hadn't enough time to reach the target. He focused his binoculars and gasped. *Tirpitz* was spewing smoke to be sure, but not from a hit. Her funnel was belching thick, oily smoke of the sort created when raw fuel oil was dumped into the boilers. She was laying a smoke screen as she turned full broadside and brought all her eight main guns to bear. Even as he watched all eight guns fired again, starting with the forward turrets and working back to the aft turrets.

"Hard right rudder!" he shouted, silently cursing himself for allowing a momentary distraction while the Doctor tended to Tovey. The ship heeled over as she leaned into her turn.

"Bridge, Radar! *Tirpitz* on course two-seven-zero, speed 32 knots. The cruiser is with her. They've shortened the range to *London*!" Halliday snatched up the phone.

"Wireless, this is the Captain! Send a plane voice signal to *London* to veer off now!"

WHHIIIRRR-BANG. *Duke of York* rocked from a fresh hit by a heavy shell. Three more shells fell to starboard in the sea.

"Damage report!" shouted Halliday. "Steady on two-seven-zero!"

"Steady on two-seven-zero!"

BOOM-BOOM-BOOM-BOOM. WHHIIIRRR-SPLASH-SPLASH-SPLASH-SPLASH. One 15-inch shell fell long, the other three short of *Duke of York*. The Germans had hit her once and bracketed her in their last two salvos.

"Enemy cruiser firing!" A lookout shouted. Halliday realized *London* was the target. BOOM-BOOM-BOOM-BOOM.

"Bridge, Radar," the intercom crackled to life. "Range to Tirpitz now 24,000 yards. She's steady on two-seven-zero." Spray erupted along *Duke of York's* port side as a salvo of shells splashed down and exploded. CLANG. THUNK. Shrapnel rang off her armored hull. The Duke's own secondary battery crackled to life as the 5.25-inch twin turrets on her port side opened fire. CRACK-CRACK-CRACK-CRACK. Each of the eight port side secondary guns hurled an 80 pound 5.25-inch shell at the enemy every six seconds

"We're in range of her secondary guns!" shouted Tovey over the din. CRASH. A 5.9-inch shell slammed home in the superstructure.

"Left rudder!" shouted Halliday to be heard over the din. "Steady on two-four-zero!"

Tovey nodded his approval. Halliday was seeking to close the range while still keeping both his remaining main turrets able to train and fire. BOOM-BOOM-BOOM-BOOM. The big guns fired as a cascade of water fell across *Duke of York's* decks from near misses. The water served to at last dampen the last of the fire burning aft among the remains of the ship's boats and the scout plane hangar.

Twelve miles away on *Tirpitz'* bridge Topp and Schniewind nervously watched their tactics unfold. With the shell hoists to her forward turrets finally repaired and operational, they would bring all eight guns of their main battery to bear. They held few illusions the smoke screen would hinder the enemy's radar directed fire but hoped it would mask *Scheer* from view as she slipped away to the east while *Tirpitz* and *Hipper* sailed at full speed due west.

CRACK-CRACK-CRACK-CRACK-CRACK-CRACK. The short, sharp bark of the 5.9-inch starboard side guns joined the deeper BOOM of the eight gun main battery in an incredible symphony. Two miles away the 8-inch guns of *Hipper* added their muted roar to the music of battle. CLANG. A 5.25-inch shell bounced off the armored hull just above the waterline. BANG. Another struck aft, on the fantail.

"Left rudder, twenty degrees, steady on two-five-zero!" shouted Topp. The ship heeled gently to port as her rudder bit into the sea and began her turn. BOOM-BOOM-BOOM-BOOM. WHHIIIRRR-SPLAT, WHHIIIRR-SPLAT, WHHIIIRR-CRASH. A 14-inch shell exploded close aboard, just twenty meters from the starboard rail. Shrapnel and shell casing rang and thumped off the hull and superstructure.

BOOM-BOOM-BOOM-BOOM. Caesar and Dora roared their defiance back at the enemy. WHHIIZZ-BANG. A 5.25-inch shell struck in the superstructure aft.

"BRIDGE, WIRELESS!" Topp barely heard the intercom crackle. He lifted the telephone and pressed his free hand flat over his other ear.

"WIRELESS, BRIDGE!" he shouted back.

"The scout plane reports we are on target, scoring hits with main and secondary batteries against the enemy battleship!" Topp flipped a switch.

"GUNNERY OFFICER! This is the Captain!" he yelled. "Did you get that message?"

"Confirmed!" came the excited reply. "Multiple hits registered! She is smoking from stem to stern!"

"WIRELESS, BRIDGE!" Topp yelled into the phone. "Do you have the signal from *Scheer* yet?"

"ARRIVING NOW!"

BOOM-BOOM-BOOM-BOOM. WHHIIZZ-CLANG. A 5.25-inch shell ricocheted off the sloped face of Anton and spun away into the sea. Heavy and light shells splashed all about *Tirpitz*, inundating her weather decks with icy water.

"BRIDGE, WIRELESS! Signal from *Scheer*!"

"AT LAST!" Topp mouthed to Schniewind. Their plan was to draw the British battleship away to the west while *Scheer* resumed her top speed and fled to the southeast, putting miles of range between herself and the pursuer in the five to ten minutes that *Tirpitz* and *Hipper* engaged the enemy.

"*SCHEER* REPORTS THREE FRESH RADAR CONTACTS TO THE NORTHEAST!" shouted the radio officer. "One battleship, two cruisers, bearing zero-two-five on course one-eight-five, range thirty miles. Her repairs are complete and she is withdrawing to the south at top speed." Topp dropped the phone to swing at the end of its wire.

"Hard left rudder!" he shouted. "Come to course one-seven-zero, all ahead full!" He turned to Schniewind. "It's a trap! There is another battleship and two cruisers to our northeast! *Scheer* has them on radar."

"Herbst!" Schniewind yelled. "Signal *Hipper*! Break off and resume base course, flank speed! Then signal the Arado. Give him the position of *Scheer's* report. Have Wahl confirm it!" The telephone Topp had dropped swung gently on its wire as *Tirpitz* heeled hard over to port. He picked it back up and held it to his ear.

"RADAR, BRIDGE!" he shouted. "Do you have another set of targets to the northeast? Bearing from zero-one-five to zero-three-zero?" He listened a moment. "Report if you find them! What range to the enemy battleship?" He hung up the phone without responding. He noticed the 5.9-inch guns were silent.

"Range to the battleship now 27,000 yards," he told Schniewind. "Our own radar has not detected the second enemy formation. *Scheer's* repairs are complete and she has turned due south at full speed."

"I should have known!" Schniewind slapped his palms together. "The British would never send just one battleship to confront *Tirpitz*! There had to be a second nearby."

"And what of the carrier that launched the torpedo planes against *Lutzow*?" questioned Topp. "Why haven't we heard more from her?"

"I don't know," shrugged the Admiral. "Perhaps a mechanical fault, like *Scheer*." He shook his head. "At this point it does not matter. All that matters is that we escape without further injury. Get a damage report. For as long as we are in range keep the aft turrets firing."

"Their crews will be near exhaustion," pointed out Topp. "The rear turrets have been in action for over an hour now."

"Time enough to sleep when we get home!" said Schniewind sternly.

"Bridge, Wireless!"

"What now?" wondered Topp.

Chapter 29

USS WASHINGTON Joins the Fight

Admiral Giffen and Captain Benson leaned on the chart table, studying the latest position reports on *Tirpitz* and *Duke of York*. A steady stream of radio signals sent from *Duke of York* and ostensibly addressed to the Admiralty in London provided a turn-by-turn, and blow-by-blow account of the battle then under way, even to the extent of conveying Admiral Tovey's guess that the German pocket battleship was damaged or suffering a mechanical fault which reduced her speed.

Giffen also understood that the frequency of the messages and the level of detail they provided, including every course change and alteration in speed were meant by Tovey to be picked up on *Washington* and used by Giffen to bring *Tirpitz* in range of *Washington's* main armament, her mighty 16-inch diameter, 45 caliber guns. The US battleship carried nine of the tremendous naval rifles, arrayed in two triple-barreled turrets forward and one triple-barreled turret aft and each of these nine, Mark 6 guns could fire a 2,700 pound armor piercing warhead an incredible 40,000 yards. *Washington* was also equipped with one of the first fully integrated radar directed fire control systems in the world. Whereas radar guided the gunnery officers of *Tirpitz* and *Duke of York* in aiming their guns and in adjusting their fire with optical observation of the fall of shot, aboard *Washington* an advanced mechanically driven fire-control computer tied directly to radar output performed this task.

The technology was based upon the British developed cavity magnetron tube, an innovation out of the laboratories at the University of Birmingham which allowed radar pulses in centimeter wavelengths and which provided much more accuracy and granularity in the return signal than was possible in the older meter length waves. Prime Minister Churchill agreed to provide this and many other British scientific innovations to the American government in 1940. In exchange, the Americans gave access to the manufacturing facilities in the USA to construct the devices in the needed numbers. While few details were known of the performance of German radar, the Allies believed their shared technology was superior to the enemy's. If *Washington* could get within range of *Tirpitz* she stood a very good chance in battle against her, especially if it were a joint attack with *Duke of York*.

Giffen was pleased with the tactical opportunity to catch *Tirpitz* in a crossfire between *Duke of York* and *Washington*, but he also knew this was a departure from accepted US Navy and Royal Navy doctrine for such a situation. The prior year, in the Battle of the Denmark Strait, *HMS Hood* and *HMS Prince of Wales* had taken on the German battleship *Bismarck*. *Prince of Wales* was a sister ship of *Duke of York* in the King George V class of battleships and carried the same set of ten, 14-inch guns as *The Duke* while *Hood's* main armament of eight 15-inch guns matched the German sisters *Bismarck* and *Tirpitz*.

Prince of Wales and *Hood* sailed under the command of Royal Navy Vice-Admiral Lancelot Holland, embarked on *Hood*. Holland was an adherent of his commanding officer, Sir John Tovey's belief that concentrated gunfire from multiple capital ships fired upon a lesser number of opponents gave the better chance of doing decisive damage. *Hood* and *Prince of Wales* sailed into battle against *Bismarck* less than a half mile from each other and when *Hood* exploded *Bismarck* had only to shift her fire a few degrees to hit *Prince of Wales* four times in quick succession, driving her to make smoke and escape with heavy damage.

Now Giffen found himself tantalizingly close to *Tirpitz*; just thirty miles separated *Washington* from the German battleship. Flashes on the horizon indicated the bearing where the battle was being fought. If he could close the range by just six more miles, he could bring his guns into the fight. But *Washington* was running at her top speed, just over 28 knots and had been at flank speed for over three hours. The strain on men and equipment could be borne, for a while longer at least, but the fuel consumption could not be sustained if he entertained any hopes of reaching safe harbor ever again. Something had to happen to bring *Tirpitz* in range.

"Let's activate the targeting radar for a few minutes," suggested Captain Benson. "These radio intercepts are fine to get the general picture, but we need to know the true range to the target."

Admiral Giffen mulled the idea. "How long from Tovey's last signal?" he asked.

Benson looked up at the clock then down at the message log. "Seven minutes," he answered. "One of the longest intervals."

"Alright," Giffen nodded. "Activate long enough to acquire and range to *Tirpitz*, but no more." He shook his head. "We needn't tip our hand before we get a shot at her."

Benson went off to give the order while Giffen stared out through the bridge windows. Despite being protected on the bridge from the wind, it was still bitter cold and he snugged his arctic parka up at the neck and stuffed his gloved hands in his pockets. The cold was unbearable for men forced to work on the weather decks, especially those exposed at the anti-aircraft gun positions. While he watched, the crew of a 20mm flak gun was relieved. They stumbled away from the gun tub flailing their arms and stamping their feet to stay warm and were replaced by a fresh, but thoroughly miserable looking crew.

"Bridge, radar," the speaker above the binnacle crackled. Benson flipped a switch.

"Radar, this is the Captain," he answered.

"Two large targets bearing almost due west look to be *The Duke* and *London*," said the radar officer. "Bearing two-seven-five, range thirty miles, course one-seven-zero, speed about 28 knots. Two large targets on the same course and speed, bearing two-two-zero, range thirty miles must be *Tirpitz* and one of the cruisers. The other cruiser is separated from them. Bearing one-nine-five, course zero-nine-zero, range 36,000 yards. One aerial target circling *The Duke* and *London*. Probably a scout floatplane."

Benson and Giffen looked at each other in amazement. Benson picked up the phone.

"Radar, Bridge, confirm the range to the second cruiser!"

"Range 35,500 yards, bearing one-nine-zero now. Course looks to be shifting. I would have to maintain the radar signal to be certain. My two minutes are up."

Benson looked quickly at Giffen who nodded his head emphatically.

"Radar, this is the Captain. Maintain radar contact on the second cruiser! Keep range and bearings coming!"

"She's in range now!" exclaimed Giffen to Benson. He stared out over the sea in the direction of the battle, but with the low cloud deck he had no hope of seeing anything on the horizon. He made a snap decision. "Shift course, Captain!" he ordered. "Pursue the second cruiser. If Tovey's signals are correct and *Tirpitz* has been shielding her for a chance to escape, maybe we can force his hand, make him come to us."

"Come to course one-eight-five!" Benson ordered.

"Course one-eight-five," the helmsman answered.

"Bridge, radar. The enemy cruiser has altered course to one-eight-zero, speed about twenty-eight knots, range 34,500 yards. She has probably detected us on her own radar." Benson snatched up the phone.

"Guns, bridge."

"Bridge, guns," came the immediate answer.

"Guns, you have the radar target for the lone enemy heavy to our south?" he asked.

"Bridge, guns, affirmative. Ready to fire on order."

"Open fire!"

Washington's six forward 16-inch guns began firing one-by-one in salvo. Accumulated ice shattered and cracked, breaking away from her hull and superstructure, especially forward. The entire ship vibrated from the tremendous recoil as her guns hurled the gigantic 1,200kg shells downrange. Developed by the US Navy's Bureau of Ordnance especially for the 16-inch Mark 6 guns of the North Carolina Class battleships, these shells were among the most powerful in the world at the time of the Battle of Bear Island and came as a nasty surprise to the Germans.

"Fairbanks!" shouted Giffen over the thunderous roar of the guns.

"Yes, Sir!" The famous Lt. materialized at the Admiral's side.

"Signal to *Wichita* and *Tuscaloosa*," Giffen ordered. "They are to take two of the destroyers on an end run to the east of the enemy cruiser.

Engage and turn her back to the northwest." Fairbanks hurried away to arrange the signal.

"Good that the German airbases are weathered in," observed Benson quietly. He was politely pointing out that separating *Washington* from her cruiser escorts deprived all three ships of mutual support in the event they came under air attack.

"We wouldn't be here otherwise," answered Giffen. "We'd have seen German bombers long ago."

"Time to signal Tovey?" asked Captain Benson.

"Yes," said Giffen. "You're right. In fact, time to signal London and Washington as well." Fairbanks hurried back on the bridge.

"*Wichita* and *Tuscaloosa* have your orders, Sir," he reported to Giffen. "They are already on their way." He nodded towards the bows. The two cruisers, each capable of nearly 33 knots at top speed were pulling away from the battleship, racing to the south to flank the enemy ship. Creaming bow waves and churning wakes showed their speed.

"Next signal is to Naval Operations in Washington, copy the Brits in London," said Giffen. "Date, time, position. Am engaging enemy cruiser from northeast, range 34,000 yards," Giffen spelled out the message content. "Use the shared code and frequency so Tovey receives it aboard *Duke of York* too."

Washington's forward guns were reloaded and began to elevate and train for their next shots. The guns fired one-by-one, shaking the entire ship, then drooping back to the reload position as each fired.

"Bridge, Radar," the bridge speaker crackled. "The enemy cruiser is changing course. Shifting from one-eight-zero to two-zero-zero, speed still 28 knots. Range steady at 34,000 yards."

"To hit her at this range would be the sheerest luck," said Captain Benson. "Radar directed fire or not."

"We don't need to hit her," Giffen shook his head. "Just force *Tirpitz* to cover her. *Wichita* and *Tuscaloosa* have 5 knots over the cruiser. They'll have her in range soon. The two of them are more than a match for her and the German knows it. She'll have to rejoin *Tirpitz* and we'll have them in a crossfire!"

Giffen lifted his binoculars and looking through the observation slits in the blast shutters he scanned the horizon, hoping for some hint, a puff of smoke, anything of the enemy. He lowered his glasses and watched the two American cruisers hurry off to the south-south-west in pursuit of their quarry. As he watched a series of six splashes fell a half mile to port, to the east of *Wichita*. In keeping with German practice these first shells were not fused to explode on hitting water.

"She's already in range of the German guns!" exclaimed Benson.

"It's the pocket battleship for sure," said Giffen. "Six 11-inch guns. She's long on this salvo, she won't be again!" *Wichita* and *Tuscaloosa* each came right twenty degrees to cut inside the arc of the enemy ship's turn, both to shorten the range and to throw off the aim of the next salvo. Six more splashes, this time the nearest fell barely a hundred yards to port of *Wichita*.

"Just over twenty seconds between salvos," said Benson, a frown of worry crossing his features. "They've got to close and get into range quickly. If the pocket can keep them at arms-length she'll tear them apart."

"Bridge, Radar. Two targets to the southwest, bearing two-two-five, range twenty-eight miles, course one-eight zero, speed 28 knots. One big return must be *Tirpitz*, the other looks to be a cruiser."

"Radar, Bridge," Benson leaned down and spoke into the receiver. "Range to the near cruiser?"

"Bridge, Radar. Range to the near cruiser, designate Target One holding steady, 34,000 yards. *Wichita* is closing the range on her. 30,500 yards. *Wichita* will open fire soon."

Scheer's next six shot salvo fell directly along *Wichita's* course, the first shell landing behind her with the subsequent shots falling progressively closer. This time the shells were fused to explode and as they hit, great fountains of water erupted around the American cruiser, obscuring her from view aboard *Washington*. *Tuscaloosa* following in *Wichita's* wake was shrouded in mist as she raced to close the range. The veil of water seemed to hang in the air suspended before it settled back onto the sea. As *Wichita* emerged from the mist, Benson and Giffen gasped. Smoke billowed from the cruiser's fantail, the bright orange and red of a fire licking up through the black, oily cloud.

"Bridge, Radar. The aerial target has widened his circle and is six miles to the south of *Wichita*."

"Third salvo and a hit!" snarled Benson. "Too good even for our radar. The scout plane is spotting the fall of shot for the pocket!"

"Fairbanks!" said Giffen. "Signal *Mayrant* and *Rhind* to ready their torpedo launchers."

Now *Wichita* finally loosed her main guns. Armed with nine 8-inch, 55 Caliber rifles in three triple turrets the cruiser packed a formidable punch. The foremost turret, designated Number 1 in the US Navy fired first, then the lone turret aft, its three guns trained all the way round to point forward of starboard and finally the Number 2 turret beneath the bridge. The nine guns hurled their 260 pound high explosive shells from maximum elevation at extreme range. *Wichita* was still out of range for the 335 pound armor piercing shells that could do real damage with a hit.

Washington fired her six forward guns again, BOOM-BOOM-BOOM-BOOM-BOOM-BOOM.

"Bridge, Radar. Range to near cruiser holding steady, 34,000 yards. Range to the other cruiser and battleship narrowing. They've altered course a few degrees to the east and are forming up with the near cruiser. Six smaller targets now showing. Two are south of the near cruiser, four are south of the heavy. Too big for destroyers I'd say. More like light cruisers."

"Six light cruisers!" exclaimed Benson. "It can't be! That's more than the whole German navy has!"

"The German destroyer classes are larger than ours or the Brits," Giffen reminded him. "More heavily armed as well. They bear watching."

Another barrage of shells fell around *Wichita*, just as she fired her own guns again. A moment later *Tuscaloosa* joined the fight. Marginally slower than *Wichita*, *Tuscaloosa* trailed the other American cruiser by nearly a half mile. Both still sustained their maximum speeds, 33 knots for *Wichita*, 32.5 knots for *Tuscaloosa*.

"Signal from *Wichita*!" shouted a lookout. A blinking signal lamp flashed its Morse encoded message from the back of the cruiser's bridge. Lt. Fairbanks hustled off to get the translated message.

"Bridge, Radar. Range to Target One steady at 34,000 yards. *Wichita* and *Tuscaloosa* between 28,000 and 29,000 yards from Target One. Range to *Tirpitz*, Target Two down to twenty-six miles. All three enemy heavies on course due south, Target One on one-eight-five, Targets Two and Three on one-seven-five."

"Their courses are converging," said Giffen, thinking aloud. "They are going to group together for mutual supporting fire." He pulled on his ear lobe, pondering his options. *Washington* was not making up the distance to the pocket battleship and all three German heavy ships were matching the American battleship's speed. His cruisers were closing the distance, but while each was a powerful ship, they were still vulnerable to the heavy caliber, 11-inch shells of their opponent. *Washington's* 16-inch forward batteries fired again, even as both *Wichita* and *Tuscaloosa* fired a nine-gun broadside. Another salvo splashed down around *Wichita*. Clearly the Germans had chosen to concentrate their fire on the nearest of the two American cruisers. Fairbanks hustled back onto the bridge.

"Damage report from *Wichita*," he said, holding up a message slip. "Hit in the fantail, two of four scout planes destroyed and burning, combat, steering and propulsion systems unaffected. At extreme range now."

Wichita emerged once more from a cascade of water falling on her decks, her guns blazing, her gun crews loading and firing, loading and firing again and again at her maximum rate. *Tuscaloosa*, with her slightly slower speed was a half mile behind, but also firing at her maximum rate. Yet another salvo of six shells fell around *Wichita*, with one exploding close aboard her starboard side. She shouldered the blast aside and sailed on at top speed to close the range, her guns blazing in defiance.

Nearly two hours into the battle, the principal ships, the cruisers and battleships of the German, American and British navies were all in action. The Allies under the command of Admirals Tovey and Giffen strove to close the range, bring all their heavy guns to bear and overwhelm the Germans. The Allied cruisers outnumbered their German counterparts three to two and held a twenty-six to fourteen edge in heavy caliber guns. The two American cruisers, *USS Tuscaloosa* and *USS Wichita*, and the Royal Navy's *HMS London* were all armed with 8-inch guns, while the German *Scheer* carried six 11-inch rifles and *Admiral Hipper* was equipped with eight 8-inch guns.

The Allied advantage in battleship firepower was even more lopsided. Even with *Duke of York's* 'B' turret and its two guns out of commission the British and American battleships held a seventeen to eight edge in heavy caliber guns. If they could corner the Germans and force them to slug it out in a protracted battle the odds of an Allied victory were very strong.

For the Germans their only hope was to keep the battle at long range and prevent the British and Americans from concentrating their fire. Should any of the German vessels suffer damage that restricted either her speed or steering or that damaged her combat power that ship would almost certainly be lost.

Aboard *Tirpitz* Admiral Schniewind was in a desperate quandary. *Tirpitz, Hipper* and his destroyers still held a speed advantage that would allow them to run away from both the Allied battleships and he was confident they could defend themselves against the Allied cruisers. Repairs to *Tirpitz'* funnel were completed and her boilers once again could push her to her top speed of 32 knots. In addition, Lt. Wahl, pilot of the airborne Arado floatplane had signaled by radio that he would continue to stay with the battle and spot the fall of shot until his fuel was exhausted. Aerial correction of fire gave the German gunners a priceless advantage, even over the radar directed fire of *Washington*. Schniewind resolved that if he should live he would submit Wahl for a decoration. Wahl knew that when he ran out of fuel he would be forced to ditch on the Arctic waters. Even a successful landing in his floatplane left little chance of rescue.

But though *Scheer's* repairs were also complete, she was at her top speed of 28 knots already. Clearly, the Allied cruisers were faster and if left on her own the three enemy cruisers then engaged were enough to finish her off, with or without the help of the enemy battleships. Schniewind was loathe to abandon her and her crew of over 900 men. The German Navy might never recover from the blow to morale of such a decision.

But if he stayed to try to protect *Scheer*, he risked losing his entire command, a defeat of truly strategic implications, for without *Tirpitz* to oppose them the Allies would be free to run convoys to and from the North Russian ports with little fear of intervention by surface ships. Furthermore, the Allies would also be able to redeploy their own battleships to other areas where they could do further injury to the German cause. Finally, the Allies could then threaten a landing in Norway that could cut off the German strategic supply of Swedish iron ore, indispensable to the German war effort.

At this point in the battle, damage that slowed any of his three heavy ships would have disastrous consequences. He searched for some solution to the dilemma and found none. He was heart sick at the decision he was being forced to make, but as much as he would have personally preferred to go down fighting, he knew he had no choice, but to make the strategic decision.

"Herbst!" he shouted finally.

Admiral Tovey received the wireless message sent by Admiral Giffen and felt success was within his grasp. With the American cruisers and battleship finally engaged, he had the firepower at his command to wipe out the German surface force. But, he knew victory was far from assured. *Duke of York* had already suffered extensive damage. Fires still burned fore and aft despite the heroic efforts of her damage parties. If she escaped the battle, she would take months in a dry dock before she was combat worthy again and she remained vulnerable to the excellent marksmanship of the German gunners aboard *Tirpitz*. If she suffered further damage that either slowed her or knocked out her remaining guns in 'A' turret forward, the balance of firepower in the battle would tilt back toward the Germans. He could only hope that *Tirpitz* was also damaged, but to this point he'd seen no indication of any falloff in either her speed or the effectiveness of her weapons.

Tovey also attempted to place himself in the mind of his German opponent. *Tirpitz* was an irreplaceable strategic asset for the Germans and if anything could be done to save her from destruction, he knew it would be done. Tovey believed that the German battleship and at least the heavy cruiser, which by now he had tentatively identified as *Admiral Hipper*, could still escape by going to top speed and running away from the two Allied battleships. Tovey would send his own Royal Navy and US Navy cruisers after them in a most likely forlorn chase that could result in his losing all three of them. His only hope was that somehow his German counterpart would make the human decision, not the strategic and refuse to abandon the pocket battleship to certain destruction.

All three forces were now on a nearly straight course due south on headings between one-seven-eight and one-eight-two. *Tirpitz* and *Hipper* were in close contact, separated from one another by less than a mile and with four of the powerful German Z-Class destroyers in close company. Almost straight north, *Duke of York* and *London* pursued them, each accompanied by a single Royal Navy destroyer.

The pocket battleship, identified as either *Scheer* or *Lutzow*, was four miles to their east along with two destroyers. *Washington, Wichita* and *Tuscaloosa* along with four US Navy destroyers were close on her heels and all three American heavies were in range to fire at her. Initial wireless reports from Giffen indicated *Wichita* had already suffered undetermined damage.

The course of both sets of German ships was such that they slowly drew closer to one another as they sailed to the south, all at 28 knots, presumed to be the top speed of the slowest ship, the pocket battleship. The two Allied battle groups were nearly thirty miles apart and could do little to provide mutual support to the other, while the Germans were moving toward each other and would soon be able to shift fire from *Tirpitz* and the pocket battleship against any of the Allied vessels posing the gravest threat.

Now Tovey's shortage of Royal Navy destroyers limited his options. With a full complement of at least four destroyers at his disposal, he could order a high-speed torpedo attack in an effort to keep the German ships from rejoining forces. But with two of his destroyers dispatched along with his other heavy cruiser *HMS Norfolk* to escort *HMS Victorious* home he hadn't enough of the small ships for an effective attack. He could only hope that Admiral Giffen would use his four available American destroyers for this purpose.

Duke of York fired her forward battery yet again. BOOM-BOOM-BOOM-BOOM. *Tirpitz* was nearly 33,000 yards down range and only the forward guns would bear. For the moment at least, until the range could somehow be shortened dramatically, the British battleship could only bring four of her eight operational main guns to the fight. Likewise, so long as *Tirpitz* fled on her nearly straight south course only her four aft guns would bear. The two battleships fought on equal terms, with Tovey thinking of both as having one hand tied behind their backs.

"Bridge, Radar!" the intercom crackled. "*Tirpitz* changing course to port, now on one-six-zero."

"She's closing the range to support the pocket," said Halliday. "She'll be firing her forward guns at the American cruisers shortly."

"Bridge, Radar. *Tirpitz* now on one-four-zero, speed up to 30 knots, range 32,000 yards. *Hipper* ahead of her to starboard on the new course, range 37,000 yards."

"She's uncovered her forward guns for us!" exclaimed Halliday. "Left rudder! Come to one-six-five!" But even as the command was acknowledged he knew he'd been slow to realize the purpose of the German turn.

WHHIIIRRR-SPLAT. The first of an eight shot salvo of 15-inch shells roared close overhead to explode in *Duke of York's* wake. Halliday never heard the second shell.

Aboard *Tirpitz*, Lt. Herbst hustled back onto the bridge as Admiral Schniewind shouted his name. Herbst was returning from the wireless office. He'd been there supervising the transmission of one of the many coded signals Schniewind ordered be sent to keep Kriegsmarine HQ in

Berlin informed of the latest developments. Now he came back to the bridge waving a fresh message flimsy.

"Signal to *Scheer*," growled Schniewind angrily. He was about to inform Captain Meendsen-Bohlken of his decision to leave *Scheer* behind to her fate in order to save *Tirpitz* and *Hipper*.

"Nein!" shouted Herbst. "Not before this!" he held out the message slip to Schniewind and steeled himself for a stern rebuke as the Admiral's eyes opened wide in surprise at his subordinate's defiance. Schniewind snatched the slip from Herbst with a glare that boded ill for the young officer.

"Captain Topp!" he shouted after scanning the message. "Come left to uncover your forward guns to fire on our pursuer." He handed the slip to Topp and turned back to Herbst who now stood at rigid attention. "Herr Leutnant!" the Admiral growled. "Signal *Hipper*. Conform to our turn to port. She is to pass in front of us then drop back to join *Scheer*. Together they can handle the enemy cruisers!"

"Yes, Admiral!" Herbst said, relief overwhelming his features. Topp slapped his thigh after reading the message slip.

"We have a chance to reach home all together in one piece after all!" he exclaimed joyfully.

"If we can hold out for thirty more minutes," agreed Schniewind, "I should say we have a better than even chance!"

As her forward guns cleared *Tirpitz* began a rolling, eight shot salvo against *Duke of York*. Four splashes erupted to her starboard as the British return fire fell on the course *Tirpitz* had been on. Her change of course had confounded the enemy's aim.

"Hold this course for two more minutes," ordered Schniewind. "Two more salvos from our forward guns against our pursuer, then resume base course and shift your forward fire against the enemy cruisers threatening *Scheer*. I want to be close enough to hit the enemy cruisers if they stay within range of *Scheer*, but far enough to her starboard that our forward guns can bear on them. We will take them under fire and either hit them or drive them out of range of *Scheer*!" Captain Topp gave the necessary orders, then came back to stand with Admiral Schniewind. Both men were aware of a limitation of the German radar technology. The German system was capable of tracking several targets but of controlling fire against only one target at a time. Only the presence of Lt. Wahl in the

Arado scout aircraft would allow for any degree of accuracy in firing against a second target. They were unsure of the Allied capabilities in this regard, but had no reason to suppose the British or Americans had a superior system.

"HIT!" shouted a lookout. "The enemy battleship is hit!"

"We have all six of our destroyers together again," Topp commented quietly to Schniewind as both men lifted their binoculars in an effort to assess the fresh damage to the enemy.

"Yes, you're right of course, Topp," said Schniewind. "No doubt the enemy is also thinking of launching torpedoes from his destroyers. Herbst!" The Lt. snapped to attention. "Order the four easternmost destroyers to make smoke and deliver a torpedo attack on the two cruisers threatening *Scheer*."

"There is still the enemy cruiser to our northeast," reminded Topp.

"We shall have to take our chances for the moment that she won't dare come within range," answered Schniewind. "Once we are back on our base course we can use our superior speed to pull ahead, then turn to uncover our forward guns against her. I tell you, Topp, we're going to pull this off!"

Herbst returned from the wireless office, a grim new expression on his face.

"*Scheer* has been hit," he said simply. "*Z27, 28, 29* and *30* are making smoke and have turned about on a torpedo run against the enemy cruisers."

German Navy destroyers launched after the outbreak of war in the autumn of 1939 carried no name other than their hull numbers. The "Z" or "Zerstorer Class" destroyers were numbered *Z23* through *Z39* and for The Knight's Gambit *Z27* through *Z30* were assigned, along with the earlier class destroyers, *Friedrich Ihn, Hans Lody, Theodor Riedel* and *Richard Beitzen*, the latter two having been detached already to accompany *Lutzow* home. All were heavily armed with the 5.9-inch guns and eight 21-inch torpedo launchers.

At the same moment, the American destroyers *USS Mayrant* and *USS Rhind* raced ahead at their top speeds in excess of 37 knots. *Mayrant* and *Rhind* were of the ten-ship Benham class and at the time were among the most modern in the US Navy. Both commissioned in the latter half of 1939 and displaced some 1,725 tons, making them rather larger than most Royal Navy destroyers, but still much smaller than their German opponents. They each carried four 5-inch guns along with a formidable anti-aircraft punch with a pair of 40mm Bofors guns and numerous .50 caliber Browning machine guns. Now their mission was to employ their 21-inch torpedoes to hit or at least force a change in course in the German pocket battleship in an effort to allow *Washington* to catch her. Each destroyer was equipped with sixteen torpedoes, with six pre-loaded in launchers mounted amidships. The remaining ten torpedoes were reload shots. Neither American destroyer carried her own radar apparatus.

The four German and two American destroyers closed on collision courses with combined speeds in excess of 70 knots. The US Navy ships held only one slim advantage to counter their enemy's superior numbers and firepower. *Washington's* radar was capable of tracking all of the vessels in the battle and a steady stream of contact reports flowed from the battleship to *Mayrant* and *Rhind* over the very high frequency radio communication known as TBS, or Talk Between Ships. *Washington* guided the American destroyers on a course that took them east of the four German destroyers in a flanking maneuver. They crossed seven miles in front of the Germans and escaped attention.

The same could not be said of the four German Z-Class destroyers. With *Washington's* state-of-the-art radar apparatus tracking them, as well as their own large size, which made them easy to track visually, the Germans drew the attention of both *Wichita* and *Tuscaloosa*. The two cruisers shifted the fire of their main batteries against the attacking Germans who were soon dodging a hail of 8-inch shells as they attempted to get close enough to launch their torpedoes. The German G7A 21-inch torpedo had a maximum range of 12,000 yards when set to run at 30 knots speed, but this was too slow to target any but the most plodding of merchant vessels. Against targets as swift as the Allied cruisers the Germans needed to close to no more than 5,500 yards (5,000 meters) and then to fill the water with as many fish as could be launched quickly to have any chance of scoring a hit.

Once the range closed to 25,000 yards the Germans shot back with their rapid fire 5.9-inch guns spitting up to eight rounds a minute and at 18,000 yards the American cruisers added the 5-inch guns of their secondary batteries to the barrage. *Wichita* and *Tuscaloosa* each carried eight of these guns, four to port and four to starboard and only the guns to starboard could bear on the German destroyers. Even so, for the ten minutes it took the Germans to close the range there were over forty guns of 5-inch caliber and larger exchanging fire and it remains as one of the wonders of this phase of the battle that only two hits were scored. With fountains of water erupting all around the six ships, *Z28* was hit by an 8-inch shell, probably from *Wichita*, that wrecked her forward gun mount and *Wichita* was hit with a single 5.9-inch projectile almost certainly from *Z27*. This hit slammed into the superstructure directly below the cruiser's bridge. Shell fragments and shrapnel tore up the deck, killing outright or mortally wounding nearly every man of the bridge watch, including the Captain who lived long enough to transfer command to the Executive Officer at the auxiliary steering station aft. The Captain collapsed at the binnacle, the telephone receiver still clutched in his hand.

Under the XO's command, *Wichita* turned away to the east for two critical minutes as the German destroyers closed the range. With only her rear turret able to bear on the enemy, she had only three 8-inch guns rather than nine in action and her secondary 5-inch batteries were ineffective as well. Moreover, as the German destroyers emerged from a hail of shells they found themselves with only one target, *USS Tuscaloosa* at a range of 6,500 yards. All four Germans turned towards her and prepared to launch their torpedoes.

Now the Captain of *Tuscaloosa* recognized his predicament and made the bold choice to turn into the German attack at full speed. With her narrowest aspect presented to the Germans, but with both forward turrets in action at a quickly shortening range the cruiser went to rapid fire and deluged the enemy with 8-inch and 5-inch shells. *Z28* was hit twice more with 8-inch projectiles; her engine room wrecked, she lost speed and launched her torpedoes at extreme range.

Several factors saved the Germans from a complete debacle. With *Tuscaloosa* and the four German destroyers racing toward each other at full speed the range closed to 5,500 yards very quickly, limiting the Germans' exposure to the cruiser's withering, point-blank fire to less than a minute. In that time the American ship fired her six forward 8-inch guns eighteen times and her eight 5-inch guns each fired five shells, but had she been able to sustain this fire for much longer there is little doubt she would have done much further damage.

Even as the German destroyers turned first to starboard, then to port to launch their torpedoes and *Tuscaloosa's* Captain began evasive maneuvers, her gunnery officer prepared to tear the Germans apart as they turned away, but at this moment *Tirpitz* and *Scheer* combined their heavy guns against the American cruiser. *Tirpitz*' after battery was still engaged with *Duke of York*, but the four guns of turrets Anton and Bruno were finally in range and able to bear on target. With Lt. Wahl still circling *Tuscaloosa* out of range of her flak guns and spotting the fall of shot the ten heavy caliber guns of the German ships quickly found the range.

Suddenly *Tuscaloosa* found the shoe on the other foot. Twenty-four torpedoes were in the water directed at her while she also zigzagged to confound the aim of the German gunners. As the surviving German destroyers fled, their aft mounted 5.9-inch guns were once more in the battle, adding injury to insult, hitting the US Navy cruiser three times. Along with several near misses from heavy caliber shells that opened plates in her starboard hull and peppered her superstructure with shrapnel it was more than her lookouts could do to spot every torpedo. Perhaps it was inevitable that she would be struck. The fish hit her starboard quarter, forward of the bridge and opened a forty foot long hole below the waterline. Tons of freezing seawater poured into *Tuscaloosa* and she adopted an immediate list of twenty degrees. Speed reduced to 20 knots she turned away as her damage control teams fought frantically to save her.

To this point, the US Navy was not doing well in its first open battle in European waters, but the American destroyers *Mayran*t and *Rhind* now avenged *Wichita* and *Tuscaloosa.* Skirting the fierce firefight between the American cruisers and German destroyers, they slipped to the east and unwittingly exploited the weakness in German radar. Unable to track more than a single target at a time with their electronic eye the German radar operators aboard *Tirpitz* and *Scheer* remained focused on *Duke of York* and *Wichita*. When *Mayrant* and *Rhind* slipped into a patch of low clouds hugging the sea they went unnoticed by German lookouts until they burst into view just 7,000 yards from *Scheer*. Fairly flying across the water at their top speeds in excess of 37 knots the American destroyers closed the range and each launched their six torpedoes before *Scheer* could even bring her 5.9-inch guns to bear. Twisting and weaving to avoid German fire, they fled back into the cloudbank as their torpedo crews worked feverishly to reload the launchers.

Scheer now found herself the target of a dozen American torpedoes, fired at close range and from two different bearings to her east. At the same time *Washington* continued her long-range 16-inch shell fire and *Wichita* turned back to the battle with all nine of her 8-inch guns in action, all targeting the German cruiser. As with *Tuscaloosa* before her, the volume and intensity of the attack overwhelmed the German lookouts and after a two minute run one of *Mayrant's* fish struck *Scheer* in her port side. Her port engine room flooding with frigid water she slowed and began to list. Only by keeping hard right rudder was she able to maintain her southerly course. The impact of the torpedo also tripped the circuit breakers in her main electrical panel that served the motors to drive her aft turret and the shells hoists that delivered ammunition to it. Temporarily defenseless and crippled *Scheer* limped south at 20 knots.

With *Washington* already in range and closing in from the north at 28 knots, only a miracle could save *Scheer* and the German fleet now.

Chapter 30

HMS Duke of York. Bishop in jeopardy.

Hit three times in quick succession by 15-inch shells *HMS Duke of York* was in trouble. All three hits caused extensive damage starting with the first hit that slammed into her armored conning tower behind the bridge. It plunged through three decks and exploded amongst the officer's quarters. Thankfully, these were largely deserted with every man and officer aboard ship at his Action Station. The only casualties were those wounded and the medical staff attending them in the ship's alternate sickbay, the officer's mess. Manned during battle by the ship's second Doctor and his aides to avoid having the ship's entire medical staff wiped out in a single blow, there were over twenty wounded and medical orderlies there with the Doctor. All were killed in an instant, with very little left to distinguish one man from another.

The blast tore back upwards, buckling decks and bulkheads, and dislodging the 15-foot optical rangefinder atop the superstructure. A flash of flame burst through several decks, reaching to the wireless office and chart house behind the bridge. The wireless operators were wiped out, seared by the flames. Fortunately for the navigator he was on the bridge at the time. Even so, every man on the bridge was hurled from his feet for the second time in the battle with numerous injuries resulting. Captain Halliday and Admiral Tovey were tossed together in a heap beside the wheelhouse, both unconscious.

The second hit followed the first so closely that few aboard knew they were separate, landing on the port side between the second and third 5.25-inch gun turrets. Both turrets were wrenched and twisted on their mountings, their crews killed outright by concussion. Fresh fires leapt instantly to life from both these hits and between them they posed a grave threat to *Duke of York's* survival, but they paled in significance compared to the hit from the third 15-inch shell to strike.

The most devastating blow of the battle to this time struck *Duke of York* ten feet to port of the earlier hit that disabled her twin-barreled 14-inch gun turret. Slamming down through decks already torn open, the shell glanced off the curved cylinder of the armored barbette of 'B' turret, leaving a three inch deep gouge in the cast steel. It ricocheted deep below decks where it exploded against the steel cap above the magazine. It is likely the energy the shell lost in striking the barbette at an angle was the difference in it not penetrating the magazine and setting off an explosion that would have sundered the ship. Its effect was serious enough for all that.

The blast rocketed up through the yawning hole left by the earlier explosion in a volcanic eruption of flame and debris that scorched the starboard face of the conning tower, perforating the superstructure with dozens of shrapnel holes. The fire just recently controlled in this area was rekindled as fresh compartments were breeched and their contents set ablaze.

With her helm unmanned in the wheelhouse *Duke of York* slewed round to port, but with her engines unharmed she plowed on through the waves at her top speed of 28 knots. After several minutes of trying to reach the bridge by telephone, the Executive Officer assumed command of the ship from her auxiliary steering station aft. He kept *Duke of York* on a westerly heading, bearing away from the guns of *Tirpitz* and he set about the task of determining how badly hurt she was. Soon he shifted to the frantic effort to save her.

Nobby Lamb came awake with the sensation of drowning. A great vise gripped his chest and a wet towel seemed pressed over his nose and mouth. Panicked, he struggled to free himself. For a moment, he believed he'd been thrown overboard and was really drowning, but he discovered a soft weight pressing him down. He squirmed out from under and gasped for breath, but found little relief. The air was foul with oily tasting smoke. He pulled his tunic up over his mouth and used it as a crude mask. The compartment was dark, with only the flickering light of flames reflected off a bulkhead from down the passageway. Nobby fished his torch out of his back pocket and pressed the switch, but no light came out. The torch lens and bulb were both shattered.

He groped around him until he found the weight that had been holding him down. It was a body and he first felt at the man's throat for a pulse or other sign of life, but there was none. He ran his hands over the man's pocket and felt the shape of a torch. He removed it and flipped it on. Shining the light around the passageway, he gasped. It was a charnel house. Men and parts of men lay everywhere around, even blasted onto the bulkhead behind him and the deck above him.

Nobby was part of a ten-man damage control party. They had been fighting the fire forward until it came under control, then shifted to making repairs. Nobby was in the process of restoring emergency power and light to the area when the explosion tore through them. Those closest to the explosion were literally ripped apart. Most others died outright.

The rest were thrown by the concussion against unforgiving hard steel with many broken limbs and fractured skulls.

Nobby heard a moan and set about finding its source, checking each of the more or less complete bodies for a pulse or signs of breathing until at last he found one man still alive. He barely recognized the burned and blackened face of his shipmate, the fatherly Chief Petty Officer Gresham. He shined the light from his torch over the man's body. He grimaced and looked away. Burnt from the top of his head down to his waist Gresham's white ribs poked through the cooked flesh of his chest. How he still breathed was a mystery.

Nobby had only the very most basic medical knowledge, nothing more than first aid for cuts and scrapes really, and he hadn't the faintest idea what to do. He knew though that it would be completely impossible to move Chief Gresham in his condition and he felt it very unlikely he had long to live even had he been delivered to the caring hands of a doctor immediately. Nobby pulled a lifejacket from a nearby locker and tucked it under Gresham's head. Burnt hair and skin came away on his hand.

"Sorry, Chief," said Nobby softly, all the while wondering at his own survival. So far as he could tell, he and Gresham were the only survivors of the damage party and aside from some bruises and a trickle of blood from his nose he did not seem to have suffered an injury. He finally decided that the bodies of the other men had absorbed the worst of the blast and that he owed his survival to them.

The torch flickered, went out, then came back on when he shook it. During the moment its light was out he noticed light from the fire around the corner in the next compartment was much brighter. He stepped to the hatchway and carefully peered through. A cheerful blaze burned there, fed by electrical wiring and the contents of a crew's mess, spilled through a ruptured bulkhead.

He was in the series of passages right below the weather deck and two decks above the steel armored deck that protected the magazine. These passages surrounded the armored barbette in a ring and were sectioned off by four heavy steel hatches. Two stairwells, known as companionways in the Navy, led to hatches in the weather deck, one each on the after port and starboard quarters of the barbettes. The starboard companionway lay at the far end of this burning passageway. Two more hatches in the deck under his feet led to escape trunks for the magazines.

The hatch he stood at had been open to permit the damage party to effect its repairs. Nobby leaned through and grabbed the hatch, pulling back at the touch of hot steel. He pulled his sleeve down and used it to protect his hand as he pulled the hatch closed and dogged it shut. The passage was plunged back into darkness and he pulled out the torch again. By its flickering light, he set out the other direction, moving forward towards the bows. He knew he was on the starboard side of the barbette for 'A' turret. Inboard of him the great cast steel mass of the barbette itself curved away into the darkness. Outboard was a series of narrow offices and equipment lockers just inside the 12-inch thick outer skin of the armored hull. Directly below his feet, beneath the 6-inch thick deck plate were the shell handling rooms where the crew who operated the magazines trundled the 14-inch projectiles to the shell hoists and up to the guns in the turret above.

Nobby stopped and listened. He counted to sixty. He could hear many noises, including the steady throb and vibration of the ship's engines, but the guns above made no sound. *Duke of York* had ceased her fire. He hurried on down the passage to the next sealed bulkhead on the forward starboard quarter of the barbette. It was still shut and he touched it gingerly, expecting it to be hot, but it was not. Next, he tapped against the hatch with the mallet hung on a chain for that purpose. He waited. No answer. He tapped again. Still no answer. Carefully he turned the wheel to un-dog the hatch and pulled it back with a dull groan on its hinges. He peered into the pitch black of the passage, then shined his light. Abandoned, the passage appeared undamaged. A dull red, battery powered light at the mid-point of the curve relieved the gloom. The standard lights were all out. He ducked through the hatch and dogged it shut behind him before moving on to the front of 'A' turret's barbette. Here he passed and for the moment ignored the hatch let into the deck that led down into the magazine. Instead, he approached the hatch that branched off the ring around the barbette and led forward to the anchor chain lockers and motor compartment on the starboard side. He felt it for signs of fire, but it was cold to his touch. He grabbed the wheel to release the clips of the hatch, but it was jammed and would not turn. He took a fire axe from its hook on the wall and used the handle as a lever, wedging it into the wheel, but it was no use. The hatch would not open.

He moved on towards the port side of the ship and checked the hatch that led to the port anchor locker. He pulled his fingers back from the touch of hot steel and guessed correctly that a fire raged on the other side. He continued to the next hatch in the ring passage. Here he carefully opened, then shut behind him the third of the four hatches in the turret ring passage.

Now he was on the port side of the barbette and the stairwell to the port side exit hatch was ahead of him, aft. The passage was lit by the dull red battle lantern and a dim suggestion of daylight around the curve, but as the one before, it was deserted and appeared undamaged. Only when he pressed his hand against the outboard bulkhead did he feel warmth. Not painful to the touch, the warm steel suggested a minor fire or one more distant than that he'd just fled. Even so, he was alarmed that fires were burning forward and aft of 'A' turret's barbette and directly above the main magazine. He hurried on, hoping to find the companionway and hatch to the weather deck above both clear and open. He skidded to a stop.

The steel framework of the stairs were twisted and bent and the deck plates above were buckled, with a clearly evident wave. He knew the steel deck was over three inches thick and the force needed to warp it in this fashion was unimaginable. Beyond the stairs a four inch gash in the deck above his head was the source of the dim daylight he'd seen and was also admitting a shower of ice cold water, residue no doubt of firefighting efforts above deck. He quickly scrambled up the twisted stairs and assessed the hatch. Its frame was misshapen. He tried turning the wheel to un-dog the clips that held it in place, but it would not budge. He grabbed the hanging mallet and banged it against the hatch. A moment later an answering bang returned, so at least he knew there were other men directly outside. He cupped his hand to his mouth and shouted towards the gash in the deck above.

"Hallo!" he shouted. "Can you hear me?"

The slit of light darkened a moment, then a voice came through it.

"Aye, we hear ya!" The voice said. "How many are ya?"

"One, plus some injured that I need help with!" Nobby answered.

"Ya'll not get out through the weather deck hatchways," the voice answered. "They're both jammed tighter'n a whore's purse!"

In spite of his situation, Nobby felt himself flush. His mates had tried many times to get him ashore to a prostitute, but he'd always begged off, for fear he'd humiliate himself at the crucial moment. The voice came through the gash again.

“Do ya ken the hatches that lead on to the capst’n flats?” the man asked him. He went on without waiting for a reply. “Go to the starboard hatch and move for’ard. The port side’s afire.”

“I’ve been there already,” shouted Nobby. “The starboard hatch is jammed. I tried to lever it open with the fire axe, but it’s jammed. The port side hatch is too hot to touch.”

“Aye, that’d be right,” replied the man. “There’s a fire for’ard on the port side. Out of bloody control it is.” Nobby tipped his head the better to hear what went on topside. Men were shouting and he could hear the crackle of flames. Tendrils of black smoke drifted over the narrow gash.

“Have ya checked the hatchway aft, the one right below me?” the man asked.

“Yes, and the one to starboard too,” shouted Nobby. “Too hot.” There was a long pause.

“There’s no other way, Laddie,” the man said finally. “Ya could go down through the bloody magazine, but they’d never open the bloody hatch for ya.”

Nobby was silent. He'd considered this possibility and had already dismissed it. The magazine was a dark and mysterious place to him. Access to the magazine was closely restricted at all times, in port or at sea and he'd never been in it. A party of Royal Marines with orders to kill anyone attempting unauthorized entry guarded entrances to the magazine. The hatches on the barbette ring passage could only be opened from the inside and were intended for use only as an emergency escape trunk from the magazine itself. While at sea these hatches were kept dogged shut and were never opened for any reason he'd ever heard of.

A torrent of water spilled down through the gash in the deck above his head and the din from the firefighting effort rose in volume with men shouting and the crackle of flames clearly audible through the narrow aperture.

"I've to go Laddie," the voice shouted. "Gettin' a bit warm here. See to your hurt mates. Move them to the for'ard passage if ya can and seal the hatches behind ya. Sit tight and dry and we'll get ya oot as soon as this bloody blaze is tamed."

As Nobby moved to do as he was told the first damage control party reached the bridge. They found it a wreck. The blast tore through the wireless office and charthouse behind the bridge, killing everyone and lighting the two compartments afire, throwing shrapnel and jagged chunks of steel forward onto the bridge. There the great armored cylinder of the wheelhouse saved several of the bridge watch crew, including both Captain Halliday and Admiral Tovey.

Both senior officers regained consciousness within minutes and set about regaining control of the ship. Halliday struggled to his knees and after helping Tovey up, the Captain went man to man around the bridge, sorting the living from the dead, cradling a broken left wrist against his body as he went. His first stop was in the wheelhouse itself where he found the quartermaster struggling to his feet. Next, he checked the state of communications. He found all telephone lines from the bridge to other parts of the ship were out of service. Whether the lines were all cut or the telephone switchboard several decks beneath his feet was destroyed he could not determine. He surveyed what he could see of his ship. The blast shutters that covered the bridge windows were blown out from the inside, with some hanging askew, others torn away completely. All the glass was gone and an icy wind with foul smelling smoke blew through the bridge.

Halliday peered down at the forward decks and 'A' and 'B' turrets. All guns were silent and sheets of black, oily smoke roiled up from the decks beneath him. Men were scrambling to deploy fire hoses and spray water on two fires. Halliday gasped. Flames burst through the shattered scuppers on the port side, forward of the breakwater that curved in front of 'A' turret. The hit *Duke of York* suffered here had very nearly separated her bows from the rest of the ship. The weather deck was cracked open with a five foot wide gap stretching past the centerline of the bows toward the starboard side and plunging down as far as he could tell directly into the sea on the port side. Damage parties were only just reaching this area to fight the fire.

He leaned out the bridge window and looked as straight down toward 'B' turret as he could manage. The situation here was even worse than forward. The base of the armored conning tower was shrouded in smoke and flames. The heat and smoke of the flames rose high above the turrets below and made his eyes water. He ducked back in the window and grabbed one of the bridge lookouts by the elbow. The boy hadn't yet collected his wits, but Halliday could not wait. He shook the boy and looked him in the eyes.

"You're to deliver a message to the Executive Officer at the auxiliary steering station," he said. The boy looked bewildered. "Come on son, do you understand?" Halliday demanded sternly.

The boy looked around the shattered bridge for a moment and the import of the Captain's command began to sink in. Control of the ship from the Bridge was lost.

"Yes, Sir," he said at last.

"What is your name son?" Halliday asked.

"Carstairs, Sir," the boy said. "Seaman Carstairs."

"All right, Carstairs," Halliday soothed him, releasing his grip on the boys elbow, rubbing his shoulder. "Tell Number One that both forward turrets are out of action, communication with the bridge is out and there are three fires burning forward, one in the bows, one at the base of the superstructure and another behind the bridge." He looked in the boy's eyes again. "Can you repeat that, Carstairs?"

Carstairs nodded, thought a moment, then repeated the message nearly verbatim.

"Good show, Carstairs!" said Halliday. "Deliver this message then return to me here on the bridge with Number One's answer. You're to be my messenger until we have the telephones working again."

"Yes, Sir!" Carstairs snapped a salute and turned to go. At first, he started back through the inboard passages of the superstructure, but realized immediately the fires burning behind the bridge cut that path off. Instead, he ducked down the exterior ladder on the bridge's port side and made his way aft.

Halliday turned back to Tovey. The ever-faithful Tembam, the Malay steward had the Admiral on his feet, leaning against the Captain's chair. The dressing on his forehead from the earlier injury showed blood seeping through from the cut and Tovey's eyes were unfocused and distant. For the first time Tembam himself appeared disheveled, his always impeccably white steward's uniform smudged and smoke stained. The right sleeve of his tunic was torn from the elbow to wrist and blood dripped from his fingertips. Tembam ignored his own injuries and helped Tovey into the Captain's chair. Others of the bridge crew were also recovering their wits, though in truth, none was uninjured and some would never recover.

At this moment neither Captain Halliday nor his Number One, the Executive Officer understood the full danger to *HMS Duke of York*. As bad as the situation looked to Halliday from the bridge he believed the fires were manageable, could be contained and the ship not only saved, but returned to action against *Tirpitz*. He rang the engine room enunciator down to 'Finished With Engines' and back to 'All Ahead Full'. A moment later the engine room responded in kind, signaling that the ship's propulsion systems were still working and that communication to the engine room was not severed. Halliday poked his head in the wheelhouse and lifted a quizzical brow to the Quartermaster at the helm.

"Aye, she's responding, Sir," the Senior Rating said, understanding the question. "On course two-five-zero."

"Come left to one-nine-zero," Halliday ordered. He planned to take the ship back on her course to pursue *Tirpitz* and at the same time put the wind behind her to assist in the firefighting efforts under way on the forward decks.

"Come left to one-nine-zero," the helmsman acknowledged.

As Captain Halliday reasserted control of his ship from the bridge, the X.O. dispatched a veteran officer forward to ascertain the damage from the most recent hits and to assess the damage control effort. First Lt. Dempsey Lloyd ran the deck along the starboard rail. Chaos reigned with men racing to and fro in seemingly disorganized madness. Dripping lengths of fire hoses ran from stanchions and valves protruding out of the adjacent bulkheads. Lloyd paused to survey what he could see of the superstructure. Smoke and flame billowed from the top of the armored conning tower, just aft of the bridge. High above on the foretop the forward radar aerial was stopped and just below it, the great optical range finder tilted at a crazy angle to port. He looked aft. The second radar aerial still rotated atop the aft mast. He assumed that *Duke of York* was at least not blind. He continued on, skirting the damage around the 5.25-inch twin gun turret and on towards the bows. He passed the remains of the two great Carley Floats. Still secured upright against the superstructure bulkhead, the steel frames, buoyant kapok and canvas webbing were shredded and blackened. Both starboard floats were unserviceable, though in truth, exposed to the elements in Arctic waters the Carleys afforded only a few extra minutes of life to their occupants if the ship should be abandoned.

Lt. Lloyd skidded to a stop as he passed the forward 5.25-inch starboard turret. Dozens of men from the ship's damage parties were scrambling back and forth, connecting fire hoses and spraying sea water onto a raging fire that billowed up through a yawning, twenty foot round hole in the deck. The hole was on the aft starboard quarter of 'B' turret barbette and extended to the very base of the conning tower. A narrow ten-foot wide strip of tilted, twisted deck was left between the hole and the starboard scuppers, but the side rails were blasted away and flames licked up out of the hole and over the side of the ship. It was impossible to go any further forward on the weather deck. He grabbed a Petty Officer and shouted in his ear.

"How long to put it out?" he shouted over the din.

"It's not just this one, Sir!" the man shouted back. "There's another bloody great blaze in the bows and one yon up high!" he jerked his head up indicating the fire near the bridge. "All three are out of control. We'd only just put down the fire here from earlier and we lost all the men and equipment still here when she took this hit," he nodded to the hole.

"Are the turrets secured?" demanded Lloyd.

"Aye, the turrets are evacuated and sealed up," answered the Petty Officer, shaking his head. "But there's no fucking telephone circuit down to the magazine. We've no idea what the situation is there. We tried to send a man down through the shell hoists of 'B' turret, but they're filled with smoke and he had to back out."

"Good God!" exclaimed Lloyd.

"Aye!" the Petty Officer said with a derisive laugh. "With smoke in the shell hoists either the barbette or the magazine itself is ruptured. One spark or ember……" he let the thought trail off to the obvious conclusion.

"What about between decks?" shouted Lloyd. "Can I get forward by going lower than the fire?"

"No!" the man answered. "I had a peek down yonder hole before the course change put the fire over the side. She's ablaze right down to the armored belt."

"So, we're cut off from the bows," concluded Lloyd.

"Aye, that we are," agreed the Petty Officer. "And sitting on a bloody great load of ammunition. God alone knows when it might go off."

"We've to flood the magazine!" shouted Lloyd.

"Aye," the Petty Officer stroked his chin pensively. "There's men trapped in the barbette ring passage. They can't pass for'ard or aft through dogged hatches with fire on either side and the hatches to the weather decks are jammed."

"Do they have access to the escape trunks?" demanded Lloyd.

"Aye, they do," nodded the P.O. "But those hatches are sealed from the inside and never to be opened in action except to evacuate. With the telephones out how will we get the hatches open?"

Lloyd opened his mouth to speak, but a violent explosion sent a burst of flame out through the shell hole, knocking both men from their feet along with all the others nearby engaged in fighting the fire. Fire hoses, ripped from the grips of the Royal Navy damage parties, flashed across the decks, propelled by the high-pressure water. The brass nozzles slammed against decks and bulkheads, ringing like bells when hitting steel, a more muted cracking sound when hitting human bodies. Seawater, barely above freezing temperatures drenched every man in the area before the survivors could tackle the flailing hoses and work their way up to the deadly nozzles to bring them back under control.

As *Duke of York* shifted course back to the south, flames took hold in the middle decks of her superstructure, threatening to gut the ship from the inside out. As yet, Captain Halliday was unaware that 'A' turret could not be operated. He proceeded on the assumption his ship would soon be back in the fight.

Chapter 31

Torpedo flight

The He 111 torpedo bomber bobbed up and down in flight with the occasional vigorous lurch or yaw as the head wind into which it flew gusted. Luftwaffe Captain Stefan Vogt struggled with the controls and with the intense concentration needed to keep his little flock of bombers in close formation without colliding with one another.

The flight from Banak airdrome in Norway's North Cape was grueling and dangerous from the very start. Vogt led the squadron's 'B' Flight off the ground in a hair-raising takeoff in near whiteout conditions. Empty oil barrels burning with scrap wood and waste oil lined the field and at least kept the pilots from veering off the runway. Even so, one of the inexperienced pilots in Vogt's 'B' flight cracked up his machine on takeoff, skidding off the runway in the fog when he missed the marker warning the runway's end was two hundred meters away.

The climb to altitude was little better. Even with his hundreds of hours flying experience Vogt fought the disorientation of flying blind in the heavy fog. Only his pre-war night flight training allowed him to use his artificial horizon instrument to keep his aircraft level until he broke free of the fog at 1000 meters altitude. That only one more of the other HE 111's with a young pilot in the Flight disappeared before reaching daylight was a wonder to him.

'A' Flight, led by his friend, Major "Mads" Wegele also lost an aircraft before the surviving twenty-three bombers formed up and headed northwest, homing in on the wireless beacon transmitted by *Tirpitz*. Conditions above the thick layer of overcast that hung over the sea were mostly sunny but a brisk and gusting headwind made keeping the bomber level difficult and the squadron was forced to spread out to avoid danger of collision. Of even greater concern, the bombers were heavily laden, each carrying a pair of torpedoes slung on either underside of the fuselage, and the headwind cut into the reserves of fuel for the return flight to Banak. Vogt could only hope the same wind, blowing from behind would push them along as they flew home.

"Are we still on the beam?" Vogt asked his wireless operator, Airman Plancke, touching the microphone button in his collar.

"Yes, Captain!" answered his wireless operator. "The signal remains steady on bearing two-nine-five and is strengthening."

Vogt took his right hand off the flight controls long enough to slap the man seated next to him in the cramped cockpit on the arm.

"Have you got our position fixed?" he shouted at his navigator, Lt. Fohn.

"Yes, I think so!" Fohn looked up from his charts with a shaky grin and pressed his throat mic. "This headwind affects the airspeed indicator and pushes us to the south, but the beacon provides the coordinates of the ships. I have used those to adjust our position. I think we are only about fifty miles away now."

Vogt nodded. Fifty miles, perhaps even fewer from the target. Little more than ten minutes separated the flight from the scene of the naval battle. He craned his neck round to port and scanned the horizon all the way to starboard looking for any break in the relentless cloud deck, but found none. The world seemed blanketed in a cotton ball. The glare of the sun above was blinding and only his tinted flight goggles allowed him to see at all. He had no way of knowing how thick these clouds were nor how close to the surface of the sea they extended at any given location. The signals transmitted from the *Tirpitz* included continuous updates on weather conditions and indicated the cloud deck lay as close as 500 meters above the sea, but with occasional patches of fog right down on the surface. His altimeter should alert him before he crashed into the sea, but the device was not so accurate that he'd gladly risk his life on it. After a moment of thought, he made his decision.

Using hand signals, he alerted the pilots of the bombers nearest to his that they were to remain at their current altitude and heading, while he ducked down into the clouds in an effort to find their bottom. He touched his throat mic.

"Pilot to crew," he announced. "We're going under the clouds to find the sea. Everyone on the alert! Sing out if you spot the water or any ships!"

From 2,400 meters altitude he pushed the control column forward with his left hand while pulling back the throttles with his right. The bomber nosed over and fell into a gentle glide slope dive, the roar of the engines fading as he lost altitude. As he plunged into the shapeless mass of cloud, his eyes locked on the instrument panel, flicking back and forth from the artificial horizon to the altimeter to the compass every few seconds, making minor corrections with the steering yoke to keep the aircraft level and on course.

The altimeter passed through 2,000 meters with no indication the clouds would break. The deeper into the clouds he dove the less sunlight penetrated and the dimmer it grew. At 1,500 meters, he allowed his eyes a few seconds to scan out the cockpit's glazed glass dome; nothing but a grey-brown murk and streaming beads of condensed moisture raced across the glass. The altimeter spun below 1,000 meters; still nothing.

"What about that damned signal?" he shouted, not bothering with his throat mic.

"Steady on two-nine-five," yelled back Plancke. "Very strong! We could be right on top of it! Certainly very close!"

Vogt eased back up on the yoke, making the dive shallower. 700 meters and he quickly scanned outside the cockpit again. For an instant, he thought he saw a brief flash of light or an opening in the clouds, but it was so fleeting he could not be certain. 500 meters and still no sign of a bottom to the clouds. His shoulders and forearms ached from the tension of holding them ready to yank back on the yoke, expectation growing that at any second he'd be confronted by the sudden horror of the sea rushing up to snatch the bomber from the sky. The navigator, Fohn tipped himself out of the right hand seat down into the bomb aimer's position in the glass nosed dome of the cockpit, staring down for any sign of the ocean below. The altimeter spiraled through 400 meters with still nothing but streaming condensate on the glass dome. 300 meters. Vogt eased back further on the yoke. Now the bomber was not really in a dive so much as a shallow glide. Finally, Vogt could stand the tension no more and began to ease back on the stick, intending to climb back to the safety of altitude.

"Wave tops!" shouted Fohn. "We're at about two-hundred meters," he added quickly, as Vogt pulled back hard on the yoke.

The Heinkel settled back to level flight as Vogt's heart rate also returned to normal. He stared hard down through the clear nose dome of the bomber, but for long seconds he could not confirm Fohn's observation. He was about to challenge it when the plane burst out of the cloudbank into open air. For miles ahead and to either side the sea was visible, with a ceiling at 600 meters. Ranks of white-capped waves marched across the sea, driven by a northwesterly wind that had freshened to a steady twenty-five knots, Force 6 on the Beaufort Scale. He checked his fuel gage; more than half expended fighting through the headwind on the flight from the North Cape. They'd have to put that same wind behind them to have any hope of getting home again. Flashes, as of lightning, lit the western horizon ahead.

Vogt smiled. "What about that beacon?" he demanded.

"We are very close and directly on the beam," answered Plancke. "Steady on two-nine-four now."

"All right!" shouted Vogt. "Back up we go to collect the chicks!"

He pushed the throttles forward and hauled back on the yoke and the He 111 responded, the crescendo of her twin BMW motors rising. Just before the nose re-entered the cloud base at 600 meters altitude the lightning lit the horizon again.

"Stay alert!" Vogt shouted using the interphone to be heard above the roar of his engines. "We don't want to collide with one of our own in this soup!" Long moments passed as they climbed back up through the clouds before they burst through again, this time into bright sunshine. Vogt scanned the sky, looking for his flight of bombers and for their companion flight led by his friend Mads Wegele. Time wasted in collecting the flock would eat away what pressure fuel he had remaining for the return flight. He needed to get all his aircraft down under the cloud deck, find the enemy, then coordinate and deliver their attack with as little delay as possible.

“There!” shouted Plancke, pointing. “9 o’clock level, about three miles.”

Vogt turned to his left and quickly spotted the black dots of other aircraft. He tipped the yoke left and the He111 turned, eating the distance quickly at full power. Soon the other crews spotted him as well and turned to intersect his course. He settled into formation and set about the time consuming task of using hand signals to deliver his orders.

Chapter 32

To save a pawn

Finally, Reggie Elkins had forgotten how cold it was. *USS Washington* was closed up, ready for battle for over a day, but when the klaxon sounded and the "Battle Stations, Surface" announcement was made it all became very real, very quickly to Reggie and his shipmates. The first time the six guns of the great 16-inch main battery forward fired in salvo he found a surprising bead of sweat trickling down his temple. Now word passed that *Washington* was coming in to range of her 5-inch secondary battery and would soon be in rapid-fire mode against the German surface fleet. Pea coats and wool caps came off and Reggie and his comrades set about confirming the readiness of their equipment for the umpteenth time. All through the ship, men exchanged silent looks. *Washington*'s baptism of fire had begun.

On the bridge of the American battleship, Admiral Giffen and Captain Benson conferred.

"We've slowed the pocket battleship and knocked one German destroyer out of the fight," said Benson, "but on the down side both

Wichita and *Tuscaloosa* have sustained damage and are at reduced speeds. Two of our four destroyers are reloading torpedo launchers now."

"Yes, and we're in range of the pocket battleship, but to close on her we'll need to divide our own fire between her and *Tirpitz*," added Giffen. "Without our cruisers to occupy the pocket we can't concentrate our own fire."

"Bridge, radar," the speaker squawked. "The enemy heavy is turning again, coming to zero-nine-zero, speed 30 knots, range closing, down to 36,000 yards."

"He's made his choice!" Giffen slapped his thigh. "He's not going to abandon the pocket. He's willing to slug it out with us to save her."

The flag officer, Lt. Fairbanks appeared at Giffen's elbow. "This just down from the radio office, Sir," he said grimly, handing Giffen a wireless message slip. "They've just finished decoding the latest signal from Admiral Tovey aboard The Duke."

Giffen read the signal, then handed it on to Benson.

"Position, course, speed," Benson said as he scanned the message, then: "'Fires out of control, forward main battery temporarily unserviceable, propulsion and steering undamaged, am pursuing *Tirpitz*.'" He looked up. "Well!" he concluded.

"*Duke of York* has taken a real beating already it seems," nodded Giffen. "And at least for the moment not even able to return fire unless she can bring her aft battery to bear."

"This explains *Tirpitz'* behavior," opined Benson. "With *Duke of York* hobbled he feels free to turn on us, one-to-one. He can mop up the Duke when he gets done with us."

"Shift your fire Captain!" ordered Giffen sternly. "Focus exclusively on *Tirpitz*. Nothing matters but to hit her. I'll let the pocket escape at her leisure so long as *Tirpitz* stays within our range."

BOOM-BOOM-BOOM-BOOM-BOOM-BOOM. One after another, *Washington's* 16-inch forward guns fired, hurling their armor piercing shells down range, one last salvo targeting *Scheer*.

"Bridge, radar, enemy course changing to one-three-five, speed still 30 knots, range down to 33,000 yards. The small cruiser is following the heavy. The large cruiser is holding steady on one-seven-five at 22 knots."

“Come to one-four-five, continue flank speed!” Benson issued his orders to pursue *Tirpitz*, cutting slightly across her course to shorten the range as quickly as possible. WHHIIIRRR-SPLAT, WHHIIIRRR-SPLAT, WHHIIIRRR-SPLAT. A three-shell ranging salvo from *Tirpitz* came down in the sea a quarter mile to port of *Washington*.

BOOM-BOOM-BOOM-BOOM-BOOM-BOOM. *Washington* returned fire with her first salvo of the battle against *Tirpitz*.

“*Wichita* and *Tuscaloosa* falling behind,” observed Captain Benson. “Should we dispatch any of the destroyers to stand by them in case they have to abandon ship?” he asked Giffen.

The Admiral shook his head. “They are on their own,” he answered softly. “I can’t diminish the combat power left to tackle *Tirpitz*. Keep all the destroyers with us.”

“Bridge, radar, range to the heavy down to 30,000 yards. She’s holding course one-three-five, now at 27 knots. The smaller cruiser is with the heavy, the larger cruiser bearing away to the south at 22 knots. Two other targets to the west at the edge of our screens must be *The Duke* and *London.* Both are following the heavy. ”

Benson snatched up the telephone. "Radar, this is the Captain. Keep range, course and speed updates coming every minute!"

"Radar, aye."

SPLAT. The first of a four shot salvo from the enemy crashed down on the sea, the closest shell falling just four hundred yards to starboard.

"Come right ten degrees!" ordered Benson, shifting *Washington's* course to avoid the next anticipated barrage. The battleship heeled over as she made the adjustment. The seas were now hitting on her starboard quarter and sheets of spray and foam flew over her bows as she shouldered into each wave top. The seawater started to freeze, even as it flew through the air, and it clung briefly to metal surfaces, but each time the 16-inch guns fired the concussion knocked further slabs and sheets from the ship until the forward weather decks became dangerous places to venture. Ice blocks weighing hundreds of pounds slid back and forth until they finally reached the scuppers and plunged over the side into the sea.

BOOM. The main battery commenced its next salvo, each gun dropping back to its near horizontal reload position as soon as it fired.

“Bridge, radar, enemy heavy and escorting cruiser holding one-three-five, speed 27 knots, range 28,500 yards.”

SPLAT, SPLAT, WHHIIIRR-SPLAT, WHHIIIRRR-SPLAT. Four shells from *Tirpitz* fell across *Washington’s* path, the first two short, the next two long, with shells two and three impacting just one hundred yards to either side of her bows.

“Straddled!” exclaimed Giffen.

“Come right twenty degrees!” shouted Benson. “The next four will be on target!” he said softly, that only Giffen would hear. The Captain knew he was at a tactical disadvantage so long as both *Tirpitz* and *Washington* held to their current courses. *Tirpitz* was bringing all eight of her main guns to bear, while his own ship’s after battery could not swing its guns round to clear her own superstructure to fire at *Tirpitz*. *Washington* could only bring her forward two turrets with six guns into the fight.

BOOM-BOOM-BOOM-BOOM-BOOM-BOOM.

SPLAT, SPLAT-CLANG, SPLAT-THUNK, WHHIIIRRR-SPLAT. Straddled again, shrapnel and shell casings punched into *Washington*. Where her armor skin was thick they ricocheted and bounced away, but in her superstructure, they left holes that briefly glowed red hot and caused *Washington's* first casualties of the war.

"Come left ten degrees!" ordered Benson.

"Come left ten degrees!" repeated the helmsman calmly.

"Bridge, radar, enemy heavy and escorting cruiser holding one-three-five, speed 27 knots, range 27,000 yards."

"We've got to hit her, slow her down!" Giffen smacked his fist into his open palm. "Once the pocket is clear *Tirpitz* will go to top speed and run away from us."

SPLAT, SPLAT, SPLAT, WHHIIIRR-CRASH. *Washington* rocked from a hit somewhere astern.

BOOM-BOOM-BOOM-BOOM-BOOM-BOOM. Her guns thundered her response.

"Come left ten degrees!" Benson snapped, then snatched up the telephone. "This is the Captain!" he snarled. "Damage report! Where are we hit and how bad."

"Bridge!" The speaker squawked. "Foretop lookouts report a hit on the enemy heavy!"

SPLAT- SPLAT- SPLAT-SPLAT. A four-shot salvo all fell short of *Washington* as she bore away to the east, but Benson knew he could not surrender any seaway; he had to keep *Tirpitz* in range. If ever the enemy battleship slipped away, he knew he could never catch her. The telephone still pressed to his ear awaiting the damage report he gave the command to stay with *Tirpitz*.

"Right twenty degrees!" he snapped.

"Right twenty degrees," responded the veteran helmsman.

Benson slammed the telephone onto its hook.

"We're hit aft," he reported to Giffen. "On the fantail. Guns, engineering and steering all unaffected. No fire."

WHHIIIRRR-SPLAT, WHHIIIRRR-SPLAT, WHHIIIRRR-SPLAT, WHHIIIRRR-SPLAT. Four shells raced overhead, one passing at angle between the fore and aft masts, all exploding long, behind *Washington* and to port.

BOOM-BOOM-BOOM-BOOM-BOOM-BOOM. The American 16-inch guns returned fire, smoke whipped away from the gun barrels by the wind.

"Bridge, radar, enemy targets holding course one-three-five, speed 27 knots, range 26,000 yards."

WHHIIZZ-SPLASH, WHHIIZZ-SPLASH, WHHIIZZ-SPLASH. A three-shell salvo of ranging shots from the German cruiser's 8-inch guns all went long.

SPLAT-SPLAT-CRASH. Benson was thrown from his feet as the third shell in another salvo from *Tirpitz* struck mid-ships on the port side. The fourth shell went unheard in the din, long.

"Left rudder twenty degrees!" Benson shouted as struggled to his feet. He snatched the phone from its cradle. "Guns, this is the Captain. I am uncovering the aft turret. Target *Tirpitz*!"

The great ship turned to port and her aft 16-inch gun turret hummed round to point its guns to starboard. BOOM-BOOM-BOOM they fired.

Four more 15-inch shells roared down to crash into the sea, the last striking just a stone's throw from the port side. Once again, shrapnel rang against *Washington's* hull and superstructure. With all eight of *Tirpitz's* main battery firing a salvo, four heavy shells fell every half minute and now the eight guns of the enemy cruiser joined the assault, firing 8-inch shells sixteen times a minute. The six 5.9-inch guns of *Tirpitz's* port secondary battery joined at extreme range. The barrage lashed the sea around *Washington* into a foaming frenzy and the sound of shells in flight and exploding merged into one mighty and continuous roar.

BANG. An 8-inch shell struck. THUNK. A heavy piece of shrapnel slammed through the superstructure. CLANG. Another chunk rang off the armored hull. Lookouts shouted and the bridge speaker kept a constant stream of reports flowing to Benson and Giffen on the bridge.

"Bridge, radar. Enemy heavy and cruiser on course one-three-five, speed 28 knots, range 20,000 yards."

"Bridge, foretop reports *London* is firing!"

"Bridge, damage control. Hit mid-ships in the paymaster's office. Fire under control."

BOOM-BOOM-BOOM-BOOM-BOOM-BOOM.

WHHIIIRR-SPLAT, WHHIIZZ-SPLASH, WHIIZZ-BANG.

"*Wichita* coming up on the port side, speed 32 knots!"

WHHHIIIRR-CRASH. Another hit from a heavy caliber shell rocked the ship.

Fairbanks appeared at Giffen's elbow, handing him a message flimsy. The Admiral scanned it quickly, then passed it to Benson.

Benson handed it back to Fairbanks. "*Duke of York* fires out of control and main battery disabled, but still pursuing," he said, shaking his head. "Plenty of guts in the Royal Navy."

BOOM-BOOM-BOOM.

"Bridge, foretop reports the enemy battleship hit again forward."

"Bridge, radar. *Tirpitz* and cruiser shifting course to one-seven-five, speed 27 knots, range 17,000 yards."

"Come right to one-seven-zero," Benson ordered, shaping a course just five degrees sharper than the enemy, still fighting for every yard of seaway. He snatched up the telephone.

"Guns, this is the Captain," he shouted. "We're in range of the 5-inch batteries forward, commence firing!"

POP-POP-POP-POP joined the cacophony as the two forward most 5-inch turrets fired, their guns aimed dead ahead of *Washington*.

"Bridge, radar, the small enemy cruiser is bearing away to the west, towards *London* and *The Duke*. Speed 30 knots."

The minds of Giffen and Benson raced to keep up with the avalanche of information thrown at them. Benson focused on the tactical situation and what he needed to do to fight his ship while Giffen blocked out the sounds of battle to puzzle over the enemy actions and what they portended. Most surprising was his counterpart's decision to turn onto an easterly heading. Even though this course put all eight of *Tirpitz's* guns in action, and in fact allowed the enemy cruiser to join the fight and get in a few licks of her own, at the same time it also exposed both enemy ships to possible damage at the hands of *Washington*. To Giffen's thinking the Germans should have had but one goal; to separate their injured consort, the pocket battleship from the battle so that she could escape further harm, then to race away themselves using their superior speed to put a finish to the battle. This should have been doubly obvious to the enemy commander when *HMS London* and *USS Wichita* rejoined the fight. Two Allied battleships and two cruisers against *Tirpitz* and a lone cruiser were long odds to be avoided, not challenged.

He considered of course that the German might still have some doubt about *Duke of York's* status, but the Royal Navy battleship's failure to fire for long minutes now, even though still in range should have given a clear indication her combat power was diminished. Could the German have dared assume *The Duke* was effectively neutralized and no longer a threat? In that case turning back on *Washington* might make sense especially in light of the Allies being temporarily deprived of their cruisers. But in that case, why turn back, fling just a few salvoes and then run again?

He pondered for other possible explanations of the German behavior and could think of two such explanations, but intelligence reports out of the Admiralty in London seemed to eliminate both. Unless London was wrong.

"Fairbanks!" he shouted. The movie star materialized at his elbow. "Find out if our destroyers have reloaded their torpedoes," he commanded. "Send all four against *Tirpitz* at flank speed. Order *Wichita* to flank speed along with the destroyers. Have her provide covering fire against the German destroyers."

Lt. Fairbanks scurried off to make the signals. Giffen turned to Benson.

"Captain," he began. "The only thing that makes sense here is that the Germans are trying to draw us down on one of their U-boats."

"Or an air attack," said Benson. "Though presumably London would have alerted us to either."

“I’m not sold on the quality of the British intelligence anymore,” Giffen answered. “Remember they told us *Tirpitz* would not venture so far north or west and would not risk battle against even odds. Our only hope of catching her was to hit her from the air first, slow her down, then take her in a surface battle according to what the Brits told us.”

Benson nodded. “Yet here we are,” he concurred. He picked up the telephone. “Pass the word to all lookouts. Double the watch for submarines and torpedoes.” He flipped a switch on the telephone console. “Radar, this is the Captain. Where is the airborne spotter aircraft?”

“The snoop is moving off to the south, Sir,” replied the Radar officer. “It has to be low on fuel by this point.”

“Maintain your aerial watch!” ordered Benson. “Stay alert to an air strike.” He hung up the phone without waiting for an answer. He turned to Fairbanks. “Go aft. Get me an assessment of where the damage control parties stand on putting out the fires there.”

Giffen nodded his approval to the signals officer. Fairbanks scurried from the bridge.

BOOM-BOOM-BOOM-BOOM-BOOM-BOOM. *Washington's* forward battery fired, though once again her three gun aft turret could no longer bear on target. Both *Tirpitz* and the American battleship were on the same course, nearly due south. For *Tirpitz* only her aft battery could fire now.

"We've hit her at least twice," observed Benson to Giffen. "Tovey's reports from *The Duke* suggest several hits as well and yet not the slightest indication of damage. No reduced rate of fire, or speed, no observed smoke or fires. Nothing!" He shook his head in frustration. "I know she's thick skinned, but she must have a weakness!"

Giffen nodded as a four-shell salvo from *Tirpitz* roared overhead. WHHIIIRRR-SPLAT.

"Hard to credit the combination of armor, armament and speed," he agreed. "Small wonder the Brits are so afraid of her."

The frenetic pace of the action eased for a few moments. As the two sides pulled apart, the smaller guns on all ships fell out of range, leaving the battle to only *Washington's* forward and *Tirpitz's* aft turrets, a situation favoring the six American 16-inch guns over the four German 15-inch rifles.

BOOM-BOOM-BOOM-BOOM-BOOM-BOOM.

WHHIIIRRR-SPLAT, WHHIIIRRR-SPLAT, WHHIIIRRR-SPLAT, CRASH.

The concussion knocked Benson and Giffen from their feet again. Smoke filled the bridge and the blast shutters slammed open and closed again over shattered windows. Benson staggered to his feet and gripped the telephone.

"Auxiliary steering!" he croaked out.

Twelve miles away on *Tirpitz,* Captain Topp fought for the survival of his ship. Hit three times by the massive shells of the American 16-inch 45-caliber guns, internal fires threatened to gut the German battleship. Admiral Schniewind lay unconscious behind the wheelhouse, struck in the back by a steel splinter that had ricocheted onto the bridge from the latest devastating hit. Tended by one of the ships' Doctors his outlook was uncertain. The American shell slammed down into the superstructure behind the armored conning tower, plunging through four decks before exploding above the 320mm thick slab of steel that capped the main magazine. Reports from the men in the magazine indicated the hit put a bulge in the deck above their heads and the steel was hot to the touch. If the temperature kept increasing, they would be forced to flood the magazine.

Almost as bad, smoke from the fires burning amidships was drawn down into the engineering spaces and threatened to force evacuation of the number one engine room. If the crew was forced to leave the boilers and engines unattended, they would quickly lose power, slowing the ship, leaving her vulnerable to the two enemy battleships that pursued her.

Topp assumed the first Allied battleship had suffered damage of her own. How else to explain that, though in range she had not fired her forward battery for over fifteen minutes. Yet, she continued to pursue and Topp also had to assume that whatever the damage or fault, the enemy Captain expected to affect repairs and resume firing. Reports from his foretop lookouts indicated this KGV class Royal Navy battleship was afire, with smoke pouring from her bows and superstructure. As such, she was the least of his worries.

The second enemy battleship was of far greater concern. Though his lookouts reported she had been hit at least twice, unlike the first enemy battleship there was no indication of any loss of combat effectiveness. Her two triple gunned forward turrets kept a steady rain of amazingly accurate fire pouring down around *Tirpitz*, and when she scored a hit, the punch was devastating. Only the extra heavy steel armor his ship carried had saved her from a catastrophic magazine explosion already. Another direct hit might spell her end.

"Come left twenty degrees rudder," Topp ordered, anticipating the next enemy salvo, trying to outguess the enemy's gunnery officer and dodge the shells.

"Left twenty degrees rudder," repeated the helmsman and *Tirpitz* began the agonizingly slow process of shifting her massive bulk onto a new heading.

The sound he'd come to dread, the high-pitched banshee howl of the American heavy caliber shells, screamed overhead.

RROAARR-SMACK, RROAARR-SMACK, RROAARR-SMACK. A three-shell salvo went long and to starboard, hitting the sea like a flat hand on a wet tabletop. A cold shiver ran up Topp's spine and he gritted his teeth. *Tirpitz* already bore the scars of the damage these shells could do. He tensed for the next three shells of the six-gun salvo, but long seconds passed.

"RIGHT FULL RUDDER!" he shouted, dawning realization bringing near panic to his voice. The American gunnery officer had held the fire of one turret back, delaying for fifteen seconds, long enough to catch *Tirpitz* on her next course alteration. The hard turn threw Topp painfully against the binnacle. He clung to the compass platform praying he had not been too late, fearing the dread howl of the enemy shells, knowing even so it was the shell he never heard that could ruin his ship.

SMACK-SMACK-SMACK-CLANG-THUNK. The second set of three shells fell short of *Tirpitz,* but all in a tightly spaced line right on her previous course and just fifty meters to port. Shrapnel rang and slammed into the hull and superstructure.

"Left rudder, twenty degrees!" he ordered, relief replacing the panic.

BOOM-BOOM-BOOM-BOOM. Topp checked his watch as *Tirpitz'* four aft guns in turrets Caesar and Dora thundered out, but their rate of fire had slowed. The guns crews and ammunition handlers in the magazine and shell hoists were tiring after two hours of nearly continuous battle.

Topp prayed for the fifteen minutes he needed to outrange the enemy battleship, that *Tirpitz* not be hit, that the internal fires not force the evacuation of the engineering spaces and that his own gun crews could sustain their efforts long and skillfully enough to force the American to dodge, to throw off his incredible aim.

It had taken many minutes to identify this new threat as American. Its profile of six guns forward in two super-firing triple turrets and one triple turret aft did not fit any of the known Royal Navy capital ships. Eventually her silhouette was matched to one of several modern battleships coming off the slipways of American yards in large numbers. Most likely, she was of either the North Carolina or South Dakota class, and was perhaps even the namesake of one of these.

Not that it mattered to Topp. He only wished to escape her before his own beautiful ship was done further harm. The teeth-gnashing howl of the American shells returned. ROOAARR-SMACK, ROOAARR-SMACK, ROOAARR-SMACK. This time Topp waited only a few seconds before ordering a course change.

"Left rudder, twenty degrees," he ordered.

"Left rudder, twenty degrees," confirmed the helmsman.

Topp's mind was processing in overdrive, considering his own options, but also those of his enemy, trying to outthink his opponent. He made a snap decision.

"Come left to course zero-nine-zero," he commanded, then snatched up the telephone handset and flipped a switch.

"Gunnery officer!" he shouted. "This is the Captain. I will uncover your forward guns to port for three or four quick salvoes. The range will shorten and the port secondary battery will be in range as well. Be ready!" He waited only long enough for his acknowledgement before flipping to a new circuit on the phone panel.

"Radar! Range to the new heavy target?" he demanded.

"Range 20,000 meters, bearing three-four-zero, course steady on two-seven-five, speed holding at 28 knots."

BOOM-BOOM-BOOM-BOOM. The aft guns fired as *Tirpitz* heeled into her turn to port, even as the forward guns of turrets Anton and Bruno swung round to their stops to port and elevated to fire. Even before the forward 15-inch guns could bear, the six guns of the port side 5.9-inch battery opened fire, adding the CRACK-CRACK of each of the three twin turrets every twenty seconds.

BOOM-BOOM-BOOM-BOOM. The forward guns lashed out. Topp hoped to hold *Tirpitz* briefly in range of his 5.9-inch guns but beyond the range of the American's smaller 5-inch secondary battery while also bringing all eight guns of his main battery to bear against the American's six.

ROOAARR-SMACK, ROOAARR-SMACK, ROOAARR-SMACK. The first three shells of the American's next salvo all flew long and to starboard, impacting the sea a thousand meters away. Topp nodded in satisfaction. At least so far, his change of course had thrown the American aim off. Seconds later three more heavy shells raced overhead to fall harmlessly to starboard. He lifted his binoculars and tried to focus on his pursuer, but the sea surrounding the American danced in a froth of shell splashes. His heavy shells were launching waterspouts high into the air, their tops obscuring all but the tips of the American's masts while smaller splashes erupted every two or three seconds around the enemy's bows. A brief, bright flash lit the American's superstructure; seconds later, another blinked in her bows.

Now all eight of his heavy guns fired again, one after the other starting with the forward turret Anton, the fire working its way all the way aft to Dora. Light shell splashes fell in the sea a thousand meters to port of *Tirpitz*. The Americans were ranging their 5-inch guns. Just another moment, thought Topp, another salvo forward then a hard right rudder at maximum speed to open the range again. By now, he was certain the American top speed was around 28 knots. He was also nearly certain that the American would ignore any chance of hunting down the damaged *Scheer*.

Topp now finally understood that the Allied battle plan required a strategic rather than a tactical victory. The Royal Navy and US Navy were never content with the prospect of merely fighting the convoy through to Russia, nor even of driving the German Navy away. The only explanation for the presence of these enemy capital ships within range of German land based air power and in the absence of their own airplane carrier based air support, was that the Allies considered them expendable. Only sinking *Tirpitz* could possibly justify the risk of two such fine ships.

He checked his watch. Another twenty seconds until his forward guns would fire again. Meanwhile the shell splashes of the American 5-inch shells were walking steadily closer, now only two hundred meters to port. He decided he did not have twenty seconds.

"Right rudder, come to course one-seven-five!" he ordered.

"Right rudder, course one-seven-five!" answered the helmsman. He put the wheel over and *Tirpitz* began to heel to starboard.

A salvo of three heavy shells roared overhead, one passing so close as to swirl the smoke from *Tirpitz's* funnel. 5-inch shell splashes continued their inexorable march towards him, closing the gap even as *Tirpitz* turned away.

"Flank speed!" Topp ordered as the ship's rudder bit into the sea. He leaned against the port bridge rail and a shudder went up his spine.

SMACK-SMACK. The fourth and fifth heavy shells of the American's latest salvo fell short.

The sixth shell was on target. It slammed into *Tirpitz'* hull on the port side just above the waterline. The ship's armor here was among her thickest skin anywhere, with over 13 inches of hardened steel protecting the magazines and engineering spaces. The massive 1,200 kg American shell struck at a plunging angle, the kinetic energy of the impact turning the armor white hot in an instant, softening it as it gouged through to explode in a machinery space housing pumps and air blowers. The blast ripped upward through an enlisted berthing compartment, mercifully empty with the entire ship at battle stations. But a sheet of flame raced through the number one dressing station, killing the ship's second Doctor, wiping out his medical orderlies and over a dozen already wounded men seeking treatment there. A spout of water erupted and fell back on deck and water poured in through a round hole, two feet in diameter left in the hull that alternately lifted out of the sea, then plunged back in as *Tirpitz* plowed on through the swells.

Topp was thrown painfully against the bridge rail just as the forward main guns thundered out their last salvo of the battle. The report of the guns rippled from fore to aft again as each of the eight 15-inch guns fired in turn.

No sooner were they done, than a hail of 5-inch shells fell on and around the fantail. Most landed in the sea, deluging the rear decks with salt water, but several struck the ship, ripping down through thinly armored decks to explode in the aft anchor capstan flats and in the Petty Officers' lounge. Blackened, smoking holes marked their points of entry.

Topp regained his balance and called for a damage report.

"HIT!" sang out several lookouts simultaneously.

Topp lifted his glasses to look at the American, but smoke and waterspouts shrouded all but a vague and indistinct view of the enemy.

"Herr Kapitan!" shouted the officer of the watch, a young man seeing his first action. "It's the Chief Engineer!" he said, holding out the telephone for Topp.

Topp snatched the handset from the junior officer. “Captain here!” he shouted. He listened intently for a moment. “Maintain your best speed!” he commanded sternly. “The next five minutes are vital! After that I may have a chance to slow.” He dropped the phone unceremoniously. It clattered against the bulkhead, swinging back and forth on its cord until the officer of the watch hung it back up.

Tirpitz strained as her mighty engines delivered every one of their 160,000 horsepower to her three triple bladed brass propellers. She surged forward into her turn, back on to a southerly heading. The decks vibrated and a low-pitched hum permeated the entire ship, as of some monstrous humming bird’s wings beating the air. The CRACK of the 5.9-inch guns fell silent, and the splash of American 5 inch shells stopped as the range to the enemy opened once more.

Topp gripped the bridge wing rail and willed his ship on, as if his silent encouragement could squeeze one more knot from her vibrating hull. Three heavy shells fell a thousand yards to the east, on her previous course, then three more splashed down a further two hundred yards to the south.

BOOM-BOOM-BOOM-BOOM. *Tirpitz's* aft turrets hurled yet another salvo of 800-kilogram shells back at the American.

Aboard *Washington,* the navigation bridge was a scene of chaos. At nearly the same moment as *Tirpitz* suffered the 16-inch hit at her waterline, *Washington* was struck as well by a 15-inch shell from *Tirpitz* that fell in the superstructure behind the armored conning tower. Splinter shields, shutters, and bulkhead hatches were all clipped shut, but the remaining glass in the bridge windows blew out, laying in tiny shards on the deck. The force of the blast was enough to rupture decks and bulkheads. A blinding flash ripped onto the bridge; the concussion knocked men to the deck with broken bones and ruptured eardrums. Captain Benson levered himself back upright, shaking his head to clear his wits. A trickle of blood oozed from his left ear. Overhead, electrical trays and conduits hung from the deck, trailing sparks. In the charthouse, the navigator lay crumpled in the corner, his uniform smudged and soot stained, his skull fractured. The chart under glass on the chart table smoldered at the corners. At the back of the armored wheelhouse, a pool of blood flowed across the deck. The quartermaster helmsman was on his knees; his two hands still gripped the wheel, but a razor sharp slice of shrapnel had neatly separated his head from his shoulders. The gruesome scene was all the more horrible as the man's head rolled back and forth on the deck with the pitch of the ship.

The two ships sailed south, each at their top rated speeds with the range slowly lengthening between them. Both ceased fire from their secondary batteries. The big 15 and 16-inch guns continued throwing death and mayhem at each other. *Washington* continued on her present course, her helmsman's slumped body holding the wheel steady such that other ships, Allied and German had no indication she was not under control. *Tirpitz'* engines roared propelling her flight with all they had. The fresh wound in her port side admitted a ton of seawater each time it dipped below the waterline, but for now this did not slow her.

Captain Benson knelt over the Admiral. Giffen was unconscious, but breathing. A phone rang, but none had the sense to answer it. The 1MC inter-ship communication speaker above the Captain's chair squawked, but, his ears ringing, Benson could not make out what it said. Lt. Fairbanks burst onto the bridge, picking his way over debris and men. He'd been aft checking on the fires there. The scene on the wrecked bridge appalled him. He stopped and stared at Benson and Giffen and then started toward them, but the incessant buzz-buzz of the telephone and the squawk of the 1MC caught his attention. He lifted the phone from its cradle.

"Bridge!" he shouted into the handset, a finger in his other ear so that he could hear. His jaw hung slack for a moment as he listened to the message. "Oh my God," he murmured under his breath. After a moment longer he said, "Acknowledged, keep your reports coming. Send a runner to the bridge if you don't get a response on the phone circuit!"

He hung up the phone and turned back to Captain Benson, still kneeling over Admiral Giffen. He knelt beside Washington's commanding officer and took him under the left elbow.

"Come along, Sir," he said gently. "You're needed." Benson looked at him and struggled to his feet, but did not speak. Noticing the blood coming from the Captain's ear, Lt. Fairbanks moved around to the Captain's right side.

"Radar report, Sir," Fairbanks spoke into Benson's right ear, enunciating each word carefully.

Chapter 33

Torpedo attack

Stefan Vogt surveyed his flight from his own He111 bomber's position above and behind the other aircraft. Arrayed below him, his ten "Chicks" bobbed in three widely spaced columns of three or four aircraft, with more than a mile separating each He111 torpedo bomber from the one in front or behind. No trace of the 'A' flight, led by his friend Major 'Mads' Wegele, could be found.

Finally, satisfied with his arrangements Stefan turned to his navigator. "All Right Fohn!" he exclaimed. "We go!"

He tipped the bomber's nose down; picking up speed, he maneuvered into position at the head of the middle of his three columns of planes. Keeping the stick tilted forward he continued his gentle descent, leaving the clear air and bright summer sunshine behind, plunging into the cloud deck that covered the sea. Once again, condensation flowed across the cockpit's glass nose bubble and it became steadily darker as he descended. It was impossible to see any of the other aircraft in his flight; he had simply to trust that they were with him in a controlled gliding dive and that they would all emerge below the cloud ceiling in time to pull up before impacting the sea.

"Bearing!" he snapped at Plancke, mostly to relieve a little of his own tension.

"We are on the beam," answered Plancke. Stefan marveled at the radio operator's calm. Plancke was flying his second combat mission, but was bearing up like a solid veteran. "Still impossible to say how far, but dead ahead, give or take a compass point either way."

Vogt's eyes flicked down to the altimeter reading 1,000 meters, then back to the nose bubble. Now on to his artificial horizon to keep the plane in level flight with no visual cues to assist. He could only pray that the inexperienced pilots following him into battle could manage the many skills needed to arrive under these clouds safely. His eyes flicking between the windscreen and his instruments he descended through the clouds. 700 meters.

"Eyes sharp!" he commanded. Tensing, he approached the altitude where he hoped to emerge into clear skies. For an instant, the somber dark grey parted in a flash of something lighter, and then the murk closed around them again. 600 meters.

He adjusted the ailerons to compensate for drift and to restore level flight. Despite his many hours of flying experience, Stefan's muscles clenched and his grip on the stick could have strangled a horse. He took a deep breath and consciously forced his hand to relax a degree on the stick. Another flash of lighter sky, then another quickly after. 500 meters.

The He111 burst from the bottom of the clouds to a scene of a serrated sea below. Though it was a mid-summer morning, the gloom from the overcast was of an autumn eve. Stefan held his glide until he was at 400 meters altitude, 100 meters below the cloud ceiling above him. The bomber bucked mildly; she was still flying into a head wind. He glanced at his fuel gauge. Well past the halfway mark now, they could only hope the head wind would hold and become a tail wind to loft them on their way home. He also knew that if the German bombers dropped their heavy loads of twin torpedoes and with the fuel already expended they would be more than two metric tons lighter on the way home.

He ruthlessly pushed thoughts of the flight home from his mind. First things first, they had to find the enemy and launch their attack against the Allies, surviving all the dangers of enemy flak fire to release the two deadly fish suspended beneath the plane.

The flashes of lightning he'd seen on his first descent under the cloud deck were much brighter this time. He now was certain they were not lightning at all, but flashes of gunfire dead ahead on the western horizon. He no longer needed confirmation they were on the radio beam.

Stefan pressed his throat button. "Plancke!" he called. "Do you see the rest of the flight?" he asked.

"They are coming out of the clouds all over the place," answered Plancke. "Seven so far. There's eight!" he exclaimed excitedly.

"Use your lamp to signal them to form up on us," commanded Vogt. He resolved to wait two minutes for the remaining two aircraft to appear before proceeding with the attack. With fuel margins so slim, he could ill afford to expend precious fuel stooging about looking for the wayward bombers.

"There is number nine!" exclaimed Plancke. "Just one still missing."

As they flew, the gun flashes grew in intensity and began to appear at divergent bearings with one set of rolling flashes slightly south of another.

"What bearing is our signal on?" demanded Vogt of Plancke.

“Steady between two-eight-three and two-eight-five,” the radioman answered. Vogt settled the aircraft on as close to two-eight-four as he could, given that the compass needle jumped and skipped about the dial. After a few moments, he confirmed the nose of the aircraft pointed at the southerly of the two origins of gunfire. He turned the ship slightly, bringing her onto course two-nine-five, just five points shy of straight north. He waited.

A nerve-wracking minute ticked by as Vogt held the Heinkel as steady as he could on bearing two-nine-five. Finally a series of gun flashes erupted almost dead ahead, rippling their reflected light off the bottoms of the clouds ahead. These flashes were just distinct enough to count. One by one, six individual flashes of orange and yellow tinged flame rolled across the horizon.

Stefan exhaled in a drawn out sigh.

“Plancke!” he shouted. “Signal the other aircraft. No one is to attack unless I give the order. I will attack first. Every plane is to attack the largest ship on scene. Golden Comb formation!”

He’d given the order for the aircraft to make their torpedo runs all from the same direction and at the same time, spread out in an arc relative to the target with every plane aiming for a hit amidships. Viewed schematically the attack formation would resemble the tines of a comb. When executed properly against a single target, by a large force of bombers, the Golden Comb could put many torpedoes into the water simultaneously, fired from many bearings. This maneuver served to complicate a ship's ability to dodge all the fish. With ten aircraft, he hoped to put all twenty of his torpedoes in the water at nearly the same time, expecting to achieve one or more hits.

"Do you see anything of 'A' flight?" Stefan asked his crew.

"No," answered Plancke.

"Nothing," said Fohn.

He briefly considered breaking radio silence to try to locate the other bombers led by his friend 'Mads' Wegele, but if the 'A' flight had not found the sea battle by following the powerful radio beacon emitted by *Tirpitz*, he believed his own much weaker transmitter was unlikely to succeed. Besides, any time spent in the effort to find Mads, whether fruitful or not, would eat up precious liters of fuel that were badly needed if they were ever to reach home again. The horizon flashed again, noticeably brighter with four flashes to the south followed seconds later by two sets of three flashes on the more northerly bearing. Vogt knew they were close now, perhaps as few as three or four minutes flying time distant and that had he been at altitude on a clear day he would already have made visual contact with the battle. But flying just 400 meters from the sea the horizon was quite close and he'd be almost upon a ship before he could see it.

Vogt guessed the German battleship *Tirpitz* and its fleet were to the south, fleeing the pursuing Allied ships to the north, but he could not be certain until he'd made a visual recognition of the ships, positively identifying the enemy. He'd have only moments to do this before either committing to a fast attack, or deciding to circle for a better sighting.

By now, he expected the enemy had detected his little flock of bombers on their radar apparatus. Every flak gun in the Allied fleet would be the scene of feverish activity. Flashes to the south were mirrored almost instantly by those to the north. He turned his bearing back five degrees to port, to two-eight-four.

"Plancke," he snarled.

"Signal bears dead ahead on two-eight-four," Plancke responded coolly, anticipating the question.

Stefan lifted his goggles from his face and rubbed his eyes and temples, then slipped the goggles back down. He shifted uncomfortably in his seat.

"Plancke! Signal the other aircraft to follow us in!" he ordered.

Reggie Elkins was shivering again, though now it was as much from fear as from the cold. *USS Washington* had been rocked by several large caliber shell hits and numerous lesser hits and the 1MC, the ship-wide communications circuit, was alive with reports from damage control teams fighting fires and assessing ruptured decks and bulkheads. Still, the hull vibrated as her massive engines strained to push the battleship forward at her maximum speed and every minute the six guns of her forward main battery thundered out another salvo of armor penetrating high explosive death.

Reggie and his mates in their 5-inch gun turret were out of range of the enemy battleship again, at least for the moment, so they were busy cleaning the guns and turret in preparation for the next command to fire. Some of the gun crew worked on removing the spent shell casings. When time permitted, as now, these were carefully set aside and preserved, as brass remained one of the key metals to the war effort in short supply. During intense action, they were simply thrown out the rear hatch of the turret to roll about on deck. Those that did not roll over the side were salvaged later. Reggie went over the auto-loader for the forward of the two guns, cleaning the rails and tracks that fed fresh shells and greasing the moving parts to assure smooth operation when the guns were called upon again. He paused a moment and caught his friend, Taylor Wynn's eye. An almost imperceptible arched eyebrow was his only answer.

At last, the compartment was shipshape and the men had time to rest. Reggie had slept for no more than two hours at a time for the past four days. He was punchy and slow-witted. Despite the regular thunderous roar of the heavy guns forward he leaned back against the auto-loader, closed his eyes and within a moment was asleep on his feet, drifting into a half dream world of warm Florida waters and bright sunshine. Pretty girls in summer print dresses strolled the boardwalk of his mind. They looked away demurely when he tried to catch their eyes.

The dream was not to last. The battle stations alarm shattered his moment of peace. As he snapped awake, he wondered why it was necessary to sound the alarm now. The ship had been in action with the German battleship for well over an hour already. There could not be a man aboard who was not already at is battle station.

The alarm ended and was replaced by the Bo 'suns whistle.

"All hands, battle stations, air attack!" the 1MC announced. "Battle stations, air attack!"

Reggie rubbed his eyes, but snugged up the chin strap on his helmet and tucked the asbestos anti-flash mask down under his collar. Everyone in the turret was already at his battle station. Aside from a nervous rustle, there was little movement.

"Starboard 5-inch guns on radar control," squawked the tin speaker. The two gunners released their grips on the elevation and deflection wheels. The turret rotated until the guns pointed outboard, directly to starboard. The gun barrels had been elevated at a 45-degree angle to loft shells at the enemy battleship. Now they dropped down to nearly horizontal.

"Looks like a low-level attack, boys," said one of the gunners, listening in on the chatter coming over his headset. "Torpedo bombers approaching at under 1000 feet altitude." He listened intently for a moment. "They are circling behind the ship for an attack on the starboard side."

Reggie swallowed hard and closed his eyes, but now sleep was a distant memory. He said a silent prayer for his soul and asked God that he not let his shipmates down. Unknown to Reggie and his mates in the turret, as the German aircraft approached *USS Washington* they found the American cruiser, *USS Wichita* and four destroyers strung out ahead and to port of the battleship. Recognizing the immense anti-aircraft firepower these five ships could add to the defense of the battleship Stefan Vogt chose to avoid them by circling behind the allied ships and attacking from the west, to starboard of the enemy.

Now was the moment *Washington* needed a firm hand to guide her, to dodge and weave to throw the aim of the enemy torpedo bombers off while her formidable anti-aircraft batteries knocked the Germans from the air. Her guns, radar, engines and rudder were all undamaged, but the death and destruction on her bridge left her slow to respond to this new threat from the sky. While the actor, Lt. Douglas Fairbanks, Jr. struggled to bring Captain Benson back to his wits and to restore order on the bridge, *Washington* sailed serenely on a straight course south and the German Heinkels lined up their attack.

Stefan Vogt could hardly credit what he was seeing. His He111 tipped over in its gentle glide-dive to reach the height just above the sea where he could release his torpedoes. The enemy ship should be turning away or towards him, altering her course to present a narrower profile, a slimmer target to reduce her chance of being hit, yet she did not deviate from her course as his altimeter spun down to 100 meters altitude. He was just moments from releasing his fish and while the starboard side of the immense battleship before him was alight with flak fire, there was no sign or indication of a turn.

Black clouds of smoke erupted all around him. **SMACK**! A chunk of shrapnel slammed into the aircraft fuselage somewhere, but the controls remained responsive and he held his aircraft on target. Another shell burst in front of him and his glass nose dome crazed and cracked. Wind whistled through several holes the diameter of a finger in the dome. He jinked to his left for a count of five, just long enough to change his bearing without also presenting the long, vulnerable aspect of the bomber's fuselage to the enemy gunners. He cut back to the right and back on target, pointing his nose just forward of the battleship's center point. He continued his descent. Away to his right a brilliant flash lit the sky and in his peripheral vision, he saw a fireball plunge into the frigid sea with a mighty splash of white water that all but extinguished the flaming wreckage of one of his chicks.

A stream of tracer shells zipped past him on his right and he adjusted course slightly to line up on the direction from which they'd come. The sky was alive with shell bursts and tracers. Shrapnel slammed his right wing and the controls wrenched in his hand, but he held the yoke in an iron grip and kept control. He reached down to his right and gripped the torpedo release lever. With a savage scream, he yanked the lever and instantly felt the bomber surge with power as its load dropped into the sea. The plane tried to jump in altitude, but Stefan pushed her nose down harder and slammed her throttles forward to the stops, even as he turned to his left. At the last possible moment, he pulled back on the yoke and the Heinkel fairly leapt over the fantail of the enemy battleship. He gasped as he recognized the American flag flying stiffly in the wind over the ship's stern. Men in gun tubs around her stern fought to track their guns on him but his airspeed for the moment exceeded 200 miles per hour and they were unable to match it. He dove for the water and turned left again as he cleared the fantail of the battleship. Now the ship's port side guns opened up, seeking to exact vengeance as he fled.

He craned his neck and tried to see the ship behind him, but the angle was too great. He whipped the yoke from left to right and back again in a desperate bid to frustrate the aim of the enemy gunners. Nonetheless, he felt the aircraft buck as it was struck by solid shot or chunks of shrapnel.

"REPORT!" he yelled. "PLANCKE! Did we hit her?"

On *Washington's* bridge Captain Benson fought through his daze to process the informational overload with which he had to contend. Damage to his ship was already extensive, though far from fatal, but for critical moments, he knew the ship was sailing on her last ordered course by inertia, not under command. As German torpedo bombers fanned out to starboard and began their attack runs, he and Lt. Fairbanks hoisted the dead helmsman away from the ship's wheel. Benson ordered Fairbanks to take the wheel while he went himself to the starboard bridge wing. He gasped as he identified at least six twin-engine bombers bearing down on his ship.

"Full right rudder!" he ordered. "Put the wheel hard over!"

At his battle station, servicing the auto loader for his 5-inch gun Reggie was sweating. The auto loader held ten rounds in a vertical stack that fed the shells directly to the gun's breech. Each time the gun fired, the recoil and ejection of the spent shell casing triggered the auto loader to drop the next round onto the breech where a hydraulic ram pushed it home, slammed the breech cover closed and fired the gun again, repeating the process every six seconds. In rapid-fire mode, the auto loader's ten shells were spent in just one minute. The Gunner's Mate's job was to feed shells in at the top of the loader to keep pace with the gun's expenditure. It was grueling, repetitive work, but a well-trained crew could keep a 5-inch gun firing continuously for many minutes. The ten guns in five turrets on the starboard side of the ship were hurling an incredible 100 rounds of 5-inch flak shells a minute at the enemy.

The din in the turret was incredible. With two guns, each firing every six seconds, spent shell casings clanged off the deck and out the rear hatch. The ammunition hoists rumbled as they delivered shells from the magazines to the guns and with the auto loader feeding shells, serving in a 5-inch gun crew aboard *Washington* was like putting one's head inside a ringing church bell. Reggie had wadded up cotton balls stuffed in his ears, his asbestos fire-retardant balaclava over his head and face leaving just a flattened circle around his eyes exposed and his helmet strapped on tight. Over his skivvies and under his dungarees he wore more of the anti-flash asbestos to protect his body, arms and legs. Heavy asbestos gloves the men called oven mitts covered his hands as he fed shells to the auto loader.

Under control of *Washington's* state-of-the-art, radar directed firing systems, the 5-inch guns tracked and elevated on their own, making tiny adjustments to the aim every second as they banged away at the enemy bombers. In one sense, the Germans were at a disadvantage. Ideally they would have coordinated the low-level torpedo bomber attack with high-level or dive bombers, to force the target ship's anti-aircraft guns to divide their fire. As it was, all ten, 5-inch guns, plus over two dozen 20mm and 40mm flak guns on the starboard side of the battleship were banging away at Stefan Vogt's flight of ten Heinkel torpedo bombers all at the same 100 feet altitude. With such a concentration of fire the Germans' chance of pressing home their attack unscathed were non-existent. The two guns in Reggie's turret targeted the aircraft closest to *Washington's* bows, hurling a blizzard of 5-inch shells at the Heinkel.

Yet, the American gunners were still months away from having one of the great technological weapons developments of World War II at their disposal. By the start of the New Year, 1943, US Navy ships at sea would employ the "VT" or proximity fuse shell. Based on British pre-war research exchanged to the Americans under the secret agreement between Churchill and Roosevelt, the American proximity fuse used a set of miniaturized radio tubes in an ingenious radar transmitter/receiver built into the tip of the anti-aircraft shell. Prior to the proximity fuse, an anti-aircraft shell had either to directly strike its target, or be pre-fused to explode at almost the exactly correct altitude at just the instant it came nearest the target. Either way, it was a matter of mere chance that a target was ever destroyed or damaged in such fashion. A shell not equipped with the proximity fuse could pass literally within inches of its target and do no harm. However, with the proximity fuse the shell needed only to pass within about 75 feet of the target at any time in its trajectory. The VT fuse would trigger the shell to explode, spraying deadly shrapnel in all directions. In its war in the Pacific Theater against Japan, the proximity fuse would destroy hundreds of enemy aircraft, saving many American ships from damage or destruction along with countless American lives.

The proximity fuse was one of the most closely guarded secrets of the entire war. So careful were the Americans to protect the secret that they allowed only ships at sea to use it, for fear that a shell that did not explode would be recovered by the enemy on land, its secrets reverse engineered and used against the Allies. Had the VT shell been available that day in the Arctic it is likely the American flak gunners could have knocked down all ten German bombers, perhaps before any had dropped their torpedoes.

As it was, the Americans directed a hail of flak fire at the Germans and the two guns in Reggie's forward starboard turret were highly effective, knocking down their first German target and moving on to share credit with another pair of 5-inch guns in the 'kill' of a second. It seemed the Americans might repulse the attack with little more bother than a wild beast flicking away flies with its tail.

On *Washington's* bridge, Lt. Fairbanks did as he was ordered. Taking the helm, he spun the wheel and held it all the way to the right when it came to its stop, but Captain Benson knew he was too late. Even as a damage party and relief crew scrambled onto the bridge, the Captain watched as at least four of the enemy bombers tipped their deadly payloads into the water. Within seconds, three of the four bombers were hit by anti-aircraft fire as they made the mistake of trying to climb for altitude, exposing their vulnerable undersides and losing speed. The fourth flew audaciously right over his ship, aft and out of his sight. Already though, the aircraft was a forgotten thought. All that mattered now were the eight torpedoes he knew were in the water directed at his ship.

Benson ran back to the engine enunciator and rang the handles to All Back Starboard, All Ahead Port, but his heart sank at the agonizingly slow and ponderous turn *Washington* made. Her 16-inch forward battery thundered out yet another six-gun salvo, her 53rd and last of the battle, even as she was struck by the first of two torpedoes.

The impact hurled Reggie off his feet. The first torpedo exploded against the starboard side below the waterline, ten feet aft of his 5-inch gun turret. The German torpedo carried an explosive charge of 250 kilograms and struck *Washington* in a place where the combination of her armored belt and torpedo blister were designed to withstand a blast from as much as 320 kilos. The blister was a series of armored compartments below the waterline, each filled with water to dampen the blast effect of a torpedo explosion. The main belt and hull were not breached, but the blister was ruptured, resulting in jagged steel plates below the waterline. Nevertheless, the battleship's seaworthiness was barely affected by this damage. Of greater concern were the effects the shock of the explosion had on the two forward 5-inch gun turrets, Reggie's and the one just aft. The torpedo exploded between the two turrets and sent a fountain of water rocketing over fifty feet in the air. It cascaded down on the two 5-inch turrets as well as several adjacent open-air guns; the fire from the

20mm and 40mm guns went out like a spent match as the gunners were instantly in shock from the deluge of freezing water. Fuses on the electrical circuits providing power to the two 5-inch turrets were blown; the guns drooped down to -5 degrees' elevation and the machinery fell silent. Had the Germans followed the attack with a second wave of bombers the American battleship would have been deprived of forty percent of her starboard defensive firepower.

Reggie rolled painfully to his knees carefully cradling a broken left forearm. He'd slammed it against the mounting bracket for the auto loader when he was thrown to the deck. Lights in the turret were out, but a dim glow filtered from the louvres used to vent gases from the guns' discharge. Other men in the turret were slowly recovering as well. Reggie was about to haul himself to his feet when the second torpedo struck.

Launched from Flight Leader Stefan Vogt's HE111 at a range of just 950 yards this torpedo first plunged to a depth of 60 meters before leveling out and beginning its rise back to its designed running depth of three meters. It performed flawlessly, racing towards *Washington's* starboard flank at 40 knots, taking just 45 seconds to cover the distance. Even so, the battleship's turn to starboard, intended by Captain Benson to give him a chance to comb the wakes of the torpedoes launched against his ship, was finally starting to bring the ship on to her new heading.

This turn had two effects on the second torpedo. First, the torpedo did not strike the ship at its intended right angle; it hit at approximately a 70 degree angle. Nonetheless, this was sufficient to trigger its impact fuse and the warhead exploded after penetrating the outer hull. Second, the foreshortened aspect of *Washington's* flank caused the torpedo to strike further forward than Stefan had aimed it. The fish burst on the third deck ten feet below the waterline, into an electrician repair shop forward of the two massive 16-inch gun turrets in a place where the heavy, armored belt protecting the magazines tapered down to just four inches. The explosion tore a hole fourteen feet by eight feet in her hull, killing eleven men outright, injuring nine more.

As with the first torpedo blast, a waterspout erupted above the impact and crashed back down, deluging the adjacent weather decks in icy water. Had the ship been only at battle stations air, the forward rail would have been lined with gunners firing an array of .50 caliber machine guns against the airborne threat, but since the 16-inch turrets forward were also firing against *Tirpitz*, the .50 caliber guns were mercifully unmanned, sparing further loss of life.

As *Washington* continued her turn, the wound in her starboard bows admitted tons of freezing seawater every minute. The water temperature made it nearly impossible for damage parties to affect any but the most rudimentary repairs, shoring up bulkheads and watertight hatches to isolate the flooding. It would require a sheltered anchorage and specialized diving gear and thermal survival suits before any men could enter the flooded compartments. Full repairs would require months in a dry dock. While the torpedo did not damage her engines, the flooding tipped the ship to a ten-degree list and slowed her top speed to just 20 knots.

As the three groups of surface vessels, American, British and German slowed, they also widened the range. *Duke of York's* forward main battery was already long out of the fight. Now the aft guns of *Tirpitz* and the forward guns of *Washington* also fell silent as the range increased to over 35,000 yards. The command staff of all three capital ships turned their attention to the fight to save their vessels, to put out fires and effect emergency repairs so that they could reach a friendly port safely.

With all three Admirals injured, the battleship Captains composed and sent lengthy wireless transmissions to their respective Admiralties, detailing the latest updates to the battle and with damage status of their ships. *Duke of York* was in by far the most serious condition. Forward batteries knocked out, several of her secondary 5.25-inch guns also out of action and with three major fires raging, she was in no condition to continue the pursuit of *Tirpitz* so long as *Washington* was no longer able to distract the German gunnery. While her engines and steering were undamaged, *Duke of York* would have been a sitting duck had she ventured back into range of *Tirpitz*, and Captain Halliday knew it. Worse still, one of the out-of-control fires on his ship was blazing on three sides of the forward ammunition magazine. Despite the intense action, the magazine still held hundreds of 14-inch shells and bales of gunpowder propellant. While the armored belt protecting the magazine remained intact, temperatures around the explosive ammunition had risen to worrisome levels, over 100 degrees Fahrenheit. Crewmen in the magazine shed their heavy protective garments and sweated as they monitored the safety of the magazine. After sending his message to London, Captain Halliday slowed his ship to 18 knots and turned her to the west. With *Tirpitz* already out of range, his priorities became fuel economy and leaving the zone of danger from air attack while fighting to save his ship.

Aboard *USS Washington*, Captain Benson did not detail the numerous shell hits his ship had suffered, but he did alert the Navy Department in

Washington, D.C. of the two aerial torpedo hits she had taken and the consequent reduction to his speed. He also turned his ship to the west and began the long voyage to a friendly port, knowing that, like *Duke of York*, he did not have enough fuel aboard to reach safe harbor. He prayed that a fleet oiler would reach him and that the difficult and dangerous job of refueling at sea would not be prevented by weather or further enemy action. For both Allied ships, the change in bearing also put the wind on their starboard sides. This served to blow flames away to port and benefited the fire-fighting efforts. Both had lost the chance to chase the German ships further. *Tirpitz* had slipped from their grasp.

As *Tirpitz* slowly pulled away from her pursuers, Captain Topp composed his message to Berlin. In doing so, he found himself on the horns of a serious dilemma. In one respect Topp and his superior, Admiral Schniewind, had fulfilled their orders, stopping the Allied convoy from delivering its invaluable cargo of war material to the Soviet Union. Topp was quite certain that at least a dozen Allied merchant ships were sunk, or bobbing about crippled on the Arctic Ocean east of Bear Island. In this sense, the German battle fleet had achieved a strategic as well as tactical victory. None of the weapons, munitions and supplies of the convoy would reach the Eastern Front, where they could have done great harm to the German war effort.

However, in a broader respect the Germans had failed their orders. Under strict instructions to avoid combat with superior enemy forces, *Tirpitz, Scheer* and *Hipper* had engaged a vastly superior enemy force of two battleships, three heavy cruisers and supporting destroyers. Even more important, the German's orders were to avoid serious damage to the heavy ships of their surface fleet, especially *Tirpitz* herself. While *Hipper* appeared to have escaped the battle relatively unscathed, both *Scheer* and *Lutzow* were limping home with torpedo damage and *Tirpitz* had suffered a battering at the hands of the heavy guns of the two Allied battleships. In fact, Topp was not even aware of how serious the damage to his ship was. Telephone and electrical circuits between the bridge and the port side where *Washington's* final hit had struck *Tirpitz* at the waterline, were cut. Topp had to rely on runners to receive information on this damage and he had not yet received the news that the ship was holed and open to the sea.

Topp made the politically expedient decision to temporize his report to Berlin, in hopes that closer inspection of his ship would reveal her damage was more superficial than he feared. In his message, Topp referred to several hits from large caliber shells, but did not mention any damage below his waterline. His message concluded with "Speed reduced to 24 knots. Rejoining *Scheer*."

The effect in Berlin was to leave Admiral Raeder with some doubt as to *Tirpitz'* exact condition, but firmly of the impression her damage was not severe or extensive. The reference to reduced speed he took as explained by the need to escort the injured pocket battleship, not by any problem *Tirpitz* had in sustaining her own speed. Raeder dutifully reported to Hitler and the Wehrmacht General Staff that the Kriegsmarine had achieved a great and heroic victory while suffering light to moderate damage and casualties of their own.

Propaganda Minister Goebbels insisted on immediate publicity and Radio Berlin issued a breathless, and largely fictional, account of the action. This report includes the first documented reference to "The Battle of Bear Island." Church bells rang across the German Capitol in celebration, as if an enemy capitol city had fallen to German arms.

In London and in Washington, D.C., the Allied naval leadership arrived at much the same conclusion as the Germans. The Allies were privy to the largely accurate damage reports from their own naval and merchant fleets, but also to the intercepted and decoded signals from the German ships, especially *Tirpitz*. They found nothing to indicate their strategic purpose of sinking or disabling the German battleship had been met, or that the risk they'd taken and damage they'd suffered already had paid off in any way. As the reports from *USS Washington* and *HMS Duke of York* indicated, the *Tirpitz* did not appear to have suffered any appreciable harm. The Allied High Command interpreted Topp's decoded report minimizing his own damage in exactly the same way the Germans did in Berlin.

Gloom descended, particularly in London as First Sea Lord of the Admiralty Sir Dudley Pound and Prime Minister Winston Churchill received the decoded intercepts. From their perspective, the convoy had been smashed with a total of twenty-one of the thirty-five merchant ships sunk or disabled and adrift, either from the previous air attacks or by the heavy guns of the German surface fleet. The survivors turned back from their destination and were still in jeopardy, headed for U-boat infested waters. The convoy's close escort of anti-submarine and anti-aircraft ships were wiped out with few if any survivors yet to be rescued. The battleships *USS Washington* and *HMS Duke of York* had each suffered extensive damage, and were low on fuel, far from safe harbor. Either or both might yet be lost. One American heavy cruiser, *USS Wichita*, was badly damaged, with her captain dead and the fate of the other*, USS Tuscaloosa* was still unknown as she had yet to rejoin the main Allied fleet.

Against all these losses, the Allies could only balance a single German destroyer out of action, though still afloat, the known torpedo hit to one German pocket battleship, correctly assumed to be the *Scheer* and the apparently light damage to *Tirpitz*. The other German cruiser involved in the surface action, the *Hipper* seemed to have escaped damage. London was also aware that a lone Fairey Albacore bi-plane bomber crew claimed to have launched a torpedo against the other pocket battleship, believed to be *Lutzow*, but they had no way of knowing how much damage, if any she had suffered. They were completely in the dark that *Lutzow* had injured herself on an uncharted rock during her passage through the Norwegian Leads.

In London, Churchill sat in an overstuffed wingback chair, pensively pulling on his cigar and sipping, some reports say gulping, brandy. Naval staff of the Admiralty war room moved about their business briskly, but quietly. When they spoke, it was in hushed undertones with many sideways glances at their war leader. They'd picked up his somber mood and reflected it. In fact, the news had made its way through the bunker and a funereal aspect descended. An orderly alternated between sweeping up the ashes from the Prime Minister's cigar and refilling his snifter.

Finally, Churchill stirred himself and swayed to his feet. He picked up his bowler hat and his cane and made his way for the exit stairwell. Passing Admiral Pound on his way, Churchill nodded.

"Keep me informed," he growled and made his way to his waiting car for the short ride to 10 Downing Street. He'd been awake for nearly two days, but now the nervous tension was gone, replaced by the most intense disappointment he'd yet suffered in the war, for now his beloved Royal Navy seemed to have let him down.

In Washington, D.C., it was still before dawn. The American Chief of Naval Operations, Admiral Ernest King had been awake all night monitoring the situation in the Arctic and the reports from Admiral Giffen aboard *USS Washington*, but his mind was also focused on the situation in the South Pacific.

Reports from Admiral Nimitz in Hawaii had alerted the US Navy command some weeks earlier that the Japanese were ashore and building an airstrip on a remote island named Guadalcanal in the Solomon Islands chain. If put into operation this airfield would allow the Japanese to threaten the convoy routes from the United States to Australia. Admiral King monitored the progress of the 1st Marine Division's preparations to seize the island and its crucial airfield before the Japanese could put it in operation. Time was very short, as was every form of equipment and supplies, most especially the troop and cargo transport vessels need to deliver the division to Guadalcanal. Incredibly, the Wellington, New Zealand dockworkers chose this critical moment to go out on strike, notwithstanding the threat to their own country from the Japanese expansion into the South Pacific. The Marine infantry battalions had to load the cargo ships themselves, cutting off their combat training. The Marines were tentatively scheduled to land on Guadalcanal in the first week of August.

Admiral King was eager for the Arctic Convoy operation to conclude and for *Washington* and her cruiser and destroyer escorts to return to US Navy command. The battleship was scheduled to return to the Brooklynn Navy Yard for a refit, then to transit the Panama Canal at the end of August on her way as a desperately needed reinforcement in the South Pacific.

King, and most of the US Navy leadership for that matter, deeply resented any diversion of American warships to the European theater. They considered the Japanese a far more dangerous naval threat, and the thirst for revenge for the surprise attack at Pearl Harbor burned in them.

King read each update from his commanders in the Arctic with growing alarm. Clearly, the Royal Navy had led his precious ships much farther east than ever contemplated when the operation was first proposed. In fact, King had initially rebuffed the Royal Navy's request to 'borrow' a US Navy battleship and escorts to strengthen the distant covering force of Convoy PQ17. Only when Churchill took the matter directly to Roosevelt and the President had ordered cooperation with the British had King relented. To put icing on the cake the Brits had also requested a US Navy fleet aircraft carrier to deliver Spitfire fighter planes to the beleaguered island of Malta and King was forced to also loan *USS Wasp* for this purpose. For the hundredth time he thanked God that *Wasp* had gotten clear of the Mediterranean before the Royal Navy sailed to disaster in their frantic and ultimately fruitless effort to relieve the Malta garrison.

"God Damn Brits," he growled under his breath. There were times when King seemed to feel the US was at war with the wrong European power. At other times, he appeared to feel the US Navy was at War with the rest of the US Military. King began working through what he would tell General George Marshall, the US Military's Chief of Staff. Marshall had delivered Roosevelt's order to loan *Washington* to the Royal Navy. A knock at King's door broke his reverie.

"Enter!" he shouted. He was in a foul mood for so early in the morning. An ensign from the Signals Office entered and approached King's desk.

"Latest signal from *Washington*, Sir," the young man said sheepishly, holding out a message flimsy.

King snatched the message from the junior officer and scanned it quickly, then took the time to read it carefully, word by word. His heart sank when he read that *Washington* had suffered two aerial torpedo hits and was fleeing the scene of battle, fighting now for her survival. Without a word, he waved the Ensign away.

"GOD DAMN BRITS!" he stormed, slamming his fist down on the desktop.

Chapter 34

'A' Flight

As the Royal Navy fleet drew away from the Germans and the sounds of battle fell silent, Captain Halliday began to get the upper hand on the fires that threatened his ship. With *Duke of York* on a southwesterly bearing the winds pushed flames over the port side of the ship and away from his firefighting crews, giving them a chance to get their firehoses near the base of the fires. They made steady progress in extinguishing them. Thick billowing clouds of black, oily smoke began to fade, replaced by lighter grey, but still dense smoke.

The most dangerous fire remained the one still burning forward, on three sides of the armored barbette of 'A' turret and the magazine below it. Damage to internal passageways continued to hamper access for the damage parties. Men remained trapped in those passages and in the magazine itself. But a damage party equipped with oxyacetylene torches began work on cutting open the mangled hatchways to the lower decks. It seemed that Nobby Lamb might soon be freed from his prison in the passage around the barbette.

As Halliday and his crew fought to restore order aboard *Duke of York, HMS London* joined the battleship, easing in just a cable length away on her starboard side. *London's* captain was prepared to assist in the firefighting effort by laying his cruiser right alongside the battleship, but for the moment, this was impractical. Hoses from *London* would unavoidably soak the *Duke's* own firefighting teams with frigid water. For the time being, *London's* contribution was limited to moral support.

Elsewhere aboard ship, men worked to assess the extensive damage done to the battleship and to make repairs. Others moved wounded to the sick bay where the ship's Doctor fought to save lives and limbs. For some, all he could do was alleviate the pain of passing. Those already dead were laid out on deck aft, in a makeshift morgue. In the shadow of the four guns of 'C' turret, the bodies were covered in canvas shrouds salvaged from smashed ship's boats. Over fifty men and three officers were fatalities and the expectation was that as interior compartments were reached, more dead would be found. A preliminary muster revealed at least eighty men currently listed as missing.

Aside from the two forward turrets, serious damage included the loss of forward anchors and chains, the destruction of the ship's observation aircraft and what was hoped was the temporary loss of the radar apparatus. Hits from *Tirpitz'* 15-inch shells high in the superstructure had unseated the mainmast and disabled the primary search radar aerial. The secondary aerial atop the aft superstructure was functional, but damage to electrical circuits prevented its signals from reaching either of the two radar offices. Arrangements were made for *HMS London* to use the short-range ship-to-ship telephone to alert *Duke of York* of any threat detected on her radar apparatus.

Thus it was, that as Major 'Mads' Wegele finally reached the scene, leading seven other remaining HE111 Torpedo Bombers he approached from almost directly due south of the Royal Navy battleship, on her port side. With *HMS London* drawn in so close to her starboard side, *Duke of York's* own massive steel bulk cast a shadow, a narrow blind spot, low on the southern horizon, in *London's* radar search radius. Wegele and his squadron aimed for the plume of smoke billowing from *Duke of York* and flew into this blind spot by mere chance. With smoke still pouring off the battleship over her port side, her own lookouts were slow to make a visual sighting of the enemy aircraft. When they finally did, Captain Halliday ordered an immediate turn to port and an increase to flank speed and with steering and engines undamaged, the ship responded as fast as a 42,000-ton slab of steel could. Even so, the Germans were less than two miles from *Duke of York* before the first anti-aircraft gun spit its first shot at them.

The air attack against *USS Washington* was a surprise for Captain Halliday, even as it was for the Americans themselves. Admiral Tovey was the only man in the Allied fleet in on "Ultra", the British code name for the intelligence they gleaned from intercepted and decoded German signals. Even so, Captain Halliday on *Duke of York* and Admiral Giffen and Captain Benson aboard *Washington* had unconsciously adopted a viewpoint that British intelligence on German intentions was very good. They never looked for any specific report, but they accepted as accurate any report they did get. Not until actually in action did either of the American officers conclude that the British intelligence might be wrong. So it was that when the Admiralty alerted the Allied fleet commanders that the German Luftwaffe was socked into their fields in the North Cape, they believed it to be true.

That Benson, injured as he was at the critical moment, was slow to react can be understood, but it seems Halliday was caught flat-footed as well. Perhaps he believed the Luftwaffe had thrown everything it had against the Americans. Perhaps he was so focused, first on chasing down *Tirpitz*, then upon damage control efforts on *Duke of York* after the battering she'd taken from the German battleship, that he discounted the air attack threat. Whatever the cause, *Duke of York* was ill prepared to fend off the Heinkels. Her own radar temporarily disabled, and with *London's* blinded in the critical sector, her electronic early warning was absent. Two of her four port side 5.25-inch twin gun turrets were out of action along with several of the smaller caliber automatic cannon in her flak array. The smoke from the fires blowing over the port side obscured the view of her lookouts and delayed their sighting the bombers for critical seconds as the Germans closed the range.

Furthermore, *London's* formidable flak guns would not bear on target until after the German bombers had dropped their torpedoes and had flown clear of *Duke of York*. The Royal Navy destroyer escort was more than a mile ahead of the two heavy ships, attention focused on a search for enemy U-boat threats.

For Mads Wegele the flight from the North Cape of Norway was fraught with hazards. Just getting off the runway at Banak in the dense, ground hugging fog was a life and death challenge that one of the least experienced pilots in 'A' Flight failed.

Once airborne, his radio operator reported that he was unable to find the promised signal from *Tirpitz*. Wegele spent precious fuel circling the airfield in a fruitless effort to resolve the problem. Finally, one of the other aircraft in his flight reported receiving the signal, though intermittently. Wegele gave the other pilot the lead in following the transmission to their target, but the weak signal meant their bearing weaved back and forth over a fifteen-degree range, wasting more precious fuel. The bombers were less than twenty minutes away before the signal strengthened and they were able to head directly to it.

Along the way, an engine fault forced one of his aircraft to turn back for base, probably sealing the fate off its crew, as the prospect of another of his inexperienced pilots finding the field and lining up for a successful landing alone were remote at best. Two more of his bombers lost contact with the rest of the flight while skirting an area of cloud that rose to 5,000 meters and were never again seen. As he approached *Duke of York*, Mads had only eight aircraft including his own of the twelve that had lifted off from Banak.

The German flight passed within visible range of *Tirpitz, Scheer* and *Hipper*, the three ships all on southerly headings. Mads used his binoculars to identify them as German, and then made his way to the north, following a course passed from *Tirpitz* in a blinkered signal.

He kept well clear of the German ships, not wanting to become a friendly fire casualty and in fact, the Kriegsmarine flak gunners had itchy fingers. The navy was still wary of attack by more aircraft from the mysterious Allied airplane carrier. Just moments after altering course to the north, Mads spotted the oily smoke from *Duke of York*. Despite the overcast, it was clearly distinguishable from the low clouds.

The bombers of the German 'A' flight were piloted by men of even less experience than those in Stefan Vogt's 'B' flight and Wegele had little confidence in their ability to coordinate the "Golden Comb" attack formation, the ideal tactic in the current situation. Instead, he ordered a simple line abreast pattern with his own bomber at the middle of the formation. He hoped this would serve to dilute the enemy's flak fire between all eight bombers, giving a better chance that one or more would successfully drop its torpedo.

Mads gave no thought to the return flight home to Banak on the North Cape. Every one of his remaining aircraft were already long past the point of no return. None had enough fuel to return to base. The best any of them could hope for was a controlled landing in water, in other words to ditch their planes, survive the impact and have enough time to escape the aircraft before it sank. Then the aircrews would have to inflate their rubber dinghy, get aboard before getting soaked by the freezing seawater and paddle clear of the plane before it sucked them down with it. Finally, they would then need prompt rescue by a surface ship, floatplane or U-boat before exposure claimed their lives. Overall, Wegele considered the chances of survival to be so slim as to be nearly non-existent. With this fatalism came a determination to sell his life and the lives of his command as dearly as possible.

Mads waggled his wings and pushed the throttles forward to their stops, then tipped the Heinkel's nose down and began the final descent to drop his two torpedoes. On either side of him his seven other aircraft all followed suit. The enemy ship's flak batteries finally opened up at a range of just two miles, with tracers flashing out of the smoke that shrouded the front half of the ship. As he closed the range, Mads felt as if every round came straight for him. Heavier shells began bursting, but above and behind his plane and they were barely noticeable. Of much greater concern were the streams of tracers, reaching across the water towards him like gigantic grasping fingers, groping and feeling to locate him and snatch him from the sky. A long rope of green hued tracer shells bent towards him and seemed to walk their way towards his glass cockpit. He pushed the stick forward, the Heinkel dove to just 30 meters above the surface of the sea, and the tracers moved on.

Wegele pulled back on the yoke and the bomber rose back to 100 meters altitude, its speed falling off to the ideal 180 miles per hour. Another stream of tracers bent towards him, flashing across the front of the Heinkel, punching a fist sized hole in the starboard wing, but he was too close now for evasive maneuvers. He reached down and gripped the torpedo release lever, even as another string of enemy shells felt for him. At 1000 meters from the smoldering ship, he yanked the lever and felt the plane bound upwards, released of two metric tons of torpedo weight.

Of the sixteen torpedoes carried by the eight Heinkels that attacked *Duke of York* that morning, none did her the least damage. Four torpedoes never dropped; the planes carrying them were knocked from the sky by the battleship's flak before reaching the release point. Panicked pilots seeing their first combat released four others far too soon. The ponderous battleship turned into the spread of remaining fish and combed their wakes, presenting a narrowed profile that left only a slim target. Only two of the fish were aimed true and these were likely the two dropped by Wegele himself. Lookouts aboard *Duke of York* reported two torpedo wakes running under her port side railing amidships. In the number one engine room, far below the waterline, members of the Black Gang heard a resounding clang above the roar of boilers and the clashing of gears. One of the torpedoes struck the ship, but failed to explode. Later examination of her hull found a dent twelve feet below the waterline, directly adjacent to the main reduction gears. Had it exploded it would likely have opened the engine room to the sea. The second torpedo ran under the ship and was seen passing under the starboard side railing. Its depth control had failed. *Duke of York's* draft was nearly thirty-five feet and the torpedo ran at least that deep to pass under her without impact.

Duke of York had been very lucky, but that luck did not extend to *HMS London*. The heavy cruiser turned away from the torpedo attack, rather than in to it and one of the fish meant for the battleship missed *Duke of York* aft and continued on to strike *London* on her starboard side, blowing a hole twelve feet wide by ten high in her bows. The one Allied heavy ship to have escaped injury to this point was now gravely wounded.

Wegele's training told him he should turn to starboard after dropping his fish, to evade the enemy flak by flying behind the ship. It can never be known why he instead chose to turn to port, towards the bows of his target. Perhaps he guessed that the clouds of smoke billowing from the bows would complicate the enemy flak gunners' task of taking aim at him.

Whatever the reason, the Flight Leader's HE111 turned left and flew into a hail of fire from the port side forward eight barreled pom-pom battery. The 40mm shells shattered the glass flight cabin, then walked down the belly of the bomber, shredding its thin skin from nose to tail. It is likely that Wegele was killed outright and his aircraft crashed out of control, but it is also possible that his dying action was to tip the nose down and plunge the twin-engine bomber into *Duke of York*.

His bomber slammed into the port side rail forward of 'A' and 'B' turrets. The starboard BMW engine skipped off the weather deck and hurtled into the 20mm gun tubs behind the breakwater on the prow. Due to the fires raging in the bows, the guns were not manned. The engine exploded, sending a hail of metal fragments and burning fuel across the weather deck and setting off a string of secondary blasts as the flak guns' ready ammunition cooked off. Mercifully, most of the damage control parties working forward were sheltered on the far side of the turrets, shielded from the worst of this shrapnel. The port side engine plunged into the area where the deck was already cracked open by the earlier 15-inch shell hit. It exploded into the port side capstan flat. Flaming fuel from the port wing's tank sprayed into the flat as the engine slammed through a watertight hatch into a paint locker. The white-hot engine wreck ignited the paint, which exploded back up through the hole in the deck and sprayed flame all the way forward over the bows and aft to the sloped face of 'A' turret. In a moment, the progress in extinguishing the fires forward on *Duke of York* was undone.

PART THREE: AFTERMATH

Chapter 35

Counting losses.

As the pitiful few survivors of Wegele's 'A' Flight fled the scene, the Allied fleet turned its attention to damage control and survival. All the principal ships of the American and British navies were damaged and in danger.

Though her Captain was dead and her bridge a wreck, *USS Wichita* was in the best overall condition. Her propulsion, steering and main gun batteries were all undamaged. Her Executive Officer conned the ship from the Auxiliary Steering Station temporarily while damage parties worked to restore function to her bridge, re-routing phone and electrical circuits. The engine enunciator and helm tested as fully functional. Firefighting teams tackled the blazes burning amidships and on her fantail, but these fires quickly consumed *Wichita's* floatplane and other flammables and burned themselves out. With the fires extinguished, the X.O. moved to the bridge to assume full command of the cruiser. Aside from her Captain, her casualties included twelve dead and eighteen wounded from a crew of 950 officers and men.

USS Tuscaloosa was in far more precarious straits. Struck by a torpedo from the German destroyer attack, she had a list of 20 degrees. Once her watertight integrity outside the immediate areas of damage was assured, her captain ordered counter flooding. Crewmen opened valves to flood bilge compartments on her port side, settling her lower in the water and reducing her speed to 16 knots, but also cutting the list down to a manageable five degrees. Both American cruisers moved to catch up to *USS Washington.*

Hit by no fewer than six, 15-inch, eight 8-inch and numerous 5.9-inch shells the crew of the US Navy battleship fought several fires and worked to restore internal telephone and electrical circuits. A puzzling fault in her main electrical panel raised alarm when several of the starboard side pumps lost power. She settled slowly to starboard as seawater slowly worked its way through, around and under damaged watertight hatches and bulkheads. With freezing water from the firefighting efforts dripping into the compartment, Maury Espinoza, an Electrician's Mate 1st Class from Albuquerque, New Mexico stood on a rubber mat and replaced fuses one-by-one in the live panel until power to the pumps was restored. He received the Navy Cross for his action.

With all pumps operating, *Washington* stayed ahead of the flooding and stabilized her list at ten degrees. Within an hour, her fires were out and she was making 16 knots. Her Chief Engineer swore she could have made 22 knots, but as *Tuscaloosa* was down to 16 knots anyway, Captain Benson opted not to drive the battleship any faster.

In the Captain's day cabin, Admiral Giffen lay badly wounded and unconscious for three days. Lt. Fairbanks and the Captain's steward tended to the Admiral round the clock, with frequent visits from the ship's Doctor. The Medical Officer could do little, but check the Admiral's pulse and shake his head. He left no doubt he held small hope for Giffen's survival. Yet, the Admiral rallied and by day four of the voyage home he was sitting up in bed sipping hot soup.

With the four American destroyers forming an anti-submarine shield, the three heavy ships made their way slowly to the southwest, following the Royal Navy's route. They caught up to *HMS Duke of York, HMS London* and the RN destroyers in just over two hours. They found both heavy British ships in mortal jeopardy.

The torpedo hit had nearly blown *HMS London's* bows off. Sailing at just 5 knots, her bow twisted and groaned every time she met one of the six-foot swells that caught her on the starboard quarter. Down by the head, her watertight hatches and bulkheads forward were in danger of collapse. The thirty-ton bows twisted and wrenched them repeatedly until water began to leak around the hatch coamings and through cracks in her bulkheads that widened rapidly. It became obvious to her captain he could not sail the ship for long into the freshening seas before the bulkhead collapsed entirely. He brought her around with her stern to the wind, put her engines to All Back, and began to sail her backwards. This relieved the pressure on the forward bulkhead, but *London* could only make 6 knots in reverse. She would be defenseless against any further attack from the air, a submarine or surface force.

Duke of York's engines and steering were unharmed and aside from a two-foot wide gash in her port bows that extended four feet below the waterline, she was watertight. Nevertheless, the internal fire raging on three sides of her forward barbettes threatened her survival. After Mads Wegele's HE111 crashed into her, her weather deck was ablaze from her prow back to 'A' turret. Damage parties were driven back by the flames and they lost all the oxyacetylene equipment they'd been using to cut their way back into the lower decks. The tanks of volatile gases ruptured and exploded, the blast propelling the tanks overboard in a spectacular display. Telephone circuits to the forward magazine were still out and the men in the magazine remained trapped and unable to communicate with the rest of the ship. Captain Halliday was certain the temperature in the magazine was dangerously high, but had no way to order the magazine flooded. He could only hope the officer in command in the magazine would judge the moment to evacuate and flood the magazine. In desperation, Halliday turned the ship directly into the wind and seas from the northwest. He increased speed to 25 knots. Soon, white water was breaking over The Dukes bows, extinguishing the fire on her weather deck. Halliday slowed and turned back to the southwest and his damage parties resumed their efforts to fight the fires that still burned between decks.

Chapter 36

Are Heroes born?

Nobby Lamb retraced his route, around the barbette to the starboard side of the ship. He took a deep breath before entering the section of passageway where his dead and injured shipmates lay. Thick, oily smoke greeted him when he opened the hatchway. He stepped through quickly and shut the hatch behind him.

First, he checked on Chief Gresham. The Cornish man's life was complete. Saddened, yet relieved that Gresham would not suffer further, Nobby said a silent prayer for him, before moving on to the other more or less complete bodies in the chamber. None showed any sign of life.

Nobby backed out of the passage, dogging shut the hatch behind him again. He retreated behind the hatch at the forward corner of 'A' turret on the port side of the barbettes below the cracked deck and the weather deck hatch the men above him strove to open. Nearly every bulkhead and deck he touched on this journey was hot to the touch. Water that entered the passage through the cracked deck above in a steady trickle sizzled and steamed on the deck at his feet. He realized it was the first time in days he'd been warm.

Above him, men continued to work to open the hatch to the weather deck. Sledges and hammers banged steadily on the hatch's hinges in an effort to loosen it in its frame. From time to time, the banging stopped and a voice called down to him.

"Do ya hearr me laddie?" queried the Scotsman's voice, characteristically rolling his 'r's.

"I do," answered Nobby. "I hear you!"

"Ya just stay put laddie," the man ordered. "We're working to get ya oot in a shake of a lamb's tail!"

Nobby chuckled at the man's inadvertent use of his own last name.

"I've nowhere to go!" he answered, with as little sarcasm as he could manage.

"Aye, that ya haven't," the voice laughed back.

The banging resumed. Nobby covered his ears against the noise. Every strike of the hammer echoed in the steel passage until he could no longer distinguish an individual CLANG from another. He moved forward, close behind the hatch that sealed him off from the passageway around the front of the barbette to put as much distance between himself and the source of the noise as he could. The hatch was twisted in its frame and smoke leaked around its edges.

The clanging stopped again and he looked up at the thin strip of daylight that fell through the twisted weather deck hatch frame. The tip of a pry bar was wedged in the crack. Two sharp cracks of a hammer drove it a foot under the hatch. Unintelligible shouting on deck, then the pry bar started to lift the hatch. The crack opened to two inches and Nobby smiled with hope that it would soon be wide enough for him to escape. A crash and a torrent of cursing from above wiped the smile from his face. The cold metal of the pry bar could not take the strain and it snapped.

Nobby went forward again and leaned against the barbette. It was warm, but not painful to touch. He was ready to cover his ears again in anticipation of the banging resuming when a different sound caught his ear. TAP-TAP-TAP. He listened intently, but his ears were still ringing from the last round of hammer blows and he could hardly be certain he was not hearing them still. Finally, he leaned down and put his hand on the top of the escape trunk hatch. He felt a vibration that corresponded to each TAP sound.

The hammer blows on the weather deck hatch resumed, drowning every other sound in the world. Nobby covered his ears again and waited for the awful racket to cease. Just when he thought he could take no more he realized the banging had stopped. He listened again for the TAP, but his ears were ringing from the banging on the hatch above. He leaned down and felt the hatch. At first, it was still, but then he felt the TAP-TAP-TAP again. He reached up, took the mallet from its hook above the hatch and tapped back on the hatch cover. Nobby did not know Morse code, so he couldn't do any more than acknowledge whatever message the men in the magazine were sending.

The banging above him resumed. Nobby, ever the conscientious seaman of the Royal Navy, carefully replaced the mallet on its hook lest it be lost or misplaced. He covered his ears again and waited for the banging to end. When it finally did, he shouted up at the crack in the deck above.

"Hello, on deck! Hello, on deck!"

"Aye laddie?" the Scotsman called down. "It'll no be long now. Be patient! We'll have ya oot in five morre minutes."

"Wait!" Nobby yelled, not wanting the banging to resume. "The men in the magazine are tapping on the escape hatch. I think they want to come out!"

"Can ya rread the message, Laddie?" the man on deck called back. "Do ya ken Morrse Code?"

"No, I cannot read it," answered the boy. "I've never learned Morse."

"Tap back to them, Laddie. At least let them know therre's men alive oot here. If they want oot it's just as well!"

The hammer blows above resumed before Nobby could say any more. He went back to the hatch and hit it with the mallet, hard this time in hopes his blows could be distinguished from the racket above. He hit the hatch cover five quick blows. He stood and put his hand on the hatch leading forward around the front of the barbette, but quickly withdrew it. The hatch was very hot to the touch with smoke pouring round its edges. He feared, correctly that the fire was burning directly on the other side. Nobby could do nothing but wait, either for the magazine escape hatch to open or for the weather deck hatch to be pried open. The escape hatch popped open an inch and a gust of hot air escaped it. Nobby peered through the tiny crack and could see a man on the underside of the hatch, trying to put his shoulder against it and shove it upwards, but standing on the rungs of a ladder, he had almost no leverage.

Nobby put his fingers under the hatch and pulled. Nothing. He squatted beside the hatch and used his scrawny legs in an effort to lift the hatch. He turned red in the face from the strain, but the hatch did not budge. Panting, he released the hatch. He leaned down and put his mouth to the gap between hatch and coaming.

"I'm going for some tools!" he shouted. "I'll be back soon!"

Not waiting for an answer, he staggered to his feet and went down the passage to the crack in the deck above him. He waited until the banging stopped again.

"Hello, on deck!" he shouted. "Hello, on deck!"

"Aye, laddie, what is it?" The Scotsman was exasperated.

"The magazine hatch won't open," he answered. "I need a lever or pry bar to help open it more. Can you pass something through to me?"

"Aye, laddie!"

A moment later a six-foot long, inch thick, steel pry bar passed through the cracked deck. He reached out, and took it. The Scotsman called out to him.

"Laddie! Do ya hear me?"

"Yes, I hear you!" Nobby shouted back. A face appeared, peering down at him through the crack.

"What is your name, laddie?" the man asked.

"I'm Ordinary Seaman Nobby Lamb!" he replied proudly.

"Well, Seaman Nobby Lamb! I'm C.P.O. MacGregor and I've a message from the Captain for you to pass to the men below as soon as you can get the hatch open."

"We already have it open, but just a crack! I can call to them, but they can't get out yet!"

"All rright, laddie," MacGregor said. "Tell them the Captain has ordered the forward magazines evacuated and flooded as soon as possible! If this fire gets any hotter, it might set off the ammunition! Do ya ken what I'm tellin' ya, laddie?"

"Aye, Chief! Evacuate and flood the magazine as soon as possible!"

"We'll worrk to get ya all oot thrrough this bloody hatch!" MacGregor concluded and the banging resumed immediately.

Nobby went back down the passage to the escape hatch. He studied the hatch, looking for the best place to apply the steel bar. The hatch was thick, heavy steel, weighing at least 300 pounds and was far too heavy for a lone man to lift on his own, even when it was undamaged. The top of the hatch was equipped with a pair of steel, spring-loaded counterweights, set such that a modest push or pull opposite the hinges would lift the hatch open to upright. A clip on the bulkhead would attach to the lip of the hatch and hold it in place. One of the springs on the counterweights was bent and twisted. Instead of helping to lift the hatch, it prevented the hatch from opening. Nobby knelt at the hatch and put his mouth to the opening again.

"I have a message from the Captain!" he shouted. "You are to flood the magazine and evacuate! The fire is out of control!"

"There's forty men down here!" the man objected in alarm.

"I have tools now!" Nobby responded. "I have to separate the steel spring on the hatch cover!" he shouted. "Stand clear!"

"Aye!" came the reply.

Nobby stood and hefted the pry bar. It was far too heavy for him to swing its full length effectively, so he gripped it two thirds down its length and swung the hooked end against the clips that attached the spring to the counterweight. Four swings and the end of the clip sheered off. Next, he knelt down with the mallet and struck the pin until it dropped clear. The misshapen spring bounded clear and smacked against his shin. He yelped and rubbed his leg.

"All right! Let's try to open it now!" he shouted down the hatch.

He slid the pry bar tip under the hatch about six inches and leaned all his weight on the other end of the bar. The hatch groaned open another inch. He reset the pry bar further under the hatch and leaned down to the crack. Hot fetid air rushed through the gap, but something else hit his nostrils. The smell of seawater was strong. The crew in the magazine had already begun to flood it.

"Push from below!" he shouted.

He stood on the end of the pry bar, balancing himself with one hand against the bulkhead. The hatch came up another inch. Now he bounced his weight up and down on the pry bar. Each time he did the hatch responded until it had opened about six inches. But now the pry bar end drooped all the way to the deck and he had no more leverage. He pushed the bar in further and stood on it again, bouncing up and down until the end of the pry bar was on the deck once more. The hatch was open about nine inches. Enough for only the skinniest of men to pass through. The banging from the hatch above him was louder than ever, and seemed about as fruitless. The hatch to the weather deck remained stuck in place. Help from that direction would be a long time coming still. He knelt to the opening in the hatch. He held out his hand and he and the burly man standing atop the ladder below him shook.

"Have you a man that can squeeze through now?" he asked. "I need help on this side."

Without a word, the burly man slid down the ladder and a moment later a skinny boy, not much older than Nobby shinnied to the top. He rolled over to his back and began to wriggle through the opening, putting his head through sideways first then reaching his arms and shoulders through. Nobby took his hands and pulled while men below pushed on the man's feet. He got through to his waist, then stuck! He wiggled and writhed but advanced no further. Nobby knelt at the hatch opening.

"His belt buckle is caught on the hatch!" he yelled. The burly man reappeared and reached up to the boy's waist. He wrestled the buckle free and pushed it past the rim of the hatch. In a moment, the boy was free and through the hatch.

Nobby now pushed the tip of the pry bar across the hatch opening and rested it on the rear of the hatch coming, between the hinges. Together, he and the boy got beneath the other end and lifting with their legs, they drove the bar and the hatch open. Suddenly, the hatch released and slammed all the way open. The two boys nearly dropped the pry bar down the hatch, catching it from falling on the men below at the last instant. Nobby earned a painful scrape across his knuckles from the effort. They cast the pry bar aside and dogged the hatch open as men began to scramble through it into the passageway. Looking down the escape trunk, Nobby saw men waiting twenty feet below in waist deep water. Hot air no longer spilled out the hatch. He shivered at the sight of the frigid water below and knew the men standing in it had only minutes to escape before they were overcome by the cold.

The burly man was first out of the hatch, fairly leaping out, then turning round to help the next man quickly through the hatch. Both of these first two were dry, but the men that followed came out of the hatch progressively wetter than the man before. Many were already shivering. It took several minutes to pass all the men in the magazine up through the hatch. Nobby directed the coldest of them to stand close to the bulkheads and hatches heated by the fire. By the time the last man, the Leftenant in command of the magazine, was through, water had reached the base of the escape trunk. The water's rise was clearly visible as it filled the escape trunk, the last void in the magazine.

"Sh-shut the hatch!" the officer stammered. The freezing water soaked him to the neck and he shivered uncontrollably. "Sh-shut the ha-hatch!"

The burly man unclipped the hatch and pressed it down against the hatch coming. But when he tried to dog it shut the clips would not hold. Nobby's efforts to release them had damaged the clips. The hatch sprang open an inch each time the burly man took his weight from it.

"Oh, my God," stammered the officer. "The valves for the sprinkler system were jammed. We had to rupture the pipes. There's no way to shut off the water."

"The only way to close the hatch is from the inside, Sir," the burly man said, terror on his face. "If we don't get it closed in the next two minutes the water pressure will hold it open forever. We'll never close it!" The officer looked around him.

"We've to close all the watertight hatches and bulkheads nearby!" he said. "Contain the flooding that way." Now Nobby spoke up.

"Excuse me, Sir," he said. "All the hatches nearby are ruptured. None of them will seal. There's been smoke leaking around all of them the whole time I've been trapped here. Even the weather deck is ruptured," he went on, pointing at the thin strip of daylight. Nobby realized there was more daylight and the banging had stopped. A dozen pry bars were under the lip of the hatch above and it was open a foot or more already. But he knew it too would never close before repair in a dockyard. He looked at the escape trunk. Water had risen halfway up the twenty-foot tube. In not much more than a minute it would spill over the hatch, and *Duke of York* would be doomed.

Nobby stepped over the hatch coaming, on to the first rung of the ladder. He gripped the hatch and pulled it down over his head.

"Lean on the hatch!" Nobby commanded the burly man.

"You'll drown!" the man said.

"The whole ship will drown if we don't close this hatch!" Nobby snarled.

"Do it!" the officer ordered.

The burly man burst into tears, but did as he was ordered and held the hatch closed. In the darkened escape trunk, as water crept up around his knees, Ordinary Seaman Nobby Lamb felt for the clips to dog the hatch closed. The first three slipped into place and locked easily. The fourth was stiff and the water was up to his neck before he slipped it in place. With the last breath he took, Nobby Lamb locked the clip in place, sealing the magazine and preventing the flood of seawater from sinking *HMS Duke of York*.

Chapter 37

Consequences

The outcome of The Knight's Gambit held profound strategic implications for Allies and Axis alike. An immediate result was that the Soviet Union received none of the supplies carried by the ships of Convoy PQ17. The manifest included over 100 tanks and other armored vehicles, 300 aircraft, 7,000 tons of refined petroleum products, 14,000 tons of explosives and munitions, 12,000 tons of food stuffs and over 650 lorries, in such critical demand for the mobility of the Red Army. Weapons and supplies to equip 50,000 Soviet soldiers were lost or returned to port undelivered.

Twenty-three of the thirty-five merchantmen of the convoy were lost, totaling 143,000 tons of shipping. Worldwide losses continued to exceed the pace Allied shipyards could build replacements. Shortage of cargo tonnage threatened to strangle the Allied war effort in every theater. For the Americans, one of the immediate consequences of PQ 17 was that it forced the US Navy and Marine Corps to reassess the planned operation to seize the island of Guadalcanal in the South Pacific. With German and Italian forces threatening the Suez Canal and Nile River Delta in Egypt,

Allied shipping requirements were on a razors balance of meeting existing demands. Already planned on a shoestring, with barely enough transport vessels to deliver the 1st Marine Division with its supplies and equipment, the War Department in Washington, D.C. ordered a reevaluation of shipping priorities with an eye to cut back on the vessels allotted for Guadalcanal. The first American counteroffensive of the Pacific War hung in the balance as the War Shipping Office weighed the competing needs of the two theaters of war.

Lend-Lease convoys to Russia were suspended for the balance of the summer. They did not resume until after the autumn equinox in late September brought more than twelve hours a day of darkness back to the Arctic, along with typically dreadful weather, allowing Allied shipping at least the chance to evade detection from aerial observation and prowling U-boats. Even then, the Royal Navy was forced once again to provide heavy escorts of capital ships to defend the convoys from the threat still posed by the German surface fleet. Through it all, the Soviets howled at the betrayal and cowardice of the western Allies.

Worse still, the Americans were no longer in a position to pass the three heavy ships they'd allotted to PQ 17 through to the Pacific Ocean. *USS Washington* spent three weeks receiving emergency repairs at

Greenock, Scotland. Temporary patches of ½-inch steel plate were welded over the torpedo damage to her hull. *Washington's* crew pumped the flooded compartments dry even as she sailed for America where she slipped into dry dock at the Norfolk Navy Station in Virginia. Shipyard gangs worked on her twenty-four hours a day for four months, but by the time she was ready for sea again it was the second week of November 1942. Another month would elapse before she passed through the Panama Canal on her way to the South Pacific war zone.

Similarly, *USS Tuscaloosa* and *USS Wichita* both spent months in the Brooklynn Navy Yard repairing the damage done them in their duel with the German Navy. All three ships received the latest upgrades to their radar apparatus and additional anti-aircraft guns, including the highly effective 40mm twin Bofors guns, then being made in America under license from the Swedish Bofors firm. These improvements aside, the absence of all three ships was keenly felt in the South Pacific.

The Royal Navy suffered its second body blow in less than a month. On top of the ships and men lost in the Malta relief effort, the Butcher's Bill in the Arctic added injury to insult. The five destroyers and numerous lesser warships of PQ 17's close escort were essentially wiped out, with only a few of the smallest ASW and rescue ships surviving. These losses further complicated the already difficult task of providing adequate escorts for trans-Atlantic convoys.

HMS Victorious, in company with *HMS Norfolk* and two RN destroyers arrived at Hvalfjord, Iceland on July 10, 1942 after a laborious, but uneventful voyage. After emergency repairs there, she sailed first to the Clyde, then on to the Harland and Wolfe Shipyard in Belfast, North Ireland where she spent seven months in dry dock receiving repairs from U-355's torpedo. During this time, the Royal Navy was without an aircraft carrier in Atlantic waters.

The two Allied battleships and their retinue made a rendezvous with a Royal Navy tanker 250 miles northeast of Iceland. A Force 8 gale made refueling a difficult and hazardous operation. Two men aboard the oiler, *HMS Welsh Dale*, lost their lives, swept overboard. With the oiler sailing in the lee of one of the two battleships, all the ships of the combined fleet took aboard enough fuel to reach Iceland where they harbored long enough to put ashore the most seriously wounded and to receive additional fuel oil to reach the British Isles.

The battleship *HMS King George V*, namesake of the class to which *Duke of York* belonged, had only just finished its repairs and returned to sea. *Duke of York* took *King George V's* place at the Gladstone Dock in Liverpool for extensive, time-consuming repairs. Dockyard cranes lifted both forward turrets off their armored barbettes and the turret ring and the gears of the motors that drove them were replaced. The ship was a beehive of activity as her bows were completely removed and replaced and her superstructure was taken down to the weather deck and rebuilt from scratch. *Duke of York's* electrical system proved especially difficult to repair, with miles of wiring replaced before all the faults were set right. She did not rejoin the home fleet until March 1943. All told, nearly a thousand Royal Navy seamen gave their lives, as did over 250 merchant seamen and 156 Americans.

The tale of Nobby Lamb took several weeks to reach the public. None of the men who witnessed his sacrifice knew his name and it was not until *Duke of York* reached Home Waters that Captain Halliday heard the details. It took him several more days of interviews with the men involved in fighting the fires in the ship's bow before Petty Officer MacGregor connected the story to the laddie, Ordinary Seaman Nobby Lamb. After his body was recovered from the flooded magazine, King George VI presented Nobby's parents with his posthumous Victoria Cross in a ceremony at Westminster Abbey. They both wept. In the coming year,

Nobby was the male child name most commonly recorded on English birth certificates.

Late in July, the Admiralty publicly revealed *London's* sinking in one of their all too familiar announcements: "The Admiralty regret to announce the loss of *HMS London*". Unable to make more than 5 knots in reverse, she'd struggled on gamely until the worsening seas threatened to turn her on beam ends. She sheltered in the lee of *Washington* and *Duke of York* as *USS Wichita* stood by and took off her crew. Once all had abandoned ship, one of the RN destroyers delivered the coup de grace with a spread of three torpedoes. She was the only major combatant lost to either side during The Knight's Gambit.

Coming on the heels as it did of the sinking of *HMS Trinidad* and *HMS Edinburgh* in Arctic waters and of the losses suffered by the Malta relief force, loss of *London* was a costly blow to the Royal Navy, which found itself with an embarrassing shortage of cruisers to fulfill its worldwide obligations. His Majesty's Government quietly directed the British Mission in Washington, D.C. to enquire discreetly on the possibility of the Americans passing any of the new cruisers then starting to come out of American yards in large numbers on to the Royal Navy under Lend-Lease.

The reaction of American CNO, Admiral Ernest King was as explosive as it was predictable. "God Damn Brits!" he shouted.

For the Allies however, all these consequences paled next to their failure to correctly assess the damage actually done to *Tirpitz.* Had they been aware of how badly hurt she was they would have borne their own losses and damage, if not cheerfully, then at least with less alarm and despair.

The interior of *Tirpitz's* lower decks were gutted by fire and her superstructure was perforated by dozens of holes from shells and shrapnel. A special salvage team flew to Altenfjord where they built a cofferdam against the side of the ship. They pumped the cofferdam dry and applied a patch of half-inch steel over the wound in her side from *Washington's* 16-inch shell. They pumped out the flooded compartments to put her on an even keel. Plywood sheets and a coat of fresh paint masked most of the damage to her superstructure and she sailed down the coast to Trondheim as if she'd been on a pleasure cruise. There, the German's worked on her slowly, affecting what repairs were possible with the limited port facilities, but it was completely impossible to fully repair the 13-inch armored belt without putting her in dry dock at home in Germany for months. They decided instead to apply a second patch on the inside of the hole and to fill the cavity between with concrete. They then buttressed the inside of this patch with steel beams welded at angles into the decks above and below, rendering the compartment unserviceable as anything but a storage closet. She was seaworthy, but less than battle worthy. A direct hit from anything as large as a 5-inch shell would likely penetrate the patch again.

However, the Germans communicated all the detailed damage reports filed after return to port via landline teletype, not subject to British wireless intercept. As time passed and Allied propaganda made no claims to have hurt *Tirpitz*, the Germans realized their enemies really did not understand the extent of her damage. They resolved to keep it a closely guarded secret, understanding that the threat of *Tirpitz* was nearly as valuable as any attack she might actually launch.

Over a period of months, British agents among the civil population in Norway gleaned details of the damage to both *Lutzow* and *Scheer*. With more extensive torpedo damage, it was impossible to mask the list each of them had due to flooded compartments. Daring Norwegians took several photographs of each and smuggled them out to Sweden. These went by diplomatic pouch on the Swedish mail packet to London where extent of the damage to the two pocket battleships was at last deduced.

Several of the Norwegians paid with their lives for this information. By the time the photos arrived in London, *Scheer* was already undergoing repairs at Danzig while *Lutzow* waited her turn for the dry dock in the outer harbor. But the truth of *Tirpitz'* wounds remained hidden for over a year.

With the conclusion of Mads Wegele's Luftwaffe attack against the Royal Navy, the active combat phase of The Knight's Gambit ended. Replacing it was a struggle in many ways every bit as grim and deadly as the warfare that preceded it. Scattered across the Arctic between the northern coast of Norway and Bear Island hundreds of men were adrift on the frigid sea. Even though it was just past high summer, temperatures were barely above freezing and a freshening wind blew from the northwest, threatening a change in the calms seas that had prevailed for days. Worsening weather would be a death sentence for many.

Duncan Butterweck and his Albacore crewmates Tim Butten and Charlie Oswald flew away from their attack on the German pocket battleship *Lutzow*, with a damaged, but still airworthy bi-plane. No wireless transmission was ever heard from them after the attack and it is not known if the radio transmitter was damaged or its operator incapacitated. The fate of these three men remained a mystery until September 1956 when a Russian scientific team on a survey of Bear Island came upon the wreckage of the Albacore. Two graves nearby made of piled stones bore the identity disks of Butten and Oswald and it is assumed that Butterweck himself piloted the plane to the island for a crash landing, then interred the bodies of his mates. It is unclear if they were killed aboard the plane or died in its crash, or perhaps after arrival on the island. Duncan's own remains were never recovered and the fate of the crews of the other two Albacores that flew the mission has never been discovered.

The Arado floatplane pilot, Lt. Wahl was much luckier. He managed his fuel supply carefully and conservatively. When he reported by wireless to *Tirpitz* on his fuel status he applied a buffer to his estimates. He and his observer succeeded in reaching a small cove with a narrow beach, sheltered on the east side of Bear Island. Earlier that summer a Luftwaffe submarine had cached a small supply of survival gear, food and critically, 120 liters of aviation fuel in 20-liter cans. Wahl and his observer landed the floatplane on the calm waters of the cove and taxied in close to the rocky shingle. Steel gray cliffs harboring tens of thousands of outraged sea birds towered over the shore, barely five meters at its widest.

Wahl rowed ashore in his inflatable dingy, and then located the cairn under which the fuel and other supplies lay buried. While the birds flew around them in screaming hordes, he and his crewman used a length of rope and the dingy to ferry two cans at a time back to the aircraft. Within an hour of landing, they were back in the air and on their way to Norway. Both received the Iron Cross for valor for their part in The Knight's Gambit.

Aboard *SS Carlton*, Willie Cipresso and his shipmates came away from *Tirpitz'* bombardment unscathed. The barrels of scrap wood and oily rags Willie set afire as the 15-inch shells began to fall were enough to convince German observers aboard the battleship that the *Carlton* was hit. Following their orders, they moved on to other targets. Captain Hansen slowed his ship to a crawl lest she be seen escaping. When the German battle fleet turned about to flee from *HMS Duke of York*, *Carlton* was the lone seaworthy vessel in a forty square mile area with over a dozen other ships either already sunk or sinking. Over a two-day period, Hansen moved slowly amongst the flotsam and jetsam of Convoy PQ17, rescuing survivors from open boats and bobbing hulks. He eventually landed 123 survivors in Iceland. Seven men died of their injuries after being taken aboard. Willie Cipresso remained in the merchant service. He survived the war, marrying and raising a family in New Jersey.

Stefan Vogt nursed his fuel and brought his damaged HE111 bomber home to Banak Airfield in Norway's North Cape, one of only five of the original twenty-three bombers to return safely. He arrived to find the field under broken clouds and easily identifiable from the air. He too received the Iron Cross and is credited with two torpedo hits during The Knight's Gambit, one against an Allied merchant ship on July 5, and the next day another hit on the American battleship *USS Washington.* He took a month's leave at home with his wife Lorelei before his next posting took him to Malta, by then a quiet backwater of the war. He was given command of his own HE111 bomber squadron, along with promotion to Major. Vogt was killed in a landing accident at Benghazi, Libya on a routine training flight that autumn.

Two more bombers of the 'A' Flight ditched near the German destroyer Z30. Five of the six aviators were rescued, but the last was dragged under when his parachute snagged on jagged metal as he attempted to evacuate the bomber. The only HE111 bomber crewman at Bear Island known to have survived the war is Stefan's hut mate, Hause, the brick-layer from Vienna.

Royal Navy Commander Broome and 13 of his men from *HMS Keppel* reached a lifeboat when their destroyer sank. The rescue ship *Zamalek* picked up over one hundred survivors of the other four Royal Navy destroyers wiped out by *Tirpitz*, but the survivors of *Keppel* were missed. They floated two days, by which time Broome and four more of his men were dead. A prowling German U-boat rescued the remaining nine. After losing many fingers and toes to frostbite, they spent the rest of the war in a POW camp in Germany.

Other U-boats came to the rescue of the crew of *Z28,* the German destroyer wrecked by 8-inch shells from *USS Wichita*. Another of the four engine Condors first located the destroyer. They found it still afloat, beam ends to the sea. In an operation that lasted three days, six submarines took aboard 184 survivors. The last U-boat put two torpedoes into the drifting hulk and finished her off. She was the only ship lost by the Germans in The Knight's Gambit. The German Navy and Air Force lost 318 men killed and another 95 injured during The Knight's Gambit.

Gunther La Baume and his U-355 arrived safely in Trondheim, nearly a week overdue and more than two weeks after they'd been declared lost by the German U-boat service. Two days of intensive diagnosis of the boat's wireless transmitter finally isolated the fault. A tiny chaff of paper had fallen into the port of one of the vacuum tubes of the device. Seaman Kubein had replaced this tube several times while the boat was at sea in the Arctic in an attempt to solve the problem with the transmitter, but he never detected the tiny slip of paper. The Kriegsmarine grudgingly credited La Baume with torpedoing an airplane carrier, but they held his failure to solve the fault in his wireless apparatus against him. No decorations came his way. He and U-355 next sailed on a war patrol into the Atlantic with Brest, France as his intended destination. The boat was to attack Atlantic convoys on this voyage, then continue its operations from its new port, replacing one of the U-boats that had transferred to the Mediterranean to support Operation Herkules, the Axis invasion of Malta. They never arrived to Brest, though this time the U-boat service waited a month before declaring them lost.

Reggie Elkins received the Purple Heart for his injuries aboard *USS Washington*. He stayed with the battleship until its return to the United States. After three months ashore to recuperate from his broken arm, he was reassigned to the heavy cruiser *USS Indianapolis*.

What of the senior leaders whose decisions set in motion and controlled the events of The Knight's Gambit? Captain Halliday received praise from the Admiralty Board for his conduct of *Duke of York*. Citing his seamanship and determination in pursuit of *Tirpitz* and his skillful ship handling that saved the ship from the many fires that raged aboard her, they brought him ashore for a posting in command of Naval Shipbuilding in the Clyde, while *Duke of York* underwent her repairs. Only when he was passed over for another seagoing command the next year did everyone realize the praise had been window dressing, designed to mask the PQ17 disaster from the public. He never commanded a combatant vessel again.

Commander of the Royal Navy's Home Fleet, Admiral Sir John Tovey died of his injuries. An embolism blocked the flow of blood to his brain while he was still at sea. Tovey was at the top of the short list of senior officers to replace Dudley Pound as First Sea Lord. Pound continued to hide his illness from the Admiralty. Admiral Andrew Brown Cunningham, known throughout the Royal Navy and to all ranks as "A.B.C.", was recalled to London and assumed command of the Home Fleet.

The Admiralty conducted a thorough, but secret, review of the events surrounding Convoy PQ17. Principal avenues of enquiry covered the decision to reverse the convoy's course, compared to the alternatives of continuing as planned for Russia, or of dispersing the convoy, with each ship ordered to make its own independent path to its destination. Ultimately, Admiral Pound's order to reverse course was deemed appropriate under the challenging circumstances.

Closer scrutiny was placed on the handling of the "Near Covering Force", the squadron of four fast Royal Navy heavy cruisers operating to the west of Bear Island. Commanded by Rear-Admiral Hamilton, this fast response fleet did not move to join the convoy in time to affect the outcome of the battle. Operating under strict radio discipline, Hamilton did not ask for guidance and the Admiralty in London offered none. By the time Hamilton received Commander Broome and Admiral Tovey's first wireless signals, his force was more than six hours away, with no prospect to reach the fight in time. Hamilton opted to obey orders and not expose his cruisers to the dangers of German land-based air for the sake of an empty gesture. But had this powerful squadron joined *Duke of York* and *Washington* in time for their confrontation with the German surface force, the outcome of the battle would likely have been much more favorable to the Allied cause.

Hamilton's supporters pointed out that he scrupulously obeyed his orders. He maintained wireless silence and did not venture east of Bear Island without orders. Hamilton's detractors pointed out that Admiral Tovey disobeyed his orders, and in so doing saved the remnants of the convoy and brought *Tirpitz* to battle, a primary objective of the entire operation. Had Hamilton joined at Bear Island with his four fast cruisers the Allies might well have finished *Tirpitz* and the rest of the German surface fleet right then and there. On the other hand, had he joined the convoy and Tovey had not, it is just as likely his four cruisers would have joined the merchant ships on the bottom. In the end, he was cleared of any wrongdoing. But the opinion lingered in the Royal Navy held that he lacked aggressiveness. Many senior officers felt he had taken the safe approach. Of course, these hindsight officers could never prove what they would have done in his position.

Admiral Giffen recovered and sailed home to America with *Washington*. He was given command of the US Navy's Great Lakes Training School on Lake Michigan. His sea-going career was over. A Navy enquiry formally acquitted him of charges of violating his orders by taking his command east of Bear Island. The board credited his defense with the argument that while operating under strict radio silence he had no choice but to follow Admiral Tovey's orders and the Royal Navy into range of land-based German bombers. With the testimony of his Flag Officer, Lt. Fairbanks it even complimented him for correctly deducing that British intelligence on weather conditions in North Norway might be wrong. Nonetheless, the heavy damage his ships suffered when they were so badly needed in the Pacific left a stain on his record.

Captain Benson came away with his reputation intact. Serving under orders of both Admiral Tovey and Admiral Benson he was not faulted for engaging *Tirpitz*. Indeed, the US Navy concluded that only his vigorous command of *USS Washington* had saved *HMS Duke of York* from a complete and humiliating defeat at the hands of the German Navy. Lt. Fairbanks stood up for Captain Benson as well, relating the condition in which he found the Captain and the bridge immediately prior to the German torpedo bomber attack. Like Giffen, Benson spent time ashore but later in the war command of *USS Illinois*, one of the last of the Iowa class battleships, fell to him.

Lt. Fairbanks also returned to the United States where his combat experience combined with his fame to make him perfect for a tour selling War Bonds. For over a year, he regaled audiences around the nation with his story of The Battle of Bear Island, carefully scripted by the War Department to cast the Navy in the best possible light. After the tour ended, he went back to Hollywood and starred as himself in a film rendering of the US Navy's heroic rescue of Convoy PQ17. Willie Cipresso and other convoy survivors refused to see *"The Battle of Bear Island"*.

Admiral Schniewind took months to recover from his wounds, by which time Hitler's anger at him over *Tirpitz*' damage had subsided.

Nonetheless, he never held a sea-going command again. He resigned his commission late in 1942 and retired, intending to garden. He was killed in an Allied air raid in July 1943.

Unlike Schniewind, *Tirpitz'* commander, Captain Topp received another sea command. Following The Knight's Gambit, the German surface Navy was in a shambles with all its heavy ships save *Hipper*, either lost in action or in dockyards for lengthy repairs. Topp took command of the battlecruiser *Scharnhorst*, then in dry-dock at home in Germany receiving repairs for damage done when she'd struck two magnetic mines. Topp will appear again, late in the Malta Fulcrum Alternate history series.

The strategic impact of The Knight's Gambit extended well beyond the careers affected and the casualty lists of ships and men. When news of the disaster reached Members of Parliament in London, they called a secret session to demand answers of the government. Winston Churchill, serving in his dual capacity as Prime Minister and War Minister was questioned mercilessly and it soon emerged that his was the leading voice that had forced PQ 17 to sail in the first place. Before the end of the month, his opponents in the House of Commons would force another Confidence Vote, challenging his leadership of the war effort.

In the summer of 1942, the western Allies' attention was focused on the Mediterranean Sea and North Africa. The Axis conquest of the island of Malta effectively severed Allied east-west air and naval traffic between Gibraltar and Cairo. The combined German-Italian army in North Africa seized the port of Tobruk in early July and moved on to threaten the British 8th Army's last defensive line in Egypt, anchored on the coast at a tiny railhead called El Alamein.

The Allies were in the planning stages for amphibious landings in French North Africa, from Casablanca, Morocco in the west to Oran and Algiers, Algeria further east. The Allies hoped to land behind the Axis forces to annihilate them in a giant pincer movement. But the possibility that the enemy could capture the Nile River Delta, Cairo and the Suez Canal could not be discounted. The threat to Suez forced the Allies to reconsider their planned landings, first tentatively code-named "Operation Gymnast", later changed to "Operation Torch". A successful Axis conquest of Suez would leave the Middle East oil fields of Iraq and Iran as the next logical target for Field Marshall Rommel's forces in the desert. The Allies began to plan that the British and American forces allotted for Gymnast be instead delivered to the Persian Gulf, at the port of Basra, Iraq and to Aqaba, across the Sinai Peninsula from the Gulf of

Suez. They would then drive overland to Gaza to block an Axis advance to the oil fields. This diversion of forces would more than double the distance these troops, equipment and supplies had to travel by ship, further stressing Allied shipping capacity. Guadalcanal slipped further down the list of priorities pending the outcome of the Axis campaign for Suez.

That story, of the Battle of El Alamein, is told in book three of the Malta Fulcrum Alternate History Series, "The Gates of Victory."

22731312R00263

Printed in Great Britain
by Amazon